REVI

"Excellent story. Mr. Brogden weav

pages turning. It really fed my love for aviation, the South and a good mystery. I would recommend this book."

By Jim Williams

"Riveting...I couldn't put the book down, yet I didn't want it to end. I loved it. I read a lot and this was one of the best. Can't wait to read another book by Mr. Brogden."

By Diane Byrd

"What a great read! The story moves along at a fast pace and the mysteries keep unfolding. The author has a masterful touch with dialogue. The characters are developed and interesting. This would make a fantastic movie!"

By Robin Koppernas

"Ted Brogden rivals DeMille and Baldacci. I have been looking for a new author and found him in Ted Brogden. Jigsaw holds your attention from the get go. I love a book I can't guess the ending. I won't use the cliché "great read" it is so much better."

By Linda Ammons

"Jigsaw is a must read for anyone seeking a compelling adventure full of wit, sorrow, humor and triumph. I could not put it down. And it didn't hurt that it was set in my familiar ground of the southeast and especially North Carolina. The Captain is gritty, sweet, flawed and alluring and proves that we all don't go through life unscathed-but we can open our eyes and finally be fearless with grace."

By Tracy Draughon

"This book is exciting and has unexpected twist. I thought Mr. Brogden did and excellent job in both character and plot development. It's a page turner and never predictable. I found myself dreaming about what might happen next. It would make a great movie. I totally see it on the silver screen!

This the cream of the crop, best of the best, of all the thrilling novels I've read. Just a gripping book you don't want to put down. Captain Cape Thomas is an awesome character. From the very start of the book you just want to know more about the mysterious woman.

By Nicole Givens

Beaufort, SC

"Jigsaw is a story that tortures your soul as you become Cape and search for the mysterious woman with him. You melt into the book, see what he sees and feel his every emotion. Once you start you cannot put it down. I read it straight through in one sitting, finishing it in the wee hours of the morning. You will not be disappointed!!! I cannot wait for the next book.

James W. Jackson

Clinton, NC

Jigsaw is an unusual novel-mixing adventure, pathos, humor and intrigue into a compelling story of betrayal and redemption. Cape, the central character is flawed but salvageable-you like him and feel for him in his quest to solve his haunting mystery. The ending does not disappoint.

The setting is romantic and alluring-the South at its best. Hints of Pat Conroy meets Jeffery Deaver spring from the pages. A great summer read and an alluring plot will hold your interest. For all mystery lovers and those who like to get "lost in literature" this is a must.

Julie Stewart Corner

Jigsaw

Ted Miller Brogden

This book is a work of fiction. The characters and dialogue are drawn from the author's imagination. Any resemblance to actual events or persons, living or dead, is entirely coincidental.

ISBN 978-0-615-36004-1

Thanks to Lt. Col Christopher Miller for the generous use of the cover picture and a special thanks to all military personnel for protecting us.

Dedicated to Maleia…you inspire by example and always leave me wanting one more day.

M E PUBLISHING

BEAUFORT SC

Jigsaw

The sandy headlands, capes, along the North Carolina coast have marked for centuries the western boundary of the Graveyard of the Atlantic. Sailors and fishermen found more comfort in the beams sent out through the Fresnel lenses of Cape Hatteras, Cape Lookout, and Cape Fear lighthouses than any woman ever could have provided on moonless, stormy nights. However, on one such night that wasn't the case. A daring young woman and skilled mariner spotted a hapless tourist being pounded by a summer squall as he tried to hand paddle his small dinghy to shore. They fell in love and later married, and somewhere near the spot they beached that stormy night I was conceived.

Rather than honor me with the time and circumstances that joined them for life, my parents chose my moniker from the geography that surrounded them during the most important moments of their lives. The initial longing glance, first touch of hands, the embryonic kiss that sparked the burning honeymoon passion which led to the consummation that made us a family all took place on the desolate headlands of the Carolina coast. Cape, Cape Thomas, an unusual name, but not a bad name considering my Mom's love of the sea and my Dad's love of the sky and the independent influences of the times. I'm told that Neptune, Poseidon, and Moon Beam, were some of the names the young Mr. & Mrs. Thomas discarded…hallelujah, and thank you Common Sense.

Back then the capes were life signals to mariners. Now, with the advent of GPS, auto pilots, and depth finders, The Capes are just reference points relative to eye walls of hurricanes that form off the Atlantic coast from June till December.

Today, I feel like the demoted Capes myself, a mere reference point. Grace, an ex-girlfriend, soon to be divorced from a bastard who ruined both our lives, is trying to pinpoint where we went wrong. "You could have tried harder, made me believe you really loved me, and none of this would have happened," she says.

Grace is baiting the blame game, but today I'm not biting. I asked her to marry me. I didn't beg but I did ask. After that she had a choice to make: marry me, a captain for AeroMax Airline, or marry the son of the guy who owns AeroMax.

Pain aside, I think I handled her decision well. After all, not many rejected lovers buy wedding gifts, and yes, my reason for giving a gift had more to do with keeping my job safe than it did with magnanimity. "Cape, your problem is that you've never cared about anyone enough to go after them--"

"No, my problem is that I don't have a job anymore, or the rating to hold a job with any airline. That's my problem."

"Jon fired you?"

I can see the guilt in her face, and I don't want that. She didn't do anything wrong, any more than I did. We're pawns, and her bastard ex-husband would enjoy this moment—and he may be--considering the evidence AeroMax used to can my butt.

"Grace, go home--"

"No." Tears well up in her eyes and roll down her cheeks. She inhales in jagged, hard, jerks that snap at her spine. Still, despite the convulsions, she manages to stay in one piece and continues to talk, "Not until I know you don't hate me. Jon said no one would get hurt, that I was just proving I loved him more than you, that's all." More tears, more stabs in the heart, hers and mine. "I would never-- if I knew you would have been hurt—never-ever, Cape, you have to believe--"

"Shh, don't do this." I hold her and a million things to say that might make her feel better run through my mind. But not one thing comes out. What she's taken from me is more than a job, more than my life really. And she's wrong about something else. I did care enough to chase after some folks once. When I was a kid, I chased my parents all the way to Death's door and tried like hell to kick it down. No need to bring that up, though. Grace has heard that story so many times she has a title for it—Pity the Poor Orphan, by the Little Matchstick Boy. She's not being cruel, Grace isn't natured that way. It's just that she knows if she doesn't stop the orphan story she'll have to hear the One that Got Away story by Cape Thomas, the story sub-titled, Why I Can't Love You Enough To Commit.

"You're not going to forgive me, are you?"

I can't talk anymore. I need time alone so I gently push Grace out the door. All I can hope is that at least her lawyers can salvage some of what they call "the lifestyle to which she's become accustomed." Sure she's hurting, but with time that will pass, it worked for me. Healing is not so tough when you have a job, a life with a regular paycheck, fellow employees that support you…not that I enjoyed any of those comforts--

"Don't do this, Cape. Right now I really need to know that someone cares about me."

It's cruel, but I have to push Grace's go button. Maybe in a few weeks I'll be able to deal with her, but not today. 5, 4, 3, 2, 1, and here goes, "So did I once, it was the saddest day of my young life--"

"I can't believe this—Pity the Poor Orphan—I need to hear that you love me, that everything will be OK--"

"Bye, Grace--"

"You're just like those stories, Cape Thomas, you never change. That's why your life is so boring--you never change!"

Grace is right about the orphan story. It never changes, no matter how much I wish it could. Damn if she's right about my life being boring, though, not once I decided to hell with Grace and set out to find the One that Got

Away. That's when I found out Death has another door, a trapdoor. And believe me no kicking or knocking is necessary to gain entry. But first let me tell you the orphan story. It's short and like Grace always said, "It defines you, Cape."

* * * * *

That day, the saddest day of my life, I was like a sea-urchin awash in a current of knees, belt buckles, and women's backsides covered in black dresses and silk stockings accessorized with toe-seeking high heeled shoes. Around and around in a maelstrom of misery we circled the room passing from one table loaded with food to the next. After a few close encounters with the spiked shoes, I broke free from the tide and found a small cove between the desserts and sweet tea tables. It was from there that I watched as the stout, well dressed woman scanned the room, then, satisfied no family members were in earshot, cupped her hand over her mouth and whispered to a man standing beside her, "I heard the old man wasn't going to bury Catherine and Allen in the same cemetery."

To her, Catherine and Allen are victims of a small plane crash, and their wake is a rich vein to mine for gossip. I knew them in a different way. Catherine was a beautiful woman who held me close and sang to me. Allen was tall man who rode me to bed on his strong shoulders every night. To me, Catherine and Allen were Mom and Dad, so naturally, I strained to hear more of what the woman had to say.

"Who told you that?" the thin man asked.

"One of Mr. Willard's law partners."

"Which one?"

"I'm not sure, one of the secretaries at the office told me. Well, she didn't exactly tell me, but I talked to the person she told."

"Ellen, how is it you always hear what nobody said?"

"Well, unlike old man Willard I don't hear the Lord, or worse, have conversations with Him. The whole family is crazy," Ellen said. "You know his wife died in a mental institution. Catherine would have eventually gone there, too, if she had lived. Just because you're pretty doesn't mean you're perfect."

Like any 5-year-old, I had no idea what a mental institution was, but the crazy remark and the backhanded insult to my pretty mother, made me feel I didn't like this woman.

"Be quiet, Mr. Willard might hear you." This time the thin man looked around the room.

"I don't care if he does. I'm not scared like you, George. If I'd known you were so spineless I never would have married you."

"Yeah, and if I'd known you were going to gain eighty pounds, most of it in your mouth, by the way, I wouldn't have married you, either."

"Wait till we get home, George," the woman snorted, then pointed down at me. "Oh, look, the boy. He's precious, do you think we can adopt him?" I ducked behind the dessert table, and watched as she devoured two more brownies.

"Why would you think he could be adopted, Mr. Willard keeps him, right?"

"That's not what I heard." She smacked, then wiped her lips. "Look at him, he looks just like Allen. If the old man hated one he's bound to hate the other. Come here, sweetie, let me hold you." Suddenly, I began to feel like I'd been baked, cooled, and slathered with double fudge icing. I scooted under the table. Concealed by lace cloth and sweet distractions I was safe….

"Now, where did you go? There you are, come here, Cape, honey." Like a pig after a truffle, she rooted me out. "Ouch…. Now that's not nice, don't hit. That's a good boy, give me a kiss…. Damn, he bit me, George! The little brat bit me!"

"Serves you right, leave him alone. You still want to adopt him?" George asked.

"No, I'd rather have a puppy." Ellen grabbed me by the scruff of my neck and pulled my ear to her mouth, "A dead one, you little brat. Dead, just like your momma and daddy--."

"Shut up, Ellen, he's just a kid. Come here, sport." George didn't seem like a very nice man, but I liked him because he didn't like fat Ellen, either.

"Watch out, George, he bites."

I couldn't be certain, but I felt pretty sure George wanted me to bite her again. As Ellen took cover behind George, I launched my next attack.

Before I reached my mark I was lifted high into the air by a big hand. "Whoa, boy, calm down." For a second I forgot about old Ellen, and I even forgot about my mother and father. All I could think about was how much fun it was to be high above the solemn misery of the room. I didn't know who this big man was who kept me dangling in mid air, but I sure liked my new neighborhood up there.

Easy, like a side of beef on a hook, I swung until I was eye to eye with the man who'd saved me. Blue eyes twinkling in a paper bag-brown face regarded me, and in a voice that warmed me like my mother's songs, he asked, "Do you remember me?" I shook my head. "Sure you do." Like a rocket I shot up in the air again, almost touching the 12-foot ceiling. "You remember that, don't you? I'm the first person who ever put you in orbit, boy. I'm Sarge, I was a friend of your dad's. As a matter of fact, I taught him how to fly." Sarge put me back on the floor and then squatted down next to me. "And one day, little Cape Thomas, I'm going to teach you how to…" Before Sarge could finish his sentence, my grandfather stepped between us.

"I doubt that day will come, Mr. Bishop. Now if you would be so kind, please leave my house."

A glint, like a small fleck of St Elmo's fire, filled Sarge's eyes and the room turned late-winter cold. "You know, Willard, I miss Catherine, too, and unlike you, I miss Allen. Whether you admit it or not, that boy will need me one day. Even the high and mighty Josh Willard can't change that."

"Why will I need him, Grandpa?"

"Cape, go on upstairs, and don't interrupt grown people when they're talking."

Like the beanstalk in the fairy tale, Sarge grew until he was a good head taller than my grandfather, "Tell him, Willard. Admit what you can't change, no matter how hard you try."

"Bishop, for the last time, you need to leave."

"I'll leave, but not before I tell him the truth." Quiet and easy, Sarge, again, squatted in front of me. "Sport, you're going to need me 'cause you're just like your daddy--born to fly."

"Get out, damn it! And don't ever come back, Bishop."

"Sarge. That's my name, boy, don't forget it. Willard, whether you like it or not, I made a promise to Allen Thomas, and I intend to keep it."

The scene with Sarge ended the wake for me, but I was later summoned from my room by Grandfather. We stood near the door and bid the mourners good-bye. While my grandfather shook hands, I suffered the indignity of unwanted familiarity. Women I neither knew nor wanted to know were compelled to crush me and smother me with their sickly floral scents. Men tousled my hair and patted my head as if I were a hunting dog that had held its point. Soft whispers ending in "poor dear" or "so young" did nothing but remind me that the sweet songs and broad shoulders were gone forever.

George and Ellen were the last to leave. After seeing how my grandfather had handled Sarge, I couldn't wait to fill him in on this pair. "Grandpa," I pointed at Ellen. "She said my mama--"

"Was perfect, picture perfect, actually," Ellen said as she stuck her big butt between me and my grandpa. "CRAZY," I yelled. "Yes, just as I told George. Crazy the way the good ones always leave so young. We're so sorry, Mr. Willard." Instead of the wrath I hoped for, Grandpa said, "Thank you, Ellen, George. And God bless."

"Oh, and by the way." Ellen rubbed the bite mark on her cheek, "your grandson is just--soooo precious."

With that George tousled my hair and bent down beside me. "You know, son, your parents aren't really gone, you'll see them again one day."

For the first time that day, I smiled. To heck with Ellen, and my Grandpa, too. As soon as Mom got back I'd tell her all about Ellen and George. She'd laugh and tell me to forgive and forget, and Dad would say how some things just aren't worth it. And we'd leave this big old empty house and never, ever, have a wake again.

Mindful not to interrupt grownups, I waited until George and Ellen were gone before I asked my question. "When will they be back, Grandpa?"

"When will who be back?"

"Mom and Dad. When can I see them again?"

"When we get to the sweet by-and-by, son. Now go to bed, I want to be alone for a while."

Years later, like my grandfather, I would learn to live in solitude. But that night all I wanted was one more sweet song and a last piggy-back ride to bed.

"When do you think we might head over to the sweet by-and-by, Grandpa?"

"When you're older."

"I'll be six next year."

"Not old enough--"

"Grandpa, why did all those people hug and pet me?"

"To make you feel better--"

"You didn't get hugged, why did they just shake your hand?"

"To make me feel better, now--"

"I didn't like getting hugged, it makes you smell funny. Maybe I'll just get my hand shook from now on. Where--"

"Cape, go to bed. I swear you're going to wear your jaws out talking so much."

From my bedroom I could see a sliver of my grandfather at his desk across the hall. Tears ran down his face as he held a framed picture of my mother. I figured there was only one thing to do…share my consolation. In the dark I found my shirt scented with ladies' perfume and crawled into his lap. With one hand I patted his head, and with the other I gently pushed the shirt under his face so the ersatz balm could rejuvenate him, since it hadn't worked on me. He held me at arm's-length, though. "Why can't you leave me alone? It's your fault, you know. If it hadn't been for you, she would have left him. She would still be here. But no, she had to fly with that fool."

"I want to fly, too," I said.

"What did you say?"

"I want to fly with my mama and daddy."

"Boy, you can stay in this house, but don't ever mention two things to me, flying or him. And one more thing, I don't want you to ever go around that Sarge Bishop. He's evil, do you understand?"

"Yes, sir."

"Promise me, then."

"I promise. Can I ask you one more question?"

"One more, Cape, and let that be it."

"Where is the sweet by-and-by?"

"It's on the other side."

"The other side of what?"

"On the other side of the river," my grandfather replied.

"The Neuse?"

"The River Jordan--"

" Is that the same river in the Bible all those people washed their sin away?"

"For the last time, Cape, go to bed, NOW!"

Staying away from Sarge was one thing, not seeing my parents was another. George had promised me that I would see my parents again, and I believed him. I waited days, then months, and finally years.

I was ten years old when a chance to fulfill that prophecy rolled into town on the wheels of a traveling carnival. I needed permission, a simple yes or no. But my grandfather wasn't a simple man, no lawyer is. His answers, as always, were based on logic and reason, the tools of his trade.

I asked and received the ambiguous response I expected. My grandfather put his pipe down and looked me over. Two ribbons of smoke the color of his gray hair rolled from his nose and layered briefly on his square chin. His bushy eyebrows knitted together, like a gunfighter's on the sunny side of the street. "Go to the carnival? What business does a ten-year-old boy have at a carnival? That place is for Philistines and sinners, so which one are you, boy?" he asked in his graveled voice.

Not sure what a Philistine was, I chose what I believed to be the more innocuous answer.

"I'm a Philistine, Grandpa."

"Philistine, are you?"

I knew he didn't want a definition of Philistine. He wanted an explanation of my convictions, so I readily complied.

"Grandpa, one of the boys at school told me there was a circus woman that could

contact people on the other side. That's got to be close to the sweet by-and-by. I want to talk to my mama, and I'm going if I have to go with the sinners."

My grandfather had his own convictions, and delivered them with the piety of an Apostle.

"Boy, the only way you are ever going to see your mama is to walk the straight and narrow path to the Lord. The same path I have to walk daily to make sure I meet my sweet Sarah when the Rapture comes. Now silence that blasphemous tongue of yours, or lose all hope of salvation. Righteousness is the path to salvation. Go to bed, and think long and hard about that."

As I waited and contemplated my salvation, the sun dipped into the cool darkness hovering on the horizon. Financing my rendezvous with the sweet by-and-by was easy thanks to my grandfather's habit of piling the contents of his pockets on his roll-top desk. I grabbed five dollars from his money clip, and folded another bill to make up for the missing five. Greased by excitement, I slid my bony frame out of my partially opened window and raced across the field.

The mysteries of the carnival beckoned me. The smell of cotton candy and popcorn tempted me like a savory Jezebel. I resisted my hunger, though. The spinning lights and loud music battled with the carnival barkers to dominate the cacophony of the Midway.

"Come one, come all. See the five-hundred-pound Bearded Lady, and the Eighth Wonder of the World, The Rubber Man from India. See Lola. She twists, she shakes, she does the hoochie-coochie-- Get out of here, boy. Come back when you grow up."

I ducked the jab of the barker's cane and hid among the tents anchored to steel stakes by paraffin-rubbed ropes. Like a predator, I searched for signs of my prey. Then I saw it. A smudgy cloth banner suspended above a tent that read, Madame Marie the World's Greatest Psychic. I eased the tent flap open and stepped inside. Bands of smoke from earlier patrons drifted atop the candles like empyreal veils guarding the secrets of the spirit world.

Inside, the fragrance of incense masked the Midway smell of onions and greasy Italian sausage. An old woman, with eyes turned milky, sat alone in this unholy sanctum. Madame Marie caressed the crystal ball with leathered, callused hands, then drew closer to the clear orb and closed her eyes.

"You seek those on the other side?"

"Yes, ma'am. But if you don't find them on the other side, you might try the sweet by-and-by, it's across the River Jordan."

"Five dollars, please."

Any fool could see the spirits were upon her, surely she could contact the dead. I plunked down my money before her trance was broken.

The world inside the crystal orb was a wondrous place of mother's love and great things to come. Then the old woman looked up and said, "You will find what you have lost, what you will lose cannot be found."

"What's that mean?" I asked.

"Five dollars, please."

Between my question and the answer was the price of a candle to be burned for good fortune. Another five dollars for answers and a candle seemed like a good deal to me.

Consumed by the prospect of finding my parents, I ran home and urged my grandfather to invest. "Five dollars! First you steal, then beg for more. You fool, get out of my sight!" he yelled.

I was trapped. Trapped in reality, and forbidden to seek what I had lost. The choice I made was easy. That night I concluded, with help from my grandfather's anger, that neither the straight and narrow, nor the spirit world would ever satisfy my depraved needs. I was a hopeless, gullible Philistine, and a thief, doomed to suffer the sinner's lot, and probably some prison time. I discarded my faith, my love of the sweet by-and-by, and my precious salvation; it was all hocus-pocus, like carnival magic, without tents and crystal balls.

*   *   *   *   *

Thirty-five years have passed since that night at the carnival, and three years have passed since I closed the door on Grace with my last rendition of Pity the Poor Orphan. As heart crushing as losing Grace had been it was nothing compared to the castration AeroMax preformed on me when they took my beloved Boeing 747.

Drunken stupor doesn't begin to the describe the days since I lost my airliner. That's why I remember this night so vividly, instead of playing my nightly game of hop-to-the-Scotch, I opted for a shot of clean and sober. I remember feeling a little smug as I slid into fresh sheets without my perpetual companion, double vision.

It was warm that night, almost summertime warm. Even though it was December, I opened my windows to enjoy the night air. Free of alcohol, I went to sleep quickly. But the breeze picked up, and the incessant clanging of wind chimes awakened me. Grace, had placed them on the deck to help her sleep. When I was snuggled up with her the sound was peaceful, but now the clanging was just a lonesome reminder of what had been. I made a promise to get rid of them.

The prosperous glow of my Rolex Chronograph, a gift from AeroMax when I made captain, illuminated the time; precisely two minutes past 2:00 a.m. Minutes and seconds are critical to pilots. Many times they are the difference between flying or dying. For me to notice the exact time was not unusual, but what happened next was.

From my bed, I can see the deck through the French doors. The moon was full, but pale shadows of trees webbed across the deck. In spite of the shadows, my view of Jimmy the yardman was unimpeded.

The reason I call him Jimmy the yardman is simple. I've never known his last name, and he helps me in the yard. An old greenhouse I never use is now his home for the same reason I have the wind chimes I don't want. Grace had a pang of social guilt, over Jimmy's low wages, and I provided the cure. It's been 3 years, and I'm still dealing with her projects.

I don't mind the blind goldfish in my pond, and I've become attached to Mex-a-peg, a three-legged Chihuahua with a prosthesis Grace rescued from the pound. Even Jimmy has become palatable, except for his habit of singing stupid songs and roaming around the yard at odd hours when he's drinking.

My unwanted guest stepped onto the wooden bench around the deck. He faced the yard and cupped his hand above his eyes, like an Indian chief peering out over the Great Plains. I was thankful he wasn't singing or yodeling. The thought that he might break out with an ill-timed and out-of-tune serenade put me on edge. By now, I was fully awake and tired of Jimmy's pitiful impression of Cochise. As I sat up in bed, he began to writhe like a man impaled by an arrow. Clutching his chest with both hands, he whirled to face me.

But the man on my deck wasn't Jimmy. The face staring at me was mine, but mine twenty-five years earlier. The younger me was dressed in a flannel shirt, jeans, long hair and a beard.

This called for an investigation, but I ignored the summons. I don't know why I didn't get up, but it might have been for the same reason people don't get up to answer nature's call in the middle of the night. The urge for relief is unbearable, but the resolution not to yield prevails, or maybe the floor is too cold. Anyway, I convinced myself that the wind and the shadows of the trees were playing tricks on me.

What happened next can't be explained away so easily. In the spot on the deck where the younger me had been standing, a young woman now stood facing the yard. She was leaning over as if searching for something. I sat up and eased to the foot of the bed. What I saw on my deck was surely a dream, but real or not, seeing her pleased me.

My consolation was knowing that once she had been real, and for one brief night she had been mine. My eyes widened and consumed her image. Her beauty pierced the darkness, and I was drawn to her light. She was dressed in jeans and a three-quarter-sleeved white blouse. Her hair was long, milk-chocolate brown, thick and delicious. The length stopped at the small of her back, and rather than the blunt cut most women with long hair have, hers was cut in an oval. Under her clothes was a perfect hourglass figure and long legs that tapered seductively to her bare feet. Her complexion was light, but darkened by a late summer tan.

She turned to face me. The bright moonlight reflected from her eyes like flame against crystal. Deep-troubled furrows creased her forehead. I let my eyes drift downward from her face. Her neck was long and graceful, and around this elegant neck hung an amulet of some sort. I strained to see what it was. In the dim light I could scarcely make it out. Then, there it was--a silver Coptic Cross in an onyx setting. Cradled in her arms was what appeared to be an infant. I couldn't see the baby, it was wrapped in a blanket, but the woman's tender stokes validated my hunch…baby.

I call this woman Faith, not because that is her name, but because that was the name she agreed to answer to when I met her twenty-five years ago.

Our one evening together was predicated upon an impromptu set of rules. I told her only my first name. "Cape," she repeated. Then held up her hand for me to stop, "I don't need to know anymore. I'm interested in the what, not the who."

I guessed it was important for her to have control over the situation. She didn't tell me why, and I didn't ask. I suspected the men in her life had controlled her long enough. She was pleased by the anonymity, and I was aroused by the intrigue.

I've had dreams and thoughts of Faith over the years. But I'd never seen her again, and the hell of it was, I wasn't sure I was seeing her now.

For a quarter of a century Faith had been absent from my life, but the mystery of her identity was as strong now as then. Little did I know this form on my deck was about to change that. This secretive lover, who would not even tell me her name, would soon unveil her reason to live and my reason to die.

CHAPTER TWO

More Riddles

Early rays from the sun scattered the events of the night across my mind like jigsaw pieces. My inability to connect them was as frustrating as the day my grandfather gave me a boxed puzzle without a picture on the lid.

"Won't I need the picture on the box to put the puzzle together?" I asked.

"No, that would be too easy. Learn to use your mind," he replied.

He was right. The puzzle wasn't easy, but hating his gift was. Each day he noted my lack of progress, and each day he urged me to finish it. Finally, I sent the gift on a short trip--unwrapped and by air.

Pipe in mouth, the old man gathered the far-flung pieces and divided them into two piles on the kitchen table. I pretended not to watch as he formed the straight-edged pieces into a frame for the puzzle. One particular detail caught my eye, a blade from a propeller. I raced to find the other pieces and didn't stop until the image of a P-51 Mustang was complete.

Whether my grandfather helped me finish the puzzle I don't remember, but I do remember what he said. "There are two ways to solve a problem, son. The one you displayed earlier is not the correct way, and starting from the ends and working toward the middle may not always work. But there is always a solution. Remember that, if you remember nothing else I tell you."

The airplane puzzle was the only artifact of aviation I remember ever being in my grandfather's house. Years after he died I realized he had allowed me to keep it not for my pleasure but as a symbol of a lesson learned. Now the puzzle, still intact, is a reminder of the wisdom of my grandfather.

My lingering doubts about Faith and the baby reminded me of the puzzle lesson from long ago. There was a solution. And in the meantime, seeing the wind chimes, now silent, I recalled last night's promise to quiet them. With a handful of remorse, I unhooked the chimes then tossed the last article of my eight-year relationship with Grace into the trash.

Certain the case of Faith's whereabouts could be solved, I secured the area like a detective at a homicide scene. In the early morning light I scrutinized each section of the lawn from the deck to the outward boundaries of the yard. Satisfied that no trespass had occurred in my little corner of the world, I turned my attention to the deck. From knee level I scoured each board of the structure with the same intensity of my yard search. No footprints, no pacifier, not even a chocolate brown hair had been left behind to confirm or refute the earlier late-night manifestation.

Case closed, the answer was simple. I was the victim of an over-active imagination.

I clung to that thought, like a drowning man to a bubble, on my way to the airport. My recent troubles with the FAA had taught me just how tenuous my job was. Pilots who see things that aren't there don't remain pilots for long.

Morning traffic on Highway 70 slowed, then stopped altogether, for a construction crew unloading a bulldozer. Horns blared, late-to-work commuters gnashed teeth, pounded steering wheels, and protested the unexpected delay with one-finger salutes for the men who had caused it. Normally, I would have joined the malcontents--but not today. Five hours ahead of schedule, I was a cut above the masses.

Oblivious to the commuters' scorn, the large D-6 Caterpillar inched up the embankment to an abandoned home site. Without stopping, the dozer sheared the front porch from the Victorian house barely visible from the road. I turned into the driveway and walked in front of the machine. Not a good idea maybe, considering the scowl on the operator's face.

"You got a problem, Bud?" he yelled.

"Nope, happy as a clown, actually."

"You the owner, then?" he asked, as he idled the engine.

"No, but I know this place. Have you got a minute?"

The operator dropped from the machine. A large ring of keys hooked to his belt rattled as he landed. "I'm kind of busy. What you got?"

"It'll just take a second, let me show you something."

We left the machine and made our way through the vines and privet that covered the lot. In a small opening behind the back porch I stopped and pointed to the backyard.

"I know it doesn't look like much now. But there's a hell of garden out here. It's an old English garden with stone walkways and a concrete water garden with an antique fountain. Along the back under the vines is a stone wall with niches cut into it. In the center of the wall is an old fireplace with a brick patio."

"So, what'd you want me to do about it?" the operator asked.

"Well, I just thought the new owners might want to save--."

"Commercial bank site, Bud. It's all coming down."

"Maybe you--"

"Hey, Bud, I gotta get to work-- time's money, you know."

"Yeah, we wouldn't want real skilled labor to stop work, now would we? See ya."

I leaned on the hood of my car and watched as the old house succumbed to the parries and thrusts of the dozer. The destruction was orderly despite the haphazard pile of broken boards, mortar-crusted bricks, and the remnants of the garden. I peered around the conical heap of trash, and observed the bulldozer blade smooth swaths of earth with each pass. The angle of the blade folded gardenias and lilac bushes under the dark brown soil like a mixing stick swirls unshaken paint into consistent uniformity.

Atop the chaos created by the blade rose the swing I piloted as a boy. Like a boat on an angry ocean, the swing fought the swell of debris and rode the crest. It was on that slatted wooden seat that Faith and I had formulated our rules. I silently admired the bravado of the swing to remain in the present. Nursed by the underdog's creed, "Swings are made for swinging," I decided to intervene, but before I could stop the machine, destiny stoked by diesel fuel prevailed. With one final crushing blow the swing exploded into a splintered memory, and the present claimed another victim.

Seeing the destruction of a place my grandfather loved so much, and the roots of my beginning, gave me second thoughts about my decision to sell the place. My home base was gone, and the thought of what its destruction meant hit me hard. If a man has a future, the course to it cannot be set without the guiding beacon of the past. I toasted that thought, then swallowed the truth--a bitter elixir.

As of today, any links to my past had all died, except one, and I wasn't even certain of that one. It was worth a shot, and I had a little time to kill. Figuring out the right route took a while, even then, each curve and dip of the secondary road played Yin and Yang with my memory. Not until I saw a mailbox decorated with freshly hand-painted letters spelling out Minnie Reynaud was I sure of my destination.

To me, Miss Minnie was a midwife-shaman who could talk the fire out of a burn, cure a cough with red rot sap, and remove a bee stinger with a dip of her snuff. I believed in Miss Minnie and her powerful medicines of herbs and signs. I believed because she saved my life once. I was eight and running the high fever of pneumonia. My grandfather called Dr. Meyer but the prognosis wasn't good. "I gave him some penicillin, Josh, but if the fever doesn't break he won't make it. You can take him to the hospital, but I don't know what good that'll do."

That's when I first met Miss Minnie. My grandfather drove me to the house down this very path. Miss Minnie boiled a concoction of eucalyptus and black snakeroot in an iron kettle over her fireplace. I leaned over the steamy cauldron and breathed in the vapors. Miss Minnie took me outside and sat with me in the freezing weather, though I was damp from the steam. The night sky was cold and clear. The stars were as bright as I ever remember seeing them. That night I learned of Orion, the hunter killed by the woman he loved; Ursa Major, the Great Bear and keeper of the Big Dipper; Ursa Minor, the Little Bear and keeper of the Little Dipper. Delirious from the fever, I imagined myself floating in the sky with the stars, and reached out to touch them. " Yours, boy, the sky is yours, always will be," Miss Minnie promised.

Then I asked the question that helped me know Miss Minnie was special, "How do I get there?"

"Why you ask me that question, boy, when you already know the answer?"

"You mean Sarge Bishop?"

"Ain't what I know, it's what you know, boy."

The fever broke and I vowed to find the man that would get me to the stars.

The shrinking and pock-marked path convinced me that I was too late. Miss Minnie, despite the new name on her mailbox, was probably dead. The bottom of my chassis scraped the sandy furrow in the middle of the path. Wax myrtle bushes overgrowing the woods path trapped the dust rolling from my car and softened my arrival.

The house looked nothing like I remembered. Instead of a neatly painted shotgun house, a hovel of weatherworn boards and a stained tin roof stood in the clearing. A thin wisp of smoke from the chimney was the only sign of life. Cluttered about the yard were old tire planters coated in fading white paint. The tires, once filled with flowers, now contained winter-dried weeds and cockleburs. I decided to yell from the yard rather than knock on the door.

"Miss Minnie, you in there?"

"Bring some wood in when you come."

I looked around the yard for the firewood pile. An axe handle protruding from a clump of red-stemmed sourwoods showed the location. The handle of the axe had been taped with electrical tape. I grabbed the sticky handle and swung at an old length of log on the ground, then ducked the axe head as it bounced back almost as fast as it went down. There was no need to look at the bark to see what the wood was--green sweetgum, and you don't split green gum.

I rummaged around the pile until I found a length of oak and split it into four pieces. Next to the logs was a chunk of fat lighter. I chipped off three hunks and headed for the porch. Most of the boards in the slat porch were gone. The remaining boards had curled from the rain, and two of those had been freshly broken. I suspected the porch doubled as a firewood source during bad weather. A heart pine joist under the porch was the only solid part left of the landing. I spaced my steps to avoid the rusting nails and walked the beam to the door. Smells of human waste mingled with the darkness of the house. Certain there was a slop jar somewhere close by, I waited at the doorway until my eyes adjusted to the dimness. "Hey, Miss Minnie."

"Did you bring the wood?"

Standing in plain view, I didn't understand the question until I saw the red-tipped cane resting by her side. The opaque lenses of her eyes told the reason for her blindness, cataracts.

"Yes, ma'am, I brought you some lighter, too."

"Good, put a piece on the fire, that ought to heat this old place up some."
I lifted the coiled stainless steel handle on the wood stove and shoved in two pieces of the kindling. The fat pine lighter sputtered, then began to roar as the pine resin ignited. "You know, Miss Minnie, they say pine will gum up your chimney if you burn too much of it."

"I don't give a damn what they say. I'm cold--been cold all winter."

It was easy to see why. Brittle shards of caulking lay under the window. Several panes of glass from the windows on the north side of the house were missing. Stuffed in their place were dingy burlap sacks. A clear plastic sheet that buffeted each time the breeze stirred covered cracks and splits on the lap siding at the opposite end of the house.

"Miss Minnie, I'm--"

" I know who you are. You're Mr. Willard's boy."

"Grandson, actually."

"He raised you, didn't he?"

"Yes, ma'am."

"His boy. Don't sass me no more."

In the South you don't "argue" with older people, you "sass" them. I was a guest, and I was displaying bad manners. The old woman was right, even if she was wrong.

"I apologize, Miss Minnie, forgive me."

The old woman smiled, and then spat out her dip of Four Roses snuff onto the door and handle of the red-hot wood stove. I watched the spittle sizzle down the front of the stove and wiped my hand on my pant leg. "Miss Minnie, why don't you ask for some help, the state could find you a better place to live."

"Been helped, don't need no more help."

"You could be warm."

"I'm warm now. Don't need nobody in my business, you included. What you want, anyway?"

"Maybe I just came by for a visit."

"You ain't been here since your granddaddy died, ain't likely you come by now to visit."

Not likely, she was right about that. I hadn't come to visit.

"Miss Minnie, you knew my grandmother and my mother-- "

"Brought your mama into this world, cared for your grandma till she went off."

"That's what I came to find out. Where did my grandmother go?"

"Hospital," Miss Minnie screeched.

"What kind of hospital?" The old woman opened up another can of snuff and poured a dip between her gum and bottom lip. I waited for her answer, and then waited some more.

"Was it a mental hospital?" I asked. The old woman hummed Sweet Chariot, but didn't answer me.

"Miss Minnie, I need to know. They say she saw things, maybe things that weren't there."

"Miss Sarah was special."

"You mean crazy? She and my mother were crazy, right?"

"I said special. Didn't say crazy, did I?"

I'd heard this story before. My grandfather said the same thing about my grandmother, special. Being a native, I can appreciate the gentility of the region as well as the next person, but I wanted--needed--the truth.

"My grandfather said she was crazy."

"Ain't no such thing, don't be putting lies in dead people's mouths. You better go now."

My lie hadn't worked, nor had I expected it to. I reverted to a novel approach, the truth.

"Miss Minnie, I saw something last night. It seemed real, but I know it wasn't. I need to know if I'm like my grandmother and mother. If I'm crazy I need to stop flying."

"Maybe you just special?"

"How were they special?"

"Depends, I reckon."

"Depends on…?"

"Depends on how you look at things."

"Miss Minnie, I need more than riddles. I know my grandmother went to a private hospital, but I don't know why. Her records are sealed. They say my mother might have ended up there too, if she had lived. Tell me how grandmother and mother saw things."

"Sometimes, what you looking at--ain't what you see."

Disgusted by another riddle, I went outside and split more wood. The situation was hopeless and, as always, beyond my control. The special-ness of my family heritage would continue to haunt me as long as the subject was taboo. As a kid the subject was never brought up directly, instead euphemistic phrases spoken in the murmurs of gossip circled the topic. For some reason I was never allowed into the loop, though I was always included in the speculation. I swung the axe with sheer malice--the destruction inflicted on the oak logs fed my frustration. One day I would pile the subject into a neat stack like the firewood I placed by the door of the old house…. Then burn it, piece by damn piece!

"Miss Minnie, I'll check back before the winter is over, just in case you need some more wood."

"Won't need none," the old woman said, as she stood in the door and felt the pile of wood to check the volume.

"Well, Miss Minnie, you'll need some next year."

"Won't be here next year."

"Are you moving?"

"I'll be a hundred come July the 4th . Plan on marching with the Saints that day."

"Miss Minnie, you can't know that, not for sure."

"Boy, don't tell me what I know. Tell me something I don't know."

I looked at the old woman with her jaw set. Determined, sure of herself, and sure of the statement she had made. "I need to know if I can be buried here, don't want to be buried in no graveyard."

"Maybe you'd better check with a lawyer."

"You a lawyer, ain't you?"

"No, ma'am, that was my grandfather," I said.

"Well, didn't you learn no law from him?"

"Miss Minnie, I'm a pilot, I fly."

"Then fly your long ass up to the courthouse and find out. I don't want to be bothered once I turn my toes up."

I nodded, then remembered she was blind, "Yes, ma'am. I'll be back"

"One more thing, make sure I get buried east to west."

"What difference does that make?"

"Knew a man once, a bad man. He got buried north to south, he near 'bout worried me to death complaining about it."

"How could he complain if he was buried, that doesn't make sense."

"Ain't you something, talking about something with no sense. If you so smart how come you here asking me questions 'bout something plain as day."

I headed back for my car. Miss Minnie, as they say, "wasn't herself."

"Boy?"

"Yes, Ma'am."

"Them things you see? "

“Yes, ma’am?”

“They tell a story, you’ll figure it out.”

“I don’t know about that, Miss Minnie.”

“It’ll come to you.”

“How do you know?”

“Cause…you special, too.”

Un-huh, I sure was. Just like my grandmother, mother, and Miss Minnie. We weren’t crazy--the rest of the world was.

CHAPTER THREE

An Old Friend in Atlanta.

My King Air came into view as soon as I turned onto the airport road. The sleek fluid lines of the aircraft sashayed across the tarmac, and my appreciation rose to meet them. Planes have always been more than machines of commerce to me. They are magic carpets that have taken me around the world many times.

Once London, Paris, Rio and Madrid had been the destinations I craved and I was certain my life as a Southerner was over. So certain that the Southern life was not for me, I sold every asset my grandfather had left me. Not until today had I regretted erasing my geographical heritage.

The South is a chameleon, a soft-spoken seductress bathed in scents of magnolia and honeysuckle. In the summer, her rivers run black and clear against verdant banks lined with thin sandy lips. In the fall, she slips from her green veil and dons a calico quilt more colorful than a rainbow. Her winters are a mixed temperate concoction, not unlike a hot fudge sundae. The extract of this wondrous place--the South-- is renowned for its therapeutic effects on expatriates come home. So far, however, the cure had eluded me.

I returned to eastern North Carolina to start over, but after three years I was more lost than ever. Faith's visit had stopped my monastic retreat, brought me up short, and forced me to face my past. My visit with Miss Minnie only reminded me of the secrets of that past, and the difficulty of engaging them.

I stopped to watch as Shane, my co-pilot, hustled the baggage of our six passengers into the various storage lockers scattered about the plane. The bang-click of the slamming lockers salted my raw nerves, and for one second I wanted to quarter his head as I had the oak logs.

"Shane, close'em, don't slam'em."

"You in a bad mood?"

I was in a bad mood. The proceeds from the sale of my grandfather's house had been sunk into this piece of machinery Shane was abusing. My bad temperament stemmed from the doubts I now had about that decision.

"What's mood got to do with the destruction of personal property?" Shane ignored me and left to retrieve the last suitcase on the ramp. To Shane this job was just another rung in the aviation ladder, a stepping stone to the airlines. To me it was the last grab hold on a tarnished world I once owned. I inspected the lockers then finished the preflight of the plane.

"Is the cabin ready?" I asked.

"Yeah," Shane slammed the last bag into the wing locker, then wisely pressed the lid into place. "It's well stocked, or stocked anyway."

"How well stocked?"

"I didn't buy anymore expensive booze, if that's what you mean."

"Good."

I'm not cheap. However, when people pay eleven hundred dollars an hour to fly, they generally recoup expenses by drinking and eating everything on the plane. Which is definitely a strain on the thin bottom line.

"I hate to bring this up, since you're in a bad mood," Shane said. "But the last charter complained about the cheap Scotch. Thought you might want to know."

"That's moderately priced Scotch, not cheap. You want to know something about the last charter?"

Shane shrugged, figuring that silence was the path of least resistance. I ignored his sullenness. I wanted someone to listen to me, and since Shane was the only one around, and on my payroll, he was nominated.

"Well, let me tell you anyway. The cheap bastard hasn't paid in full yet, and you want to know why?"

"Because he deducted for the Scotch?" Shane asked.

"Heck, no. It's because he's using my money to buy old houses and paying bulldozers to tear up gardens. And the banks that buy the land don't care if an old woman is cold, crazy, or needs help. She doesn't count, I don't count, and you don't count, because we're deducted from the bottom line. That's why he doesn't pay. He's using my money to screw up my life."

"I don't know, I think he just wanted better Scot-"

"Yeah, well the next time he does, maybe I'll take it out of the co-pilot pay, then I won't have to buy the cheap stuff."

"Austere but charming Scotch, I believe you meant." I ignored Shane's facetious comment. But he was right. It was the Scotch. The world's ills could be cured if we all drank better Scotch.

"Fine," I gave Shane my bag. " Put this and the rest of the goodies on the plane, maybe they'll make up for the booze."

"Oh man, expensive Krispy Kreme donuts and a pot of exquisite instant coffee… must be another slow payer."

"Shane, you know you're wasting your talents in aviation. Comedy. Stand-up
comedy--there's where your fortune lies."

Shane was twenty-one and bulletproof. A hot-shot flight instructor ready to move up to the airlines. His chance for an airline job was a long shot unless he could get some turbine time. That's where I came in. Turbine time was the ticket to the big leagues, and without it you couldn't get hired by the airlines. I couldn't pay Shane much money to fly, but I could punch his ticket to the next level. So, I guess you could say we had a true symbiotic relationship. I got my required copilot, and he got turbine time flying the King Air.

"You want me to fly left seat today?"

"Sure, Shane, why not, I've lived a good life."

Left seat on an airplane is the captain's seat. I've spent over twenty thousand hours in left seats as pilot in command. A lot of those hours were as a 747 captain. The world was good then, and I was on top of it. Now I can't even fly solo, not for hire anyway. I'm a pilot with clipped wings.

"Do you ever miss the 747?" Shane asked.

Now there was a dumb question. Left seat on a King Air was a world away from the left seat on the 747 I flew as a captain for AeroMax, and the differences were more than subtle. Both planes had a crew of two and they both burned kerosene, but there the similarity ended.

A Boeing 747-400 carries 57,285 gallons of jet fuel. That's 343,710 lbs., or more than the gross weight of 29 King Air B100's like we were flying. With a full load of passengers, and a complement of 15 flight attendants, the weight of the 747 balloons to 875,000 lbs., roughly equal to the weight of a 1,000-head herd of prime beef cattle. Once this aerial behemoth is airborne, the captain has sole autonomy over a populace of more than 500 people. More than many of the rural towns it flies over in excess of 560 mph. Pretty heady stuff, that made for a very long fall back to the left seat of the King Air.

"Nope, it's just another plane to me," I lied.

"I'd kill to fly a 747. The bullshit wouldn't bother me."

That was the airport rumor: I had given up my cushy airline job because of the bullshit. Hey, it sounded good, and besides I wasn't obliged to tell them that nothing could be further from the truth. I gave it up because I had two options--resign or be fired. Discretion being the better part of valor, I chose resignation. AeroMax was noble enough to be discreet, and I had enough sense to follow their lead.

The FAA mandatory retirement age is sixty. I should have had fourteen years of good flying left. But none of that mattered anymore. As far as anyone in the aviation industry was concerned, I was finished. Shane made sure our passengers were belted in, locked the door, and then slid into the left seat.

"You ready?" Shane asked.

"Yeah, sure. I was just thinking about mandatory retirement."

"Why you've got a long way to go. What are you now, fifty-nine?"

"Forty-six, Butthead."

We taxied out to the departure end of runway five. Shane lined up on the centerline and checked the instruments one last time before departure roll.

From the cockpit window I watched as the fields and woods below lost their identities and melded into a patchwork quilt of boundless geography.

Somewhere, probably within my field of vision, lay the remains of my family. Buried with them were the answers to my questions.

My grandfather was my last link to my ancestry, and his answers had been as meaningless and enigmatic as Miss Minnie's. My father, as far as I knew, was an alien cast down from a strange planet called, Up North. If he had family living, I knew nothing of them. I was certain they knew even less about me. This makes me the last denizen from planet Up North and the final link in a Southern helix--proud but conflicted. My bloodline stops with me because of my bad choices. Grace didn't want children, but she knew all about my one evening with Faith, even how my mystery lady felt about kids. Her dig about not chasing after the one I loved wasn't new, hackneyed, well-worn, but sure-as-hell not new.

I think what Grace never understood is that Faith was like my parents. In my mind they were perfect. Perfect, only because they were unknown and unspoiled by association. Unfound, Faith was the perfect one-that-got-away. Over the years it became easy to make her the benchmark no other woman could attain. I invoked her stature anytime the prospect of commitment arose in other relationships.

Now my ideal woman had come calling. OK not physically, but I took Faith's visit as a sign that maybe the good times were back, maybe I was back. That, or else my family legacy of insanity had mutated and come to claim its last victim.

Once we reached cruise altitude I grabbed the copy of the A.I.M. (Aeronautical Information Manual) to research the events of last night. I not only wanted to know the reason for the visit--I had an obligation to find out what it was.

"Why do you need the AIM?" Shane asked. "I thought you wrote it with Wilbur and Orville."

"I'm paying you to fly, not to insult me. Do you mind?" I studied Shane for a moment. Yes, I decided he would look good quartered and stacked on Miss Minnie's woodpile.

"What F.A.R. (Federal Aviation Regulation) do you need, I bet I know it."

I looked down and opened the book. "I doubt it."

"Try me?"

"Shane, I'll look it up. Do you mind if I do a little reading on my own?"

"Nope, I'm all for higher education."

"You keep running your mouth, and that'll be the only way you get higher."

"Just kidding."

"Kid quieter."

"Right."

According to Part 67.302 of the F.A.R. "A pilot can have no established medical history or clinical diagnosis of any of the following: delusions, hallucinations, gross bizarre or disorganized behavior is not qualified to hold a second-class medical certificate."

Clinical diagnosis? If the dead could talk that would be a good question to ask. Were the two women responsible for my life certified crazy, or just crazy? My grandfather said they were special, but my grandfather had a way with words. It was his job to make words serve him. Funny I never wanted to be like my grandfather. Now it would be good if I had his talents. I read the paragraph again and pondered the meaning of clinical diagnosis--Grandpa could use those two little words in a way that would keep me flying.

I made a mental note not to talk to a psychologist, because avoiding a consultation would at least keep me from being officially diagnosed. Next, I would give the phenomenon a name, a harmless word that would raise no red flags. I searched for a word or phrase to describe my phantom visitor. "Figment of my imagination" sounded too much like mental illness. What harmless word or phrase could describe the visit by Faith and the infant?

"Vision." I verbalized the word and instantly regretted it.

"What?"

"Nothing. Just thinking out loud."

"You said vision. Losing the old eyesight, Cape? You can still fly as long as it's correctable."

"I know that, see how you like this word… fired."

"Fired?" Shane asked, with a wounded look.

"Just checking your hearing."

"You want me to shut up?"

"Yeah."

Vision, good word and a safe distance from psychosis. My grandfather would have used that word, vision; it sounded almost Biblical. After all, people in the Bible were always having visions, and nobody ever stuck them in a nut house, or worse, grounded them.

I watched as Shane's chin played tag with his neck. The vibration of the plane was putting him to sleep, a phenomenon more common than the flying public would ever believe. Good, the quiet would give me time to think. No, that wouldn't do, I had a better plan. I turned the volume up on the crew intercom.

"It's over! Both engines are on fire, we're going down." I yelled.

"Oh no… Mama!" Shane's recovery was neither graceful nor dignified.

"Mama?"

"Jesus," Shane muttered as he determined the plane was still flyable. "What was that all about?"

"You were sleeping."

"Huh? Sleeping…naw, I was day dreaming. I had one eye open."

"Right… While we're on the subject, have you ever dreamed something that seemed real?" I asked.

"Just for the record I didn't say Mama, I said Mayday."

"Uh huh, sounded more like Mama to me."

"It was Mayday." Shane rubbed his eyes. "What was the question? Oh yeah, dream. Sure, let me think. Yeah, I dreamed one time I was caught robbing a bank. Man, I woke up in a sweat."

"I guess you woke up screaming Mayday?"

"I didn't scream. I very calmly said Mayday."

"Whatever....But, you remember waking up, I mean you knew it was a dream?" I asked.

"Yeah, I knew it was a dream, I wouldn't rob a bank."

No doubt Shane would never break a rule. He would fly by the numbers, and retire at sixty.

"Hey, is that the mental section of the F.A.R. you're reading--?"

"Just fly, Mama's boy."

Shane wasn't any help, and I needed to quit talking about the vision before Shane determined this was more than idle conversation.

Sure I'd had weird dreams, not robbing-the-bank weird, but weird. Some pilots have premonitions about crashes--they could also be construed as visions. Maybe my vision was related to aviation?

"I hate to bother you. But do you think you might act like you're awake, just in case the passengers look up here." Shane was nodding off again.

"Sorry, my dad made me work with him last night."

"Is your dad paying you fifty bucks an hour?"

"Nope."

"Then sleep on his time."

"I'm really sorry, Cape, maybe I need some coffee."

"You fly, I'll get it for you." I got the coffee and checked on the passengers, they were sleeping, too.

"Here."

"Thanks…Yuk," Shane wiped his tongue on his shirt. "Boss, this coffee tastes like crap."

"You want to fly cheaper? I can get you some Starbucks."

"Ummm….Good coffee, what kind is this? I may get some of this for my private stock, you know the really good stuff for when I need to impress Miss. Right."

"Funny." I waited for Shane to set his cup down. "Hey, what do you know about symbols?"

"Not much," Shane made a gagging sound and handed me the coffee. "Well, maybe one thing. This junk is not even symbolic of coffee. Can you pour it out for me?"

"Drink it, it's not that bad."

"Cut my pay, Boss, but I can't drink it. If I do, I'll leave a symbol of my breakfast on the cabin floor," Shane said.

"Fine by me, the co-pilot cleans up the mess."

"I thought I was the captain, left seat, you know?"

"Right up until you puke."

I watched the clouds building from the southeast. Flight service weather had missed the forecast again. We would be in the clouds in a few more minutes.

"So what kind of symbol were you talking about?" Shane asked.

"Nothing." I couldn't see a reason to continue the conversation. Shane hadn't lived long enough to recognize a symbol if it was tattooed on his forehead.

"Come on, I may know something about symbols, my grandmother was part Cherokee."

"Interesting, did she have blonde hair and blue eyes too?"

"Okay, she was German, but--"

"Go back to sleep, Shane, or can't you sleep without Mama tucking you in?"

"Mayday," Shane mumbled. "I said Mayday."

"On second thought get the approach plate out for two zero left."

"Why? Weather called for a visual, right?"

"Kid, you're old enough not to believe in the tooth fairy, Santa, and weather forecasts," I said. "I'm going to wake the passengers, it's going to get bumpy. Set up for the approach."

We had six souls to get safely on the ground and off to whatever important business they needed to conduct in Atlanta. The last thing they needed was a bunch of pop knots on their heads. I made sure the passengers were belted in, and returned to the cockpit.

"I checked the ATIS (Automated Terminal Information Service). You were right, boss, we've got weather in Atlanta."

"Well, what's the weather?" I asked.

"Five hundred overcast, visibility one mile." Good, at least Shane was back in the game.

I acknowledged the information with a nod, and handed Shane the plate. The chart for the approach procedure, from the Jeppeson book. He deftly tucked the plate under the chart holder on the yoke and set up for the approach. I watched as he executed a perfect approach and landing. This kid was a good pilot, sleep disorder and all. The majors were definitely in his future. One of these days I'd have to talk with Shane, and explain the aviation facts of life. He could get in the big jet, but that didn't mean he would stay there. One mistake and that plush digital flight deck on the jet can turn back into the cockpit of a King Air. And he'd be damn glad to have that.

We taxied up to the SegFlight FBO, Fixed Base Operator or airplane service station, and parked under the big canopy that would keep the rain off our execs.

Shane grabbed the bags and put them in the waiting limo, while I gave the fuel guy instructions on how much fuel to put in the plane. I met Shane in the FBO after our clients deplaned. We both headed for the weather room to check the radar and ascertain where this unpredicted weather had come from. Areas of low pressure off the Georgia coast and an Alberta Clipper blasting out of Canada were about to collide over the Carolinas. The flight home would be anything but normal.

As I left the weather room and walked up to the fuel desk, Shane called flight service to get an update on the weather.

"Can I help you, sir?"

The young girl behind the fuel desk was nice enough, but not who I had expected. Once the person behind this same counter wouldn't have called me sir. But that's life, like it or hate it, things change. Some people adapt and move on, others get caught in a time warp, and life passes them by. People move in and out of your life. Some you never miss, and others leave a void that becomes vague memory. I felt that void now, but like always the feeling would pass soon enough.

"Well, Cape Thomas, this could mean only one thing." The words came from a distance, but the voice was familiar. So, she wasn't going to be just a memory after all. Good, I've never cared much for memories anyway.

"Let me guess. Hell is going to freeze over?" I repeated the last words I used when Linda questioned me about coming back to Atlanta.

"If memory serves me, that would be a fair assessment." Linda's memory was serving her well. I'd said it, and meant it too, Atlanta had turned its back on me, and I felt obligated to do the same.

"It's been a long time, so what made you come back?" Linda asked.

"Business."

"Why, Cape, I'm hurt, I thought it was me."

"Couldn't be that, I still don't have my medical license."

"You bastard."

I've known Linda a long time. We met years ago when I was building time hauling checks in and out of Augusta.

Linda was younger, about seventeen, married and madly in love with an airplane mechanic. She had life all planned. Two kids, boy first then a girl, and she would live in a big mansion with all of the perks. It was a good plan except her choice for a mate. Airplane mechanics, like pilots, for the most part don't buy large mansions. That thought must have dawned on her at some point. She ditched the mechanic, married a doctor, and became a member of the Southern B.e.l.l.e.s. (Beauties Evading Low Level Economic Scale.)

"Since you brought the subject up, let's talk about flight attendants. Let's talk about the real reason I married a doctor--"

"Let's do it from your office, unless you have a need to discuss your life in public," I insisted.

"I don't mind discussing this in public," Linda said. "As a matter of fact, let's tell the whole story and let the public decide my guilt or innocence." The people in the FBO were looking in our direction. I looked around for a rock to crawl under.

"Linda, I'm sorry. Let's go back to your office."

"I can't hear you, speak up."

"Linda, I'm sorry."

"Say it louder, I want everybody to hear that Cape Thomas is sorry--"

"Linda--"

"Say it out loud, or we have this conversation in the lobby."

"This is stupid--"

"Say it louder, or I will."

"Fine--I'M SORRY, I MADE A STUPID COMMENT… THAT I REGRET… Satisfied, or do I need to write it in blood?"

"No, I've seen that scribble you call handwriting. Come on, we'll go to my office," Linda said. "Now that you've found your manners."

On the way to the office I thought about the events that led up to this little tiff. It all started when I got Linda a job as a flight attendant on a commuter that I captained for AeroMax. Back then I was her knight in shining armor, heck I even counseled her on marrying someone who could help her reach her goals in life. I guess she took my advice seriously, or maybe her genetic Southern programming took over. One thing was certain; her goals in life changed after her divorce from the mechanic. Oh, she still wanted the children she didn't have, but at least she had her mansion.

The flight crew on the commuter called her "The Prospector." Unlike the prospectors of old who panned for gold from the silt and alluvia at the bottom of ore rich streams, Linda's search was for a more refined form of gold. She never missed the layout of embossed 24-carat gold lettering on leather bags. Every guy who got on the plane with any luggage that resembled a doctor's bag received special treatment from Linda at least until she found out the bag contained Fuller brushes rather than medical supplies. Once the imposter was identified, he not only received the lackluster amenities of coach, but the full complement of Linda's reserve.

When she couldn't find a doctor on a flight, we would hang out during the inevitable layovers. Things had gone pretty well between us until she came in on another flight and found me in bed with an attractive redhead new hire. Linda said I hurt her. I don't know whether it was the fling with the redhead or my going-away gift that was the reason for her complaint. I bought her a miner's helmet with the little light on top, and a small gold plastic shovel. It was just a gag gift that seemed funny at the time… I guess funny is like beauty, best judged by the beholder.

Linda stopped at the door to her office and put her face close to mine, "I'll tell you one thing. If you'd brought up your second-favorite subject, you wouldn't have gotten off so easy."

"I don't have a clue what you're talking about."

"Your favorite little pet name for me. Prospector, ring a bell?"

"I haven't thought of that in years."

"You lying dog, if the word Doctor comes up, Prospector is never far behind."

I followed her into the office and remembered Linda when I first met her. She hadn't changed that much--tall, slender, and still blonde, albeit not the same shade of natural blonde. Now her hair had that brassy, cover-the-gray, blonde sheen.

Linda sat down behind the desk and cupped her aging, but still attractive face in her hands. "So what are you thinking about, another insult?"

"No just the opposite, a compliment. You still look good. I like the new editions, by the way."

Linda pushed up her breasts, "What, these old things?"

"Can't be that old, they weren't there the last time I was in Atlanta."

A perfectly sculptured, provocative pair of enlarged breasts now replaced the small firm ones I remembered. Then again I wasn't really surprised. Boob jobs in Atlanta are as plentiful as dogwood blossoms in April.

If you've ever had the pleasure of sitting in the bar that adjoins the Phipps Mall in Buckhead, you know what I am talking about. It seems like every woman in the mall has the exact same breasts. Not that it's a bad thing. You marvel at the scenery, and then you want to toast the unknown plastic surgeon responsible for this wondrous phenomenon. But I'd never met this prince of aesthetic augmentation. Linda, sporting the latest status symbol of Atlanta, no doubt had.

"It's been three years," Linda said. "Why haven't you called?"

"I didn't think the good doctor would appreciate it."

"I've told him all about us. He knows we're just friends now."

"Just curious, Linda. How long were we ex-lovers before we became just friends?"

"My husband has always thought we were friends."

"So, you told him all about us? Omitting the juicier parts, right?"

"Why would anyone want to tell another about past loves? I'm sure you don't mention that to anyone, do you?"

"Hell no, someone always beats me to it," I yelled.

"Is that another insult?"

"No, that is a statement of fact. You made a career out of keeping my love life front and center at AeroMax."

"I only did it after the Redhead, and the Prospector thing."

"And Grace?" I asked.

"I did that to save you from yourself. I told you from day one she was trouble."

"So, I should thank you?"

"Excuse me." Linda picked up the phone and called the front desk. "Julie, discount the King Air fuel ten percent, thanks." Linda cradled the phone and savored her coup.

"No, but now you can thank me, Cape."

Like always, when I thought I could make a point, Linda stole my thunder. That's the curse of being intimate with someone. You always reveal your weaknesses, and Linda could spot mine, like a submariner could spot a leak.

But instead of plugging the leaks in my psyche, like a good shipmate, Linda stood back and blamed me for each and every one.

"So why did you discount me?" I asked.

"I thought you could use the help."

"Well, thanks but no thanks, my business is doing just fine." Pride, an ill-placed Southern male attribute--often confused with indignation.

"That's not what I heard," Linda said.

"Did you hear it from AeroMax?"

"No, not officially."

"Rumors?"

"No," Linda said, "The rumor is that you quit to scratch an entrepreneurial itch."

"What's the AeroMax version?"

"Officially, the same as the rumor."

Linda didn't work at SegFlight for the money, the good doctor saw to that. He could also be credited with Linda's being able to socialize in the same circles as the Atlanta-based AeroMax executives.

"Okay, then what's the cocktail-party, keep-this-under-your-hat gossip?" I asked.

"They wanted to fire your butt, but decided to give you a chance to resign. Which one is true, by the way?"

"You, of all people, Linda, know that gossip and truth are synonymous. Did the gossip say why they wanted to fire me?"

"The Bitch," Linda hissed.

"I suppose you mean Grace. How is she, by the way? Well, I hope." Hypocrisy, another ill-placed Southern trait--often confused with good breeding.

"She's divorced and looking for a free ride."

"Really, I didn't know that."

"Liar. You were the reason for her divorce."

"That's an absolute lie, and you can put that in the gossip mill." I turned so Linda couldn't read my face. " Let's talk about something else."

"Okay, we can do that, just answer this one question. Was she worth the trouble she brought you?"

"I'll answer that with a question. When has love ever been worth more than the trouble it brings?"

Linda toyed with a small model of a Boeing 737 on her desk.

"I'll have to remember that, Cape. But that should be easy, I've lived it."

I wasn't sure if Linda's remark was meant for the doctor or me. I supposed both. I thought of my parting gift to Linda--it had been a bad idea. Maybe becoming a Southern Belle was a more difficult task than I thought. If it was, at least she had the courage to go on with her life and play the hand she was dealt. Grace had knocked me down, and three years later I was still trying to find the nerve to stand back up. Seeing Linda was good. If she could get on with her life, so could I.

"Are you dating anyone?" Linda asked.

"No."

"Why don't you move to Atlanta? We have scads of beautiful women. Besides, you could get on with United or Delta."

"It's hard to fly without your ATP (Airline Transport Rating). I'm finished in the majors."

"Cape Thomas without an airliner. Doesn't sound possible. I used to think you were born in a captain's uniform."

I wasn't born a captain, but she knew I always wanted to retire or die being one. Fat chance now, no one would hire me. AeroMax was blackballing me, not officially, but efficiently.

"Does the line know I was almost fired?" I asked.

"No, everyone I talked to said you quit."

"You said everyone, you mean the few you talked to, right?"

"No, I think everyone covers it better. We just can't get enough of your exploits down here, Cape. But don't worry, the gossip will die down when something juicier comes along. Got anything for me?"

"Sure, I know this ex-airline pilot that's a serial killer. He uses an axe, quarters up mouthy co-pilots and rumor-spreading ex-flight attendants. Something just drove him over the edge. Want to guess what that was?"

"Let's see, couldn't be flying or too much money," Linda paused for effect. "Ah ha, it has to be a woman."

"God, you're good. It's two women actually, one talks all the time. She lives in Atlanta, married to a doctor, I think. The other woman doesn't talk at all."

"Let's don't talk about the talkative one. I'm sure she's perfectly adorable." Linda fluffed her hair. " Let's talk about the other one. Let me guess, she's a deaf mute locked away in your basement?"

"You and Shane should team up, Tweedle Dee-mouth and Tweedle Dumb-ass."

"I'm going to let that slide," Linda said.

"Thanks, I didn't want to have to stand in the corner."

"That wasn't the punishment I was thinking of." Linda made a scissors motion with her fingers, then pointed at my crotch. "So who is this silent woman that pushed the pilot over the edge?"

"Before I answer…your husband, Arnold--"

"Aaron, his name is Aaron, Dr Aaron Jessup," Linda said.

"Whatever. He's a shrink, right?"

"Psychiatrist-- Aaron, you might want to jot that down."

"Doctor, how's that?" I asked.

"Good enough."

"Has he ever had a patient that sees things that aren't there?"

"You mean the kooks?"

"No, I mean normal everyday people who see things that may not be real?"

"Sure, the kooks." Linda twirled her index finger around her temple.

"Cape, are you seeing things?"

"Yes, and I'm not a kook," I twirled my middle finger around my temple, saluting Linda and the medical profession. "Were people in the Bible kooks when they saw a burning bush or Jesus walking on water?"

"So this woman, does she walk on water or hang out in a burning bush?"

"She hangs out on my deck with a baby. She doesn't talk. Not to me anyway, she's just there. Do you think it means something?"

"Maybe she wants child support, and you don't want to hear it. Don't pay, get your friend with the axe and save a buck or two."

"Nice talking to you, see ya."

"Cape, sit down." Linda leaned across the desk to grab my hand. "You're serious, aren't you?"

"No, it's just that I have this need for ridicule, come on, lay some more on me. Ummm good stuff, more, more."

Linda suppressed a smile, and no doubt another comeback. Maybe she figured I had enough problems. Whatever the reason, I was grateful for a moment of silence between us.

"Aaron doesn't talk about his clients, not by name, anyway. How long has this been going on, by the way?"

"Just once, but it was real, Linda. I saw what I saw. Since the Homeland Security changes I feel obligated to report it. I finally get over Grace and now this…."

"Cape, I'll talk to Aaron about it--wait a minute, this wouldn't be about the love-at- first-sight girl, would it?" I had used Faith to break things off with Linda, and sensed this was not a good subject to bring up.

"No…. I didn't tell you? I finally found her, she's married now, six kids. Divorced three times. It's a sad story, but let's save it for a day when you need a little pick me up."

"You are such a fool, love at first sight, ha. I bet she married right after she met you."

"Come on, Linda, give me a break. I was young."

"Oh, but you had all the right answers for me. You're a real piece of work. I take your advice, to date wealthy, stable men, and you throw it up in my face every time you see me. "

"History. Let's get back to the present. I don't think talking to Aaron is a good idea, either. He'd love to keep me from being a pilot."

"Don't worry, I won't tell him it's you. I'll lie, say it's a friend…. I might even make you a dear friend. Besides, I wouldn't worry about it--"

"Of course you wouldn't, it didn't happen to you."

"It happened one time, big deal." Linda said. "Chances are it will never happen again, it could be stress."

"What if it does happen again?"

"I'd lose the stress or make an appointment with Aaron. Do you think this could be hereditary?" Linda chose her words carefully. "Does mental instability run in your family?"

"No." I was just as careful. My family wasn't crazy, or insane. Hell, we were special.

CHAPTER FOUR

Hello…Good-Bye

Seymour-Johnson Approach Control picked us up on radar at 7000 feet on our return flight from PDK. I anticipated Seymour's instructions and reduced power while I waited, "King Air six niner Bravo Charlie descend and maintain 3000 ft." I acknowledged the clearance, "Six niner Bravo Charlie out of seven for three."

It was still snowing as we descended to our assigned altitude of 3000-ft. "King Air six niner Bravo Charlie. Ten miles from STALS intersection, fly heading zero eight zero, descend and maintain 2200 ft. cleared for the ILS runway 5." The required read back of Seymour's approach clearance was the copilot's job, but since mine was sleeping, that duty fell to me. "Six niner Bravo Charlie heading zero eight zero, down to 2200 ft. and cleared for the ILS 5." ILS, or Instrument Landing System, may sound like Star Wars stuff, but it's just an electronic signal, sent from the runway to instruments in the plane to help guide it to the runway. One signal, called the Localizer, lets the plane know if it's right or left of the runway. Another signal, the Glide Slope, lets the plane know if it's too high or low. It works really well, especially when the only thing you can see from the cockpit is the inside of the clouds.

We broke out of the overcast at 400 ft. and the runway lights were on our nose, just where they should have been. Shane awoke and nodded approval as we touched down.

Warmer air blanketed the ground, and instead of the snow at altitude, a cold rain was falling on the ramp. Before we reached the FBO, I instructed Shane to get the umbrellas from the rear of the plane and try to erase our client's hard feelings over bad coffee and stale donuts.

Shane secured the plane, and I headed for my car. "You're not going to wait for me, what if I get mugged?" Shane asked.

"Then, I suppose history will be made."

"How's that?" Shane asked.

"It will be the first time in recorded history that a sleepwalker has been mugged."

" I wasn't sleeping, I've trained myself to be awake even when it looks like I'm sleeping."

"Knock out the snoring, and you're there," I said.

Home at last, I headed straight for my bar and poured my usual. As hoped, the booze knocked the chill from my bones. Sunny Orlando, Florida, was my next destination, and that was fine by me. Now that the weather had finally turned cold, I wanted no part of it.

Dr. and Mrs. Harvey Klein had chartered the plane for December 23rd through the 27th .

The Kleins were an older couple, easy-going, low-maintenance, and never complained about the $600.00 per day I charged for layover time. Having a profitable charter pleased me, but not nearly as much as being out of town for Christmas.

My grandfather didn't abide by Santa. His idea of Christmas was celebrating the birth of Christ. I could appreciate the reason for the season, but like all good little boys and girls, I appreciated toys more. Now, Christmas was just a reminder of the family and girlfriend I didn't have, so Florida suited me just fine.

Shane, the sleep-trick artist, was luckier. As a surprise I made arrangements for Cynthia, his girlfriend, to make the trip with us. The Kliens had been reluctant to share their charter with a stowaway, but when I referred to her as our flight attendant, everything was fine.

Jimmy the yardman could hear clinking ice and smell a drink from two miles away. I wasn't surprised to see him standing in front of the window, nor was I surprised when he cupped his hand to his mouth and signaled for a drink. As was Jimmy's habit, his mouth opened at the same time the door did. "Damn, it's cold out there--Got Scotch?"

Before I could answer, Jimmy was behind the bar pouring his drink. "Good to see you too, Jimmy."

"Sorry, Cape. How's it going?"

Jimmy's question opened the door for me to ask him about what I had seen on the deck the night before, deciding whether I should or not took a little longer. "I'm glad you dropped by, I've got a question for you."

"Shoot, bud."

"Did you see anyone in the yard last night?"

"Nope."

"How about on the deck, did you see anything out of the ordinary?"

"Nope."

Most of the time I like one-word answers, but this time I wanted him to expand upon it a little. Something simple that would verify my sanity. Like "No, other than the hippie on the deck, the lady with the baby, and who's that damn Indian, anyway?"

"Are you sure you haven't seen anything unusual?" I asked.

Jimmy's dirty fingers combed through his greasy beard. His chin came to rest on his thumb and index finger. For a moment, a brief moment, he looked like a man with deep thoughts to reveal. A notion I discarded as soon as Jimmy responded with his next one-word answer, "Nope."

"Heard anything unusual?--and don't say nope," I said.

"Yeah."

"You did, what was it? I mean I saw them, but I didn't hear anything."

"Saw who, Cape."

"The people you heard, that's who."

"I didn't hear any people."

"Well, what did you hear, Jimmy?"

"Nothing."

"Nothing? You said, 'Yeah.' You heard something."

"I said yeah, 'cause you told me not to say, nope."

"You know, Jimmy, Grace could have appreciated this little conversation, I don't. Why didn't you leave when Grace left?"

"She didn't ask me."

Jimmy left, and I checked my deck for visitors, nothing. Two more drinks and I was down for the night, or so I thought. Like the night before, Faith and the baby were on my deck. Remembering what Linda had said about stress I took a deep breath and closed my eyes. When I opened them Faith and the baby were still there. I grabbed the phone and called Linda, "Linda? The woman's here again, what do you think, I'm crazy, right?"

"Hell no, you're drunk go back to bed."

Good advice. Since I was already in bed, I passed out.

So far Faith had been pretty territorial. I hoped she stayed that way. I didn't stay home the next night, even though it was a short drive to the airport. I rented a motel room, and called Linda, "Hi--"

"Cape Thomas, have you lost your mind?"

"Well, that's why I called last night to get your opinion, besides you've already told the good doctor all about us."

"Don't say another word until you apologize."

"I'm sorry. I know it was a stupid thing to do, but this woman is really getting to me, did you talk to Aaron?"

"Cape, not many people see things like you described."

"Not many normal people, you mean?"

"Yes."

"So, I am crazy?"

"Why don't you make an appointment with Aaron, maybe you just have some issues you need to talk about."

"Linda, if I know I'm crazy, doesn't that make me sane? I mean, crazy people don't know they are crazy, they think they're sane."

"Oh really? I thought they just had a problem with advice--get some help, Cape."

Linda was convinced I was no longer stressed, but crazy. In spite of my asinine statement about crazy people, I needed more proof.

I once knew an airline pilot who had some problems because his circadian clock had gotten out of whack. Instead of checking himself into a nut house, he reset his clock with melatonin. On the outside chance the melatonin didn't work, I decided to rest rather than play on this trip. While I was reducing my stress, I would also read up on visions, weird dreams, and…mental illnesses.

Cynthia was indignant at first when I mentioned she would have to play the part of flight attendant. When faced with the price of an airline ticket and the unlikely event she couldn't get one anyway, we were set. Intent on playing her role, Cynthia delivered the pre-flight speech. You know the one, how to buckle a seat belt and put the little mask on that drops from the ceiling, standard equipment on a King Air. Even I was convinced by her flight attendant act, until she mentioned in-flight meals, movies, and a two-drink limit. After assuring the Kliens they would arrive in Orlando, hungry, movie-less, and drunk if they so desired, we departed.

The winding Neuse River below us slithered out of the shroud of convection fog like a snake shedding its skin. The scene below reminded me of myself; like the river, I wanted out of the fog. The little bottle of melatonin in my pocket would help with that. Old Cape was just a few hours away from recovery, life would soon be good again.

I made a mental note to send Linda some flowers at work. At least she would know I was a well-mannered psychotic. In a way I would miss the visions because without them I had no excuse to talk to Linda. In spite of our spats, I would miss her. But it was time to move on, like she had done. AeroMax, Linda, Grace, and any other baggage I had carried around was about to be checked, for good.

A tail wind favored us, so Orlando was a dot on our windshield in less than two hours. Somewhere during the flight Cynthia lost her professionalism, and by the time we landed in Orlando, she and the Kleins were best friends. Strains of a slightly slurred "Jingle Bells" was background music for the Orlando tower as I cleared us from the runway. Shane and Cynthia headed off for Disney World. The Kleins instructed me to be ready to depart at 8:00 a.m. on the 27th and, for a change, even I was in the Christmas spirit.

I headed to the library to find a book on visions or temporary insanity. The librarian snipped out a rule which prevented non-residents from checking out books. Since I didn't live in Orlando, the "policy" applied. Rather than tell her it was also "policy" not to roll a Boeing 737 and further explain the Cape Thomas Policy of breaking "policy," I wished her a Merry Christmas. Pleased by my wish, the librarian apologized, and I decided to do more Merry Christmas wishing.

I purchased a magazine from a bookstore on paranormal psychology, and headed for the pool to read up on what, I was certain, was a short-term problem. None of the articles dealt with my situation, except for a few on mental illnesses. I tossed the magazine beside my chair, and decided to sort this thing out on my own--something a crazy person wouldn't have done. A thought I reveled in, now that I was cured.

Convinced I wasn't going to be bothered by the vision anymore, but still consumed by my desire to see Faith, I gave the magazine one more chance, and skimmed the pages for articles on dream interpretations.

"Skeptic or believer?" I hadn't noticed the woman when I sat down, but now it was hard to see why. Her eyes were dark, bedroom eyes, intense and piercing. I checked behind me to make sure the question was for me. No one else was by the pool, so I engaged her.

"Pardon me?"

The woman notched her pool chaise erect, and faced me.

"Your magazine?"

"Oh, this?" I lied, "It was in the lobby, I just picked it up." She reclined the chair, and lifted her face toward the sun. Her skin was bronze, firm, and undamaged by the sun she appeared to worship. A small puddle of perspiration filled the navel of her flat stomach. I waited for her to respond to my remark. Instead, she pressed one side of her navel and a rivulet of sweat coursed across her waist then spattered onto the pool apron.

"How about you," I asked. " Skeptic or believer?"

"Believer, definitely."

"Would that be in psychology or the paranormal?"

"I believe in things that can't be explained."

She moved to the end of the chair, I decided to do the same.

"I'm Cape Thomas."

She smiled, shook my hand, and flicked her tongue across her even white teeth. "MarKay Devoreaux, pleased to meet you."

"French?

"In a round-about way, via N'Orleans to be exact, I'm Creole."

"I thought you guys believed in Voodoo?"

"It's unexplained, no conflict."

I couldn't see her punching pins into dolls--too sophisticated. "Are you a psychologist?"

"No, I thought you were," she said.

"Nope, fertilizer salesman." I didn't want her to know pilots could be crazy, and besides it was only a white lie--the bull I was selling made great fertilizer.

"I'm a drug rep," she said. "Guess we're sort of in the same line of work. I sell chemicals to keep the body healthy, you do it for plants."

"Yeah, I guess it's all related. So, do you believe in ghosts?" I asked.

"I guess, but I have premonitions, see things that happen before they happen."

A kook, Linda would think her a kook. She seemed nice enough. Maybe I could get us a two-for-one deal from Dr. Aaron Jessup--group therapy, no shrink could resist it.

"Do you ever have dreams?" I asked.

"People might call them dreams, but I call them--"

"Visions?"

"Insights, actually, but vision is close. Why, do you?"

"No, but I had this dream, a couple of times now. That's why I bought--I lied about the magazine by the way--I bought it."

"I know, I saw you take it out of the bag earlier. Why did you lie?"

"Kook, a friend thought I might be a little nuts. I didn't want you to think that."

"Tell me about the dream," MarKay said. "Then I'll tell you if I think you're a kook."

I told her about the dream, and about being awake.

"Weird, huh?"

"You don't know the woman?"

"Yeah, she's the woman of my dreams, literally and figuratively. We met once, neither of us were big on names," I said.

"Now that's weird. Tell me about it."

I told her about Faith and our rules. Then I told her about the things I knew nothing about, the baby and the necklace. I didn't tell her about being cured because what had once been a problem was turning into a nice conversation piece.

"The baby and necklace are clues," MarKay said.

"Clues, for how I can find her?"

"What makes you so sure she's alive? Most of the time only the dead choose that medium. Maybe your vision has to do with the child, you haven't seen it, that could be the most important clue."

Markay's suggestion that Faith was dead chilled me, even in the hot sun. "No, she's alive. I'm beginning to think what happened might have to do with my guilt for not finding her, but she's alive--I know that."

Markay nodded her head, "You're right, I'm sure she's alive. But, if she keeps doing the same thing over again, she's told you what you need to know."

"You don't understand. She doesn't speak, she just stands there."

"The dead--ah, sorry, I misspoke, she--what was her name, Faith?"

"Yes, Faith, as in living and breathing," I said.

"Okay, Faith, as in alive and well, is speaking to you with signs."

I thought of Miss Minnie and her conversation with the man who had complained about the way he was buried, and smiled.

"You think I'm crazy, don't you?" MarKay asked. She had misread my smile as mockery rather than the humor I felt.

"No, it's just that I'm not good at this vision thing, it's my first time. I thought maybe I could find her and she could explain the 'signs.' Too logical, huh?"

"Depends on how you look at things." MarKay's comment seemed so final, so closed; and, again, it reminded me of Miss Minnie and her solution.

"This wouldn't have anything to do with, 'What you looking at--ain't what you see,' would it?"

"Excuse me?"

"Nothing, I just had a bad memory."

"Believe what you want to believe," MarKay said, and reclined in her chair. "I don't care."

"I'm sorry, it's an old habit. Logic has worked pretty well for me. It's a hang up I developed at an early age. My family had an aversion to it, I rebelled and embraced it over their protest."

MarKay forgave me and sat back up. "Someone in your family…had insights?"

"No, some of them were crazy, the big question is whether they were certified or just freelancing."

"Maybe they were logical and you are crazy?"

"Oh, I'm beginning to think I'm crazy, too. As a matter of fact, I was thinking about checking into the nut house."

"Why haven't you?" MarKay asked.

"Modesty."

"Why would modesty stop you from getting help?"

"With my luck I would graduate with honors. That would make me the only member of my family to complete the Mental School of Health. The rest of them are stuck in the lower grades, struggling with Mumbo-jumbo 101. The professors at Nut U. would probably give me a certificate of some sort for acing the program. I have no modesty, so I would frame it, maybe even hang it on my wall. I just can't imagine the old family reunions being the same after that."

"You are crazy," MarKay flipped over on her stomach. "But I like crazy people."

"So does this mean we're an item, now?" I asked, only half joking.

"It means I can help. Logical people bore me, besides they never need help."

I tried to imagine my new Creole friend drawing circles around me with lime and chanting Voodoo prayers. "Thanks, so what do I need to do now? Round up a live chicken or two, I think I have straw and some pins in my room."

"Voodoo doesn't work on skeptics. Let's try something you are more comfortable with, logic." MarKay leaned over my chair and pushed me down. "This is called association. Lie back, close your eyes, and go back to when you first met the girl."

Her hand rested lightly on my chest. Through the slits of my eyes I soaked her in. She leaned down, her dark locks fluffed against my face. The smell of coconut and aloe drifted above her silky skin.

"Come with me, I have a better idea." MarKay said.

This woman might have been a Kook, but she had read my mind. We left the pool and went to her room. MarKay stopped in front of her closet and pulled out a briefcase, from the briefcase she retrieved a deck of Tarot Cards. "I'll do a reading for you, maybe that will help, you lie on the bed."

"MarKay, you don't really believe in those things, do you?"

"You don't?" Her ebony eyes sparkled and teased.

I thought of Madame Marie, not that MarKay reminded me of the old lady. One was a low two on the ten scale, and my companion was a solid ten, but the situation was similar. "I'll hang around for the cards, but I must warn you, I'll bail when the crystal ball comes out."

"That's funny," MarKay said, "My grandmother had a crystal ball."

"Let me guess, her name was Marie?"

"How did you--oh my name, the Mar is for Marie. Most people think it comes from Mary."

"The Kay, it isn't some French name for Carnival is it?" I asked.

"No, that was my godmother's name," MarKay said, "Why does a crystal ball bother you, anyway?"

"Ah, it's just something an old gypsy said once. At the time I didn't think it meant anything, now I'm not so sure."

"What did she say?"

"Nothing much, but one thing she said keeps gnawing at me," I said.

"And that would be?"

"She said I would find what I had lost, but lose what I couldn't find, or something like that. Maybe Faith is what I lost, the other part doesn't make any sense."

"The gypsy, she didn't tell you what it meant?" MarKay asked.

"Naw."

"Why not?"

"I didn't have five dollars."

"Cheapskate. Five dollars to solve a riddle, and you wouldn't pay?"

"Hey, I was kid, five dollars was a lot of money then. You don't think it meant anything, do you? I asked.

"I doubt it, it was a hook. For her same price, I'll give you the answer."

"Get outta town, you're a gypsy?"

"No, my grandmother was a gypsy, and I wrote my thesis on the occult."

"Why would a drug rep write a thesis on the occult?"

"I have a master's in psychology, the drugs I sell are for the mind."

"So that's why you know so much about this stuff, huh?" I asked.

"Yes, and why I know the answer to the gypsy's hook, are you game?"

"Well, I don't know, Madame Marie was the World's Greatest Physic. You've got some good credentials, but you're hardly in the same league. Maybe we should negotiate the price?"

"Still a cheapskate, are you?"

"Frugal. Cheapskate, sounds…oh, I don't know, cheap."

MarKay laughed. "I'll tell you what, let me finish the free stuff first, then we'll talk about my fees."

"Okay, if you're any good at it, we may not have to dicker."

MarKay shuffled the cards and placed them on the bed in three rows, three cards to each row. "Lie down, relax, think about the girl."

"It won't help, I don't know her name. She didn't tell me, it was one of the rules."

"I will help, close your eyes."

I closed my eyes, I could hear her breathe as she flipped the first card.

"She's blonde." MarKay looked at me for confirmation. "Was she blonde?"

"Brunette, but if she's been to Atlanta lately, she could be a blonde with big boobs by now," I said

"You are crazy."

"Good, then you really can help me." I would do the next eight cards, then ask MarKay to lunch. Now, that my old baggage was checked, it was time to start living again. MarKay was fun, no ring, and probably alone over the holidays. Christmas, and I had been presented a nice present. Thanks, Santa, all is forgiven.

MarKay flipped the second card, "Oh no, the girl is a man, she had a sex change."

"Get out of here, that's not in the cards," I sat up.

"I'm kidding, the cards have nothing to do with it, they're a prop. I'm saying things to help you--association…remember?"

"Sounds like doctor stuff to me."

"My grandmother taught me how to do this," MarKay said.

"Okay, but let's stick with the traditional stuff, beauty queens, topless dancers, call girls--"

"Shh." She turned the third card over, "Nun."

"What? We made love, I told you that."

"I know, but you've already mentioned all the good seedy choices."

"Belly dancer, I left that one out--"

MarKay smacked me on the stomach. "That was my next choice, I'll have to skip that card. You need to be quiet. I'm still in the student stage, my grandmother was the professional."

Then it hit me. The garden, the swing, Faith was a student. The night I met Faith, I had been on a date with Marilyn, another Southern Belle, and I had taken her home early for that very reason. When I got home, my roommate was there with his girl friend, Faith, and some dip-wad. The guy became angry at Faith and left. She and I went outside to talk. I made a fire in the outside fireplace and burned my hand. She bandaged my hand. The bandage looked professional, and I mentioned that. Faith told me it was no big deal, she was just using her training.

"Slut."

"Hold on, that's it." I yelled as I sat up.

"She was a slut? I knew it."

"No, she was a student, you're great."

"I told you I could help." MarKay wrinkled her brow. "A student. That's it, and you know who she is?"

MarKay came from New Orleans, lots of people there. I could understand her thinking. I came from Podunk U.S.A. where five people were a crowd. Faith had to be a nurse, and I remembered the school. East Carolina University and she was a junior.

"Trust me, I can find her now."

"Well, tell me about her," MarKay said. "You owe me that, I helped you find her."

Twenty-five years had just disappeared, and she was right, I did owe her the story.

"When Faith and I met, who she was, or where she was from wasn't important. I guess that's why I couldn't remember those things. I remember her beauty. It was so obvious, but mostly I remembered how she and I felt about the same things. I think both of us wanted to be together, but there was a problem. Faith had a fiancé and I had to go to flight school. The time and the place weren't right, but we were. Faith and I would have been good together. She felt right, for the first time in my life someone made me feel like I belonged--"

"Your parents didn't make you feel like you belonged?" MarKay asked.

"Look, that stuff I said about the family reunions?"

"Yes."

"It wasn't true, MarKay. My grandfather is--was--the only family I had, and we didn't get along that well."

"Why?"

"He was a religious man, and I committed a sin he couldn't abide."

MarKay rubbed my arm, "What was your sin, Cape?"

I didn't want to get into family history, but MarKay's eyes opened me up. "Tell me, what was your sin?"

"You won't understand this…but I committed the one sin my grandfather could never forgive. I turned out just like my father." I stared at myself in the mirror and for a moment my grandfather and I were alone in the room, a place I didn't want to be.

MarKay had a nice way of changing the mood, and she never pressed me to get in touch with my feelings, like some women. "So, if you have five dollars I'll answer the gypsy's hook for you."

I didn't linger in my depression and responded quickly to MarKay's offer, "Okay, five bucks, now free me from that old woman."

"Tell me exactly what she said."

"I did."

"No, you adlibbed, I need to know exactly what she said."

"She said, 'You will find what you have lost, what you will lose cannot be found.'--heavy, huh?"

"Much too heavy for a child, how old did you say you were then?"

"Ten."

"I'm glad you didn't pay her, Cape, she was a charlatan. That hook is used for extortion, it's used to keep people coming back once they find out the answer to the hook."

"Well, come on, give it to me--I paid for it."

"Lost for now
In days of dark
Fated doom will soon endow
Eternally yours in lifeless heart."

"No offense, MarKay, but that really clears thing up," I said, as I wrote down the riddle.

MarKay's eyes danced with mirth, "Okay, this is where the gypsy comes out in me. The answer is in code, there is one word that can break it."

"Geez, you gypsies are all alike, how much?"

"The price is steep, you may not want to pay it."

"Try me."

"Dinner, in a really nice place, and a wonderful bottle of wine, then you get the secret word."

"You know, MarKay, you may not be in the same league with Madame Marie when it comes to the psychic stuff, but you're on equal ground when it comes to extortion."

"Ahh, too bad for you."

"Okay, you beautiful blackmailer…you're on, what time?"

The knock at the door wasn't ominous, or hostile, it was just a knock. MarKay reacted differently, though.

"Are you expecting someone?" I asked.

"Yes, it's my ex-husband, but don't worry--he won't hurt you. It's me he's after."

MarKay started for the door then stopped and turned to face me. "Cape, there's no charge for this--if you don't give up, you'll find Faith. I want you to promise me that you won't stop until you do. Promise me."

"MarKay, maybe I'd better talk to him, you know. Explain that we weren't doing
any--"

"No, you can't change anything. Hurry promise me you won't stop searching."

"Geez, MarKay, we can talk about this over--"

"Promise me, now!"

"Okay, I promise I'll find her. I swear to you I'll find her"

MarKay opened the door and I grabbed a lamp.

"I knew, I knew damn well you were with a man." The voice came from a man I would never know, but one I would hate till my dying day.

"It's not what you think, Jerome, I hardly know him." MarKay's voice was high and frantic.

"Lying bitch!"

An explosion from a gun filled the room, and time blasted out into another dimension. MarKay, mortally wounded, walked toward me like a Voodoo zombie. Her dark fluffy curls were matted with blood, her eyes gathered the last offerings of life. I reached for her outstretched hand, then her head, warm and wet fell against my chest. She did not speak; her eyes fluttered then froze in a fixed stare. Her warm blood pooled in my shirt and the waistband of my shorts.

Jerome Devoreaux stepped around the partition wall and leveled the gun at my head. I stared into his eyes, eyes that were as dead as his beautiful wife's. His arm curled up until the chrome gun barrel rested against his own temple. "You bastard."

I don't remember hearing the second report of the gun. In slow motion his head swelled, and his eyes protruded to make room for the bullet in his brain. Bits of flesh and bone spewed from his skull in a torrent of blood, like water from a whale's blowhole. I watched as his blood showered the lamp in my hand. A wedding band, MarKay's wedding band lying on the night table, cupped the blood and symbolized well their vows, Till death us do part.

CHAPTER FIVE

Grounded.

The blood on my shirt, warm and sticky, had started to congeal. I rubbed my arms to ease the chill from the room in the Orlando Police Annex. The door opened and the officer called out "Ramone Vasquez." A Latino in the chair at the far end of the room rose and followed the police officer through the door. A woman seated next to me moved into the vacant chair, then picked up a magazine and blocked her face from my view. An old man in the chair one down from me gave me the once-over, then stared straight ahead.

"Cape Thomas." The cop who called my name was the homicide detective who had questioned me at the hotel. I followed him down to an office with Interrogation Room stenciled on the door. With a wave of his hand the detective motioned for me to have a seat at the Formica-topped table.

"Here's some paper, write out your statement, I'll be back in twenty minutes." Before I could reply, the door slammed and the detective was gone. I had never been asked to write a statement before, so a little instruction would have been nice. As I considered whether to put the pool conversation in the report, the detective came back. "I hope the piece of ass was worth it." The detective's hair was cut high and tight, ex-military. Probably a marine, maybe army, but not navy or air force. Something about his face looked familiar, silver blue eyes, reflective, like mirrors. His nametag read R.H. Carter. "Detective Carter, where do you want me to start the statement?" Carter poured himself a cup of coffee.

"Leave out the screwing part, Casanova. We know what happened, murder-suicide, we just need your statement to verify the facts." I scratched through the beginning of the pool conversation and handed him the paper.

"Is that all?" I asked.

Carter looked over the statement, "Put your name and phone number on here in case ballistics don't check out. You cleared the gunpowder residue test, but your ass is still guilty, Casanova."

I wrote in the information and put the pen back on the table. Carter noticed the address, "North Carolina, huh? I've got people up there, Greenville."

Nothing about Carter's familiar looks made me want to engage him, I moved toward the door. "Will that be all?"

Carter moved close to my face, "Yeah, nice ain't it, accessory to murder and you walk."

"I'll need a ride, I left my wallet at the hotel."

"Too freaking bad--walk, asshole."

I walked by several small restaurants on the way back to the hotel. Any of them could have been where MarKay and I ate lunch. None of them was where I wanted to be at the moment. I stopped by the pool and looked at the chairs we had sat in earlier, two small kids occupied them now. "Look, Mommy, that's the man the police took away."

The young mother gathered up her kids and headed for their room. "Is he a bad man?" the little girl asked. "Come on, kids, we have to go." I watched the trio leave and thought about the little girl's question. Technically I wasn't a bad man. I just felt like one. MarKay was dead and I had some responsibility, Carter was right about that even if his reasoning was wrong.

I showered, then checked my messages at the front desk. The Kleins had left a message, with a request. Mrs. Klein's college roommate was living in Long Boat Key. She wanted to visit her friend and had made arrangements to stay there a few days. The Kleins were willing to pay extra money for the change in plans. We would be going back on the 2nd of January.

Florida is one of my favorite places, but the thought of spending more time in the state bothered me. I wanted to get as far away from the Sunshine State as possible. I returned the Kleins' call and feigned a potential schedule conflict with another charter. In reality I had no more flights until the 6th of January. The Kleins increased their offer and I reluctantly agreed to stay the extra days. We arranged to meet at the airport at noon the following day.

Morning broke, and despite the melantonin, my night had not been a good one. There were no visions this time, only dreams--nightmares of MarKay's murder. The vision I had tried so hard to trivialize had new meaning, someone had died and, either directly or indirectly, the vision was involved.

R.H. Carter was certain I was partially to blame for the deaths of two people. I thought about it and decided he could have been right. I could have made some different choices, like reading the magazine in the privacy of my own room. There are hundreds of hotels around Orlando, I should have chosen a different one. Or maybe I shouldn't have been born. No, the decisions I made were nothing more than bad timing.

MarKay's choices were as innocent as mine. Why should either of us have done anything differently? Shared curiosity about the vision, not lust had brought us together. One choice stood out though. MarKay had chosen to marry, a choice millions of people make. But, how could she have known that marriage, an institution supposed to be based in love and trust, could generate hate and jealousy powerful enough to kill?

In spite of what Carter thought, we were innocent. Jerome Devereax was the only person who had had a specific choice yesterday, and the sanctimonious R.H.Carter would figure that out one day. My regret was not being able to help that day come sooner.

I called Shane several times, but didn't have any luck, so I left a message. Legally, because of the deal with the FAA, I couldn't fly the Kleins without a copilot. Rules that once were sacrosanct now seemed petty. Right and wrong had little heft compared to life and death. Still, it was my duty to operate by the rules, I figured it shouldn't be hard to find a co-pilot in Orlando to fill the bill.

I stopped first at the FBO to ask about flight crews. Sure, there were plenty of them, but it was Christmas. Most were busy or had taken time off for the holidays. On the ramp, a coffin was being loaded into the belly cavity of a twin turbo prop. It may, or may not have been MarKay. It didn't matter. I was getting out of Orlando, Shane could meet me in Sarasota for the return flight.

Walking down a row of hangers, I spotted a man washing a Cheyenne, "Hi, partner, is this your plane?" I asked. The man put his brush down and turned to face me, "Yeah, well, I own it with three other guys, but yeah I own it."

I explained my situation, and offered him $500.00 for an hour's work.

"What kind of plane did you say you have?"

"King Air."

"What's the tail number?"

An odd question, but I gave it to him anyway, "6-9-6-9 Bravo Charlie."

"Oh yeah, it's parked on the ramp. I saw it when I drove up this morning, nice plane."

Some pilots are picky; they don't like to fly junk. I usually like that in a pilot, now the only thing that mattered was if he could fly.

"I'd like to help you out, but I have to leave in an hour. I'm taking my grandkids down to Key West." The guy was squeezing me like a Florida orange, "I'll pay you a thousand, I need to get out of here," I offered.

"Can't do it, I already have plans."

This guy was bandit, "Look that's my final offer, to hell with the FAA, I'm getting out of here."

"I don't think I'd do that if I were you."

"Well, you're not me," I almost yelled. Maybe the guy was on the level, no need to make an enemy. "Hey, how about one of your partners? Maybe they could do it."

"They're all out of town."

"Do you know anybody that could help me out?" I asked.

He did the obligatory thoughtful look, then shook his head, "Sorry."

The potential trouble with the FAA seemed small in comparison to what had already happened. Besides, it was a short hop to Sarasota SRQ, maybe thirty minutes tops. The weather was VFR, that's Visual Flight Rules, and it doesn't get any easier than that in the flying business. The turbo prop with the coffin on board lifted off the runway, and my mind was made up. If I couldn't leave the state, I could at least change cities.

The Kleins were punctual as usual, and in high spirits. Each had a thermos of eggnog, both were singing Jingle Bells. As my passengers boarded, I gave Shane another call, no answer. The guy on the Cheyenne was busy talking on his cell phone, and rounded up what I supposed were his grandkids, I waved as we taxied past.

Our flight to Sarasota did nothing to lift my spirits. Usually when I fly my problems are left on the ground, but today was different. I had absolved MarKay and myself and put the blame where it belonged. But R.H.Carter's remark still bothered me. I hadn't thought about it before but he had insulted MarKay, the bastard had spoken ill of the dead, and I should have punched him.

I listened to the ATIS and set up for a visual approach, landed, then taxied to the FBO. Bright rays from the mid-day sun poured into the dark cabin as I opened the door. Heat trapped in the engine nacelles burned into my already bleary eyes. While the Kleins stayed in the cool cabin, I removed the baggage from the wing lockers. With me playing the part of a pack mule laden with designer bags, we headed for the taxi I had prearranged for them. Dr. Klein, as always, insisted on carrying his medical bag, and for some reason, I thought of Linda.

Two men in suits were heading away from the FBO, I stood to the side to let them pass, they didn't. Like two dancers following a perfectly choreographed routine, they reached inside their jacket pockets and pulled out badges, "We're with the FAA, Air Carrier Safety Inspections. Mind if we see your pilot license and passenger manifest?" The two men folded the badges and stuffed them back into their coat pockets. " This flight is under Part 135, isn't it?"

The Kleins were already inside the FBO. Both turned to see what had happened to me, and more importantly their bags. I'd been ramp checked before--this wasn't a typical ramp check. Asking what type of flight you were on was not a question I had ever been asked before. "Sure guys, let me get my passengers on their way and I'll be right with you."

My request didn't seem unreasonable, at least to me, but the two FAA guys didn't seem to think so, "That's fine, but you don't mind if we ask your passengers a couple of questions, do you?" The inspector who had asked the questions moved back toward the FBO and held the door open for me. His actions let me know he wasn't really asking my permission to talk to the Kleins, he was going to speak with the Kleins.

We stood in the lobby of the FBO. The two Inspectors did their little synchronized badge pulling routine again. The Kleins ignored the badges, and instead looked at me. I felt like a counterfeiter surrounded by cops and covered in wet green ink.

The inspector who had asked to talk to the Kleins did just that. "Folks, I'm John Stennis, Federal Aviation Administration, Air Carrier Safety Inspector. Do you mind if I ask you a few questions?"

Before answering, Doctor Klein looked at me for instructions. I shrugged my shoulders and waited. Dr. Klein introduced himself and his wife to John Stennis, then asked the obvious, "What's this about, have we done something wrong?"

"I apologize for the inconvenience, folks, I'd just like to ask you a few questions."

John's smile faded as he turned to face me, then continued his interrogation of the Kleins, "It's probably nothing; I just wanted to make sure you are paying this gentleman to fly you here." The Kleins and the fuel guy behind the desk in the FBO followed John Stennis's nod in my direction. With all eyes focused on me, I began to commiserate with the tennis ball in a championship match at the U.S. Open.

"Yes we are, but we didn't know it was wrong."

"Well, you didn't do anything wrong, Dr. Klein, but your pilot might have. We just want to check and make sure."

John Stennis had his job to do, and so did I. My clients were on vacation, not fodder for the Gestapo. I stepped between the Kleins and John Stennis, "Well, Dr. Klein, here's your cab, I'll get this straightened out, it's just paperwork, you know how the government is, no need for you and Mrs. Klein to hang around here."

The good doctor wasn't buying it, "If you don't mind, Mr. Thomas, I'd like to make sure everything is in order." Mr. Thomas? I had flown the Kleins many times, I was always Cape, now I was Mr. Thomas. My sudden elevation in status wasn't uplifting.

John lost his interest in the Kleins and made me the focus of his attention, "May I see your pilot's license, Mr. Thomas?" I reached for my wallet. I'd lost my Airline Transport Rating as part of the deal with the FAA. My new license read Commercial Pilot, which would have made the flight legal. But, unfortunately, I had agreed to have a restriction from single pilot commercial operations added to the rating.

John read the restriction, inhaled deeply, and pronounced judgment, "Mr. Thomas, you are in violation of an agreement you have with the FAA. We're rescinding your part 135 certificate." Before his remarks had time to register, he turned to Dr. Klein,

"Doctor, in case this goes to court we may need your testimony, is that a problem?"

"That won't be a problem." Doctor Klein faced me, then snapped, "And by the way Mr. Thomas, you're fired."

I offered to put the baggage in the taxi, but Dr. Klein and his wife scooped up the bags and jumped into the taxi without a good-bye. The inspectors and I watched them leave. My throat was parched, and small patches of perspiration spread across my shirt. "Look, you bastards, I'm a twenty-thousand-hour pilot, I was a captain with AeroMax, and I flew 747's internationally. What the hell is this about?" The words coming out of my mouth sounded like they had been scrubbed by extra-coarse sandpaper.

"Mr. Thomas, I don't care who you flew for. As a matter of fact, I don't care if you ever fly again." John Stennis shifted his weight and edged closer to me. "The guy in the Cheyenne in Orlando was in charge of our FSDO, Flight Standards District Office until he retired last week. That may not mean much to you since you have a total disregard for rules, anyway. But with his testimony and the doctor's, I think I can safely say your flying days are over. As for being bastards, I know both my parents, Mr. Thomas. Can you say the same? "

John Stennis and R. H. Carter had the same government-issued haircuts and attitudes. I'd let Carter's comment slide, damn if that was going to happen twice, "Go to hell and take your damn rules with you."

John Stennis and his partner smiled at one another. Stennis's partner was a tall man, a good five or six inches taller than my six-foot frame. His deep voice seemed to come from the sky rather than his mouth. "Oh, we're going to take something, Hotshot, but it won't be rules, it'll be your 135 certificate. You mouth off again, and we'll take your damn pilot's license and your plane....What do you think about that, Mister I-flew-747's-for-AeroMax ?"

Both men waited for me to respond. I was in trouble, and saying any more would only make it worse. I turned to walk to my plane. The fake snow and tinsel on the FBO window reminded me of the season, "Merry Christmas."

"Is that supposed to be funny?" John Stennis asked.

"Nope, from the bottom of my heart, Merry Christmas."

Neither man responded to my comment, and I continued my walk to the plane. By the time I was in the cockpit both men were in their car. From the safety of my plane I dialed Shane's number, this time he answered. "I got your message, I'm at the airport but I can't find the plane." I looked at my watch, if I had postponed the flight for one hour; none of this would have happened. "Shane, I'll be there in about an hour, meet me at the FBO, we're headed back home." I was grounded from flying Part 135, but not from flying my personal plane.

I didn't explain any of the details to Shane. It was obvious something was wrong, the return leg wasn't supposed to be a deadhead leg. Before he could ask any questions I gave him a reason to think about something else. "Shane, I'm going to get you a job on a Citation. A friend of mine needs a co-pilot."

"Jet time, all right." Shane was quiet for the rest of the trip. Propellers had just stopped being a part of his life, and he was savoring the loss.

We landed at ISO, and by the time the plane stopped Shane had loaded his personal effects into his flight bag. "Hey, Cape, I forgot to ask, who's taking my slot?"

"No one, Kid, I'm going to take a little break, relax a little, maybe look up some old friends."

"That's good, Cape, you've been looking a little tired lately. By the way, I appreciate the hookup, Merry Christmas."

I secured the plane, poured myself a cup of the shitty instant coffee, punched through my phone, and found the number for the Kleins in Sarasota. A woman answered my call, and I asked to speak to Dr. Klein. "Doctor Klein, I'd like to pay for your flights back home. It's the least I can do." There was a pause, then the Doctor responded, "Go to hell, Mister Thomas, go straight to hell." The line went dead; I went home.

CHAPTER SIX

Pictures from the Past.

For the first time in twenty-five years, I stored my luggage in the attic. Over that same period of time the bags had always been as close and as ready to travel as my wallet.

Now, I wondered when, or even if, I would ever use them again. Like a distant storm on the radar screen, this day had been on my mind. The thought that it could be so sudden and unexpected had never been part of the process, though. I wondered if MarKay had had death on her radar screen.

Dying is part of aviation, it comes with the job, and it happens fast. The altitude of the flight determines the amount of time you have to pray. And they all pray, I'd heard enough NTSB tapes to know that. MarKay hadn't been given that luxury. In the attic, where no one could see, I knelt in front of an old steamer trunk that had once belonged to my grandfather. What had come so easily for him felt foreign to me. My prayer was woefully inadequate, but heartfelt. I hoped that being close to the property of a pious man would, somehow, give the prayer more weight with the Almighty. MarKay deserved that.

My desk was scattered with paperwork and bills. Paying bills had never been one of my favorite activities, even when I was gainfully employed. Now that my earning power had dwindled to zero, the chore was even more detestable.

Losing the security and income of a captain with AeroMax had been an adjustment, socially and economically. As bad as losing my job had been, I was still left with the option of making a living flying. This deal wasn't as attractive, I had two options: pity myself or do something about it.

I made a pot of strong coffee and telephoned Tom Butterfield, an aviation attorney the Aircraft Owners Pilots Association recommended. My first call was answered by his voice mail, so I left my name and pilot certificate number. Tom's call back came within the hour.

"On the face of it, things don't sound good." Tom was brief and to the point. I liked that about him though I didn't like what he had to say. Tom was priming the pump, and to get the water flowing would be costly. What he didn't know was how shallow the well was, money was definitely an object. My opposition, the FAA, would be drawing from a deep reservoir.

"Tom, what's the cheapest way to get out of this?"

"Do you have any friends in high places?"

Either Tom had a sense of humor or a sadistic streak.

"How high are the places we're talking here, Tom?"

"The White House maybe?"

"The only person I know who had any political connections was a girl I dated in high school."

"How well connected was she?" Tom asked hopefully.

"She was a page in the North Carolina House."

"A what? A page….Oh--hey, that was a good one."

"Yeah, I know, the really funny part is--that's the truth. Think she would work?" I asked.

"Maybe, but not nearly as well as a high-priced call girl who's into serious discounting."

This guy wasn't just a lawyer, he'd lived life. At some time he'd been in a tight situation, lived on the edge, and laughed about it.

"Let me guess, you're a real aviation attorney--pilot, right?"

"Yeah, instrument with a commercial, how'd you know?"

"I used to hang out with a lawyer a long time ago."

"Sorry to hear about that, Cape, I hope there were no long-term ill effects from the relationship."

"Nope, I never listened to a word he said." And wasn't that a smart choice? Sure would be nice to have a law degree to fall back on now.

"Good for you. I wish I'd done that, but my dad insisted I get my degree. It's a sad story, by the time I finished law school I was married to a beautiful woman and blessed with a great kid. Terrible life, huh?" Tom asked.

"Pathetic."

"I can see why you would say that. I was just looking over your employment record. 747 captain with AeroMax, great job. Says here you resigned, why…? Never mind, lost your ATP, what happened?"

"Long story, I'll tell you about it sometime."

"You weren't charged with anything, why would you agree to forfeit your ATP?"

"Let's talk about my 135 certificate, the other stuff is personal." My comment wasn't open-ended, the subject was closed.

"Yeah, whatever you say, Cape. I was serious earlier, if you know someone it might help. The 'good old boy network' is still alive and well in Washington, contrary to what you might have heard. How about AeroMax, would they be willing to help? They can throw some weight around in Washington." Tom said.

"I'm very aware of the weight they can throw around. Back to your original question, I don't know the President, a U.S. Senator, or a Congressman. That leaves us with the violation, what'd you think?"

I knew my comments sounded cold, but when it came to AeroMax, I couldn't think of one thing that was funny.

"What you did wasn't so bad as far as flying is concerned. Unfortunately, you made a promise to the FAA, for whatever reason, and failed to keep it. They don't like that."

"Yeah, I know, but there's no regulation against what I did."

"Technically, you're right, but you entered into an agreement, and the rules changed once you signed that paper."

"Temporary insanity, I signed under duress, there has to be a loophole."

"I'd need some background on the AeroMax subject, and that sounds off limits," Tom said.

"Tom, if I open that can of worms, I may never fly again. How about we get them all an apple, or write a thousand times 'I will not fly without a co-pilot'?"

"How about a little paddling from Marion Blakey? That might work," Tom added.

"Hey, if the head of the FAA is into that, and I can fly again, put me down for forty lashes."

"Maybe we better start with a few feelers. I'll begin with the 135 certificate, and if that doesn't work, we may have to deal with the worms." Tom said.

"Okay, in the meantime, I'll try to find someone with some political clout, or that high-priced call girl you mentioned," I told him.

"Good deal, we gotta start somewhere."

Flight plans are a mainstay of aviation. Not only do they insure that nothing is overlooked, they also eliminate surprises. I decided to incorporate them in my personal life, because the stakes were too high to justify flying by the seat of my pants.

I had saved a good portion of my earnings from AeroMax for a rainy day. That was a good thing, I was going to need it.

Until now a rainy day had been a metaphor for a bad day, maybe even a bad week. Now it was becoming painfully clear that that rainy day could mean a lifetime.

Discounting my personal bills, I was paying out over $6,000 per month to operate my business. Household and other expenses brought my total to over $9,000 per month. Even if I committed to spending the little less than $250,000 in my ill-invested mutual fund, I could maintain my present existence for only two years.

The King Air would have to be sold. With any luck that could happen fast. The Research Triangle, usually flush with cash, had recently tightened its belt due to a blip in tech stocks. Until that happened my Suburban or the Jaguar convertible would have sold like Super Bowl tickets in late January. Now, such luxuries might be as unwanted as office space off Miami Boulevard in the RTP.

I would need a job. All unemployed people needed one of those. Then again, most unemployed people had some type of vocational training. Discounting my flying ability, I was vocationally bankrupt. Then there was the long shot, the FAA could turn out to be a kinder and gentler entity than I gave them credit for. I could get lucky and get off with a fine, or a temporary suspension. Then again, the sun could rise in the west, and water could run up hill, and if all that worked out, I might even snag a little sack time with Cleopatra.

I placed an ad in the paper for my two vehicles, then decided to wait on selling the King Air. In the interim, I had an old friend to find.

East Carolina University was in the midst of the holiday season, only a skeleton staff remained behind to answer the phones. I was transferred to an assistant of the assistant of the Admissions Administrator. I surmised this assistant was a grad student. A person I was sure could care less if I was able to locate a nursing student who had graduated twenty-five years ago.

The assistant was Judith, and she sounded as I expected, uninterested. "Do you have a name?" she asked.

It was a good question, and one I knew she would ask, "No, and I know this is crazy, but I do know what she looked like."

"Mr. Thomas, I'd really like to help. But unfortunately, we don't input former students by pictures, and I don't know of any school that does."

Fair enough, but not good enough. "Judith, maybe I asked the wrong question. Let's start again. Is there some pictorial archive, or maybe a yearbook that I could look at, so I could learn her name?"

"Hold please, I'll check." I listened to elevator music until Judith came back online with an answer. Finally, a number and a place I could go to review old yearbooks.

I drove over to Greenville in the Jag. The campus was pretty much deserted, so finding a parking place was easy. I took one look at the yearbook, and realized how big this task would be. East Carolina University is considered a small school by most university standards, but the size of the yearbook undermined that assumption. Thousands of faces stared up at me from the pages of the yearbook and despite the era's reputation for rebellious students, all of them looked the same. Men with long hair, and women with hair parted down the middle. This yearbook idea was a long shot, and the more pages I flipped, the deeper that notion sank in.

The 1976 yearbook didn't yield my mystery woman but damned if it didn't have one thing going for it, a plethora of beautiful women. I made a comment about that to some kid that was in the library with me. He gave me a little tidbit I didn't know.

"Yeah, we got a lot of them, you know Sandra Bullock graduated from here?"

I didn't know that, but I made a note to look for her picture. Damn if she wasn't in there, too.

I finally finished looking at the junior class of 1976. No luck, Faith wasn't there. Then a brainstorm hit me. Maybe nurses had class pictures taken? I walked over to the information desk in the library and made my request. The assistant pointed me in the right direction, and I was off again.

I took one look at the class picture and realized I had another problem. I don't know if nursing classes still do this or not, but they did in 1976 and 1977. Each student wore those little white nursing caps, except for one guy. I eliminated him, women of color, blondes, and redheads, but still no luck. The process of skipping over the culls was annoying, I needed my own copy. I returned to the desk and inquired about obtaining a copy of the class pictures. My new friend at the desk, Ellen, was destined for a great career in public relations. Not only did she answer "yes," she was nice enough to lead me to the media room.

I left the school with two enlarged photos of the nurses graduating classes 1976 and 1977. On the way home I stopped by an office supply store and picked up a magnifying glass.

I poured myself a glass of port and sat down to scour the photos. Some of the girls resembled Faith, but none was a dead ringer. One particular girl had possibilities, but with the cap hiding most of her hair, I couldn't be sure. After three hours, the pictures became a fuzzy blur, it was useless to continue. I put the photo on a shelf in my closet and went to bed.

Images of Jerome Devoreaux and John Stennis swirled in my brain. Soaked with sweat and unable to sleep, I stared outside at the deck. Faith and now MarKay floated in my mind. The deck was empty. The event, or lack of it, should have been comforting....It wasn't. I needed to see the vision once more. Markay said I had all the information I needed, but after my visit to ECU, I was sure there had to be more clues. I tore from my bed, and raced out onto the deck.

"It's not enough, dammit, I need more information....I don't understand, talk to me," I screamed into the darkness.

"Hey, you all right?" I jumped back inside and stumbled over my shoes. Sitting flat on the floor, I heard again, "Hey, you all right?" The long silence was broken, but I was too shocked to respond. I could hear footsteps on the deck, my eyes locked on the still opened door. Slowly the steps stopped and a head poked through my door. It was Jimmy the yardman. Relief and anger found me at the same time. "Damn, Jimmy, don't ever do that again, you scared the shit out of me," I shouted.

Jimmy grinned, then spoke, "I thought you were hollering at me." I must have made a pitiful sight sprawled on the floor. Jimmy began to laugh.

"I guess I was dreaming," I jumped from the floor and tried to regain a measure of composure, " or sleep walking." Jimmy stepped away from the door and back onto the deck.

"I dunno, sounded more like hollering to me." Jimmy lit a smoke.

I notched my bathrobe up and joined him outside.

"Want some?" Jimmy asked.

"You know I don't smoke."

"Ain't that kind of smoke. This'll help you sleep."

Just what I needed, something to remove me further from reality. "I sleep just fine, and I told you I don't want drugs on my property."

"Want me to put it out?"

"Yes....No, hell I don't know....Put it out!"

"Still say you need something to relax you, you don't look so good," Jimmy said as he snuffed the joint out in the callused palm of his hand.

"What do you mean?"

"You look stressed, want to talk?"

"It's called life, Jimmy, not stress, it's what most people who are productive go through sometimes. You don't worry about things?"

"Nope, what happens, happens....Why worry?"

"What if I lost this place and you had to move out, that would worry you--wouldn't it?"

"Naw, just be a matter of moving on, no big deal."

"You're sick, Jimmy."

"Might be, but I sleep okay."

"You sleep okay? You're up now and it's"....I glanced at my bare wrist. "Whatever the hell time it is....Way past midnight, and you sleep okay? Gimme a break."

"Night ain't the only time to sleep," Jimmy explained.

"Well, it would be if you had a regular job."

"That's why I work for myself, no clocks. Life's good, if you keep it simple."

It was an asinine statement. What if everyone felt that way, where would the world be? Still, at that hour it sounded profound.

"Hey, Jimmy, have you ever seen things that weren't there but you thought they were?"

He tilted his head back and jerked his jaw from side to side. "Yeah."

"You have, what was it?" Finally, someone I could identify with.

"A pink elephant."

"A what?"

"A pink elephant, then one time when the judge sent me to dry out, I saw some fish on my arms." Jimmy nodded as he shared his vision, "Yeah, I'm pretty sure the elephant was there, but I think I imagined those fish. Don't see how a fish could live without water. It happened to a friend of mine, he tried to quit and he saw fish on him too. I was drunk, but I didn't see no fish on him. You been seeing fish, Cape?"

D T's-- that might be it, maybe I had the DT's? That couldn't be, I just had one glass of port.

"No, I haven't seen fish or an elephant. Besides, that's not what kind of things I'm talking about. I'm talking about seeing things when you haven't had a drink, or maybe just one drink. Have you ever been sober, and seen a person that wasn't really there? That's what I'm asking you."

Jimmy thought a second, then answered, "No, Cape, I ain't ever seen that, but I know the reason why." I should have known better than to ask the question, but I was having a weak moment, "Why is that, Jimmy?"

Jimmy was almost down the steps and into the yard, but without smiling he answered me,

"Hell, that's easy, Cape, I'm a drunk. I ain't crazy." I thought about killing him, then thought about the DNA evidence that would send me to prison. "Yeah, well, if you stick your head in my door again you'll be a dead drunk--smart-ass."

Sleep was out of the question. Peace and quiet weren't going to be options for me, either. They might be options, but only if I sought professional help, or found Faith.

Reluctantly, I pulled the pictures from my closet and went over them again, and again. My search kept ending with the girl that resembled Faith. I circled her picture and stared out of my window. The bottom of the eastern sky was streaked with the rays of the dawn-red sun….Dawn, maybe her name was Dawn? As before, I tried to recall whether Faith had left a clue to her identity when she visited me on the deck. No, that wasn't the case. Whatever the clues were…Her name wasn't among them.

I concentrated on what I had learned when we sat by the outside fireplace. She was engaged, and her fiancé had cheated on her. She broke off the engagement, or she could have reconciled. Either way she would have sought guidance before she made her decision. Who would she have confided in? Family for sure, and friends, some of the women in these pictures might have been her friends. Even if all of them didn't know Faith, some of them would.

I poured over the pictures with newfound resolve. What types of girls would she have made her friends? Attractive girls, of course. Pretty people hang out with pretty people. The same as rich people, or poor people, associate with one another. It's the common thread of life. We all seek things that are familiar to us. Lawyers hang with lawyers, engineers with engineers, pilots with pilots.

I highlighted fifteen of the most attractive women in the class pictures. Including my Faith look-a-like, I now had sixteen candidates to help me. Showered and refreshed, I headed back to ECU to put names with the faces. Ellen wasn't in the library, just my luck. The one person willing to help me was gone. No problem, I could work around that. The yearbooks were all I needed and I knew where to find them.

It took me four hours, but I identified twelve of my choices by cross-referencing them with the yearbooks. Armed now with names. I headed for the Admissions office.

Even before I heard her nasal twang, I theorized that the thin, pale girl in the office was Judith. The nameplate on her desk confirmed my hunch.

Judith Speidecker had a shock of unruly red hair that fought against conformity. Underneath this mass of confusion was a pinched-drawn face of someone who had eaten a persimmon before the first frost, on purpose. Tweety Bird glasses perched on the end of a pointed nose, magnified her eyes. Her aloofness started at the door and thickened the closer I came to her desk.

"May I help you, sir?"

"Hi, I'm Cape Thomas. I called here the other day for some information on a former student." I smiled what I thought was a charming smile, but Judith didn't smile back.

"You would be the guy that wants information on people who doesn't have names." I would be, and you would be the person I spoke to with no interest in helping me?

"Yes, Judith, that would be me."

Despite her tempered steel posture, Judith swirled to face her computer screen. Without looking at me, she cut right to the chase, "I can only assume you at least have a name now?" With all the disdain in her voice, it was hard to tell if she was asking a question, or making a statement.

"Beverly Robertson."

"Year of graduation?"

"1977."

Judith squeaked the same response for each of my inquires, "No current information."

After the fifth identical response to those on my list, I needed clarity.

"Excuse me, Judith, I don't mean to intentionally slow our little game of 'let's get to the end of the list as quickly as we can… But--?"

"That means Mr. Thomas," you dumbass, was omitted but implied, "…the only address or information I have on them is from 1977. Which means, they could have since married, changed their names, moved or died. If you would care to have the old information, I can give you that. But since you are obviously trying to locate these persons, I thought I might just give you current information only."

I didn't know exactly what information I wanted, but maybe current information would be the best, " Well, I guess that makes sense, Judith," Bitch was omitted, but implied. "But what would cause these persons to have current information?"

Judith droned out her answer, "If one of these persons would have bothered to fill out the alumni survey…that we, the University, send out each year, I could give you that information."

"I see. Moving right along, Carol Kornegay."

"Spell it."

I obliged, "I-t."

"Mr. Thomas, you may not believe this, but I enjoy humor. I do not enjoy pathetic attempts at humor."

"K-o-r-n-e-g-a-y."

"Thank you."

After a brief pause, Judith started to spout more information than I could write down.

"Married to John Edward Pate, 1977-- divorced 1984, remarried 1987 to Dr. John Lee. Divorced 1994, currently resides in Boca Raton Florida--Nurse R.N. Two children, Katlin and John Lee, Jr."

To my credit, I did get down John Pate and the divorce date. "OK, and she remarried when?"

"If you prefer, I can print that out for you?"

"Why thank you, Judith, that would be nice."

From my twelve requests, only five had updated information. Three were from the 1976 class, the remaining two from the 1977 class.

The odds weren't in my favor, and if this didn't work out I had no alternative plan. What if Faith had married? Most people did marry, she could be happily married with children and there was also the possibility that she wouldn't remember me. What would the vision mean if either of those scenarios was true? The answer was simple, I would be spending a lot of time with Linda's husband, Dr. Aaron Jessup.

CHAPTER SEVEN

Bad Leads…Good Leads.

The first name on my list was Carol Kornegay Pate Lee, possibly Kornegay again. Married to John Edward Pate 1976--divorced 1983. Married to Dr. John Lee 1987- divorced 1994. Two Children, Katlin Pate, and John Lee, Jr.

Each marriage had lasted seven years, Carol could have suffered the seven-year-itch in her relationships. She might have also had a failed relationship while in college, a perfect person to counsel Faith.

I dialed the number, it rang once. "Hello, may I speak with Carol?"

"No, this is Katlin, may I ask who's calling?"

I hadn't thought about reaching someone other than Carol. "She doesn't know me but-- I was hoping she could help me find someone from her past--from college."

There was a pause, "She isn't here now, but if you want to leave your name, I'll give her your message."

"I'm afraid she wouldn't understand the message. I wonder if I might call back at a time when she will be home?"

Katlin paused again. I guessed she was waiting for the long-distance phone service pitch, but it wasn't coming.

"She gets home around seven, you could try then."

I gave her quick thanks, and looked down at my list. Next on my list was Janis Williamson, married to Arthur Kramer--1980, New York, New York, one child Brian.

The phone rung once and a man answered "Hello, Kramers."

I was torn between Brian or Mr. Kramer, then went with the breadwinner, "Mr. Kramer, I was wondering if I might speak to Mrs. Kramer?"

"Concerning?"

"Well, I don't now how to explain this, but I was hoping she could help me find an old classmate of hers from ECU."

"What the hell is this. Oh, I get it, you're with one of those companies that charge to find people. Get lost, pal, and take me off of your damn list."

Click. If the Kramers had caller ID, twenty percent of my odds had just dropped off line.

Next on my list was April Mitchell. Married to Adolfo Manuel Saa--married 1976, divorced 1977, no children--lives in Beaufort, S.C.

She picked up on the fifth ring, "Hello."

"Hello, is this April?"

"Yes it is, who's calling, please?"

"April, my name is Cape Thomas, I live in North Carolina. I'm trying to find an old classmate of yours from ECU, and I was hoping you could help." I crossed my fingers to hex a hang-up. It worked, and April responded,

"I'll try. What is the name of the person you're looking for, sir?" The name problem, how could you look for someone you didn't know? I kept my fingers crossed, and gave it a shot, "Well, that's where the problem comes in, I don't really remember her name. You see, I met her only once."

"You didn't get her name? When did you meet her in college?" April asked.

"I didn't meet her at ECU, but she was in school there when I met her." Dumb, I should have thought of something better to say.

"That was a long time ago, why wait so long to follow back up? I can tell you I wouldn't like that, I can't imagine she would."

"I know, but--"

"I don't know. I might talk to you, but you would need a good excuse. I suppose if we had fallen in love, you know, at first sight that might be a little different. I fell in love with someone once, but it wasn't at first sight. Well, I think he loved me at first sight but he wasn't a stranger. I knew his name, Allen Rogers. I've often wondered what happened to him. Maybe I should try and find him? You know, with the Internet and all the information they have now I suppose I could. Is that how you found me, on the Internet? Wouldn't you think that might be my best place to find--Allen? "

"Anything is possible, Ap--?"

"I think I will. I'm so happy you called. If you would not have called I might not ever have thought of finding him. He was such a wonderful man. Well, I suppose he wasn't quite an adult when I knew him. I just assume he is a wonderful man. Wouldn't you think a wonderful person would still be wonderful? But some people change as they age, maybe Allen changed, I hope not. We got along so well. But Adolfo came along and I dumped Allen for him. Allen was heartbroken, do you think he would even talk to me if I found him?"

I was drawing a big X across April's name as I answered her questions,

"Maybe, April. You seem to be a nice person, I would talk--."

"Really? How old are you? What do you look like? North Carolina, right?"

The thought of talking to April wasn't as satisfying as it had been.

"April, do you think you might--?"

"Oh, I'm sorry. Sometimes I just get carried away. Adolfo said I never listened. But I did listen, he never shut up. Have you ever met anyone like that, they just won't shut up?"

"Just one."

"Just one, really? I know lots of people like that, but Adolfo was the worst. You can't imagine how it is to have to hear someone talk about themselves all the time. That's why I divorced--"

"April, the lady I was looking for--"

"Oh yes, your friend. What was her name again? That's right you didn't know her name. Well, you'll have to tell me what she looked like--"

I gave a physical description and personal information in one breath. When you get your shot, you take it.

"That could have been a lot of people. Well, maybe not a lot of people. Not everyone is pretty and thin, I certainly--"

" My friend was engaged, her fiancé cheated on her. They may have called the engagement off," I said.

"Was she pregnant?"

While April rattled on, I thought about the blanket and MarKays' statement--You have all the clues.

"Yes, yes, April, there may have been a baby."

"Oh God, that could have been me. I've never told anyone this, but I cheated on

Allen….I had an abortion." April's voice faded as she retreated into her thoughts.

I used the moment of silence to assess my own situation. The blanket? I was sure the blanket contained an infant, but I never saw it. Maybe the blanket that hid the baby symbolized an abortion. If Faith had had an abortion, why would she come to me in such a strange way. An abortion? No, Faith would have called, or gotten in touch with me….There was no abortion. I mulled over the other option. Faith and I were together one night, could she, did we have a baby?

"April, do you remember anyone like that….A girl that broke an engagement and had a baby?" I asked.

From somewhere in her past, surely a tormented past, April joined me.

"No, I'm sorry. I mean, there were girls that might have looked like your friend, but I don't remember anyone breaking an engagement. If there is one thing I know, it's about breaking engagements. Although Allen and I weren't engaged, but we were so close. We would have made a good couple, I would have made a good mother…. I'm sorry, I can't talk anymore, I don't know this woman."

April, once talkative and annoying, was someone I wanted to comfort, but I could not think of the right words to say. I'm sorry, wish things had worked out differently, came to mind, but April hung up before I could express them.

My hands shook as I picked up the phone to make my next call. These revelations and their possible consequences gave what once had been a search to find my soulmate new meaning. For the first time the consequences of one night together twenty-five years ago had become serious, very serious. I could be a father, or worse I could be a man that had left a young woman in a bad situation. My excuse for not hunting Faith down seemed weak.

For years I was satisfied that I was abiding by Faith's wishes. Now, I was forced to face the truth: Responsibility had never been my strong suit. I hadn't sought Faith out because to do so would have meant commitment. Part of me wanted to forget the whole thing, the better part of me decided to continue. I went into the bar and poured myself a drink. Inches from my lips was a liquid that could make me forget and help me hide from responsibility. I poured the drink out, then emptied the rest of the bottles into the sink. I had hid long enough, no more drinking, no more hiding. I was better than that.

I had planned to save the Faith look-a-like for last, but I ditched that plan and dialed my best chance: Allison Moore, married to W. Cronos Kress-1978, Charlotte, NC-no children.

"Hello, is this Mrs. Kress?"

"No, this is her maid, hold please."

I waited and thought of Faith's voice. Would I recognize it, had it changed?

"Allison Kress, to whom am I speaking, please?"

Allison Tyra Moore Kress sounded as if she had just stepped off the set of Gone with the Wind. She was blessed with a country club drawl, still Southern but with great diction. The endings of her words were pronounced, rather than elided, as most Southerners were inclined to do. If Allison wasn't Faith they had one thing in common, both were pure Southern aristocrats.

I explained my reason for calling. Allison had no interest in helping me find one of her old classmates. Until I explained the reason she might know my mystery woman.

"Let me understand this…. Mr. Thomas, was it?" Afraid Allison might turn into April, I quickly affirmed her memory, "Yes, Thomas, Cape Thomas."

"You say this person broke an engagement. Then perhaps had a child with her paramour?"

I hadn't used the word paramour or her scenario about the child. Since Allison was on the right track, I let her continue. "This friend of yours, Mr. Thomas, I assume she later married her former fiancé?"

"Well, Mrs. Kress, that was something I was hoping you could tell me."

"Mr. Thomas, if indeed that is your name, you strike me as a very clever person. Most clever people that I know generally have the answer for the question they ask."

I didn't speak. I had a feeling Allison had more to say. Unlike my conversation with April, I didn't want her to stop talking. Allison broke the stalemate, "I'll talk about this, but not over the phone. Where do you live?"

The questioned surprised me. All I wanted was the name of an old classmate. Still I needed an answer. To get one, it looked as if I would have to provide some answers myself. "In the eastern part of the state."

There was another pause, then Allison continued, "Very vague, Mr. Thomas. But I suppose that is a requirement for someone in your line of work. Do you know Raleigh?"

Not only didn't I have a line of work I also had no idea where this conversation was going. "Well, not like the back of my hand, but I can find a few places."

Allison lowered her voice, almost to a whisper, "Do you know Café Moon?"

What luck. One of the few places I did know in Raleigh. "You mean the one across from Moore Square?"

"One and the same, Mr. Thomas. I'll be there tomorrow at 1:00 p.m., ask for Ally Moore."

I wanted to be sure of the name so I repeated it, "Ally Moore?"

"Yes Mr. Thomas, Ally Moore, I'm sure you can appreciate why I wouldn't use the Kress name." I didn't have a clue why she wouldn't use the Kress name. But I wasn't about to ask. "Ally Moore, 1:00 p.m. Café Moon."

"Until then, Mr. Thomas." Allison Kress, a.k.a. Ally Moore, hung up without a good-bye.

I tried to remember her entire conversation. That wasn't a problem, but the suggestion of a meeting was. I could think of only one reason.

Allison Kress might be my mystery woman, and if not she knew her.

I looked at my watch--7:00 p.m.. I had roughly eighteen hours to find out a little about Allison Kress. I typed the name into the web, but nothing came up. Then I typed in W. Cronos Kress. Bingo! Graduate of Harvard Law, Rhodes Scholar, Oxford, and a former member of the Federal Reserve Board. W. Cronos Kress had more accolades than I had hours flying. This guy was to banking what Donald Trump was to real estate.

I considered calling Carol Kornegay Pate Lee, but I couldn't see where it would be necessary. I was certain Mrs. W. Cronos Kress had the answers to all my questions.

CHAPTER EIGHT

A Woman to Remember.

I didn't wake up until 8:00 am. My new life didn't require a schedule, but it did however, require money. Money I apparently wouldn't be getting from my unused unemployment benefits from AeroMax. I listened intently as the unemployment claims representative explained my predicament, "Three years have passed, that removes AeroMax from the picture. You have been self-employed and have deducted payroll taxes. Unfortunately for you, owners of a company cannot draw benefits. Do you understand, Mr. Thomas?"

I did understand. I was screwed and no amount of explaining would change that. No job, no benefits.

That left me with two options, win the FAA hearing, or flip hamburgers at MoBurgers. I called my lawyer, Tom Butterfield.

Tom asked me a few questions about the AeroMax suspension. I filled him in on dates and times, then faxed him a copy of my bid sheet for the dates in question. He briefly mentioned the hearing--things were still not good.

I mentally started preparing myself for my change of careers from flying to frying. As I showered I sang parts of the Big Burger ditty, " A Big-beef burger mustard, bacon, something, something on Texas Toast-Ye-Haw..." Maybe that wouldn't be a question on the MoBurgers employment application. Besides, airline captains have great voices, so I could do the drive-up window. With my training I was a lock, "Good morning, ladies and gentlemen, thank you for stopping at MoBurgers. We'll be frying your hamburger at five hundred degrees and the estimated delivery time will be two minutes. If any of our younger patrons care to see the kitchen action, I'll be glad to give you a tour. As is our custom at MoBurgers you will receive our lovely gold plastic spatula pin. "

I thought of my days as captain with AeroMax, I'd given out many gold plastic wings and tours of the cockpit to kids. The speeches I made weren't that much different than the facetious one I had just made up….Damn, I missed being an airline captain.

It was 11:00 a.m. by the time I finished my pre-employment practice session and shower. I tried on three different sports coats before finally deciding on a black coat, black slacks and a blue shirt. It had been a long time since I had worried about how I dressed. This woman was about to solve my vision problem. The least I could do was dress well. Besides if she was Faith, I wanted to look successful.

I rolled into Raleigh at 12:30. The lanes on the outer loop were filled with mid-day traffic. My driving skills, unfortunately, didn't parallel my flying skills. I began to worry that I wouldn't make Café Moon by 1:00. As I turned onto Wilmington Street, the traffic finally began to move. I found an empty parking space, gave myself a once-over, popped an Altoid, and headed inside.

The hostess met me at the door. "Yes, sir?"

"I'd like to be seated with Ally Moore."

"Ally, right?"

"Yes."

"Right this way, sir"

The perky little hostess guided me to a table in the back of the restaurant adjoining the patio. But the table was empty. "Is this the right table?" For a second I thought she meant Ally was a passageway between two buildings.

"Don't worry, sir, Ally will join you shortly." She assured me with a smile. I glanced over the menu even though I wasn't hungry. The menu listed the typical bistro items--most contained sun-dried tomatoes, basil, or pine nuts. I would have been happier with a cheeseburger, but unfortunately, nothing that simple existed on the menu. I declined the offer of a cocktail and sipped on my glass of water instead.

The room was full of talkative diners. The din from the different conversations conflicted with the peaceful setting of the room. I fidgeted with my silverware, and kept my eye on the ladies' room. Soon a tall blonde came from the room and made her way toward my table. I had never seen Ally Moore, except in the old class picture from ECU. She was a brunette who would now be in her mid forties. This blonde wasn't much over thirty, thirty-five tops. I tried not to stare, but she was striking. She made eye contact, so I smiled. Maybe after I finished with Ally I would try to get her number. The blonde gave me a weak smile, then stopped at my table. I stood, gave her another smile and spoke,

"Hi."

She extended her hand, "Mr. Thomas, I presume?"

I tried not to look surprised. This woman couldn't be Ally Moore. She had sent someone in her place, maybe a friend or, more than likely, her assistant. A woman like Allison Moore Kress would have an assistant. I took her hand and introduced myself,

"Yes, I'm Cape Thomas, and you are…?"

"I'm Ally Moore, Mr. Thomas." I nodded and studied her more closely. Her hair didn't have the brassy sheen of Linda's, and her face was smooth, no age lines, even close up. I looked down at her hand that I still had cupped in mine. Her nails were perfect and real. I had learned a long time ago to notice women's hands. They were the first place that age could be detected. At least that's what I had always believed, but Ally's were as youthful looking as her face.

"Time has been kind to me, Mr. Thomas, but I can assure you, I'm Ally Moore."

She answered the question my expression had asked. I regained my composure and pulled the chair out for her. Allison Kress was used to being attended to, pampered. I wondered whether she would have seated herself had I not offered. She thanked me, and sat down. No, had I not offered to seat her, she would have stood. Faith, like Allison Moore Kress, had stood until I offered her a seat by the fireplace.

"Mr. Thomas, if that is your name? May I ask you a question?"

I could sense her distrust. I wanted to dispel it, because without trust this meeting was going nowhere. " I don't mind you asking questions, if you don't mind calling me Cape."

She smiled another weak smile, "As you wish, Cape, and you may call me Ally."

The emphasis she placed on my name made it sound dignified, important. It was fitting. I suspected that Allison Kress spoke to very few people who were unimportant.

"Ally? You know, you really look more like an Allison."

She smiled again, this time a real smile, "I prefer Ally, but most of the time I don't get what I prefer."

It was hard to imagine Ally not getting anything she wanted.

" I know I don't appear to be deprived, but Mr.--Cape, sorry--appearances can be deceiving."

The voice, her mannerisms, all of it seemed familiar, but add in twenty-five years and even the well-preserved Allison Kress could hide behind the anonymity of time. The thought that we might have made love, long ago, pushed me forward, "You wanted to ask me a question, Ally?"

She looked intently into my eyes, "You have a kindness about you. It shows in your eyes, and I hope you are honest as well."

I hadn't given much thought to being honest, but if Ally Moore wanted me to be honest then I would be honest.

"I think for the most part I'm honest," I said.

"Good, then I guess I'll appeal to the 'most part' of you." There was a brief smile, then a serious Allison Kress asked, " Do you work for my husband?"

I hadn't expected a question concerning her husband. I'd hoped she would recognize me, but no such luck--time had changed me, too.

"I'm sorry to be direct, but I need to know. Of course you can lie, but I don't think you will."

I had lied before, but lying wasn't on the agenda today. Lying would distance me from Ally Moore. I didn't want that. I liked Ally, so far anyway.

"Ally, I don't even know your husband."

"There are many people who work for my husband who don't know him. Do you work for W. Cronos Kress?"

"I don't work for him. The only thing I know about him is what I read on the Internet last night."

" I appreciate your honesty, but may I ask why you would search for my husband on the Internet?"

That was an easy question, and one I could answer without raising any red flags for Ally.

"You mentioned that you didn't want to use the Kress name. Most people refer to a name. There are plain names, like Jones, Smith, and Thomas. Then there are The Rockefellers, The Astors, and The Vanderbilts, and I was curious."

She leaned back in her chair and relaxed her rigid posture before continuing. "That's fair. I must confess that I looked for your name on the Internet, too. It didn't come up, so I wondered if you were using an alias."

This time it was my turn to smile, "I apologize for that, It's my father's fault, I guess."

"Your father's fault? You'll forgive me, but I don't understand."

"Well, my middle name is Allen. If my father had had a little foresight, he would have made it, The." I was trying to make a play on words, but she didn't get it.

"I'm sorry, why would that rather than Allen have made a difference?"

I spelled it out, "T-H-E as in The Rockefellers." She still didn't get it. Maybe humor was a bad idea, so I put it to rest, " I just meant-"

"Oh, I see, cute."

She got it. It wasn't, so I moved on. "Ally, do you have any more questions?"

"I really do want to trust you, but would you mind?"

Why not answer questions? I had nothing to hide, "Fire away."

"Are you a detective?"

"No."

"Do you work for a newspaper, magazine, or one of those horrid tabloids?"

"Nope, nope, and nope." I shook my head with each denial.

The waiter brought Ally a glass of wine she had apparently ordered before I arrived.

She accepted the wine without a thank you. She wasn't rude, it was good breeding. I had read once in a book of etiquette that one shouldn't thank staff for performance of duty. I had had to learn that, but it had been bred into Ally.

The waiter was poised. I knew the question he would ask, and I was sure Ally did also.

"Would you care to hear the specials?"

She looked to me to handle the question. I shook my head no, and tossed the ball back in her court, "I don't think that will be necessary. I will have the salmon, and you can bring another glass of pinot with that," Ally said.

The waiter nodded his approval then turned to me, "And for you, sir?"

"I'll have the salmon, and water to drink."

The waiter didn't nod approval this time, "Very good, sir." I couldn't blame him, water didn't add a lot to the tab. The tip would be smaller without the wine.

"A man who doesn't have a cocktail or at least a glass of wine could be perceived as working," Ally said.

I wanted Ally to trust me, but I had never drunk during the day. I was facing the fact that I wouldn't be drinking anymore. "Or a recovering alcoholic," I interjected.

"Oh, I'm so sorry, Cape, I didn't mean-"

"I'm not. I think I'm a better person for it; at least, I hope I am."

She frowned, "I'm too suspicious, I apologize."

When I was fired by AeroMax, I was at worst a social drinker. Now, six years later, I was a recovering alcoholic. My beautiful companion accepted my affliction with no reservations, but I knew my acceptance wouldn't come as easily.

"Apology accepted, any more questions?"

"Well, I do have some more questions, but not about who you are." Her voice was soft and gentle. I was no longer a stranger, but a patient on the road to recovery. " This person you described over the phone. How do you know her?"

Finally, a question I was prepared for, "I met her a long time ago. Something made me think of her, but I couldn't remember her name. I was hoping you could help."

Ally traced the rim of her wineglass with her finger, "This person whom you are looking for does remind me of someone. But you know that already. Tell me, what led you to me?" I explained about my trip to ECU, the time line, and the chosen profession of my mystery lady. I omitted the vision I had had on my deck.

"I thought, hoped, this was long forgotten. But if you could find out, I suppose anyone could." She paused, "You do know Walter is up for an ambassadorship?" How was I supposed to know that? Hell, I didn't even know who Walter was, "Ally, who's Walter?"

"Walter, my husband, Walter Cronos Kress." I should have figured it out. Except W. Cronos Kress was my first encounter with anyone who used an initial as his first name.

"Is that why you came?" I asked.

" Yes, when you called I thought you might be from the press. You know when one accepts public life, one's life becomes public, any skeletons from one's past come out. Walter has no skeletons, that can be found anyway, he's very good at hiding his faux pas. I'm afraid I'm not. I came here today to make you an offer, but first I had to find out who you are."

This was starting to sound more like marital problems, not what I wanted to hear.

"Ally, I can't see how this concerns me, Walter, ambassador, an offer? I'm just a guy that knows a situation concerning a lady, and a baby. I don't even know any names to--."

"It would be only a matter of time before that happened. If you know my story the names will come. That's why I wanted to meet with you. I want you to stop digging for those names, stop and go no further--."

"Ally, I--."

"Please, let me finish while I still have the nerve. I'm prepared to pay you five hundred thousand dollars to stop searching for this person."

The amount of money Ally offered, five hundred thousand dollars, bounced around in my head like a pinball hung between two angry bumpers. What the hell could I know that was worth five hundred thousand to forget? For five hundred thousand dollars I could almost be talked into forgetting to breathe…forever.

"Look, Ally, it doesn't take some maven from Langley to figure this out. You had a baby that wasn't Walter's--then you married Walter. Obviously, he still doesn't know about the child. But--."

"Can't you just take the money and forget about this?" she begged.

I wondered if Ally had five hundred thousand dollars, but I had no doubt that Walter did. But did she? I noticed her diamond ring as she sipped her wine, four, maybe five carats at least. Probably top quality worth at least fifty thousand, maybe more. Platinum necklace, ten, or twelve more thousand. Yeah, she could raid her jewelry box and find a half a million dollars.

"Ally, I don't know exactly what I'm trying to find, but I know it doesn't involve money. Maybe a few days ago, if you had made me that offer, I would have accepted. But things have changed, I made a promise to a friend and I intend to keep it. I can't stop now, not even for a half a million dollars, sorry."

"I think I know who your 'friend' is. Excuse me, I'm going on the patio for some fresh air." Ally stepped from the room and onto the adjoining patio. I watched as she dug in her purse and produced a pack of Nat Shermans'. Fresh air with tar and nicotine, that was a new twist on an old cliché. The wind blew and Ally Moore, in spite of her best efforts, could not ignite her expensive silver lighter.

I rose from the table and joined her on the patio. Without speaking I pulled my old Zippo from my pocket and gave her a light. Ally's hand touched mine as she guided the cigarette into the guarded flame.

"I thought I was the last smoker, thanks," she said.

"Ex-smoker. I quit a few years ago. The lighter was a gift, so it's been a little harder to put down than the cigarettes."

"Let's see, ex-drinker, ex-smoker, and for sale to the highest bidder. Is there anything else I should know about you, Mister Thomas?"

"I understand two out of your three, but I'm not for sale, Mrs. Kress."

"The hell you're not. Do you think I can't figure out who your friend is? You're not a liar, Mr. Thomas, but you are devious. You answered my questions like a lawyer. You don't work for my husband, not at the moment. But you will work for my husband, soon. I'm curious, how much will he pay when you connect the dots?"

"Ally, I don't know your husband and I don't give a damn about what he's willing to pay for what I find from this search. I do know I won't stop until I find out what I need to know.... The friend I mentioned is someone who died because she got mixed up in this. I made her a promise, and I intend to keep it. The Rockefellers, The Vanderbilts, and please forgive me, but even the high and mighty Walter Kress can't stop me from finding this woman," I said.

"Why is that, Mr. Thomas? What could be so important about this that you would reject a half a million dollars, or more if Walter is involved? Let me guess. You're rich and you take great pleasure in meddling in other people's lives? No, you're too devious for that. It's political, isn't it?"

"No, not even close. I know this doesn't make much sense to you, it didn't to me either. At first I thought this was about a woman, but now I think it has more to do with the baby. Do you know where the baby is?" I asked.

"You leave her out of this, Mr. Thomas." Ally hissed the words.

" So it's a girl?"

Ally leaned over, her face inches from mine. "That's right, Mr. Thomas. A girl, an innocent person, who has every right to lead her life without interruption."

I moved away from Ally, "Look I won't bother her, I just want to see her. I never thought I would have a child."

"Why on earth would you think she's your child?" Ally asked.

"Because twenty-five years ago I think we spent the night together. From this little union, I think we produced a child."

"Mr. Thomas, twenty-five years ago I did some things I might not remember. But one thing I do know for certain. This child is not yours." I had been so close to having my vision in the flesh. Now I was as far from the answer as I was the five hundred thousand dollars Ally had offered. "What makes you so sure? I mean, twenty-five years is a long time. I don't remember you either," I said.

Ally planted her cigarette into an ashcan on the patio, and leaned closer to my ear,

"Because, Mr. Thomas, this child is a mulatto, and I know who the father is. You can do whatever you want with this information, I'm tired of hiding from the truth."

Ally left the patio, passed by the table and out the front room of Café Moon. I looked at the bill and the untouched food, then threw down my only hundred to cover the tab. I caught up with her in the entrance as she stopped to pay her bill. "The bill's taken care of, the money's on the table," I said. The cashier nodded and Ally headed for the door. I quickly pushed the door open for her.

"I'm perfectly capable of opening a door, do you mind?"

Ally walked fast, I had to jog to catch her, "Mrs. Kress, wait, please--"

"I asked you not to use that name."

"Ally--"

"Don't call me Ally, either."

The traffic was heavy, and we waited for the light to change. "I'm not a threat to you." I rushed the words before the light changed, " Back on the patio, you defended your daughter. I assume you love her, even if she was a mistake--."

"You can stop assuming, Mr. Thomas, I love my daughter, very much, and she wasn't a mistake," Ally said.

"You say that, but if Walter doesn't know about her, then didn't she get swept under the carpet in some way?"

"Your point, Mr. Thomas. What is your point?"

"My point is, that you and I are alike in some ways--"

"Hardly."

"Wait, please….You had something that happened in your life twenty-five years ago, and I did, too. You were able to deal with it, I wasn't. All I want is the same chance you had, that's it, nothing more," I explained.

"I hope you get that chance, but I can't help. I don't know the woman you speak of, I'm sorry."

I wanted to believe her, but Ally could be lying about the child's father. She couldn't buy me off. Maybe she was trying to put the toothpaste back in the tube.

"Okay, I believe you. But what would it hurt for you to answer a few questions? I'll be satisfied and your secret will be safe, I promise you that."

The biting wind stirred the chill in the air. I could see Ally shaking from the cold. In spite of the cold she hadn't left me, and that was a good sign.

"Suppose I don't answer your questions, then what? You go to Walter with the information and collect considerably more than thirty pieces of silver….Sounds like blackmail to me."

"Mrs. Kress, I'm not a lawyer. I didn't go into law for good reasons, or business for that matter. I could never defend someone who was guilty, and I would never destroy anyone for greed. So I guess the answer to your question is this; whether you talk to me or not, your secret is safe. Thanks for meeting with me." I had tried, but it just wasn't working, it was time to hanger the plane. I headed to my car parked near an Irish Pub on Moore Square.

"Mr. Thomas, I can think of another reason you couldn't have made it in either of those fields," Ally said.

"Yeah, what's that?"

"Your negotiating skills are woefully lacking....And I think you are a very honest person. I'll answer your questions."

"So do you want to finish lunch?" I nodded toward the doorway of Café Moon.

"No, I think we made a little scene in there. Let's go somewhere else and have a cup of coffee, I'm freezing."

Moore Square in Raleigh is just that, a square block park. I looked over at GraniteShields, another restaurant that adjoined the Square, "How about there?" I pointed to the south end of the Square. She nodded and we started walking toward GraniteShields. We hunched over against the wind but Ally was still shaking. I draped my coat over her shoulders. "Thank you, I left mine in the car."

The lunch crowd had thinned. I wanted a quiet place--I asked the hostess for a table upstairs. There was only one group, of five women, left in our section of the restaurant. We could hear them as they divided the tab, "I only had a salad, you had a salad and dessert. Yes, but you had wine, I only had coffee." I've never understood why women always divided the bill. Men just took turns paying. When the group was satisfied each had paid a fair portion of the bill, they left.

I seated Ally, then ordered a cup of coffee for myself and a cappuccino for her.

" Do you want your coat back?" Ally asked.

"When you warm up, just hang it on your chair, you still look cold to me."

"Thanks, I'm ready for your questions."

It was important to phrase the question in a way that wouldn't upset Ally, and the time I spent thinking about how to do that caused an awkward gap.

"Ally, I mean….What should I call you, anyway?"

"Ally is the name I prefer, and you may call me that."

"Good, that means I can be Cape, right?" Ally nodded and waited for the question.

"Did you ever have a Coptic cross?"

"No, I don't even know what a Coptic cross is."

So far so good.

"Do you like outside fireplaces?" I asked.

"I love them, why did you ask that?"

"Just a hunch."

"I thought these would be personal and probing questions. Are we making small talk, or are you leading up to the hard questions?"

"I didn't want to upset you. I figured if I did, I'd have to revert to calling you…Oh, I don't know…. 'The tall attractive blonde woman, since you don't like given names once you get angry."

"Cape, I'm not that fragile, give it your best shot. I have to leave soon."

"Did Walter cheat on you? Is that what caused you to have a one-night stand with this person, or paramour, to use your terminology ?"

"One-night stand? I didn't have a one-night stand. I had a yearlong relationship with a man I should have married. It happened while Walter was in Oxford. This situation you have described does not involve me, I'm certain of it now. I know you want me to be your mystery woman, but I'm not the one you are looking for, sorry." Ally glanced at her diamond encrusted Chopard watch, an item I had overlooked when I inventoried her earlier. "Are you satisfied I've told you the truth?" Ally asked.

She was truthful, Ally wasn't Faith, and it was back to the beginning for me.

"Yes, and thanks, I won't hold you any longer," I said.

"Summarily dismissed, that reminds me of Walter, I don't like that--"

"No, I didn't mean it like that. You kept checking your watch, I thought you might need to go."

"Oh, I have a few minutes, and I'd love another cappuccino."

"Excuse me," I looked around the room for the server, no luck. "I'll get it for you."

When I returned to the table a lone diner had joined Ally and I upstairs. I glanced at the headlines of the News and Observer he was reading--'America Intensifies Campaign against Insurgents.'

"Ally, I have a little confession to make."

"Don't you think we've had enough confessions for one day?"

"Maybe, but let's squeeze in one more. The money, it was on my mind quite a bit. I struggled with not taking it."

"I know. You don't play a lot of poker, do you, Cape?"

"I play a lot of poker, I just don't win a lot at poker."

"You might think about giving it up, your feelings have a way of showing up on your face."

"It was that obvious, huh?"

"Well, for just a second I thought you might be a jewelry appraiser, or perhaps a jewel thief. If you are going to keep playing poker, maybe you should wear a mask."

I liked this woman, and in spite of my questions she liked me, I could feel it.

"Ally, I'll tell you what I'll do. I'll give up poker, if you'll give up attempted bribery."

"You've got a deal, Cape, no pun intended."

"You wouldn't consider making one last attempt at it before you quit, would you?"

"Forget it, buster." Ally was a perfect woman. Beautiful, witty, and--damn it all-- married.

"Ally, I'm sorry you weren't my mystery woman, it might have been fun."

"Fun, there's something I haven't had in a long time."

"Yeah, I guess it would be tough for you to have fun on your budget."

"Money doesn't make me happy, not any more. But back to your mystery woman.

Why are you looking for this person? You couldn't have loved her--you don't even remember her name."

I trusted Ally but not enough to go into my vision, so I put it in the context of a dream. She listened as I rushed through my explanation.

"One night, that's it? Why are you so sure you fathered a child with this, this--?" She searched for the right word then finally settled on "lady."

It was a fair question, but one I was hoping she wouldn't ask. "I don't know, Ally, I guess it's the only thing that makes sense. Yeah, before you say it, most dreams aren't logical. Maybe this one isn't, either. Maybe it means something entirely different from what I've perceived. I don't know, any ideas?"

She stirred her cappuccino before she spoke. "Perhaps it's something you want? Do you have children?"

"No."

"Have you ever been married?"

"No."

She sipped the hot drink, then continued, " You seem nice, why didn't you marry?"

This was one question I could answer without thinking about it. "I guess I never found the right girl."

She wasn't buying it, "That's a pat answer, I suppose you've been asked that numerous times?"

"Yeah, a thousand times, maybe more." She searched my face for a reaction. I turned away, and stared at the naked oak limbs scratching against the cold gray sky. The hair on my neck bristled, and I could feel her eyes.

"You don't like talking about it. Were you hurt by someone?" Ally was right. I didn't want to talk about it. Why bring it up? Let it stay buried in my past.

"You know, I told you a lot about me, it's only fair for me to find out a little about you," Ally said gently.

Yeah. That was true, considering what Ally had revealed, and so I was obligated. "I almost married once. She found someone else, end of story."

" The someone else? Was he a friend of yours?"

"Hardly." Did I really want to go into this? Why not, though? I'd never see Ally again. "No, the guy was--is a jerk. He's in management with AeroMax, we all worked there."

Ally didn't understand AeroMax.

"AeroMax-Technology?"

I smiled, for fifteen years there had only been one AeroMax to me. "No, AeroMax Airlines. I was a captain, she was a flight attendant, he was a jerk."

"Sounds like an interesting story, but why don't you say what you really think about this jerk?"

I smiled back, "I thought I had."

"You were being polite. I like that about Southern men, but sometimes I think it's a cop out."

I sipped my coffee before responding, "Asshole, he's an asshole, and I apologize for the language."

Ally laughed. It was a good laugh, refined. "Do you feel better?" she asked.

I nodded, "A little. In retrospect, I think some more derogatory adjectives could have described him better. I know a more detailed description would have heightened my euphoria."

Ally made a mock frown, then continued with her inquiry, "I think 'asshole' really said it all, good choice. Did you love her?"

Grace was becoming a popular subject but still not something I relished. "I think I did, I've never had much experience with love. I've known a lot of women. But I've never known much about love. I thought that one day….Poof! Wife, kids, and a minivan in the garage, you know, like in the movies. Now, I'm beginning to think it's more about time and place, than the people involved."

"I agree, timing is everything." Ally stirred her drink. "I've known love only once myself." Her eyes filled with tears and for a second I thought she might cry.

"The guy that fathered your child?" I asked.

She almost whispered her answer, "Yes, Caesar. We met at ECU. You're from the South, that doesn't bother you?"

"What?"

"That I loved a black man."

"Ally, I've been all over the world. Seen a lot of things, met a lot of people, happiness is where you find it." I hadn't always felt that way. My copilot on my first 747 job was Jake, a black man who became my best friend. He died a few years back in a crash in Taiwan. Good man, I still miss him.

Ally was comfortable with me; she wanted to talk and I let her. "People didn't feel like that years ago, not here anyway. My father almost disowned me. He and Walter's father were college roommates. Walter was serious about life, I guess he had to be. His life was planned out for him before he was born. The Kress family is big in banking-."

"Yeah, I read that in Walter's bio."

Ally continued, "Anyway, Walter knew he would take over his father's banking concerns. Caesar was an artist, a person who saw the beauty of everything. I bought him an ant farm once, and he was fascinated by it. Walter has never been fascinated by anything other than the bottom line. I needed someone who shared my interest."

" Speaking of interest….Why nursing, by the way? It doesn't seem like a choice you would have made."

"My father was, is, a doctor, a surgeon actually. His desire was that I become a doctor. I didn't have the constitution or the grades. Nursing was a choice he could live with. That's what all little Southern girls strive for, I guess."

"What's that?" I asked.

"Their father's approval, Cape, it's an old Southern family tradition. I'm surprised you didn't know that?"

I didn't want her to stop talking, but I had to answer, "I don't know much about family tradition. My mother and father died in a plane crash when I was young, and my grandfather raised me."

Ally looked at me with pity I didn't want.

"I'm so sorry, it must have been hard on you?"

" I was five, I'm fine with it, go on, please."

Ally hailed the waiter and ordered another cappuccino. "Long story short. Walter left for Oxford, I met Caesar, my father sent me away to have the baby. Everything was covered up. I married Walter. We have known one another since childhood. I think our wedding was planned just after we were baptized. Walter and I have never loved one another. But our parents are happy, isn't that what life is all about, anyway?"

I ordered another coffee, "I suppose that would be more of the family tradition thing?"

"Exactly." Ally looked at her watch. "I have to leave soon."

"If you aren't happy why don't you leave?" I asked.

"Have you ever known a drug addict?"

"No," I lied. Jimmy was the only drug addict I knew, and one I didn't want to talk about, or know for that matter.

"Wealth is like a drug, perhaps worse. It's addictive, private jets, limos, exclusive spas, shopping, and the best seats at any function. Being Mrs. W. Cronos Kress is something I fight to hold on to daily. Not for the status, but for the protection."

I knew it was a stupid question, but that had never stopped me before, "Why don't you just find Caesar, and pick up the pieces? He could protect you, right?"

A bitter look came over Ally's face, "Walter found out about Caesar when he returned from Oxford. Walter destroyed Caesar's dream of becoming an artist. The Kress family contributes heavily to the arts. Walter couldn't destroy

Caesar's talent, but he could destroy his dream of becoming an artist. Caesar thought he had no talent because none of his art sold, Walter saw to that." A single tear spilled over the rim of Ally's eye and she flicked it away in frustration.

"Caesar killed himself, he couldn't live without his art. That was my punishment for having an affair on Walter. He has been punishing me ever since, in one way or another. He has blatant affairs, makes cutting remarks, and the worst part, he isolates me from my emotions. He would love for me to just go away. We haven't slept in the same bed for almost ten years. Walter wants me to make a mistake; I won't because I'm trying to rectify one I made twenty-five years ago. I hurt him, and in an indirect way I killed Caesar."

Beautiful, rich, and miserable, Ally was an unfortunate irony.

"Yeah, but is having the wealth worth all the pain? And protection, why would you need protection?

"Cape, it's not just about me. Walter knew about Caesar, and you were right, he never knew about the baby. She's an actress, if I told you her name you would know her. The protection I spoke of is for her, not me. If Walter found out about her, he would destroy her, too. I stay in this wonderful hell I've built, because of that. Isn't there an old saying about keeping your enemies close at hand?"

"I think so."

Ally sighed then continued, "I keep dreaming maybe one day Walter will think I've suffered enough and forgive me. I guess my dream is a little different from yours, Cape. I know the who, why, and what, but not the when. You, on the other hand, know the when, but not the who, why, or what. I have to go. Good luck, don't give up the search."

I stood and offered to walk her to her car. She insisted that she go alone. I wasn't expecting the hug or the quick peck she gave me. "Whoa, was that payment for lunch?"

"No, that was for being a good man. They're hard to find, I hope when you find this mystery woman of yours she realizes that. Good luck."

I sat back down and stared at her. From the stairs I heard Ally call out.

"Cape, thanks for listening, and I trust you, by the way." With that, Ally Moore was gone.

"More coffee, sir?" the waitress asked.

"No thanks."

"You look sad, ending a relationship?"

"No, not really, just regretting that I didn't have one."

CHAPTER NINE

Requiem for a Friend

The phone was ringing when I got home. I fumbled for and found the light switch, only to be rewarded with a brief flash of light as the bulb blew. Stumbling around like a drunk at last call, I barked both shins and my knee before I made it to the phone.

"Hello!" I yelled into the wrong end of the receiver.

"Cape, Tom Butterfield. Can you hear me?"

"Yeah, we had a bad connection, but I can hear you now."

"Good, I'm glad I finally caught you, I tried a few times earlier."

"What's up, Tom?"

Tom paused, "I put out those feelers I talked about."

"And?"

"It's not good, Cape. If we go any further I'll need a $10,000.00 retainer. To be honest, I think you'll be wasting your money."

An honest lawyer? I pondered the oxymoron before I responded.

"So how long do you think the suspension will be?"

"Permanently, they're pretty angry with you, Cape."

"Can't we work a deal?"

"They did that once, and you broke it, remember?"

" Well, Tom, that was before I realized I didn't know all the ingredients of a Big Burger."

"What the hell does that have to do with the hearing?"

"Just that I'm not qualified to work at MoBurgers. I'll get you a check." I said.

" A Big-beef burger, mustard, jalapeno , bacon, lettuce, and a few more things I forgot…" Tom sang. "Not bad, huh?"

"Not bad? What were you doing, strangling your cat?"

"No, I was trying to provide some information to my client," Tom said.

"Yeah, well, if that constitutes legal advice, I'm suing you if I don't get the job at the drive-thru window. Of course you may have nothing left if MoBurgers hears your rendition of the jingle."

"Cape, you can buy a lot of Big Burgers for ten grand, then again, send the check. I could use a nice vacation. We'll talk about my fees when I get back."

"Tom, you may want a nice vacation, but you need singing lessons."

" Seriously, this case is stacked against you. I've got a better chance at winning a Grammy than winning this case, but I'll give it my best shot," Tom concluded.

"I know you will, I just hope you defend better than you sing, thanks Tom."

I cradled the phone and looked out my window. It was raining. My recorder light was blinking; I pushed the play button, "Mr. Thomas, this is William Johnston. I'm an attorney with Johnston, Ballard & Hearst, in Charlotte. Could you give me a call, please?"

I was sure I didn't know William Johnston, but the reason for his call wasn't hard to figure out. The FAA violation represented an opportunity to supplement a meager caseload for some under-worked aviation attorney, so I erased the message. My case, as bad as it was, was in capable hands with Tom.

I replaced the light bulb and found my list of names from Judith. Then I jabbed Carol Kornegay's number into the phone. This time I was luckier, and Carol answered. "Hello, Mr. Thomas, is it?"

"Yes, I called yesterday."

Carol seemed nice, at least she was willing to talk. "Yes, my daughter told me someone called. I believe you wanted me to help you find someone?"

I explained everything to Carol, and waited for her response.

"You know, Mr. Thomas, twenty-five years is a long time. But I don't remember any of the nursing students breaking an engagement. I mean there were a lot of break-ups. Kid stuff mostly, but no one in our class broke an engagement that I can remember."

I expected her answer, but still felt disappointment. "Thanks, Carol, it was a long shot. I appreciate it--"

" I don't know if this relevant to your search or not. There was a girl who broke an engagement, but she wasn't in nursing."

"Did she look like the girl I described?" I asked.

Carol laughed, then explained, "Exactly, but I don't remember the jewelry you described. She was a friend of my suitemate. That night I met her was the drunkest I've ever been, but I'll never forget her name."

"And that would be?"

Carol laughed again, hard this time, "Laura Fisher. Every time I have too much to drink, I always say 'I pulled a Laura Fisher.' She was the only one that got drunker than I did that night."

I pressed her, "You say she wasn't a nurse, but do you remember what she majored in?"

Carol paused, before responding, "I believe she was pre-med. I'm almost certain she became a doctor. It's been so long, and I'm afraid I've lost touch with everyone at ECU. I've lived in Boca for over ten years now. God, those were good times."

"Do you remember where she was from?"

Carol was still laughing, like a woman well on her way to another Laura Fisher .

I waited as she composed herself and answered my question, "I'm not positive, but I think she was local. I could look up my suitemate's number, she would know."

Laura Fisher. Likely a useless name, but a name, and old prune-face Judith was big on names. I got the number and thanked Carol.

After the pay dirt I had struck with W. Cronus Kress I was feeling lucky. Laura Fisher's name remained on the computer screen, but no information followed. She could have married, I thought of Ally's sad union….And maybe she hadn't.

The campus at ECU was teeming with life. Students with backpacks swarmed over the grounds in various modes of transportation, some walked, and others used in-line skates and bicycles. Small groups were scattered about under trees, on stairways, and even street curbs pecking away on laptops to finish assignments.

Parking wasn't an option, walking barely was. I parked at the airport in Greenville and called a cab. The driver dropped me off at the Admissions Office and left me his card.

Judith was in her usual place, sporting her trademark sour face. No need to be nice this time, I had the fix she needed….A name.

Judith, buried in the paperwork of new applicants, looked at me and rolled her eyes, "May I help you?"

I cut right to the chase, "Laura Fisher F-I-S-H-E-R." I sounded each letter with emphasis. Judith typed in the name, "No current information."

"Well, Judith, why don't you just print me out that old useless non-current information anyway." Judith hit the print button and drummed her fingers on her desk. "Hey, Judith, do you like persimmons?"

"I don't think I've ever had one, why?"

"Just curious, but if you ever get a shot at one make sure it's after the first frost."

"Huh?"

Laura Fisher's address was in Greenville. I asked the cab driver for directions, and he complied. Then added, "Millionaire's Row."

"Excuse me?"

"That's what they call that section of town, Millionaire's Row."

I thanked him, jumped in the Jag and headed out to talk to Laura Fisher. The cab driver wasn't kidding. Anyone who lived in this part of town hadn't worried about paying the power bill lately. An old plantation house with imposing white columns loomed up from the stately acreage surrounding it.

I drove to the front door and hopped out. An older man washing an antique Lincoln stopped and looked at me. "Hi, I'm Cape Thomas, is this where the Fishers live?"

The man dropped the soapy rag in the bucket, and wiped his hands before we shook, "I'm Gustavo Jobim."

Not sure if he had heard me, I repeated myself, "Cape Thomas. Is this where the Fishers live?"

Gustavo corrected my question, "Mr. Fisher resides here, no others."

Mr. Fisher would do. "Great." I bounded up the steps and rang the doorbell.

Gustavo stood at the bottom of the steps staring at me while I waited. I rang the bell again, waited, and then repeated the process.

"Mr. Fisher doesn't hear very well. If you desire, I can inform him that you are here?"

I nodded, "Yes, thank you."

Gustavo opened the door, slowly, the same way he had climbed the steps. "Wait here, I will advise Mr. Fisher that you are here."

"Thanks, Gustavo, that's mighty nice of you." Gustavo did a half bow, then disappeared down the long hallway.

The foyer was where I had been deposited, and where I should have remained. But the huge room to my left drew me to it. The windows stretched from the floor to the twenty-foot-high ceiling above. At one end of the room sat a grand piano. A balcony extended the entire length of the room, and a curved staircase descended from each end of the balcony. At the far end was a roaring fireplace, topped by an enormous mantel. Over the mantel was a portrait of two young women. I walked over to the fireplace to get a better look. Both of the women were beautiful, and more importantly, one of them was Faith.

"May I help you, sir?" I turned around to see where the voice had come from.

Mr. Nathan Hale Fisher stood in the foyer looking every bit the Titan I had imagined he would be. His flowing mane of gray hair and full beard fused together, making it hard to tell where one stopped and the other started.

"YES SIR, I'M CAPE THOMAS. I WAS HOPING YOU COULD HELP ME FIND YOUR DAUGHTER."

"Mr. Thomas, why are you yelling at me?"

"I'm sorry, Mr. Fisher--ah, Gustavo said you didn't hear very well."

"I hear perfectly well, Mr. Thomas. It is Gustavo who doesn't hear well."

"My mistake. I apologize, sir."

Fisher made his way to where I stood. "I believe you asked the whereabouts of my daughter? May I ask why?"

"I met her a long time ago. I was hoping I could talk to her."

Fisher shuffled forward then leaned on his cane. "Bianca isn't here, nor will she be. Did you try her at her office?"

I was confused about the name Bianca, we were both staring at the woman in the portrait I knew as Laura.

"Laura, is that her middle name?" I asked without yelling.

Fisher continued to look at the portrait, "Yes, it is a nice frame."

I immediately suspected Gustavo's hearing was fine.

I waited till Fisher faced me, then repeated the question. "Good frames are hard to find, but I was just curious, is Bianca's middle name Laura?"

"Are you interested in frames, or Bianca, Mr. Thomas?"

"Sorry, Mr. Fisher, sometimes I lose my concentration. Bianca, I was just wondering if her middle name was Laura?"

"No, Laura was my other daughter."

"Was?"

"Laura has been dead for sixteen years, Mr. Thomas. The exact amount of time I've been dead."

Laura, my Faith, was dead. I had been prepared, or at least had come to terms with the fact that Faith might be married. But dead? I was mistaken. The girl in the portrait couldn't be Faith. Once again I looked at the woman, but there was no mistake. The portrait had been made when Laura was in her late teens or early twenties.

"Mr. Fisher, that can't be, it doesn't make sense."

"Oh, of course I didn't actually die, but I quit living that day, Mr.--err-- Thomas, was it?" The old man followed my gaze, and our eyes locked onto the image of the beautiful young woman.

"Yes sir, Thomas, Cape Thomas."

"Anyway, I should have died. Instead, I stopped working, sold my business, and quit living. Laura was everything to me, she was a dear girl, so loving and kind. The only time I leave this house now is when Gustavo takes me to Forest Lawn to visit her."

I could see the pain in the old man's face, and I was sure my face mirrored his. I wanted to say something to make him feel better. I wanted someone to say something that would make me feel better. But no words could cure our loss.

"You said Forest Lawn, is that where she's buried?" I asked.

Fisher stiffened, then snapped out his reply, "Mr. Thomas, I don't care to think of her in that way….Not today. You see, today would have been her birthday. I have only thoughts of her being alive on this day. Gustavo will show you out, good day."

"Mr. Fis--"

"Good day, Mr. Thomas, please leave."

Gustavo appeared from the shadows of an adjoining room. "This way, Mr. Thomas." I looked back at Mr. Fisher before I turned away, and tears were running down his face.

Gustavo led me down the steps to my car to make sure I didn't further disturb Mr. Fisher.

I deserved an answer, someone who would talk to me. "Gustavo, do you know Bianca's number, or last name if she's married?"

"I'm sorry, I do not. It would be best if you left now, Mr. Thomas."

I opened the door of my car to get in, but I couldn't leave without asking the most important question. "Gustavo, where is Laura's child?"

"Child? Miss Laura did not have a child, good day."

Laura Fisher was definitely the girl on my deck but she hadn't had a child. My conversation with April ran through my mind. The blanket, the reason I couldn't see the baby, was it a symbol of an abortion? Why did a dead woman visit me to let me know she had had an abortion? To punish me for not finding her….For honoring her request to forget her? To not trace her?

I drove around Greenville aimlessly for an hour or so. The search was over, but if that was true, I had one thing left to do.

I stopped for a traffic light and noticed a Greenville police car beside me in the turn lane. I tooted my horn, rolled my window down, and did something no woman has ever witnessed, "Excuse me, officer, but could you give me directions to Forest Lawn Cemetery?"

Forest Lawn was an old cemetery located in the middle of town. Large magnolias covered the grounds and tombstones clustered around the trees like marble saplings. The lane through the cemetery was a large circle. Walkways lined with mondo grass spread from the circle in radial symmetry. The small office at the gate was made from cinder blocks covered with stucco. Opaque glass blocks lined the door on either side, and through the blocks I could see the silhouette of a figure. I knocked on the door, and heard from within the sound of a slamming desk drawer and the screech of a chair sliding across the floor. The guy behind the desk was younger than I expected. "I'm trying to find the grave of someone, are you the person I should see?" I asked.

"I guess…. Who you looking?"

I eased in the doorway and closed the door behind me. The office smelled of Lysol and marijuana. "I'm trying to find Laura Fisher."

The young guy pulled out a worn and weathered account book. Its obvious exposure to the elements made it almost as thick as War and Peace. "We got a lot of Fishers. What year did she die?"

"I don't know--No, wait. Sixteen years ago." At least that's what I thought Fisher had said. I waited for him to subtract the date on an old envelope he had on his desk.

"They would be about 1976, let's see--."

I could see why he was working in the graveyard. I corrected him before he could finish.

"1986."

"Huh?"

"1986, the year she died would have been 1986," I said.

"Oh yeah, I musta carried a two."

I nodded agreement.

"Well, she won't be hard to find," he said as he stepped to the door. "You see that mausoleum over there by the big magnolia tree?"

"Yes."

I waited for him to say something else. Then decided that wasn't going to happen, so I left without saying thanks.

Laura's final resting-place was a Greco-Roman style mausoleum. Moss had grown over the north side of the marble building. The wrought iron gate at the entrance was locked. I peered inside the darkened cubicle. Ten sepulchers, four on each side and two at the rear framed an obelisk engraved with a cross that stood in the center of the building. The top left drawer was engraved with the name Laura Fisher, but the two rear panels were engraved with names I couldn't read. I took out my lighter and held it as far as my arm could reach through the door. Calis Fisher rested in the lower of the two sepulchers in the rear. The top sepulcher, the one above Calis Fisher, was engraved with Nathan Hale Fisher's name.

I figured Calis Fisher to have been Laura's mother. The dates on her crypt bore out my assumption: Born 1929 Died 1956. I looked at Laura's dates: Born 1956 Died 1986. No month and day. I couldn't be sure, but Calis could have died during childbirth. I was pretty sure of one thing, Laura Fisher never knew her mother.

"Hi."

Startled, I jumped and turned to face the speaker. It was the other woman in the portrait over Fisher's mantel.

"Sorry, I get a little jumpy in graveyards," I said.

The woman pulled her long dark hair from her face with her free hand, "You gave me a little start there, too. I'm Bianca Jenkins."

She shifted what looked to be a supermarket bouquet of flowers to her left hand, and we shook.

"I'm Cape Thomas."

Bianca gave me the once-over, and must have decided she had never seen me. "Are you one of Laura's old friends?"

It was a simple question, but not an easy one. I was almost certain I had slept with her sister, but I wasn't an old friend. "Yes," I decided. "I'm an old friend of Laura's."

Bianca gave me a quizzical look, " I thought I knew all of Laura's friends, but I don't remember you."

"We met a long time ago."

" Mr. Thomas, you must have been fairly close--I mean to visit on her birthday. You did know today would have been her birthday?"

Bianca was getting nervous, I could sense it. I needed to tell her something. "Well, actually I didn't until I talked with your father a little earlier."

"You saw my father?"

"Yes, just a little while ago."

"So you know my father then? How is he?"

Her question was not one I thought a daughter would have asked.

"Bianca, I know this looks and sounds a little strange. But, I don't really know your father. I'm not really sure I knew your sister. I thought I did, but now I'm not so sure."

She stepped back. "If you were trying to explain why you are here, you might want to try again. I'll be honest, I'm getting a little nervous," she said glancing at the caretaker's office.

I knew what I was about to tell her would make even less sense, but she deserved an explanation. I told her about the dream of the woman and the baby. "So you thought my sister was the person in the dream?"

I just wanted to get this over with--coming by the graveyard was a mistake.

"Bianca, I don't even dream much. But this one seemed so real. I arrived at my conclusion about your sister by the process of elimination."

She seemed more curious than nervous. "How did you do that? If you don't mind explaining, I would love to hear about it."

I explained the time line, the broken engagement, and why I didn't know her sister by her name.

"But my sister did break off an engagement during that time."

What was the point in my being here? Faith….Laura was dead and she had had an abortion. Or the woman in my vision was someone else, it was the only other logical explanation, I had no right to intrude any further. "Yes, but she didn't wear a Coptic Cross or have a baby, did she?"

Bianca paused, then shocked the hell out of me.

"Yes."

"She did? But Gustavo, your father's friend, said she didn't have a child, why would he lie?"

Bianca glanced at her watch. "You didn't mention the child to my father, did you?

"No, but I upset him, I'm sorry to say."

"But you didn't mention the child, you're sure about that?

"Yes, I mean no. No, I didn't mention the child. Why would that make a difference? I don't understand."

Bianca's reaction was odd, she smiled.

"I know you're confused. I can explain, but it would take a little while, do you have time to get a cup of coffee?" she asked.

Nothing was making sense. Fisher had almost tossed me out of the house, now his daughter wanted to spend time with me. Maybe a little explaining wasn't such a bad idea.

"Where do you have in mind?"

"Are you familiar with the Hilton? It's quiet there," she said.

"Yeah, I passed it on the way out here, but maybe I should follow you, I'm not sure I could find it again."

She looked at the mausoleum, "I can give you directions, but I need a little time alone with my sister. Would you mind?"

I thought about writing the directions down then decided against it. After two wrong turns I finally made it to the Hilton. While I waited for Bianca, I had a cup of coffee. The restaurant was quiet, and I used the moment to sort things out. Why had Gustavo lied? That was fairly simple, two scenarios came to mind. Gustavo hadn't been around when Laura was alive. But if that were so, he would have said he didn't know her. Hired help? Gustavo was hired help, not a relative as I had suspected earlier. If Laura's pregnancy had been a secret they certainly wouldn't have told the hired help. Then there was Bianca's reaction when she realized my dream had been so accurate. She hadn't been surprised at all. That was one question I would definitely ask.

I had two more cups of coffee, and began to think Bianca wasn't going to show. Before that thought sank in, she drove up. I watched her as she got out of the car, a Lexus. She wasn't tall, maybe 5'4" but well proportioned. I couldn't see any resemblance to Laura though. Laura, if my dream was correct and I had every reason now to think it was, had blue eyes. Bianca's eyes were brown, almost black. Her skin wasn't tanned from the sun. She had the complexion of someone from the Mediterranean, or perhaps South America, but she was definitely not Anglo-Saxon. Her lips were fuller than Laura's and her nose more aquiline. I stood as she approached the table and seated her. Bianca was appreciative of the gesture, but unlike Ally, she hadn't expected it as her due.

"Sorry, this is the only day of the year I visit my sister's grave."

"Why is that, do you live far away?"

Bianca thought before she answered. "No, as a matter of fact, I have an office here in town. This is the one day I know my father won't be there."

It seemed obvious, but I wanted to know for sure. "I take it you and your father don't get along very well?" She sighed, and I knew the reason why. I responded the same way when I was asked my least favorite question. Why didn't you marry? It wasn't the question, it was the complexity associated with answering.

"I love my father." Bianca fumbled with the condiment rack on the table, "Mr. Thomas--."

"Call me Cape, please?"

She smiled, then spoke, "Very well, Cape. As I was saying, I love my father. I know he loves me, too. But I remind him of my mother."

"Calis?" I asked.

"How did you know about Calis?"

"She was in the mausoleum, next to where your father will be entombed, father--mother, right?"

"No, that was Laura's mother. My mother was Maria Paulo. She was my father's housekeeper before he married her."

"Is she dead too?" I asked.

"No, I suppose she's in Brazil, I haven't seen her since I was a child. She hurt my father, let's say their parting wasn't amicable. You see, Cape, there are two sides of the Fisher family. Laura, who was perfect, and adored by my father. Then Laura's mother, Calis the saint, whom my father also adored. Then there is me, and my mother."

"Okay, they were saints, and you and your mother were…?"

"I don't mean perfect and saint in the traditional sense. Laura and Calis, from all accounts, did everything to please my father. Laura became a doctor to please him, Calis was like his handmaiden. I, on the other hand, led my own life. My father always worried that I would grow up to be like my 'tramp mother', as he put it. Anyway, we have our differences."

I thought about Ally, "I guess that must be a thing with most Southern women?"

She looked puzzled. "I'm sorry?"

"Pleasing their fathers, I guess that must be an endemic trait of Southern women?"

"Most, I believe you said." Bianca smiled a wonderful naughty smile.

The family history was nice but I really wanted to know about Laura. "So how did Laura die? She was so young, car wreck?"

"No, Laura died of kidney failure."

"You'd think a doctor could have done a transplant or something?"

"Transplants weren't the norm when Laura died, Cape."

I should have known that, "Does Laura's child live with your father?"

"No, my father has never known Laura had a child. She gave the baby up for adoption."

That definitely didn't make any sense, "How is it that your father didn't know about the child?"

Bianca paused, "That's why I'm here, you can't tell him. I promised Laura he wouldn't know."

"Okay, just curious. How did you and Laura keep him from finding out?"

"Laura hid her pregnancy well. She had the baby while she was in med school in Florida."

It still didn't make sense to me, "But why not tell her father?"

"I told you earlier. Laura didn't want to disappoint him. My mother and father were married for a very short time. She was young and full of life. My father was older, more settled, and much too involved in his business. She made a mistake, and Laura and I paid for it though out our childhood."

Even I could figure this one out, "Let me guess, she had an affair?"

Bianca nodded, "Good guess. But there's more. She became pregnant by another man. That made my father bitter. All he talked about when we were young was how despicable that was. So you see, Laura had a choice; the baby or her father."

I thought of another option, "Abortion?"

"You didn't know Laura well, did you?"

Why lie? "No."

"Laura gave the baby away, but she was still concerned about her welfare. It was her final wish that her child never be confronted with her father's anger. I guess she knew he would never forgive the child, either."

I figured it was a slip of the tongue. But after years of confirming read backs, I felt obligated to correct her, " You meant our father's anger?"

"Of course, our father…."

"So the baby was a girl?"

"Yes."

"Bianca, who was the father?"

"I never asked, but I would imagine Jim Rogers."

I hadn't told Bianca about Laura and my little tryst yet. "Jim Rogers, that would have been her fiancé?"

"Yes. "

"When I told you about my dream you weren't surprised, why?" I asked.

"I guess what you described isn't so unusual for me to hear."

I was game, "And that would be because?"

"Because,--I'm a psychiatrist."

"So you became a doctor in spite of your independence? That didn't make your father happy?"

"I became a psychiatrist for myself, I could care less what he wanted me to do."

Another doctor, and another chance at being diagnosed. Not that it mattered much, but it couldn't help things with the FAA. "I won't tell your father about the baby. But you can't tell anyone I told you about this dream thing."

She smiled her sassy smile again, "That's easy, I'll send you a bill."

"What?"

"If I bill you that makes you my patient, and everything will be confidential then."

I didn't smile. "So what's the going rate for a psychiatrist now, by the way?"

" $150.00 per hour, but you can stand it, you're wearing a Rolex." She fingered my watch.

"I'm paying for it on time, seriously I don't need for this to get out." Linda knew I was a pilot who saw things, but in spite of our differences she wouldn't talk.

"I was just kidding. It's only a dream. What harm could be in someone knowing that?"

I had to talk to someone but I hoped she was only kidding about sending me a bill.

"I didn't have a dream. I saw Laura on my deck--in a vision, and another thing, I don't think Jim Rogers is the father."

Bianca leaned over the table exposing most of her full bosom. I tried to avert my eyes, but I couldn't help but admire her. "What did you call this experience involving my sister?"

"I don't know the psychological term for it. I call it a vision, maybe you guys call it an insight."

"Insight?....Doesn't ring a bell," Bianca replied.

"You still don't think it's strange that I knew so much about Laura?"

Bianca gave me a soothing look, "Cape, all you knew about Laura was what a lot of people who knew Laura could have known. The break-up was common knowledge in Greenville. The Coptic Cross, she always wore that. I gave it to her when she graduated from high school. The baby, you said yourself she was holding a blanket. You thought it was a baby, you could have just as easily guessed it was a puppy."

I wasn't buying it. Even if it did sound feasible. "Yeah well, that's all fine and good, but I had to hunt Laura down. I couldn't even remember her name."

Bianca looked at me with that condescending look doctors have. "Cape, subconsciously you knew who Laura was. It was just in your conscious you didn't know her."

I still didn't think I remembered that many details about Laura consciously or subconsciously. " So, why did you want to meet for coffee then?"

"Simple, you made a lucky guess about the baby. I came here to make sure you don't tell my father about it. Besides, you're kind of cute."

A come on. An attractive woman was coming on to me, and I could think of nothing but Laura.

"But the thing, the dream, it seemed so real."

"Cape, take it from your doctor, it was just a dream. All the pieces of your puzzle fit into a logical explanation. It's quite universal. But if you really need to talk about it, stop by anytime, I'll give you a cut rate." She smiled, gave me her business card, and left.

CHAPTER TEN

A Meeting, but not of the Minds.

On the ride back from Greenville, my emotions swung back and forth like a pendulum on a Salvador Dali clock. The high side was that I wasn't crazy. After all, a psychiatrist had just certified me sane. I thought of Bianca's diagnosis. "All the pieces of your puzzle fit into a logical explanation." That much was true, but I wasn't satisfied with the explanation.

The low side was that Laura was dead and a child was in the world that might be mine. If she was adopted I was certain she had found a good family. But why not make sure? I decided to pay Bianca a visit.

The new message light was blinking on my office recorder.

"Mr. Thomas, I need to talk to you. This is William Johnston of Johnston Ballard & Hearst in Charlotte, please return my call." Either William Johnston was hungry or I was wrong about his reason for calling. He could represent the FAA. Maybe they wanted to make another deal? I picked up the phone and dialed William Johnston's home number.

"Hello, this is William Johnston."

"Mr. Johnston, this is Cape Thomas returning your call."

He paused, "Thomas? Oh yes, Mr. Thomas, thank you for calling. I'm calling on behalf of a client of mine, W. Cronos Kress, perhaps you've heard of him?"

I had, but I was wondering how he had heard of me. Why would Ally be so secretive about our meeting, and then tell Walter that we had met?

"I've heard of him, Mr. Johnston, but never had the pleasure of meeting him."

Johnston cleared his throat. "Many people are in the same boat. Mr. Kress is a very busy man. As am I: therefore, I'll get right to the purpose of my call. What is your schedule for tomorrow?"

"I'm flexible, what'd you have in mind?"

Johnston cleared his throat again, it was annoying. I couldn't imagine he did that during every conversation. He was an attorney, a professional mouthpiece, so I suspected his vocal glitch showed he was nervous. Why would a lawyer for W. Cronos Kress be nervous to talk with me? Johnston continued, "I prefer to talk to you in person. It just so happens I have to be in Goldsboro tomorrow on business. I was wondering if you might be able to meet me there. It is close to you, isn't it?"

"Very."

"Do you have a preferred meeting place, Mr. Thomas?"

I wasn't sure what this was about, but I was fairly sure I wasn't going to like it. "I'm an old airport bum, but I suspect you know that for some reason, Mr. Johnston. How about we meet at the Goldsboro airport?"

"Ex-AeroMax Captain I believe, Mr. Thomas. Shall we say 9:00 a.m.?"

Charlotte was a four-hour drive from Goldsboro. Johnston would have to leave by 5:00 a.m. I wondered about that. "That puts you leaving pretty early in the morning, I'm open later if that's better for you, Mr. Johnston?"

"Nine is perfect. That was very kind of you, by the way, but it's just a twenty-five-minute trip. I'll be on a Citation 10. See you at nine. Good night, Mr. Thomas."

I knew what a Citation 10 was--an exec jet. The only plane faster in civilian aviation was the Concorde. I had never shopped around for one. They were certainly out of my league at $18,000,000 per copy. I knew some attorneys who owned planes, but none who owned jets. The pay scale for attorneys in Charlotte must definitely be on the high end. This one trip would cost in the neighborhood of $10,000.

I arrived early at the airport. Sarge Bishop, the airport manager, and as he all ways liked to brag, "The first one who'd ever put my butt in the sky." was at his usual place behind his desk. Sarge, had been a P51 crew chief during World War II. Most people thought of him as a crusty old curmudgeon. Some, like my grandfather, thought he was an evil old S.O.B. Me? I knew he was all buzz and no sting, a benevolent grouch, who had given me more hours of flight time than I could have ever bought.

Weeks had slipped into months since I'd seen him, but he hadn't changed nor had I expected him to. The trademarks of his profession adorned his frame like the chest full of medal he had earned in the war. Oil-stained leather bomber jacket and aviator glasses made up the same uniform he had worn when I first met him. An ever-present cigar was clamped in his stained yellow teeth. "Well damn, Cape Thomas, someone told me you died. Maybe you are dead, you look like a corpse."

Yep, same old Sarge. As welcoming as a fireplace on a cold winter's day, but pesky.

"I may look like a corpse, but at least I don't smell like one."

Sarge grinned. "You go straight to hell, Cape Thomas, I washed day before yesterday. How are you sport?"

I'd never been one to talk about my problems, but it was a little different with Sarge.

"Things could be better."

Sarge came from behind his desk. "I heard about your problems with the FAA, don't let it get you down, sport. You wouldn't know anybody looking for a job, would you?"

I knew what he was up to, and I appreciated it. "Just so happens I do, Sarge."

"It doesn't pay much, but the work is steady. I got a Lance. I need someone to fly checks and some freight. You still have your commercial ticket, right?"

Flying checks is an entry-level job, or 'time builder' as it's referred to in aviation vernacular. To me, at this point and time, it meant salvation.

"I guess I do. I know I lost my Part 135 certificate. I suppose I'll find out what else I lost at my hearing," I said.

Sarge pushed the phone on his desk toward me. "Give the FSDO office a call, and if you still have your commercial, the job's yours."

I didn't ask about the money. Sarge would pay more than the job was worth, still it wouldn't be much. I checked with the Fed's, and found my commercial was still intact, but I couldn't fly any passengers for hire. "I've still got it, Sarge."

Sarge gave me the old bear look he saved for new-hires. "You bust up my plane, and you pay for it."

"How would you know? I've never seen a plane you owned that didn't look busted up."

Sarge feigned mock hurt. "Hey, it needs a little paint, some radios and maybe a new seat, but other than that it's like brand new."

"Let's see if I can translate that. The plane has corrosion, I need to bring my hand-held radio, and I might need to find a seat for a Lance. Sound about right, Sarge?"

"Ahh, cry baby pilots."

"Thanks, Sarge, I appreciate it."

"Don't think I'm doing this out of the goodness of my heart. I can't find a damn soul that can fly."

Not a likely scenario. Sarge would say anything to keep the offer from sounding like a favor. There were at least twenty young Turks around the airport that would kill to have a job flying. "When do I start?"

"Today, you lazy bastard. Providing you can still find your way to Richmond."

Before I could explain about my meeting, the FBO Unicom radio crackled to life.

"Goldsboro traffic Citation Zero One Whiskey Charlie Kilo final approach ILS Two-Three." The transmission described the approach and tail number of the Citation 10. The tail number 0-1-W-C-K stood for Walter Cronos Kress. Johnston wasn't coming in his plane.

"Sarge, I have to meet with this guy. I don't think I'll be long, then I'll be ready to go."

Sarge rolled his eyes and went back to his desk.

I watched the big jet as it taxied to the ramp. Sarge stared out at the plane. "Damn, that's a pretty S.O.B.…High Rollers, huh?"

I nodded in agreement with Sarge's assessment. "Yeah, Big-Time High Rollers."

William Johnston was a short, stout man in his fifties. Who looked more like a Weeble-Wooble than a high-powered attorney, not exactly what I expected. His suit was expensive, but ill fitting. His tie was too short, and his trousers were too long.

Johnston ambled down the airstairs of the jet and waddled into the terminal. I was his first stop. "Mr. Thomas, I'm William Johnston."

Johnston knew what I looked like. No inquiries were necessary, I wondered about that. The reason would come shortly, I was sure of that. Johnston glanced at Sarge and nodded recognition. "Is there a more private place we can talk?"

Sarge pointed to the hallway. "Use my other office, Cape. Do you need any fuel in that bird, Mr. Johnston?"

Johnston shook his head no, and moved in the direction Sarge had pointed. It was time to test the water before Johnston and I talked, and besides I wanted to help Sarge. "You know, Mr. Johnston, it's considered good manners to buy fuel when you park at an FBO."

Johnston glared at me, then smiled. "My mistake, fill it up. Is that better, Mr. Thomas?"

I didn't know what the meeting would be about. But I did know one thing, I had some leverage.

Johnston tossed his heavy briefcase onto the table. "Mr. Thomas, I know you're a busy man. So I'll get right to the point if you don't mind?"

I thought I detected some sarcasm in his voice, I assumed he knew I wasn't a busy man. "That'll be fine, Mr. Johnston, and I do have some work to do today."

"Oh really?"

I probably shouldn't have told him, but I was a busy man, I had a job.

"That's right, I have a flight as soon as we finish."

Johnston ignored my statement and opened his briefcase. Then slapped a large manila folder down on the table. Inside the folder were six 8x10 glossy photographs. He pushed the pictures in front of me. They were pictures of Ally and me in Raleigh.

The first picture was of us walking down the street. It appeared as if I had my arm around Ally. I knew it was when I draped my coat over her. The other pictures had been taken in GraniteShields. Pictures of Ally and me talking, our heads close together in what appeared to be intimate conversation. The last picture was of the kiss Ally had given me for being a good man. Pictures don't lie, as the old adage goes, but they don't always tell the truth, either. Johnston waited as I smoked the pictures over.

When I finished he spoke. "Do you wish to explain these, Mr. Thomas?"

I did, but I had seen pictures such as these before. My job at AeroMax was put in jeopardy over 8x10 pictures just like these. It was only when I tried to explain them that I lost my job. "I don't know what there is to explain," I said.

Johnston smirked. "I almost agree with you, Mr. Thomas. On the face of it, the pictures appear to be two lovers enjoying their time together. That's fine and good. All the world loves a lover, right?"

I knew the question was a statement, so I let him finish. "But when one of those lovers is married, it's then called adultery. Then one, specifically my client W. Cronos Kress, is entitled to an explanation. You do know the woman in the photograph is Allison Moore Kress, the wife of my client, don't you, Mr. Thomas? Now, do you wish to explain these?"

I didn't wish to say anything. I especially didn't wish to say anything wrong. As soon as I opened my mouth both my wishes were crushed. "I met Ally one time, a brief encounter, that's it."

Johnston was on my statement, like a hobo on a ham sandwich. "Ally? I've known, Allison Kress for almost ten years. But I've never called her Ally. How is it that someone whom has met Mrs. Kress only briefly knows her as Ally?"

I didn't care for Johnston, yet I was giving him all the ammunition he needed to sink Ally. I tried to redeem myself. "Ally is the name she used when

I met her, had she told me her name was Fat Ass Johnston, I would have known her as that."

Johnston's face turned red, and he tugged at the tie that seemed to be choking him. That's when I decided the tie was the only article of his clothing I liked.

"Mr. Thomas, you are viewing me as an adversary, but in fact I may be your only salvation concerning the FAA. If I were you, Mr. Thomas, I would be very careful of what I said."

"That's a private matter between me an the FAA, butt out."

Johnston spoke in a soothing tone. "On the contrary, Mr. Thomas, it's a matter of public record, but that's not important. What is important is that I can make your problems with the FAA go away."

"How?"

Johnston placed the photographs back in the folder before he spoke. "You have an attorney, Tom Butterfield. He's a good person, and probably a good attorney. Unfortunately, he has no clout. I'm sure you've heard the adage, 'It's not what you know, but who'?"

Johnston waited for me to answer, instead I turned to look at the big jet on the ramp.

"Anyway, we have a law firm in Washington, D.C. which specializes in dealing with various branches of the government. This firm, Mr. Thomas, stands ready to provide Mr. Butterfield with all the resources he will need to solve your problems with the FAA."

I turned back toward Johnson. "So, you mean to tell me that this firm can get my 135 certificate back?" I snapped my fingers for emphasis. "Just like that?"

Johnston moved toward my chair. " No, Mr. Thomas, not your Part 135 certificate, this firm can get you back in the cockpit of a 747."

"That's bullshit!"

"Mr. Thomas, are you aware that W.Cronos Kress is the single largest stockholder of AeroMax Airlines?"

"No, and what does AeroMax Airlines have to do with the FAA?"

Johnson looked through me, as if I were a sieve incapable of holding the polity he commanded. "Mr. Kress also contributes heavily to many politicians across the country. There are many favors owed by these politicians to Mr. Kress. The matter you have before the FAA is an insurmountable mountain to you and Tom Butterfield. I can assure you that your problem is but a molehill to Mr. Kress. Do you follow me, Mr. Thomas?"

I had accepted that I might never fly for an airline again, yet this man held a promise.

"Mr. Johnston, I'm sure that if everything you say is true--there's a hell of a price to pay."

"The price for you is very small, Mr. Thomas, as a matter of fact, the payment doesn't involve money. Mr. Kress wants you to do him a favor in return for his favor. That's fair, isn't it?" Johnston concluded with a fake smile.

On the surface it did sound fair. "OK, what would this favor entail?"

"All we want you to do, Mr. Thomas, is say you have been having an affair with Allison Kress."

I didn't know exactly what the favor would be, but this was more devious that I had imagined. "That would be a lie, Mr. Johnston. You already know that, hell you know everything about me. What if I say no? Then you use the photographs anyway to try and prove I having an affair with Ally, right?"

"Precisely."

"I don't know much about the law, Mr. Johnston, but I'd think even with the photographs you'd have a pretty weak case. They were all taken in very public places. Seems to me, if someone wanted to prove an affair they would have to have more incriminating evidence."

Johnston turned red again. "You know, Mr. Thomas, that's a good point. Our case may be weak, but we still have a case. Conversely, Mr. Thomas, without us, you have no case at all against the FAA. You help us with our case, and we help you with yours."

"You need more evidence, or should I say better pictures?" I asked.

"No, Mr. Thomas, not you, and not us, we need better evidence. Then we win, and you fly away." Johnson used his hand as an imaginary airplane shooting off into the sky.

"And while 'we' are winning and flying away--what happens to Ally?"

I was standing on a greased razor, and Johnston knew it. The question wasn't whether I would fall, but when and to which side. If I went against Johnston I would lose my butt, against Ally and it was my manhood.

Johnston put the file back in the briefcase and snapped it shut. "Mr. Thomas, Allison Kress is not who she seems. Let's just say her past is colored. Do you really want to lose everything for a chance to help someone who cares absolutely nothing about you?"

I didn't care for the remark about Ally's colored past. He had no way of knowing I knew the truth about Ally, but he did know I was mad.

"Mr. Thomas, you're upset, and it's not good to make a decision in anger. Before you make a choice, give Tom Butterfield a call. Cool off, think with your head, and not with some antiquated notions of chivalry. You did that once. She kept her husband, and you lost your job. Was it really worth it? Good day, Mr. Thomas, I'll be in touch."

I didn't like Johnston and I didn't like W. Cronos Kress, but I was impressed with the knowledge they had. The FAA violation? A matter of public record, the incident with Grace and Asshole, definitely off the record, yet they knew. Ally? I could give her a call to see what she knew. The thought perished as paranoia set in. Such a shame, too, and just after I had been certified sane. Despite my paranoia Ally had nothing to do with this, she was the victim of this scheme. Her home phone had to be tapped. But I hadn't mentioned any of the things Johnston knew, not over the phone. I thought of the remarks I'd made about Grace and Asshole. I'd never told Ally the complete story, even in GraniteShields.

The pictures? The lone diner who was reading the News and Observer had to be the one taking the pictures, but he wasn't recording the conversation. Johnston couldn't have gotten his information over the Internet, Ally had already tried that. No, Johnston had a direct connection to my past, and it had to be the Asshole. My employment record? Asshole was in management, and he had first-hand knowledge about Grace and the AeroMax incident. History, all of it was history if not a matter of public record. I needed to deal with the future.

I had choices: help myself, or help a woman I hardly knew. I thought of Ally's parting words. "I trust you, by the way." My grandfather had been an avid reader. Rather than give advice he quoted great minds to help me come to the right decisions. One quote from Despreaux came to mind. "Honor is like an island, rugged and without a beach; once we have left it, we can never return."

Stand on solid financial ground or languish in a sea of turmoil? The choice should have been easy, but it wasn't. I needed time, flying time, and then the answer would come.

I picked up the Lance at the Mt. Olive airport. The check haul to Richmond and back was a milk run--the plane was a dog. I tied the plane down for the night, and headed to Oliver's Railroad Grill for a drink. The restaurant was crowded, the bar was empty. I eyed the Scotch, forgot about it, and drank a cup of coffee before heading home.

I needed some advice, but not particularly legal advice. Tom Butterfield was the only advisor I had, so I called him at home. "Hello, Tom.... Cape Thomas."

Tom sounded excited. "You lying devil. I thought you didn't know any people in high places?"

"What are you talking about?"

Tom was ecstatic, not excited. "What am I talking about? Cape, I have a certified check here from Johnston Ballard & Hearst's Washington office in the amount of $10,000. They want to join us in our case against the FAA. Me working with Johnston Ballard & Hearst, can you imagine that?"

For some reason I couldn't. "So that's a big deal, huh?"

"Big deal? Cape, this firm doesn't do anything without at least a $100,000 retainer. This is the big league. How did you pull this off? That's not important. Thanks for keeping me on case. I don't know why you still need me, especially if you have the resources to hire Johnston Ballard & Hearst….But I appreciate the chance."

I knew there was more to the offer. "Tom, what strings came with the deal?"

"Strings? The only instructions that came with the check was for me not to deposit the check until I was told to do so by Mr. Cape Thomas. I assumed that's why you were calling. That is why you are calling, isn't it?"

I didn't want a grown attorney to cry, but my mind wasn't made up, not yet. "Tom, don't deposit the check."

"Cape, they aren't trying just to get your Part 135 back. They intend to get you back on with AeroMax, with back pay for wrongful dismissal. That's $600,000, hell, maybe more, if we can get you some punitive damages. What's the problem?"

"It's a little matter of honor, Tom. I have to think about this."

"This is Johnston Ballard & Hearst, this is your life back. This firm practices in the Supreme Court, like most attorneys practice in district court. What price do you put on honor? Let me remind you, honor is an intangible quality, this is real," Tom said.

"I know it's a once-in-a-lifetime thing, but I want to smell the milk before I drink it. Find out how much time I have."

"Cape, these are important people. I don't think they'll take kindly to your indecision. What's this honor related to, a criminal activity?"

"No, it's about a lady's honor, and it's about my honor."

"As your attorney, I'm advising you to work with these people. Without this firm you will be taking orders at the drive-thru…. I can promise you that "

"Tom, just find out how much time I have, thanks."

"I can't believe this--you--you're insane."

"Not really, I'm sane, I just had my sanity validated by a beautiful sexy doctor. Stupid, that would be the word you want."

"Cape, if this beautiful doctor finds out about this, she'd change her diagnosis--."

"Good night, counselor."

CHAPTER ELEVEN

Good Doctor--Bad Sister.

My visit to the Goldsboro airport the next day wasn't exactly social or business. I'd have called it good manners, but my old mentor would have called it brown nosing. Sarge was in his usual place with a fresh cigar in his mouth. I watched as he patted his pockets and shuffled papers around on this desk.

"Give me a light, Cape, I can't find my damn matches."

I reached in my pocket for my lighter only to realize it was gone. "I must have left my lighter at home, you want to use the one in my truck?"

Sarge grumbled something about quitting smoking and threw the cigar in the trash.

"I'd like to know who moves everything around on my desk. I can't keep a damn thing. Pilots are the worse thieves in the world."

I spotted a box of three torch matches in the out box on Sarge's desk and gave them to him. He retrieved the cigar from the trashcan and lit it.

"Well?"

"Well what?" Sarge snorted.

"I'm waiting for an apology, Sarge."

"What the hell have I got to apologize to you for?"

"That little remark about pilots."

Sarge puffed on the cigar, until small rings of smoke circled his head. "I stand by that remark."

"I'm still waiting, Sarge."

"Well, you better stand over there by the heater then."

"Why's that, Sarge?"

"Cause hell's going to freeze over before that happens. You know pilots steal. Tools, pens, matches, coffee cups, and anything else they can stuff into those little fancy flight bags. What do you want, anyway? "

I put the matches in my pocket when he turned his head to look at the runway. "I just wanted to thank you again for the job, that was nice of you."

Sarge turned back around to face me. "I told you I couldn't find anybody else. A damn hotshot jet jockey was my last choice."

"I'll take that as a 'you're welcome.' You know, Sarge, if you aren't careful, people may start thinking you're half-way decent."

"Decent? Cape, you wouldn't know decency if you found it on the bottom of your shoe. And if you did, you'd try to scrape it off."

"Sarge--ah never mind….When's my next flight?"

"In the morning at 4:00 a.m. and don't expect a wake-up call."

The cigar was out, Sarge hunted for the matches again. "Cape, did you get a good look at those matches I just had?"

"What are you talking about?"

"I didn't notice it, but they must of had legs on 'em….Sons of bitches have walked off."

I laughed as he did the paper shuffle boogie on his desk again. " Yeah, I did notice that. I think the matches hooked up with a pen and a coffee cup, then hauled butt."

"Get the hell outta here, you smartass jet jockey."

I left Sarge grumbling about smoking and headed back home to get my lighter. I had quit smoking years ago. The lighter was a gift from the 737 crew I piloted before I moved up to 747. It was an old Zippo engraved with a picture of a Boeing 737. It wasn't worth a lot, but it was important to me.

I searched the house for the lighter with no luck, then remembered the mausoleum in Greenville. I must have dropped it when Bianca came up behind me. I had nothing else to do, so I headed to Greenville. I was fairly certain my lighter wouldn't be there, I suspected it was being used by the gatekeeper to light joints.

This time I didn't stop at the office at Forest Lawn. I parked as close as I could to the mausoleum. As I neared the structure I thought of Laura, and regretted that I hadn't gotten to know her better. The drawer that covered her sepulcher was an aggregate of mixed marble chips that matched the building and concrete. I looked behind me to make sure we were alone, then put my hand on the cool surface. Laura, I've always wondered if you felt about me like I did you. Now, I'll never know. But you came to me for a reason, is it the baby? Give me a sign, come back and give me a sign. Talk to me.

Seeing Laura's grave helped me accept her death....Coming to terms with a world that would never be would take longer.

My lighter was lying inside the wrought iron door. I scooped it up and turned to leave. A magnolia cone crunched under my foot and twisted my ankle. I grabbed onto one of the plant urns in front of the building and held my balance. From my genuflecting stance I could see a bouquet of flowers down next to the urn. I picked them up and noticed a price sticker on the cellophane wrapper, $6.95 ring as produce. I was certain the flowers were the same ones Bianca had carried the day we met.

Several questions came to mind. Why would Bianca buy a cheap bouquet of flowers to bring to a place she visited only once a year? Maybe if she were poor I'd have understood the cost of the flowers but, Bianca was a doctor.

If this were an annual pilgrimage to visit someone she professed great love for, why hadn't she ordered a florist's arrangement? Why hadn't she at least placed the flowers in one of the two plant sconces on either side of the mausoleum door? With that thought I put the flowers into one of the sconces.

The flowers had obviously been bought in haste.
Why had she tossed the bouquet on the ground? Bianca had remained behind to spend time with her sister, and she wasn't in a hurry. I had almost given up on her at our meeting at the Hilton because she was late.

I pulled Bianca's business card from my pocket. My first thought was to call her, then I remembered her invitation to drop by anytime. I made up my mind to do just that. On the way out I stopped by the gatekeeper's office. The gatekeeper was behind the office stacking old wreaths against the wall. "Hi, I was here the other day, you helped me find someone."

The guy recognized me. "Yeah, I know. Do you need to find someone else?" He started for the office. I motioned for him to stop. "No, but I would like to ask you a question. Do you remember seeing a lady in a Lexus, I met her at the mausoleum?"

He grinned, "Yeah, the good-looking one on the white Lexus?"

I nodded. "That would be the one." I wasn't sure, but I was almost certain he had watched Bianca and me the entire time. "You don't remember how long she stayed after I left, do you?"

The gatekeeper was interested in Bianca, but uneasy. "Is she your wife, or girlfriend?" he asked.

"No, I hardly know her." My answer seemed to put him at ease.

"She left right after you did. I thought she was trying to catch up with you, she was in such a big hurry."

I thanked him and started to leave, then I thought of another question. "I know you get a lot of visitors here, but have you ever seen that lady out here before?"

"I don't remember many people, but I'd remember her. I've never seen her before, she was hot." Having said that, the gatekeeper touched his finger to an imaginary red-hot stove.

"One more thing, how long have you worked here?"

"Ten years next month," he said.

Bianca's office was in a strip mall complex on Greenville Boulevard. I recognized the old Lincoln parked in front of Bianca's office, it was the one I had seen at Mr. Fisher's.

I decided to wait before going inside. Maybe she and Mr. Fisher were patching things up? I waited thirty minutes, then decided to join the little family reunion.

"May I help you, sir, do you have an appointment?"

I regretted not calling earlier. "No, but Doctor Jenkins told me to drop by anytime. I just need to speak to her for a moment."

Before the receptionist could respond, Bianca's office door opened. Gustavo was standing in the partially open doorway conversing with Bianca in whispered Portuguese. I wasn't fluent in Portuguese, but I'd spent quite a bit of time in Rio and Sao Paulo, compliments of AeroMax. I heard Bianca say "love you" and a word that sounded like papa, or maybe poppy. The rest of the conversation I wasn't so sure about. Gustavo eyed me, then slipped back into the office and mumbled something in Portuguese too softly for me to understand.

Bianca came to the door. "That will be all, Gustavo, tell Father I love him." Gustavo ignored me and went straight to the parking lot. Bianca followed him to the lobby, I gave my ear to Bianca, but kept my eyes on Gustavo.

"Cape, I see you took me up on my offer, come in."

I watched the Lincoln until it cleared the parking lot.

"I apologize for not calling. I was riding around and found myself at your office, so here I am," I said.

Bianca tapped her watch. "I'm just a few minutes from my lunch hour, have you eaten? Do you have time for lunch?"

I wasn't hungry, but I did want to talk. "Sure, what do you have in mind."

Bianca smiled her naughty smile, then gave me my choices. "MoBurgers, Tex-Mex or a tax deductible three martini lunch, you decide."

A martini wasn't an option, nor was trying to talk over the noise of a fast food joint. Besides with the stupid choices I was making lately there was a good possibility I would get my fill of fast food places soon enough.

"How about the Mess Café?" I asked.

"I'll be back by 3:00, Judy. Have Angela interview my new patients." Bianca snuggled my arm against her breast and guided me outside. "A three-martini guy, good choice, Cape."

I started to explain my decision to quit drinking, then thought of something better.

"The tax-deductible part was the deciding factor."

She laughed. "Fine, since you need the deduction… you buy, I'll drive."

Nothing seemed out of the ordinary in the packed restaurant, but I tried to notice each person in the place. One lady with a camera partially hidden by a newspaper caught my eye. Bianca noticed me checking her out.

"Cape, I'm hurt. I thought you only had eyes for me, do you know her?"

"Sorry. No, I thought for a minute she might work for a guy I know from Charlotte."

"Sure you did."

Bianca ordered a martini, I asked for water.

She spoke first. "You know, Cape, if you don't have the martinis, the deduction won't be as sweet."

I didn't bother with the long explanation. "I have to fly a little later, drinking is against the rules."

"Too bad."

The chit-chat was nice, but I wanted answers.

"So, you and Laura became doctors, I guess that made your father happy?"

Bianca corrected me. "Laura never became a doctor, she had some problems in a couple of courses, besides she died before that happened."

"I apologize, I thought you told me she was a doctor."

Bianca shook her head. "I suppose we bestowed that honor on her posthumously."

"We?"

"My Dad and I."

Bianca stirred her martini as if she were in deep thought. "Cape, is this entire conversation going to be about Laura?"

During any other stage in my life, I would have never mentioned another woman while I was on a date. Especially when my date was as attractive as Bianca. "I'm sorry. I just can't seem to get my mind off of the--the…."

"Dream, Cape, the word you are looking for is dream."

I nodded. "OK, dream. I just feel like there are some answers for what happened. I haven't gotten them, do you mind?"

"I'll answer your questions, if that's how you really want to spend our time together. But first let me ask you a question."

"Shoot," I said.

"Even if Laura were alive and here, do you think she would have admitted to you to having your child? A child she desperately wanted to keep secret?"

It was a good question. Almost good enough to end my curiosity, but not quite. "I don't know. Since you put it that way, I doubt it."

"Cape, you're making this dream more important than it is. Once you knew Laura had died, you made this dream more mysterious. Why? Because you can't get answers. The dead tell no tales, don't you see?"

Maybe I did need to hire Bianca. She was making a lot more sense out of this than I was. "You make things seem so simple, logical, but as soon as I leave you I'll think of some question I should have asked."

"If it will make you feel better, let's talk about it. I generally get paid to listen to people, but I don't generally listen to people and sip on martinis. Pour your heart out, please," Bianca said.

I felt like a jerk. For three years I had been without the company of a woman who interested me, with the possible exception of Ally. Now all I wanted to do was talk about a dead woman. "You and Laura were close, right?"

"My mother left when I was young. Laura was five years older, so she became more of a mother to me than a sister."

"Your Papa said--"

"Papa? That sounds so….So, third world, where did that come from?" Bianca asked.

"I don't know, sorry. Okay, your father said…. He died after Laura's death. That couldn't have been easy for you."

A flash of anger came across Bianca face. "You wanted to talk about Laura, not our family history."

"Sorry."

"Laura and I were close. I am the executrix of her estate. What are you driving at, that I didn't love my sister?"

I was upsetting Bianca. If she was the executrix of Laura's estate, that spoke volumes.

"I'm done, let's enjoy lunch."

"That's it? I was prepared for a two-hour session. But not so fast, Mr. Cape Thomas, my turn."

"OK, but let me do a quick bio then you can ask questions. I don't get paid to listen to people, and I'm not sipping on a martini. Not a bad job by the way."

I explained my life as quickly as I could, but Bianca still had some questions. "You left AeroMax to start your own company, how is that going?" She answered the question before I could. "Obviously well, or you wouldn't need the tax deduction. I'm done, no more questions." The gatekeeper was right, Bianca was hot.

We spent the rest of our lunch laughing and talking, and it was nice. Then Bianca looked at her watch.

"Come on, Cape, let's leave."

"Are you sure?"

I checked my watch, only 1:12 p.m. Bianca didn't have to be back until 3:00 p.m. I didn't want to leave, I wanted to go to the beach or maybe walk in the park. Just hang out and spend more time getting to know Bianca.

Our route back turned into a tour of the town. Greenville's avenues and boulevards were examples of a small Southern town on steroids. Growth and progress gobbled up open spaces like cancer cells in full-blown mutation. The changes on the side streets were more subtle, but even there, a battle raged to hang on to a modicum of Southern Comfort. On one of these side streets Bianca's luxury town house was located.

"Come in, I want to show you my house," Bianca said.

My tour of her home was delayed as she instructed me to wait in the marbled-floored foyer. I watched as she turned down the hallway. Restroom? She needed to use the restroom. For a second I thought she had something else on her mind. Music began to play, jazz, my favorite. I walked over to the window overlooking the pool. The late winter sun had attracted a few sunbathers, but none were hardy enough to brave the sparkling water.

"Cape." I turned around. Bianca was standing in the middle of the room with her blouse partially unbuttoned. I wasn't sure at that exact moment, but I would later find out I didn't need to sing praises to the enigmatic plastic surgeon of Buckhead.

Bianca moved down the hall letting her blouse fall to the floor, then her bra. I followed her garment trail, like a kid on an Easter egg hunt for the chocolate bunny. She stood in front of the bed naked and succulent. I peeled off my shirt to join her.

"No wait, first tell me what a bad boy you are."

I didn't feel like a bad boy, I felt like a lucky boy. "I'm bad, really bad."

"Then what should I do with my bad boy?"

Hey, I'm wasn't into kinky but…. "I'd say about thirty minutes of good, hard aerobic exercise would be just punishment."

"Just what I was thinking my bad boy needed."

We were like two savage animals fighting over a fresh kill. She the lioness and I the lion, her body supple and firm thrust against my hard-lean frame. I pressed deep and thrust in long slow strokes. She parried with frenzied gyrations stoking our passion in a heated fervor until we melted into one. Our glistening bodies pulsated in unison, until we exploded into sexual oblivion.

My chest heaved as I sucked the cool air of the room down my lungs. I ran my hands over her smooth shape and gathered her in my arms.

Bianca pulled away and sat up in the bed. "So how was I?"

"Wonderful." One of those one-word answers I really liked.

Bianca wanted more than a one-word answer. "No! I mean how did I compare to my sister?"

I had thought lovingly of Laura an hour earlier, then gone on to make love to her sister. Now I was blindsided by incestuous guilt. "Fine…. You were fine."

Bianca still wasn't satisfied. " No, compare us."

"It was a long time ago. I barely remember your sister," I said impassively, now lying on my back, forearm heavy across my eyes.

"My breast, Laura's breast were smaller. My skin, my complexion….All real, nothing is phony about me. Laura had to stay in the sun for hours to have what I have naturally. Say it, Cape, tell me how much better I am than my sister."

My relationship with Laura was nonexistent, but I felt as if I were betraying her. I found no joy in this game that Bianca seemed to relish.

"You were fantastic. Come here, let me hold you."

"No, I want to hear it," she demanded, turning fierce.

"Bianca, I've been with a lot of women. You're the most exquisite woman I've ever known."

Bianca snarled, "I don't care about the other women, tell me I'm better than my sister, say it."

"Your sister is nothing compared to you. You're everything she could never be." Bianca snuggled her body against mine and slowly gyrated her pelvis against my thigh. Her nipples, firm and ripe, pushed into my chest. I nuzzled her head into my neck.

"Jim, oh Jim."

I looked at her as she moaned the name again with her eyes closed. "Oops." She opened her eyes and looked at me. "Oh Cape, I'm sorry--that was my husband's name. Please forgive me, you were wonderful."

Bianca dropped me off at my car. "I hope I see you again, Cape. I still feel terrible about calling you Jim…. Call me."

I didn't mind the slip of the tongue, who hasn't done that? The other things she had done bothered me, though.

Her demand that I compare her with Laura, and the quick changes in mood and actions. Why? Almost sixteen years had elapsed since Laura's death. Why would a woman as beautiful as Bianca be intimidated by anyone? Much less a woman, though her sister, who had been dead for so long? Her reaction was too intense for someone who supposedly loved her competitor deeply. Sibling rivalry couldn't explain it away, either, too vicious.

Approval? Bianca suggested at our first meeting that her father hadn't approved of her lifestyle, yet he had adored Laura. That was a possibility.

My reference to Papa? The statement was loaded and Bianca had jumped all over it. I had thought she said, "I love you, papai." dad in Portuguese, when she spoke to Gustavo, but I was wrong. She had made it very clear that papa wasn't one of her favorite words. Then there was Gustavo. No speculation necessary, he was definitely a liar.

One more thing bothered me. Bianca had said, "I am the executrix of Laura's estate." I wasn't a lawyer, but wouldn't an estate have been settled before now. Shouldn't Bianca have said "was"? I was the executrix of Laura's estate. A grammatical error?

Logically, except for Gustavo, each point could be explained. But add them together and the total begged for more questions.

I decided to call Michelle Davidson, Carol Kornegay's suitemate. I suspected she had known Laura before ECU. I would know for sure as soon as I got home.

CHAPTER TWELVE

A Friend with a Cross to Bear.

It was just after 4:00 p.m. when I arrived home. I would need to be in bed by 8:00 p.m. to be ready for my early morning flight. I checked my fax and found the manifest and destination of my flight. My destination was the Columbia Metro airport in Columbia, S.C. I would be hauling a cadaver to the University of South Carolina.

I don't care for hauling bodies. Oh, if they are curvaceous, hot, and alive no problem. But dead, cold, and stiff, no way. We flew lots of bodies when I was with AeroMax, but they were always tucked away in the cargo area of the jet. That wasn't so bad. On a small plane like the Lance the body would be up close and personal. Not good.

I found Michelle Davidson's number and called.

"Hello, is this Michelle?"

"Yes."

"Michelle, this is Cape Thomas. Carol Kornegay gave me your number."

"How is Carol? I haven't seen her forever. Is she still married to John?"

"Michelle, I don't know Carol that well, but I don't think she is. I'm really calling about Laura Fisher."

There was a pause. I thought for a moment that Michelle was trying to remember Laura Fisher. I was wrong.

"Laura Fisher. I was just thinking of her today. I still miss her, life can be so cruel sometimes."

No sense wasting time, she knew Laura, and she would help me or she wouldn't.

"Michelle, what I really called about is Laura's child?"

"Laura didn't marry, and she never had children."

That was the answer I was expecting, but not the one I wanted.

"I talked to her sister, Bianca. She did have a child. I thought since you knew her so well you might have known about it."

"That bitch. I told Laura not to trust her."

"Michelle, I found out about the child. Bianca only confirmed it."

"That still doesn't change the fact that she's a bitch."

I couldn't understand the animosity Michelle felt for Bianca, but I felt it was caused by more than the perfidy.

"What did you say your name was?"

"Cape, Cape Thomas."

"Why are you looking for her child?"

"I met Laura once, I think I might have something to do with her having the child."

There was another pause. I prepared for the next question.

"I do know that Jim Rogers wasn't the father. Laura was so despondent when she found out what he had done to her. She did some things after the breakup that were so out of character for her. Tell me, what makes you think you are the father, and why are you looking for her now?"

I didn't want what had happened to sound cavalier.

"I met her…things clicked."

"Mr. Thomas, Laura wanted to hurt Jim like he had hurt her. She did some things that she regretted. I can tell you this, you are not the only candidate that could be that child's father."

The odds of my being the father had just decreased. I felt something, but it wasn't relief.

"If you're having feelings of guilt, because you didn't pay child support or something like that, I think you can forget it. After all, it's a little late to try and be responsible now, don't you think?"

I explained why I wasn't able to find Laura, the dream, and my search. I also told her about Bianca's explanation and why it should all seem logical.

Michelle had some questions. "Wait a minute, did you say Bianca told you she gave Laura the Coptic Cross for her high school graduation?"

"Yes."

"Why would Bianca tell you that? That's a lie. Laura did get the Coptic Cross for her graduation, but it was her college graduation, not high school."

"Are you sure about that, Michelle? I mean, it was a long time ago."

"Mr. Thomas, I'm certain of that."

"Why so certain?"

"Because I gave her that cross. Laura loved antique jewelry, I found it at the big flea market in Charleston."

"Michelle, I met Laura one time almost twenty-five years ago. I remember a few things she said, but I can't be sure if I remembered them correctly. I thought she was in nursing. When, in fact, she was pre-med. Was Laura a junior in college when the breakup happened?"

"Yes."

"So, I couldn't have subconsciously remembered seeing the cross. Because Laura never had the cross when I knew her?"

"Exactly, and you want to know another little interesting tidbit, Mr. Thomas?"

I did. "Call me Cape, if you don't mind."

"Okay, Cape, the person that Jim Rogers had sex with? That was Bianca."

"Why would Bianca do that to someone she loved so much?" I could understand why, after the bedroom episode, but I wanted Michelle's take on it. " It doesn't make sense."

"Did Bianca tell you that?"

" What? That she loved her sister? Yeah, at least a couple of times," I said.

"Cape, that's a damn lie. I could tell you much more, but I have to pick up my kids. Can you call back?"

"Sure. Where do you live, anyway? I have your number but I never asked Carol where you live."

"Augusta, Georgia."

Columbia, South Carolina, was sixty miles from Augusta. Even on the Lance I could be there in less than thirty minutes.

"Michelle, if I could be in Augusta in the morning could you meet me at the airport?"

"Which one, Bush or Daniels? We have two."

The weather was forecast to be crappy so I would need Bush because it had a precision approach. I remembered that from my Linda days.

"Bush Field, at the general aviation terminal, is 8:00 a. m. too early for you?" I asked.

"Eight is fine, let me leave my cell number with you."

Sarge rented one of the new corporate hangers at the Mount Olive Airport. It would come in handy this morning, the rain was pouring down. While I waited for the body to be delivered, I called the flight service station to check on the weather. The rain would last all day in the southeastern part of the country. The forecast also called for light to moderate turbulence, and the freezing level was 4500'. That meant it would be bumpy and I would have to stay low to avoid the ice.

The ambulance was pulling up to the hanger as I hung up the phone. The fresh bodies, not embalmed, we flew at AeroMax were stuffed into lightweight aluminum coffins. The corpses were dressed in whatever clothes the deceased was wearing when they died. I know that because once in Rio I had been asked to check a body before it was loaded.

The dead guy looked like a business executive. Except he was dressed in a DKNY skirt with a matching blouse and a lovely pair of black pumps.

The body I would be flying today was dressed in a white hospital gown open in the back. He was an older gentleman, somewhere near eighty years old. The attendants removed the body from the stretcher, then placed him on a fiberglass board with six hand hole slots, three on each side. A plain white sheet was then draped over the body.

Three straps where strung into the handholds to secure the body. I opened the cargo door on the Lance. Then moved to the front of the plane to help guide the body into place.

The seats from the plane had been removed, but not the seat belts. I used two of the belts to hold my cargo in place. Rain buffeted the plane as I taxied out to runway two-three and departed. I checked in with Seymour-Johnson Approach Control then looked behind me to check on my passenger. The wind had blown the sheet from the old guy's face. His eyes were open, and I wondered if he was alive. I tried to reach the sheet to cover his face. The turbulence had increased, so I forgot about my passenger and concentrated on flying the plane.

Somewhere near Florence S.C. the turbulence lessened. I decided to cover my passenger. I turned around to see the old man sitting up. Corpses do strange things, muscle spasms sometimes cause movements of the dead body. I knew that, but this guy was sitting straight up. Apparently, one of the attendants had forgotten to buckle a strap. Maybe the doctor had screwed up. This guy looked alive to me. I yelled at him over the noise in the plane. "Hey, are you alive?" His eyes were open and I could swear his mouth moved. I could hear Florence Approach Control through my headset. "Lance 5426 Whiskey, say altitude."

I quickly turned around in my seat to look at the altimeter that read three thousand feet. I didn't need to be busted for an altitude violation. Two hundred feet off my assigned altitude would have constituted that. I was a thousand feet off. "This is Lance 5426 Whisky I've got a runaway auto-pilot."

Florence Approach automatically became sympathetic. "Lance 5426 Whiskey, do you want to declare an emergency?"

My lie worked. "This is 5426 Whiskey, I think I have it under control now, climbing to assigned altitude."

Florence Control responded, "Florence altimeter Two-eight-three-eight."

I did have an autopilot on board, but it had been placarded out of service. If I didn't get ramp checked again, I would live to fly another day.

Rain and clouds filled the windshield as I set up for the ILS Runway 29 at Columbia Metro. I taxied to the ramp and was met by an ambulance. "What's this?" the attendant asked referring to the old man sitting up. "Oh that, he's an old pilot--been telling me how to fly all the way down here. See ya."

"Is he dead?"

"Says he is."

"Say what!"

I went inside the FBO grabbed a cup of coffee and filed my flight plan for Augusta. I would have to pay Sarge for the plane and fuel to Augusta. He would moan and groan, and probably threaten to fire me. In the end I would get a warning, and Sarge would get another story to tell about us sorry-ass pilots.

Augusta Approach gave me vectors for the ILS for Bush Field as soon as I was airborne. The needles centered on the localizer and I flew the crosshairs down to minimums on the ILS Runway 35 at Augusta, it was 7:46 a.m. when I broke out. By the time I taxied to the FBO it was close to my meeting time with Michelle.

The fuel attendant and a heavyset older woman were in the FBO. I dialed Michelle's cell phone. The heavyset woman received a call almost as soon as I dialed.

"Hello."

"Michelle, this is Cape Thomas."

"I think I'm looking at you, Cape?"

Michelle had changed from her picture in the ECU photo. Besides the weight gain, her hair had changed from jet-black to gray.

"Hi, Michelle, thanks for meeting me."

"Hi."

I asked Michelle if there were a place we could grab a cup of coffee and talk. She suggested a Waffle Shoppe a couple of miles from the airport. I had coffee, she had bacon, eggs, and a Belgian Waffle.

"Is that how you stay so skinny you don't eat?"

I hadn't eaten, but I didn't want Michelle to feel badly about eating. "I'm not hungry. I had something before I left North Carolina."

She nodded and munched on her bacon.

"Michelle, you said you had more to tell me?"

She swallowed and sipped her coffee before she answered.

"I've been thinking about this.... Are you going to tell Mr. Fisher about the baby?"

"No, but I got the feeling Fisher was lonesome. Why is everyone so sure he would be opposed to the child?" I asked.

"I'm with you. I've visited with Mr. Fisher a few times since Laura died. You know that Laura was in the process of finding the baby before she became ill, right?"

I didn't know that, but I wasn't surprised. "No, but why didn't she at least tell her father about the baby?"

"Laura was a wonderful person. She wanted everyone to be happy, except maybe herself. She never told me, but I think she had planned to tell her father about the child."

I ordered another refill on my coffee and asked Michelle if she needed anything. "No I shouldn't be eating all this. I know you won't believe this, but at one time I was attractive."

I could and I told her, "You're still attractive. I saw your picture from ECU, I looked it up after I spoke with Carol. You've changed, but not that much."

She smiled. "You're nice, but if you fly planes, you're not blind."

"Laura was lucky to have a friend like you. Did you meet her in college?"

"No, Laura and I were best friends from kindergarten, we lived only a few houses apart."

"That means you knew Bianca, too. I get the feeling you don't like her?"

"Cape, let me fill you in on a little Fisher family history."

I didn't want to rehash much of what I had learned from Bianca. I divulged all that Bianca had told me.

"Well, most of that is true. Except the part about Bianca loving Laura. Laura was like a mother to Bianca. I guess you noticed the lack of family resemblance?" Michelle asked.

It was hard not to spot. "Well, other than the hair color, they didn't have a lot of similarities."

Michelle nodded. "Laura was a natural blond. She dyed her hair and stayed out in the sun to become darker. She did that so she and Bianca would look more like sisters. When Bianca was a small child, it upset her when people thought they weren't sisters. As I said, Laura was a wonderful person."

"Sounds like some very good reasons for Bianca to love her sister?"

Michelle pushed her empty plate away. "Oh, Bianca acted as if she loved Laura. It worked on Laura, but I never bought it, and Bianca doesn't like me for that reason. We haven't spoken since the funeral."

"Is that because you knew about her and Jim Rogers?" I asked.

Michelle got her coffee refilled and continued. "That, and a little disagreement we had over some personal belonging of Laura's."

"So Laura forgave Bianca for the Jim Rogers fling?"

"No, Laura never knew about that."

I wanted to believe Michelle, but it didn't make sense. "How did you know about it then? Bianca couldn't have been much over sixteen when it happened. That's pretty young to lay all the blame on her, isn't it?"

"If you really knew Bianca I wouldn't have to explain this to you," Michelle said. "Bianca, learned how to wrap men around her little finger the day she was born. She was just like her mother. If you think Jim instigated the sex, you're wrong. Bianca was very experienced by that age. Just to keep the record straight, she was fifteen, barely, but very active. As for how did I know? I caught them in bed together. I didn't tell Laura about Bianca, because it would have killed her. Sometimes I wish I had told her. Maybe then Laura wouldn't have made Bianca her executrix."

I was shocked Michelle knew about that. "So, you know about that, too?

Michelle smiled again. "You're not from Greenville, are you?"

"No."

"Cape, that was the talk of the town in Greenville for years. You know Laura's will still hasn't been probated yet, don't you?"

I didn't know that either, but it explained the, am Bianca had used when she told me about being the executrix. "I thought that was something that had to be done in a specific length of time?"

"So did everybody else. Jim Rogers became an attorney, and he's also a friend of Zeke and Bianca Jenkins. He's the attorney helping Bianca probate the will. I've never read the will, but I've heard it can't be probated until a certain date."

I was curious about something else. "You said Zeke Jenkins, but you meant Jim Jenkins, right?'

Michelle was puzzled now. "Who is Jim Jenkins?"

"Bianca's ex- or late husband, right?"

"Bianca's ex-husband is Zeke Jenkins, period."

I needed a little clarification. "So when did Bianca marry Jim, whatever his name is?"

"Bianca has been married once, and never to anybody named Jim."

I thought of Bianca naked and moaning the name, Jim. I was certain of the name, she had even apologized for calling me Jim. Why would she tell me Jim was her husband, when the truth would be so easy to find out?

"You look like you've seen another ghost. What's wrong, Cape?"

"Nothing, I was under the impression Bianca's husband was named Jim."

"Bianca's had so many men she probably can't remember her own husband's name."

I didn't care about that right now. I wanted to know more about Laura.

"Tell me, why would Bianca wanted to break up Laura and Jim Rogers?"

"Bianca never gained the approval from Mr. Fisher that Laura did. Rightfully so, I might add. She was jealous of Laura. She wanted to have anything Laura ever had or wanted. Bianca competed with Laura on every level.

Laura didn't see it that way. She was the most popular in school, home-coming queen, and Miss Greenville at one time.

You name an accolade and Laura had it. Beta Club, class valedictorian, and most of all, the undying love and respect of her father. Bianca wanted to out do Laura in just one thing. But the only thing she ever out-did Laura on was the number of lovers she had. God she's such a tramp. I wouldn't be surprised if she was full of diseases," Michelle said.

I wasn't feeling good about having had unprotected sex with the red-hot Doctor. But the things Michelle said helped me understand the little comparison episode in the bedroom.

"So, Bianca will sleep with anyone?"

"Man, or woman, I would imagine."

I wasn't feeling special, and I thought Bianca had really liked me, too.

"You say, you and Bianca had a dispute over some of Laura's personal items. What were they?"

"A box of stupid stuff mostly, yearbooks for one thing. Laura always wrote me a little note in my yearbook, then I would write something under that note. We did the same in her yearbook. Mr. Fisher wanted me to have them, but Bianca didn't."

"Anything else?"

"Yes, the Coptic Cross locket you described on the phone."

"Do you still have it?"

"Of course I do," Michelle said.

"Could I see it?"

"Why? It isn't worth much, sterling, but still not worth much."

"I still want to see it, if you don't mind? Just to make sure it's the one I saw in my dream."

"I thought you had already seen it. It's on the mirror of my minivan. I'll get it."

Michelle returned with the cross and handed it to me. It was exactly like the one I had seen in my dream--vision--damn it, I was holding the proof. "You said it was a locket, can you open it?"

Michelle flipped the locket open. Inside was a picture of Michelle in her younger days. She was attractive, very attractive. "Cape, I don't want you to think I'm vain. It's the picture Laura always had in it. I seldom open it for that reason."

I rubbed the picture with my thump to press it into the locket. There was a lump behind it.

"Do you mind if I pull the picture out for just a second?" I used my fork to coax the picture from its setting. Behind the picture was a small key.

"Is that a key? I never knew that was in there--let me see it," Michelle said. I handed the key to Michelle.

"You don't know what it fits?"

Michelle still looked surprised. "No, this is the first time I've ever seen it. It looks like a diary key or something like that."

"Did Laura keep a diary?" I asked.

"You know, I'm not sure. I keep a diary. They are private things, I doubt my husband even knows I have one."

"The box of Laura's things--does it have a diary in it?"

"No, I know everything in that box, no diary."

"Do you know where she might have kept it?" I asked.

"In her room, I suppose, that's where mine is. At my parents' house."

"Yeah, but Laura's room has bound to have been cleaned out by now?"

"No way, Cape, Mr. Fisher doesn't let anyone in that room unless he's with them, not even Bianca."

"I think I need that diary." I thought of what MarKay had said, You have all the clues. The key had been hidden, but I was sure it was a clue.

"What do you expect to find in the diary?"

"I don't know, Michelle, maybe answers. Maybe questions that I need to ask. Why would Laura have on the cross in my dream, when it's something I wouldn't have recognized? There has to be a reason and I have to find out what it is, I know that."

Michelle face was serious. "Cape, with the exception of the Coptic Cross, Bianca's explanation makes sense. Maybe you just had a dream? Forgive me for this--I don't really know you. You know that the Fisher family is the richest family in Greenville, and maybe one of the richest families in North Carolina. You could have another motive, like money, right?"

It was a hard question, but a fair one. "Michelle, when this first happened to me, I thought it was about Laura. She's dead, and has been for over sixteen years. If I had motives to try and steal the Fisher family fortune, why did I wait so long to make my move? I think you have sensed that I may need your help to figure this out. I respect your concern. I'm convinced this isn't about Laura, but the child. With or without your help I'm going to find her. Likewise, whether you help me or not, I'm going to put this puzzle together."

"Why didn't Laura visit me? I was her closest friend in the world. If the dead can return, what you're saying isn't logical."

"I don't know, all I know is this. Since I started this quest, I've found nothing but roadblocks. Yet I've gotten this far. Bianca says what happened to me can be put in a logical box. You say nothing I've said is logical. Me, I'm in the middle, still looking," I said.

"Well, at least I'm on the right side."

"How's that?"

"I'm on the opposite side from Bianca, and that has to be the right side. What can I do to help?"

I promised to call her after I did a little more checking. Then I flew back to Goldsboro to face the wrath of Sarge.

CHAPTER THIRTEEN

Prayer Meeting in Charlotte.

Sarge's promised to fire me if I every pulled another stunt like the Augusta trip on his airplane. Not that he meant it, but I wouldn't do it again just in case.

I turned William Johnston's business card over and over in my hand. It was only a name, only a card, but now I wanted to go wash my hands. Ally needed to be warned. I could call William Johnston, he would be happy to make the arrangements and the electronic surveillance to cover the event. Not something I relished.

I had thought about how to contact Ally without getting on the wrong side of the W. Cronus Kress juggernaut. It wasn't a good idea, but on the other hand, it was better than going through William Johnston.

When I was based at the Charlotte Douglas Airport, I dated a woman who was an aspiring actress. I had kept in touch with her over the years, but we hadn't spoken in a while. I looked at William Johnston's card again. Then decided that my plan, though a long shot, was worth a try.

I called Joy Meredith, her given name was Martha Higgenbottom. She changed her name for professional reasons, a good idea. The phone rang once and Joy answered. "Joy, this is Cape Thomas. How's my favorite actress doing?"

"Good, and my very favorite airline captain?"

"Oh, getting by. Are you still acting?"

"A little regional stuff, but mostly waitress work, why?"

"Any starring roles in the regional stuff?"

"No, actually I haven't had a part in a few years. Why? Do you have a lead for me, Mr. Coppolla?"

I wished the best for Joy. I felt guilt for being relieved at her lack of success at doing something she loved. I understood all too well how it was to be unable to participate in a chosen field. Fortunately for me, Joy's failure would lend itself to my plan's accomplishment. After all, Ally or some of her friends could have known Joy if she was prominent in Charlotte theatre.

"Actually, I do have a role for you, but it's good and bad?"

"I'll bite. What's the good part?" Joy asked.

"The good part is you will have the starring role."

"And the bad?"

"There's only one character."

"Damn, Cape, that's cruel. You had my hopes up."

"Joy, I'm serious. The job pays three hundred dollars for about thirty minutes worth of work, interested?"

"Do I have to take my clothes off? Not that it matters, anything for the arts, I was just curious."

"Taking your clothes off is the last thing this role requires. Do you think you could pull off being a Jehovah's Witness?"

"Amen, Brother, Amen."

Joy's slipped right into character and that reminded me of why I had called her. She could pull this off.

I filled Joy in on my plan. I had Ally's address from her phone number. She was to visit Ally's house. If it was a gated community, and I suspected it was, the acting job would pay more. A starving actress could manage to get into Fort Knox for that amount of money.

Her mission was to get a message to Ally that I would write. If Ally were out of town or not available, she was to postpone the plan. Ditto if a man answered the phone.

Should Ally's maid answer the door, a high probability, Joy would have to act her way inside.

I gave her Ally's phone number and instructed her to call before her debut.

"Joy, can you meet me at the Concord Airport around noon today?"

"Yes sir, Mr. Coppolla, sir. Noon it is at the Concord Airport."

I hung up the phone and left for the Goldsboro Airport to see Sarge.

"Sarge, I need to rent one of those Rent-a-Wreck airplanes you have on the ramp."

Sarge was in a rare good mood. "What's wrong with the Lance?"

"You just told me an hour ago not to use the Lance again for personal business, and this is personal business."

"Since when have you ever listened to anything I say? Be back by 4:00 in the morning, you have another flight."

"God, Sarge, not another body."

Sarge smiled, that wasn't good. "Naw, its some skunk from Europe going to the Nashville Zoo, you pick it up in Wilmington."

"Does it still have the ability to spray?"

"What difference does it make? 4:00 a.m., no wake-up call, Jet Jockey."

Considering the ungodly hours and unusual freight, I began to suspect Sarge really had had a hard time filling the job.

I rushed back home to type the message to Ally. En route to the Mount Olive Airport, I scanned the note.

Ally Moore,

We need to talk. I have been contacted by Walter's people, and I think your phone has been bugged. Nothing that you have planned is more important than this meeting. I will be at the Charlotte Coliseum parking section ZZ1 in the rear of the building. Do not drive straight to the coliseum, and at some point along the way, notice the cars around you. Find a city block, turn four times to the right then find another city block and turn four times to the left. As you know, this will put you at the point on the street where you started. Make sure no car behind you makes the same maneuvers. If one does, call the number at the bottom of this note. The person who will answer the phone is Joy. Pretend she is someone you met at the theater. Make a date to have coffee or drinks. The last time I saw you, you wanted my trust. I'm asking for yours now.

Bring this note with you or memorize the number and destroy it.

I read over the note, deciding it looked like something from a cheap spy novel. I didn't have time for nuanced prose, I only hoped it would work. The last line was too melodramatic. It beat out my second choice hands down, though. Should you choose to accept this mission….

I decided not to file a flight plan for my trip to Concord. For as much as I knew they could be public information, too. I landed in Concord at noon . Joy was waiting outside in her car as I had instructed.

"Cape, what the hell are you up to? I checked out the address. I'm assuming this would have something to do with a woman? Any woman in that neighborhood is way out of your league, Buster."

Women, natural-born matchmakers, go figure.

"Is it a gated community?" I asked.

"Yes, with a guard and everything. The price has gone up."

"OK, five hundred," I said.

"Six, they have a guard that rides around on a golf cart, too."

"Six hundred! Geez! You should try out for a part in Ali Baba and the Forty Thieves. Damn, six hundred dollars," I bitched, then agreed to it.

"Well, that's a possibility. Speaking of thieves, will I go to jail if they catch me?"

"Not if you can act one iota. Just be a Jehovah's Witness."

"What if I get caught before I get to the house, do I still get paid?" Joy asked.

"Sure, but only a hundred dollars."

"One hundred fifty."

"One hundred twenty-five, or I find myself another star that can get it right."

"Done. You said you had some more instructions?"

"When you get to the door make sure it's a tall blonde woman. She will look to be in her early thirties. Once you identify her say, 'Ally Moore, Cape wants you to read this page.' Got it?"

"Ally Moore, Cape wants you to read this page."

"Repeat it," I insisted.

"Duh--I'm an actress it's just one line. What page?"

"This page." I let her see the note. "Did you get the Bible?"

"Yes."

"Good, give it to me."

"Why Cape, I didn't know you were a religious man."

"The Bible, Joy, I need to cut the note to fit the book."

She handed me the Bible. " I don't think this is a good idea."

"Joy, I know it's not a good idea. It's a dumb idea. I can't tell you any more, other than this is my only chance. Remember, if she calls, pretend you've known her for a while."

"I get it. 'Ally, dear, it's been a while let's do lunch at the club, darling.' Now back to the bad idea. I don't like you using The Good Book to set up a sordid affair. That's low even for you."

"Joy, this is not a sordid affair or any other type of affair. Besides, I've changed. I can't tell you any more. Can you get in?"

"Piece of cake. Now what was the price again for the role?"

"Six hundred, and no arguments. Did you rent me a car?"

"Enterprise has already delivered it…Cape, can I ask you something?"

"Sure."

"You really like this woman, don't you? You're doing this for a good reason, right?"

"Joy, do you want this job or not?"

"Yes, and an answer to my question. Do you love her?"

" Joy, I hardly know her. If you want to know the truth, helping her may end my career in aviation."

"Then why do it?"

"Hell, I don't know…I suppose because it's the right thing to do. Now, can we please get this done before I change my mind?"

"Cape--."

"Joy, I swear, if you don't shut up I'll dress up like a Jehovah Witness myself."

"I'm--."

"Shh…not another word."

I dropped Joy off near Ally's house and watched as she made her way over a brick fence and to Ally's front door. What happened next came from conversations I later had with Joy and Ally, it goes something like this: Joy rang the front doorbell and was greeted by Louise, Ally's maid. Fortunately for my plan, Louise looked nothing like Ally.

"Yes ma'am may I help you?" Louise asked.

"Yes, I'd like to ask you where you'll be when the salvation day comes?"

"Sister, I'll be sitting at the right hand of Our Lord Jesus Christ."

"Bless you sister. Tell me, will everyone inside your beautiful home be there with you?

"You talking about this home? One of them won't make it, I'm pretty sure of that. He's a heathen," Louise said shaking her head.

"Well, I'll have to talk to him, and get him right for judgement day," Joy said.

"He's not here, but I'll get you his office address, just don't tell him I sent you. Wait here I'll be right back."

Louise closed the door, but didn't lock it. Joy stepped inside and starting singing
Hallelujah as loud as she could.

Ally came running from her study. "Louise, what on earth is going on here?"

Joy changed the refrain of the old spiritual "Al-ly-lu-jah, Al-ly-lu-jah, Ally Moore."

Louise hustled back to the foyer out of breath.

"Louise, remove this woman from this house at once!"

"Yes ma'am. Sister, you got to go, now. I don't won't to hurt a Christian, but I will if I have to," Louise said.

Joy pretended to become faint. "Praise Jesus, I get woozy when the Spirit moves me. Water, water, can I have some water, please?"

"Louise, quick get her a glass of water before she faints here in the house," Ally said.

"What kind of water do you want, sister, bottle or tap?" Louise asked.

"Holy, if you have it," Joy said.

"Huh?"

"Louise….Just get her some water, please."

Louise left for the water. Ally had a question, "How do you know my name?"

Joy held the Bible for Ally to see, and whispered, "Ally Moore, Cape wants you to read this?"

"Cape? Cape Thomas … wants me to read the entire Bible?

"I knew I would blow my lines. Ally Moore, Cape wants you to read this page." Joy opened the book and revealed the note.

Ally finished the note just as Louise returned with the water. "Louise, I'm taking this lady to a medical facility, I should be back in an hour or two."

"You want me to come with you, Miss Ally? The Spirit might jump on her again, but I can beat it out of her."

"No I'll be fine," Ally said.

Ally dropped Joy at her house and arrived at the Coliseum at 2:14. I stopped her and instructed her to park her car behind a Dumpster.

"Cape, what on earth is going on here? I feel like Mata Hari."

"I'm sorry, but I couldn't think of any other way to contact you."

"Why do you think my phone line has been tapped? Who are Walter's people?

And last, but certainly not least. Why would you pay someone to be a Jehovah's Witness, then send them to my house?"

"Ally, it was a dumb idea but it worked, you're here."

"I almost called the police. Although it was funny. How much did you pay Joy, by the way?" Ally asked.

"Six hundred dollars. Did I get my money's worth?"

"Double it, the poor woman earned every dime of it." Ally laughed. It was a dumb plan but worth the investment to see Ally laugh.

"Cape, don't give up your flying job to be a spymaster, you'll starve."

I didn't know how long Ally could stay. I wanted to talk more, spend more time with her. Instead I pushed ahead with my mission.

"That's the reason I needed to talk to you. I've been offered my old job back with AeroMax."

"That's wonderful. I know you're happy about that."

"I would be, but I didn't care for the strings that were attached to the job offer," I said.

"I don't understand."

"Ally, I was contacted by William Johnston, of Johnston Ballard & Hearst. Ever heard of him?"

"Yes, but why on earth would William Johnston contact you? No offense, Cape, but William Johnston doesn't work cheaply."

"He offered me my job back in a round-about way. It won't cost me a penny if I do a little favor for them."

"I don't understand. How does this concern me?"

"I supposed to admit that I had an affair with you," I said.

"Why would he want you to do that? You and I have met only once for lunch and coffee, for God's sake."

"He has pictures of us together in Raleigh. They look incriminating. Johnston knows the truth, but I don't think that matters."

"How bad could they be? We were in public."

"Do you remember when I gave you my coat?"

"Cape, I'm sorry, but how could that be incriminating?"

"It looks as if I had my arm around you. The picture of the little peck you gave me? It's worse."

"Why would they…how did they get pictures?"

"My guess is a private eye. You were being followed," I said.

"How did they know where to find me? The phone…God, I'm so glad I didn't talk to you over the phone. William Johnston is such a dirt bag."

"Ally, I agree with you, but he told me he was contacting me on behalf of his client, W.Cronus Kress."

"My husband? Sorry, I can't believe this. Walter is behind this whole thing? That creep!"

"If you need some adjectives to go along with that creep, I'm pretty well stocked," I offered.

"I must leave. What if they see me talking to you again? Walter will have some more evidence. I can't afford that. I have to stay married to him."

"Even if I don't go along with their plan, they have an alternate. They're going to use the pictures they have to try and prove adultery regardless. It would be a weak case. But they're convinced they would prevail," I said.

Ally looked shocked, who wouldn't? Childhood sweethearts aren't supposed to hurt one another, are they?

"Will you give a deposition?"

"I guess, but they want an air-tight case. Maybe more pictures in a private place, perhaps something a little more provocative. A video, recorded conversations, something that will strengthen their case. I don't know, but I do know this. Whether we talk or not, W. Cronus Kress is going to have a divorce on the grounds of adultery."

"Why adultery, why not just settle?

"You tell me, I'm just a pawn in all this," I told her.

"It has to do with Walter's ambassadorship, I expect."

"Understand, Ally, I am only quoting William Johnston, but he said, ' Mrs. Kress has a colored past.' I thought of politics when he mentioned that."

"That bastard, I should call the Charlotte Observer. Yes, I could tell them all about Walter. He hides his affairs so well from everyone but me. I can't believe this. Walter, of all people, would try to win a divorce trial on the grounds of my purported infidelity. I haven't slept with a man in ten years, and just for the record, he was that man. He knows that, he can't be that stupid."

"Ally, are affairs all you know about Walter? I mean most people don't think you are a politician if you don't have an affair or two."

"Well, I wouldn't vote for him for that reason, but I can't think of anything else bad that he's done."

"Yeah, you're right, we're still in the Bible Belt. I guess that would be reason enough to want to keep you quiet. It would be nice if you had some dirt on Walter."

"Thanks for telling me, but now what, Cape?"

"We need a plan, that's why I'm here. I have a plan."

I told Ally my plan. It was better than my Jehovah Witness plan. She was still nervous about trusting me and I was nervous, too. My stake in this game had just increased, considerably. I was betting everything I ever loved on a woman I hardly knew.

"Cape, why are you doing this? I can't see where any of this benefits you. Your best bet is with Walter. Everyone's best bet is to be on Walter's side. Are we being photographed now, is this a setup? Should I cry so you can hold me?"

"This isn't a setup. William Johnston and W. Cronus Kress have the resources and money to have both of us in the same place at the same time. Cameras at the ready, I'm sure. Do you really think they would be dumb enough to plan a setup using the old Jehovah Witness ploy?"

Ally didn't answer, not right away. She was cracking up, and I chuckled a little then waited for her to finish. Then I waited a little longer.

"Hey, I know it was dumb, but like I said, it did work."

She laughed again. "The note, the last line. I thought the note was going to ignite."

I pulled my shoe off and placed it against my ear like a phone. "That's it, Ally, I'm calling the chief."

"Stop it, my sides are hurting. Oh God, and poor Louise, she was going to beat on Joy. Knock the Spirit out of her! Then Hallelujah became Al-ly-lu-jah. I wish you could have been there, " Ally said.

"I'm sorry I missed it." I was getting a little embarrassed after realizing how dumb my thinking had been. Ally looked as if she felt sorry for me and finally stopped laughing. "I did like the driving instructions, though. That was a good part."

"I saw it in a movie once. Except they only drove around one block. I figured the more the better," I said.

"Cape, why didn't you marry? You're funny and clever. You could have made some woman very happy."

"You know, that's the first time anyone has ever said that to me. Besides, I told you in Raleigh."

"You told me an abbreviated version. I want to hear the whole story. I don't even care if the breakup was your fault. Not that I think it was. Tell me something about Cape Thomas. You certainly know a lot about me."

"This story will take a while. Are you sure you should be gone this long?"

" I am rarely at home. Nobody will miss me. I do tons of charity work. Tell me please."

" I'll try and keep it brief. No interruptions, no questions," I said.

"Deal."

"It was six years ago. I was forty, Grace was thirty-four. I was a captain on the 747. She was one of the flight attendants. We knew each other from my 737 days, Grace and I became close then--things heated up later. It was the first time I'd ever felt that way about a woman. She talked about having kids, a family, and I guess I bought in to the dream. I mean at forty it's time to start a family, so I asked her to marry me. I thought she felt the same way, but she didn't. We had fun, a lot of good times, but Grace didn't take me seriously. I had a little credibility problem when it came to staying with one woman. To be honest, I had earned my status as a man about town.

"Anyway, she asked for a little time. Seems she had been dating the Asshole. His father was the CEO of AeroMax. Grace had a choice me or Asshole. She chose the Asshole. After they were married, I guess he heard some rumors about Grace and me, but they were only rumors. He confronted her about it. They separated, and Grace was miserable. She wanted to be with him. They made peace, and moved back in together. Grace--."

"--I think I would have chosen you over the a-hole," Ally interjected.

"Thanks, but you promised no interruptions, remember?"

"Sorry."

"As I was saying, before I was so kindly interrupted, Grace never quit her job after they were married. She and I wound up on the same flight to Paris. He found out about the flight, and I guess his imagination got the best of him, he thought we had slept together in Paris.

"But we never even talked on that trip. They had a fight, and she was upset for being wrongly accused. Grace stopped by my house one night. She wanted me to assure her husband, Jon that was his name--that it was over between us. Grace had this idea…if I talked to Jon, and explained everything. You know, that we weren't together in Paris, or any other time since they were married, everything would be fine in their lives. I didn't touch her that night at my house. She just wanted me to set things straight between them.

"I wanted to help Grace, so I gave Jon a call. I thought he was fine with it. A few weeks later we had another flight to London, we landed on New Year's Eve.

"The flight carried a double crew, the pilots called it 'bunking for bucks'. The first crew flew over. I had a push back time of 7:00 a.m. the next morning.

"FAA rules require that a pilot have eight hours from bottle to throttle. I've flown planes when some of the crew reeked of alcohol. But my personal rules were ten hours from bottle to throttle.

"Grace wanted to thank me for calling Jon. She suggested we have a New Year's drink. We went to a pub, a place she knew. I'd never been there before.

"Grace knew I was very strict about my ten-hour rule, but still she insisted I toast her at 12:00 New Year's Eve. At 9:00 p.m. I quit drinking. My bedtime was ten that night, and even though the whole bar begged me to stay and toast her, I refused.

"Anyway, since I wouldn't be with her at 12:00 she asked the bartender to set the big clock in the bar to 12:00. I thought it was funny. I didn't want to order a drink so I asked the bartender to give me a bottle from the bar. We had a fake countdown in the bar. I pretended to drink from the bottle. Grace was beside me with a drink.

"After the flight returned to New York, I was called into the office the next day. On the CEO's desk were some 8x10 glossys of the scene in the London pub. I tried to explain the situation. The CEO pulled a typed and notarized statement signed by Grace affirming that it was midnight, not 9:00 p.m. I was shocked--hurt.

"I was given a choice, resign or be fired. I chose resignation. I think you know the rest."

"Did you talk to Grace?" Ally asked.

"I called her later. She explained that on the night she came to my house, to get me to talk to Jon, someone had taken a picture of us hugging good-bye on my doorstep. Jon had it in his possession. He accused her of sleeping with me, though she denied it, of course. Why wouldn't she? He threatened to leave her again unless she helped him get me fired. He told her it would 'prove her love for him'. That's all, end of story."

"Are they still married?"

"That's the ironic part. He soon after used the photographs in my house and at the pub to prove adultery. He made out like a bandit, I don't think he paid her a dime. I guess that's why when Johnston gave me the photographs, I knew I couldn't be on his side.

"You see, Ally, I know first hand that pictures can tell the truth, but not the whole truth. I also know the price of not fighting back."

"Do you ever see Grace?"

I just stared at her. "Ally, Grace took the one thing in my life that I loved, and the one thing in my life that loved me back. I can't forgive her for that."

"Dumb question, huh?"

"Almost as dumb as the Jehovah Witness caper."

"I better leave, Cape."

"Remember, we use Joy as the go-between, stay in touch with her."

"Bye. Thanks for fighting back."

CHAPTER FOURTEEN

A Useless Will, Hidden Codicil, and a May Day Baby.

I delivered the skunk to the Nashville Zoo. The vet who anesthetized the critter erred on the dosage. Somewhere over the Smokies my furry passenger triggered his defense mechanism. I wasn't a happy aviator when I got back to Sarge.

"Sarge, do you think it might be remotely possible to spread some of these exotic freight trips around with the other guys?"

"Geez, you smell like shit. Let's go outside and talk."

We went outside to continue our conversation. Sarge stood off at a distance, and upwind.

"Yeah, I know you've had some bad trips. But those were the last weird loads I have for awhile. I've got some milk runs, UPS and FedEx freight out of Greenville. How about I put you down for that, sport?" Sarge asked.

"Thank you, thank God."

"I gotta go, Cape, I have to fuel this King Air. Be in Greenville first thing in the morning with the plane. Get there around eight," Sarge sniffed. "And think about taking a shower…you really smell like shit."

I returned to Sarge's office and removed a ceiling tile. Then I placed my soiled clothes in the ceiling, replaced the tile and drove home in my shorts and tee shirt.

Greenville was a good place for me to work. My time was being eaten up by my two projects, Laura and Ally. From Greenville I could work on both projects. I packed an overnight bag, picked up the Lance, and flew to Greenville. I used the FBO courtesy car to get around town for the next couple of days.

My first stop was at the Greenville Courthouse. I wanted to read Laura's will. The information Michelle had given me could be nothing more than rumors. I had spent a large part of my life in a small town, and rumors were a way of life there. I wanted nothing but facts from here on out.

I stopped at the Register of Deeds office with my request. They directed me to the Clerk of Courts office. The woman in the clerk's office pointed me to a couple of thick books titled Devisee and Devisor. I didn't have a clue which was which. I searched for thirty minutes in each one with no luck. I gave up on my search and any hopes I had of a second career in law. I was over my head. Finally I asked the woman for assistance. The document materialized in seconds, and I got the feeling this wasn't the first time the request for Laura's will had been made. The office staff gathered in a small group and eyed me as I waited for the copy of the document. I paid for the copy and returned to my motel room to peruse it.

The first page was made up entirely of legal jargon. The only thing of any consequence in the entire document was one sentence in legalese, which stated the estate couldn't be probated until May 1, 2002. Then there was an advisory statement: See Unrecorded Codicil. I called Tom Butterfield for some legal advice since he was on my payroll or maybe W. Cronos Kress's payroll, if my plan with Ally worked out.

"Tom, this is Cape."

"Cape, you've finally come to your senses. Tell me you called to have me deposit the check from Johnston Ballard & Hearst."

"Nope, but I'll let you know something before, too long. I want to meet with some people--."

"You're looking a gift horse in the mouth, you need--."

"What I need is some legal advice, but not more coercion. What is a codicil? More specifically an Unrecorded Codicil?" I asked.

"What does this have to do with our case?"

"Nothing, but I need to know something about a codicil."

"I'm not an estate attorney, maybe you better ask one of those guys."

"You mean you passed the bar, and you can't answer one little old legal question?"

"Cape, there are tax attorneys, estate attorneys, corporate attorneys, aviation attorneys and the list goes on. I fall in the last category, by the way, and estates are not my field. You want legal advice? Here's some, deposit the damn check."

"Your advice is duly noted. Now, how about a textbook definition? You don't have to be right on the money, just in the neighborhood."

"I'd still advise you to see an estate attorney…and deposit the check."

"Tom, are you going to give me an answer, or do I need to call Johnston Ballard & Hearst?"

"Fine….A codicil would be a supplement or an appendix to a will. That's as far as I'm going on record. I know as much about estates, as I do Eskimos."

I ignored the Eskimos comment and pressed on. "Just curious, where or how would I find a copy of this Unrecorded Codicil?"

"Without knowing the whole story, and I don't want to know the whole story, by the way, I wouldn't think you could, not in the public records, anyway. Someone, perhaps a lawyer or even a family member, may have it. I doubt they would show it to you, either," Tom said.

"This Unrecorded Codicil. Could it spell out the entire terms of the will?"

" I suppose it could, ask an estate attorney they can explain it to you. I can't…. You got anymore off-the-wall legal questions?"

"Oh yeah, while I've got you on the line, is there a legal term for burying someone in the backyard?"

"Cape, believe it or not, I can help you with that one."

"Great, give me the Latin--and spell it, so I can look it up on the Internet. I don't want to tax your limited legal knowledge, too much."

"That's kind of you--ready to copy?"

"Ready."

"M-U-R-D-E-R."

"Thanks, Tom--F-U-N-N-Y, real F-U-N-N-Y."

"I have my moments, but back to something more serious. We need to start work on this FAA case, time is running out, let me know something," Tom said.

"Just do your work, use the check I sent you. If and when I decide to use Johnston Ballard & Hearst we'll be delighted to spend their money. Happy?"

"Sure, but we need to work with those guys, I wish you could understand how important that is for us."

"Be careful what you wish for, Tom. It might not be all that you think it is."

"What do you mean?"

"Thanks, Tom. I'll be in touch, good-bye."

I had a copy of a will that was useless, and no way to get a copy of the codicil in the public records. That left two means or maybe three to get my hands on the codicil. I could use Jim Rogers, the attorney who prepared the will, Bianca, or the old rumor mill. I decided to work from last to first.

I called Michelle. Hoping she could fill me in on the facts as well as rumors about the Fisher family.

"Hello, Michelle, Cape Thomas here."

"Cape, how are you?"

"Michelle, do you have a few minutes for us to talk?"

"Sure, if you don't mind the noise. Lee Davidson Jr…do not bounce that basketball in this house again! Sorry, Cape, I had to do a little mommy duty. Let me change phones, it's quieter in my office….Are you still there?"

"Yes."

I filled Michelle in on the bad news from Greenville. "Do you know anything special about May, 1, 2002"

"May Day Baby. If you know what I mean," Michelle said.

"I know what that means, May Day. It's an aviator's term for emergency. That wasn't what I meant."

"That wasn't what I meant, either. May 1st was the day Laura's child was born. That's what we called her, May Day Baby."

"So, the date of the will's probation and the baby are tied together? What year was the baby born, late seventies I know."

"May, 1st 1977. She'll be twenty-five this year. God, it seems like yesterday."

"Michelle, we have to find the codicil or the diary, without those we're lost. I've been thinking about how to do that. I think I need a brief history on the Fisher Family. I can ask here, but I'll just get rumors and few facts, so can you help me out?"

"Do you want a family tree or just knowledge of the family?"

"Knowledge for now, but we may need the other later. How did Fisher make his money?" I asked.

"He started in timber and land, then moved to real estate and development. He owns lots of land and properties. Motels, shopping center, car dealerships, you name it."

"So he's self made?"

"Yes, Laura was really proud of that, too. What else do you need to know?"

"Gustavo Jobim, what do you know about him?"

"Not much, Gustavo has been with the Fishers since I can remember. He's from somewhere in South America. Chile, Argentina, or maybe Brazil, I forget."

"I think he might be Brazilian. He speaks Portuguese," I said.

"I think you're right, it was Brazil. Gustavo is Mr. Fisher's manservant. He drives him, takes care of the yard, horses, everything. I was never close to him. He was nice, but hard to get to know."

"How did Laura get along with him?"

"She never said anything bad about him, but I don't think they were close."

"Bianca?" I asked.

"That's a different story, he had some pet foreign name for her. They were close."

"Does Gustavo know about the baby?"

"No, I'm sure of that. If he knew, I'm almost certain Mr. Fisher would know."

"The baby was born in May. That would be the same year Laura graduated, how could she hide that from Mr. Fisher?"

"When Laura knew she was pregnant she doubled her course load and graduated early. I told you Laura was brilliant, she could do anything. She had the baby at Med School in Georgia," Michelle said.

"Georgia? Bianca told me Florida. She also told me Laura had some grade problems and didn't graduate."

"Cape, Bianca is a bitch. Lying is just one of her many bad traits. I could name them all, that's part of the Fisher family history."

"We'll get into that later. Did Laura put the baby up for adoption in Georgia?"

"Yes, the child went to a foster family here in Georgia, then the family moved to Oklahoma."

"How do you know that?"

"I guess you assumed I was a nurse, you never asked me. I couldn't deal with it. Nursing pays well, but the cost is too high. I kept leaving pieces of my heart with each patient--it was too much for me. I've been in Social Services most of my career. I helped Laura with that information before she died."

"Do you know where the girl is now? What's her name?" I asked.

"Jana was her name when she was adopted. I do know she was removed from the foster parents' home while they were in Oklahoma, but then the trail grows cold. Oklahoma seals adoption records."

"How did you find out she was removed from the home, then?"

"Bureaucrats for the most part are a bane to productive society, but if you work from within it pays," Michelle said.

"That would mean?"

"From one bureaucrat to another, I guess you could call it professional courtesy."

"I see. So, Michelle, the bureaucrat obtained a favor from an Oklahoma bureaucrat in return for a favor?"

"Exactly."

"You said she left the foster family, do you know why?"

"The father molested her when she was six," Michelle said.

Jana's lineage became less the point; more important now was her right to innocence. The image of a terrified and confused child, curled up seeking safety from a world gone mad, saturated my thoughts. I gritted my teeth, and asked my next question, "Do you know who that bastard is, or where he is?"

"I know who he is, not where he is. If I did I would go out there and do the same thing you are thinking. Makes you sick, doesn't it?"

"Damn right. We need to find him, so I can molest his ass," I said.

"I'm with you, but I don't think he's in Oklahoma anymore. I'll find him. I just haven't put all my resources to work yet. I think he might have changed his name, but don't worry, I'll find him. He might know where Jana is."

"The will, Michelle, do you know anything about it. I wouldn't imagine Laura could have had a huge estate, she died so young."

"Wrong, Mr. Fisher left Laura a very large trust. It was in the millions way back then. There's no telling how much it is worth today. I'm not sure of this part. There's a rumor in Greenville that Mr. Fisher finally had enough of Bianca and gave Laura most of his money before Laura died. That's just a rumor, but you might want to check it out.

"If that's the case, we are talking about an enormous amount of money," I said. "How many heirs does Laura have?"

"That's the sad part, only one, Bianca. Nathan and Calis Fisher were only children, and that's not a rumor, that's a fact."

"The will can't be probated until Jana's twenty-fifth birthday. If Laura tried to find her
before she died, she has to be mentioned in the will. If she is and if she's found, Bianca's
status will change--Right down the totem pole for her."

"Ah--you mean from heir apparent to heir presumptive. Looks like we have until May 1, 2002 to see that justice is done or that bitch, Bianca, will be out of the townhouse, and into the Big House on the hill," Michelle said.

"What about Jana? If we're lucky enough to find her, will Mr. Fisher accept her?"

"I can't say. He's from the old school, I just don't know."

"Michelle, I think we might have hit a dead end here. The will without the codicil is useless. I don't think Bianca will be any help, since the information in the codicil can only hurt her. But how about Jim Rogers?"

"Cape, Jim Rogers loved Laura. He tried hard to make up for his mistake. Laura never forgave him, but they remained friends. He drew up her will."

"So he might be willing to help?"

"Cape, if Bianca wasn't in the picture I would say yes."

"He still loves Bianca then?"

"No, and she doesn't love him, but Jim Rogers is scared of Bianca. I don't know what she has on him, but you couldn't pay Jim Rogers to cross Bianca."

"Do you know Jim very well?" I asked.

"Sure, we all went to school together. Jim always thought a lot of me for not telling Laura it was Bianca. He wasn't happy that I told Laura he had cheated on her. But he was thankful I didn't tell all."

"Do you mind if I use your name?"

"No, but he won't tell you anything. I've asked."

"Okay, Michelle. We need the diary, since the codicil might be out of the equation. Good luck with your search."

"Keep trying, Cape, and if you need my help up your way I'm not afraid to fly. Anything I can do to help, I will."

"Michelle, I'm glad you said that. I have a favor to ask."

"Shoot."

"This has to be between you and me, okay?"

"You can trust me."

"It's not about Laura or Jana. It does concern my welfare, and someone else's. There's a woman in Charlotte…she's an old classmate of yours, Allison Moore. Remember her?"

"Sure, I remember Ally. God, I haven't thought of her in years, she was nice."

"Michelle, I want you to call her. Ask if she has talked to Joy, and no matter what the answer is tell her in the conversation that she needs to talk to Joy right away. Will you do that for me?"

"Cape, I haven't thought of Ally lately, but I know she's still married to W. Cronus Kress. I'm not sure I want to be a part of this. Not if it's what I think it is."

"It has nothing to do with a relationship. I trusted you enough to tell you about it. I want you to trust that I'm doing this for a good reason."

"I trust you, even if you don't have a good reputation at the Augusta Airport," Michelle said with a laugh.

"I don't know what you heard, but more than likely it's true. All I can say is I'm not the same person I was, I think…I hope…I've finally grown up."

"I'll call Ally, and I'll be sure not mention your name. You did want to warn me against that, didn't you?"

"Thanks, Michelle. I'll keep you posted."

I liked smart people, and Michelle was smart.

CHAPTER FIFTEEN

Fighting Two Battles from one Front.

My motel room in Greenville wasn't home, but it was convenient to the airport and the Fisher information source. Unlike Orlando, I avoided the pool and had taken to eating meals in my room. Other than missing Mex-a-peg, and my fish, solitary confinement wasn't too bad.

I made up two progress charts, one titled Jana, the other Ally, both were blank. I scribbled out a to do list and finished just as the phone rang.

"Cape, this Is Ally. I talked with Michelle. I guess that was code for me to call you, not Joy, right?"

"I was hoping you'd remember."

"It would be a lot easier if you'd let me write down the plan, but I understand the reason now."

"Yeah, no writing, no record--."

" No, that wasn't it. I'm beginning to think you flunked out of spy school and aviation was your second career choice," Ally said. "And by the way, should we be letting other people in on our plan?"

"You mean Michelle?"

"Yes."

"Michelle can be trusted, she likes you."

"Cape, liking a person is one thing. This is my life--and yours too, now. Don't you think it's a bit reckless?"

"Ally, we can't do this alone. Michelle is a good person, and she also provides me a direct link to you. I don't think people will buy you and Joy becoming fast friends, but at least you and Michelle were classmates. Where are you calling from, by the way?"

"The country club."

"That'll work…hey, I talked to the guy I told you about. Do you have a pen and paper handy?" I asked.

"Yes, and my secret decoder ring, I pulled it out of storage. I'll be careful with the information. One more question, when can I stop driving around two blocks? It's adding an awful lot of time to my trips."

"When my shoe stops ringing, but not a minute before….Are you ready to copy?"

"Is that more spy talk?" Ally asked.

"No, 'ready to copy' is aviation talk. This is spy talk….Ken Bateman, Private Investigator. He was a detective with the Wayne County Sheriff's Department, and a very good one. I guess that's why he went into business for himself."

"I think it is a good idea not to use a Charlotte detective--but we're not going to use this Ken guy to investigate Walter, right?"

"No, the only goods you have on Walter, are his affairs. But you don't have any proof. As you said, he hid it well in public. I thought we could use Ken as a consultant. You know, let him tell you how to gather information in your house. Who knows, he may be able to tell you how to find some better dirt on him," I said.

"Yes, but can we trust Mr. Bateman? You know money is a very persuasive tool. Except on airline pilots, money doesn't faze those guys. Well, at least one anyway."

"Yeah, us ex-airline pilots hate money. Heck, I've even gotten to the point I can almost live without the dirty stuff."

"I never said money was dirty. It comes in very handy sometimes," Ally said.

"I wouldn't know. Back to Ken. I've known Ken a long time. I taught him to fly when I was a flight instructor. There's a powerful bond between a student and a flight instructor--he's a fine person. His number is in the book, but don't call him from your house."

"I know I'm junior in this spy game, but give me more credit than that. Oh, before I forget, I've already had a little luck from my internal snooping," Ally said.

"Good, tell Ken what you've found, and I'm sorry about pulling rank on you. But if you feel the need to move up to the senior spy slot, it's yours."

"What do you mean?"

"Look, Ally, we're both amateurs, but we have to play a perfect game, no mistakes. If I come across like I've got it all figured out, I don't."

"Cape, I was just kidding, so far your plan is working just fine."

"I know, but if you think of something, don't hold back."

"I won't."

"Even if this turns out like we hope it does, you'll still be the former Mrs. Walter Cronus Kress. Can you deal with that?" I asked.

"It was never about the money or Walter, I told you that. Even if I get nothing from the divorce, I'll be fine. What worries me is that Walter won't stop, even after it's over. He takes great pride in not leaving his competitors standing. He'll stay after us even if we pull this off, and you may never fly again. Can you deal with that?"

"Haven't thought about it. How about your daughter?" I asked.

" I don't care if he destroys me. I just hope he doesn't find out about her."

"I take it you're close to her?"

"Not as close as I would like to be. She knows I paid for her education at Vassar. The same with the years of acting lessons. She's been my rock. She accepts that we can't have an open relationship. I suppose the best part is that she understands why. If the worst happens, we still have each other."

Ally Kress, in spite of her opulent surroundings, had spent many years in solitary confinement, I could see. I hoped my own sentence would be shorter.

"Cape, what happens to you?"

"I'm a pilot, so I don't even try to think about life without aviation. My grandfather always told me to be positive. I guess that's why I haven't come up with any options."

"I know one field in which you might excel."

"What?" I asked.

"Espionage."

"Funny, very funny…. Ally, you know people in high places, right?"

"I suppose you could say that."

"How about important people in Oklahoma?"

"I know the Governor on a first-name basis, if that helps."

"I'll let you know. Call me every couple of days," I said.

"I will. I look forward to our little chats."

"Be careful, Ally. Bye."

Ratings in aviation are earned after many hours of training and numerous tests. In order to prove proficiently, the aviator must take a federally monitored check ride. This process not only adds to the safety of the industry. Beyond that, the pilot who passes this final, federal test gains in confidence himself. Sometimes that confidence becomes extreme. Pilots can be cocky for that reason, and fighter pilots are the cockiest of all. I didn't come from the military side of aviation, though. At this moment, I wished I had.

I'm plenty cocky about flying a plane. I think I'm good at it. The spy business, as Ally put it, was another ballgame. But the game wouldn't start until the other team showed up. I assessed the two teams; ours was weak in all the positions.

Conversely, our opponent's roster was loaded with superstars and experience. This certainly wasn't the first time either of them had played this game. W. Cronus Kress could eat the likes of us for a mid-day snack, without getting indigestion. William Johnston, in spite of his Weeble Wobble looks, could smack one over the old legal fence at any time. Not to mention the resources, if that could be equated into home field advantage….Oh-man, the game would be a rout.

If Ally and I had a chance it was the element of surprise. A lot of praying and a little luck wouldn't hurt either. I thought of the 1969 Mets, the Miracle Mets. Miracles happen….

CHAPTER SIXTEEN

Finding Hidden Clues.

Greenville's rumor mill provided little insight into my search for Jana. Any hopes of finding her rested with two people, and neither of them were promising. Jim Rogers would be bound by client-attorney privilege and even if he wasn't, there was no reason for him to help. Bianca held more promise, but only slightly. If a family member had the codicil or the diary it had to be her, and finding them was the problem.

I didn't relish the thought of going to jail for burglary, so that left one option. I had to see Bianca again. Michelle's assessment of the hot doctor's sexual promiscuity made that choice more difficult.

How to see Bianca and not have sex depended on a malady I was cursed with as a kid, a condition that caused me embarrassment when I played sports in high school. I don't know the reason for it, but when I ingest salt tablets I puke. If I was still afflicted, gaining access to conduct my search would be safer.

I called Bianca and arranged a dinner date, and then stopped by a drug store on Greenville Boulevard to purchase the tablets. Thoughts of the voluptuous Bianca were beginning to weaken my resolve not to have sex, though. That's when I noticed the condom display at the checkout counter. "Let me have a pack of those condoms."

"Any particular style?" The clerk asked.

"Iron clad, if you have'em--Rhino skin if you don't."

If the salt tablets didn't work, maybe the Trojans would.

Dating wasn't on my agenda when I had packed for the trip to Greenville. Luckily I had a sports coat. A clotheshorse I wasn't, but I could pass for a suitor. When I arrived Bianca was standing at her door. "Cape, where's your car?"

"The Jag? It's at my house. I'm using the airport courtesy car."

The car was an old Greenville police cruiser. One of the doors had been replaced with a door of a different color, a typical courtesy car...ugly.

"Cape, you don't mind if I drive, do you?" Bianca asked.

"I don't know. I've become quite attached to this sled. I think the siren still works-- you want me to check?"

"I'll drive, no arguments."

While Bianca was busy negotiating the traffic, the strobes of light from the passing cars flirted with her sexy attributes. We rode in silence as I admired the woman I had promised to avoid. Limpid black almond shaped eyes pooled in lagoons nestled in her soft olive skin. Shadows cast from her chiseled cheeks and nose teased the light that shimmered from her moist lips. Her black knit dress, struggling to hide the curvature of her body, heightened my prurient thoughts. It was easy to understand how a man could surrender to her temptations. I tried to think unpleasant thoughts of her, but it was difficult.

Sure she had lied, but maybe she had lied for a good reason. She did promise Laura she wouldn't tell about the baby. As for the Jim Rogers affair, that could have been one of those youthful indiscretions we've all been guilty of at one time or another. Hell, could she have been misunderstood?

"Cape, you look like you're in deep thought. Please tell me you aren't thinking of more questions about Laura. I was hoping we had settled that."

"Actually, I was thinking about how beautiful you are," I said.

"That was a nice thing to say. Thank you."

"Bianca, if I asked someone that knew you what kind of person you are, what would they tell me?"

"I suppose we are talking about a hypothetical person?"

"Yeah."

"Male or female?" She asked.

"Would that make such a difference?"

"Cape, men and women are different. They can see the same thing and describe it completely opposite." She pulled the visor down and checked her makeup in the mirror. Satisfied she was perfect, Bianca finished her answer. " If this person is a man. He would see what you just saw, a beautiful woman."

"No, I didn't mean physically. I meant what would they say about you as a person. Good, bad, or no opinion?"

"From the man's prospective--he would say I am passionate, driven, intelligent, and sexy. Conversely, a woman would say, I'm cold, greedy, aloof, and a slut. I told you I've led my own life. There are things in life I want. I've never shied away from going after them."

"Such as?" I asked.

"Money, power, prestige." She looked at me for a reaction. " I could have said a little white house with the white picket fence. Because that's what you want to hear. It's what all men want to hear, but not what women want, not really."

"Assuming you have all men figured out," I said, "what do men want?"

"Simple, men like to control. Have you ever noticed men never give a gift?"

"I've got you there. I've given plenty of gifts to women, a small fortune's worth, as a matter of fact," I said with a smile.

"No, Cape, just like every other man, you've traded gifts, but never given one. It's not in the nature of a man to do that. There are always strings attached to the gifts. My father gave us money for getting good grades, my husband gave me jewelry but he expected me to hop into bed with him to pay for the gift. Sorry, but you aren't any different. You gave, but you expected something in return."

I thought about that and decided she was right. Something for nothing had never been an M.O. of mine. "Ok, maybe you're right, but come on, women do the same thing."

"Do they?"

Typical psychiatrist, reverting to questions to trap their intellectual prey. I was surprised she hadn't used the, How do you feel about that, question, always a winner. So I tried to avoid the trap with another question, "So you don't like gifts, is that what you're saying?"

"I'm saying I'm my own person, and I don't want anyone to give me something if I have to conform to certain expectations," Bianca said.

"I've seen where your family lives, and you don't strike me as someone who shunned the advantages. Which means you conformed."

"There were lots of advantages, but I rebelled. A birthright is just that, one shouldn't have to pay for it. Like I said, you pay for gifts, nothing is free. I have been constantly reminded of that my entire life."

"By your father?"

"My father, my ex-husband and some lovers I've had. I want to be my own woman. A woman who is born to or marries wealth will always be chattel. Have you ever known a woman like that, Cape?"

I thought of Ally. "Yes."

"Was she happy?"

"I don't think so."

"Then you see my reasoning?"

"Yeah, I do, but when your father dies that all changes, right?"

"Cape, my father uses his wealth much like a taskmaster uses a whip. If I were more like Laura, I could toe the line and avoid his threats of poverty. I'm not like that, I'm not a conformist. No matter what you think."

"So life at the Fisher mansion wasn't wonderful?"

"Hardly, and if you want to know the truth, I doubt my father will leave me one penny. I hate him for that. I've earned some inheritance for my years of suffering."

"What about Laura, did she feel the same way?"

"No, Laura, was taken care of very early in her life. She died before she could use it."

I wanted to ask the obvious question, but I didn't want to anger Bianca. "Did she leave her money to you?" It didn't work.

"Cape, I suspect…. No, I know you have read the will."

"How did you know that?"

"Greenville is a small town. People talk, especially about the Fisher fortune. Everyone at the courthouse knows you now. Oh, maybe not your name, but they know what you look like. You're not an original, Cape. Just one of many fortune hunters, and there have been many."

"I'm not a fortune hunter, how could I possibly hope to get anything Laura had?"

"Well, let me think of some of the ploys your predecessors have used. There was the one secretly married to her. One had a bogus unrecorded codicil, and one woman was a supposed jilted lover. I could go on, but you get the picture."

"You think I'm a fake?"

"Cape, a vision? That's your explanation for being here. Maybe you met my sister, and maybe you even slept with her. I can tell you this, though, you never had a child with her."

"You sound so certain. Certain that I'm a fake, and certain that I'm not the father, why?"

"Because, Cape, I know who the father is. Surprised?"

That was an understatement, but considering the source, probably an overstatement as well.

"Bianca, that may be so. If it is, I'd advise you to find the child and bring her home, because that's what I intend to do if I find her."

"You don't need to find her. We, her father and I, know where she is. You will ruin everything if you keep following up wild leads."

"How?"

"In this unrecorded codicil Laura left explicit instructions. She loved her child and I can assure you she is well taken care of financially. If my father finds out about the child, he'll see to it that she doesn't get a dime."

"Is your father really that big a bastard?"

"Total bastard, and a control freak."

Maybe the old man was so bad that not even Laura had wanted him to know about the child. But people change. My grandfather hadn't wanted me in the beginning, maybe Fisher could change, too?

"Why wait until her twenty-fifth birthday? Maybe she's already had troubles, troubles more stressful than living in a mansion." I wanted to tell Bianca what had happened to her niece. I wondered if she would have felt so burdened by her gifts of bribery if she knew Jana had been molested.

"How do you know it's her birthday? Who have you been talking to, Cape?"

"Nobody."

"Cape, on May 2, 2002, this child will be very happy, I can assure you."

"What's her name?"

"Nice try, but that's privileged information ."

"Bianca, I'll tell you what I am willing to do. If you can prove to me that what you say is true--I mean proof that will stand up to legal scrutiny, a legal and binding document that says Laura's child gets an heir's share of her estate, I'll stop the search."

"I can't do that. I made a promise to Laura, and I intend to keep it."

"You're the executrix--of course you can."

"Cape, let's just have dinner. We'll talk about this later. Okay?"

We went back to the Mess Café. Bianca and I had a little light conversation, then got back to the matters at hand.

"Cape, while you were snooping around in the Fisher background, I've done a little snooping of my own. You have serious trouble with the FAA. More than likely, you won't be a pilot much longer. You should have taken me up on my offer to let me bill you before you told me about the 'vision,' I believe you said? In light of the events that happened on 9-11, I wonder what the FAA would think about a pilot who has visions?
I would think that information would be well received. Especially if that information came from a doctor."

"Is that a threat, Bianca? If it is, let me assure you I have no false hopes of retaining my status as a pilot. You want to talk to the FAA, be my guest. You're dealing with a man who has nothing to lose. Threatening to take away something from a man like that is a losing proposition, don't you think?"

"Why are you so hell-bent on finding this child, and why do you think I don't have her best interests at heart? I might remind you, if it hadn't been for me, you never would have known about her," Bianca said.

I hadn't thought about that, but she had already given me the reason--so I wouldn't ask her father about Jana. I wondered whether the old man would hurt his own blood, blood of someone he loved dearly.

"Then why not let me see the codicil or let me know the girl is taken care of, what could it hurt?"

"God, Cape, to be an airline pilot, a man who's seen the world, you're not too bright, are you? Right now this child, woman, is safe. She has no idea what kind of wealth she's about to come into, nor does anyone else. If who she is or where she is becomes public knowledge, all of that will change. If you find her you will be putting her in danger, and I won't let that happen."

"You mean someone might kidnap her? Come on."

"If you read the papers or listen to the news, is that so hard for you to believe?" Bianca asked.

I hadn't thought about that. Maybe Michelle was wrong about Bianca, she could be telling the truth. But she also admitted to being greedy, as well as hungry for power and money. I would back off until I had more proof. The last thing I wanted to do was bring harm to Laura's child. "Okay you win. I won't stop searching for her, but I won't tell anyone who she is, fair enough?"

"I'd prefer that you stop looking for her altogether, but if this is the best deal I can get, I'll take it. One thing, will you stop trying to find her until after her birthday?"

"I will if you put in writing,--legally--that Laura's daughter gets a child's share. Then I'll stop."

"Cape, I stand to inherit a lot of money if things stay as they are. Laura was much more generous than my father is. You're not in this for the child. You're broke. I've checked your financial records. I'll pay you to stop searching. How much is fair?"

The real Bianca Jenkins had just shown up. I was more determined than ever to find out the reason for the change. One thing was certain, her niece's safety wasn't her primary concern. She had said as much herself. Bianca wasn't interested in gifts with strings attached. The only gifts that met her criteria were the ones she could give herself.

"Bianca, you're right. I'm broke, but whatever deal I make would have to be tied with the girl's right to her inheritance."

"She'll be taken care of, so will you, and so will I. What could be fairer? Everybody wins." Bianca squeezed my hand. "You're smarter than the others. It's good you stuck up for the child. If you hadn't, I couldn't have trusted you. Someone has to find her, why not you?"

Did she think I was really buying that? Somebody wasn't going to be taken care of in this deal. The only thing I was sure of was that it wouldn't be Bianca.

"Bianca, before we talk terms, who loses if we all win?"

"What difference does it make? You'll be a millionaire, and the girl will have more money than she can ever spend, I will, too. What does it matter who loses?"

"I don't guess it does, but humor me," I said.

"The East Carolina School of Medicine. They are one of the benefactors of the will, but I can change that before it's probated."

"How?"

"Trust me, the codicil will read as I want, that's all you need to know. Except for your payment. Had time to pick out a number?"

The figure didn't interest me. I already knew neither Jana nor I would never see a dime.

"Why don't you surprise me?"

"Two million dollars. That would solve your problems wouldn't it?" Bianca asked.

"How can you assure me that I would get paid?" The question was a waste. I already had that part figured out. My payment would be in Monopoly money or a bad check. I expected that, but Jana's payment had better be by certified check.

"I have a friend who is an attorney. I'll have him draw up a document stating what I have said. Of course, we need to keep this among the three of us. My father must not find out about the child or she loses, big time, and so do we. He's already given his money to that damn school, but this money is mine….Ours." Bianca raised her wineglass. "Partners?"

I clinked my water goblet to her wine glass. "Partners."

"You've finished eating, haven't you?"

"Yes."

"Good, let's go to my house and celebrate," Bianca suggested.

We would be celebrating for different reasons, Bianca for her victory, I for going back to her house. If I found nothing else out during our conversation, I had learned one thing. The codicil wasn't in Bianca's possession; if it were, it would already have been altered. No, the document was safe, for the moment anyway. Jim Rogers knew something about the codicil, but if he controlled it, Bianca would already have it. I was sure the diary had more clues. There had to be a reason for the key.

I felt for the salt tablets in my pocket. When Bianca turned into her parking space I popped three in my mouth. Instantly my saliva production increased, and I felt like a hungry dog standing in front of a butcher shop window. The same feeling I had had just before I puked playing sports. We walked in the door and I asked for the restroom. Two seconds later, and I was heaving my guts out.

"Cape, you're ill. Do you want me to call a doctor?"

"No, but do you mind if I lie down? I need to rest a minute."

Bianca led me to her bedroom and helped undress me, then unrobed and climbed into bed with me. A beautiful woman naked and I was platonic. I kept reminding myself of Michelle's description of Bianca. Each time an urge to touch her entered my mind, I popped another salt tablet from my pants on the floor. I spent the night shuttling from the bathroom to Bianca's bed.

Morning came, finally. I popped two more tablets and puked again. "Cape, why don't you stay here awhile. I have to go into the office, but I'll be back as soon as I can."

I pretended to be much sicker than I was. "Are you sure you don't mind?"

"No, of course not. If you don't feel better when I return, I'll take you by the hospital."

While Bianca dressed for work it occurred to me that I had never before watched a woman dress who I hadn't had sex with. There was something sensual about it. Bianca was magnificent. Her sculptured body was a testament to her workout ethic. Bodies like hers don't just happen. I felt around in my pocket for the Trojans, but before I found them she kissed me on the forehead and left for work. It was a nice gesture. If I hadn't known what was inside her heart, I could have fallen hard for Bianca.

The door closed, but I waited a few minutes before I started my search. There is something sinister about invading one's privacy. Particularly, someone you like, and in spite of Bianca's faults I almost liked her. If for no other reason than her honest male-female assessment of her passionate and cold attributes. The kiss on my forehead before she left only confused me more.

I began my search for the diary in Bianca's closets. When that proved fruitless, I moved on to her desk, kitchen, and garage, with the same futile results. Her bedroom yielded some sex toys, and a whip with leather cuffs. I pictured Bianca standing over her helpless prey demanding submission, but thankfully I had been spared that role.

I was down to one place left to search, her bathroom. I turned my focus there with little hope of finding anything. I started by moving some personal hygiene items in the bottom of her vanity. An old tube of lipstick rolled out of sight and through a roughly carved-out notch in the bottom of a shelf. I put my finger in the hole and lifted the shelf, then quickly removed the items on the shelf and removed the board. A file folder covered the bottom of the space. I lifted it out. At first I thought it might be a high-profile client's psychological file she had tucked away for confidential reasons until I read the name on the file folder tab--Jim Rogers. In the folder were numerous copies of canceled checks and a letter written on the personal stationary of James Howard Rogers, III. I put the letter aside and arranged the checks by date. The first check dated September 30, 1976, was in the amount of five hundred dollars. The last check dated September 30, 2001, was in the amount of twenty thousand dollars, and was stubbed for "professional services."

I read the letter:

Bianca, I feel so badly about what happened between us. I am older and should have known better. I don't know what happened to me that night. I wanted to stop myself, but the more I saw and felt you I had to have you. Now I'm afraid my passion has ruined everything between Laura and me. I have obtained a promise from Michelle. She will not tell Laura about us. I have lost Laura. I can only hope you can maintain your relationship with her. She loves you so much. The thought of you and I making love together would crush her. According to my dad, a girl under sixteen is a minor under North Carolina law. I didn't know I was breaking a law. As you know I hope to one day become a lawyer and then a judge like my father. If he finds out about this he will be so disappointed. Look at the lives I've hurt--Laura's, yours, my father's and even my own.

Please forgive me for taking advantage of your youth.

I want to do what is right. I can't remove that night from our lives.

I don't want you to have to go to your father for help. In case any problems arise from our union, pregnancy or medical, use the enclosed check to solve them. I know it isn't much but I can provide more if it is needed. We should cease any contact and keep this our secret. I feel so rotten I thought of ending my life, but my mother would die from grief. She is so proud of me and I have betrayed her as well. I hope you can put this behind you and lead a normal life.

Please forgive me.

The letter was signed Jim. I felt sorry for the guy. If Michelle was right the fault was Bianca's as much as Jim's. I turned my attention back to the checks and re-sorted them according to the stub remarks. September 30, 1986, was the first check stubbed for "professional services" the amount was ten thousand dollars. Unless I missed my guess, Bianca was blackmailing Jim Rogers. I stuffed the folder in my shirt.

I heard the door to the townhouse open. I quickly shoved the items back on the shelf. Before I could finish Bianca was in the bathroom with me. "What are you looking for, Cape?"

"Pepto-Bismol, I need something to settle my stomach."

"Poor baby, it's on the other side. I'll get it for you. I'm going to make you some soup, it will make you feel better."

I've never liked soup, but if Bianca wanted to make it I would have a few sips and leave. I needed a little more time to arrange the file in my shirt. "Ah, I hate to ask but can I have a moment alone?"

"Sure, I'll fix the soup. Extra rolls of toilet paper are on the top shelf."

Bianca left. I waited, then flushed the commode, re-arranged the file, and joined her in the kitchen.

"This is an herbal soup you'll feel better in no time," she said.

I stood behind her and watched as she prepared the soup. She wore a laced apron reminiscent of a sexy French maid's outfit I had seen in an old movie. The only things not sexy about her were the sheer latex gloves she wore. I wore the same gloves when I did preflights, at least we had something in common.

"Thanks, Bianca. You know, you wouldn't do half-bad in the little white house with the white picket fence."

"Forget it, Cape. I'm a sucker for sick loved ones, that's all."

Bianca watched as I sipped the soup. It wasn't that I didn't appreciate her efforts, but the soup tasted like shit. I couldn't eat much more or I would be puking without the salt tablets.

"I hate to ask, but do you have any root beer?"

"No. Why do you want root beer?" Bianca asked.

"My grandfather use to give it to me for an upset stomach. Would you run down to the C-mart and get me some. Please?"

"I told you I'm a sucker for sick loved ones, any particular brand?"

"Yeah, the one that's in the glass bottle without the screw-off cap, if they have it."

Bianca kissed me on the forehead again before she left.

My morning search had not only produced the letter. I had also peeled away a layer of her protective veneer. I was beginning to know her. I poured the remaining soup down the drain, washed the bowl, and made her bed.

"Well, looks like you've made a speedy recovery. What's that in your shirt?" she asked.

The outline of the file folder was visible in my shirt. "It's my flight plan and freight manifest."

"Have you ever heard of a briefcase?"

"That's for wussies, real men do it in their shirts." I thought of the whip and leather cuffs, Bianca would like that statement. It would also make me more of a challenge in case I needed to return.

"I suppose you have to leave?"

"Yeah, I need to be at the airport in ten minutes. Thanks for taking care of me."

"When will I see you again?"

"Soon," I said.

"I'll contact my friend the attorney and have the paper drawn up. You haven't changed your mind have you?"

"No Baby, we're still partners, right?"

"Yes, till the end. Bye, Cape."

I fired up the Lance and headed for Goldsboro to pick up a fresh change of clothes. The take off was normal, but just after I was airborne vertigo hit me. I was thankful to be in VFR conditions. My vision blurred and the instruments were hard to see. I fought to keep the plane level. The flight was only ten minutes, but it seemed more like an hour. I lined up on final for runway two-three at Goldsboro. The plane bounced to a landing and almost ran off the runway. I taxied to the ramp, flung the door open, and heaved. I couldn't make up my mind if it was from the salt tablets or the lingering odor of the skunk. Sarge met me at the plane.

"What the hell's wrong with you?"

"I'm sick, Sarge. Do you have anybody that can take the flight?"

"Yeah, I've got a kid that can handle it, but I need to check this plane before I let him fly it. That was a hard landing you just made, damn near a crash landing….Go to the doctor, you look like shit."

I wanted to go to the doctor. My body wanted me to go to the doctor. But I couldn't do it. At times like this I wished I had a family of some sort. Someone I could call and there would be no questions. "Sarge, do you think maybe you could run me by the doctor's office? I don't think I can drive."

"I'll call Betty, she can take you there. I need to get this freight on its way." Sarge paused and walked back to check on me. "Are you okay, son? You really don't look well."

Betty, Sarge's wife, was a heavy-set woman in her seventies and a saint. I waited in Sarge's office for Betty, but the smell of the skunk was making me sicker. I made it to a couch in the terminal, and faded in and out of consciousness, until I was awakened by an angelic voice.

"Cape, wake up, are you okay?"

I shook my head to clear the murky veil hanging over my face.

Betty drifted in from the fog. "I didn't think you were going to wake up. I thought you were dead."

We stopped several times before we arrived at the Doc in the Box off Berkley Boulevard. It would be embarrassing to tell the doctor about the little stunt I had pulled the night before. The doctor was a young woman, early thirties tops. I tried to make out her nametag, but my eyes wouldn't focus. "How long have you been ill, Mr. Thomas?"

"Since last night. I've been puking all night long."

"I think it's safe to assume that you are dehydrated. What did you have for dinner?"

I knew where she was heading, but this wasn't food poisoning. My illness was self-inflicted. I listed the items I had eaten. The oysters I had at the Mess became her focal point.

"Sounds like you may have picked up a bacteria from the shellfish. I 'll run a toxicology test and we'll see what turns up."

I knew she wanted to do a good job, but the test wasn't necessary. I looked at her nametag again, Dr. Eva Benson.

"Dr. Benson, I think if you can get me over this little episode it won't happen again."

"Giving up on shellfish, are we?"

"Yes," I lied. I loved oysters, I was giving up salt tablets.

"I can get you a prescription that will make you feel better, but I still think you need to run by the hospital just to make sure," she said.

I appreciated her concern, but had she known the truth, I didn't think she would have been in the mood to waste any more time on me. There were plenty of people in her office who were ill, and I doubted any of them had made themselves that way.

"If you could just get me that prescription, I'll be fine," I said.

"I'll note in your record that I did recommend the hospital."

I knew what she was doing. We call it C. Y. A. W. P, Cover Your Ass With Paper, in aviation. I nodded agreement with her strategy. I felt bad enough about taking up her time. I wanted even less to tie up busy hospital personnel. "Thanks, Dr. Benson, I appreciate it."

"Do you mind if I take a blood sample? I won't charge you for the test. I plan to specialize in toxicology."

"I guess you're just doing the Doc in the Box thing to help make ends meet, then?" I asked.

She smiled. "Something like that. My goal is to be a pathologist."

"Well, I wish you luck. No offense, but I hope we don't meet again after you become one."

"Same here, Mr. Thomas."

"Doctor, I don't think you'll find any earth-shattering revelations in my blood sample." Since salt is a fairly benign substance, I was sure the good doctor had seen worse.

"Oh, I don't expect to, I just want to verify my suspicions. We see a lot of shellfish poisoning here. Even with the medicine I prescribed, you will still have some nausea, I suggest you stay in bed until this passes."

"Thanks, Doc."

Betty drove me to the drugstore, then dropped me off at home. I stayed in bed most of the day. Dr. Benson was right. I was nauseated, but by that night I felt like my old self.

CHAPTER SEVENTEEN

Out of the Fire and into the Pressure Cooker.

Rays from the morning sun shot across the sky in bands of optimism. My search had finally become productive, and now blessed with good health I had a rare moment of invincibility. The phone rang and I reached over to the nightstand for it.

"Hello, Mr. Cape Thomas, please."

"Hello?"

My first thought was telemarketer, my next one was to hang up. "Yes it is, and I wouldn't be interested."

"Mr. Thomas, this is Bob Mitchell with BancEast. I need to talk with you, do you have a moment?"

There are three entities I can always make time for: The Internal Revenue Service, The FAA and The Bank. "Sure, Bob, what can I do for you?"

"Mr. Thomas, this concerns your loan at the bank for your airplane."

My partner and I had always made the payments on time. Bob was calling with a better offer. "Yeah, I know the rate is high. If you have something lower we might be interested," I said.

"The rate isn't the problem. With the bank's approval, your cosigner has removed himself from the note, I'm afraid you don't qualify for an $800,000 loan with your credit."

"Why would he do that?"

"You'll have to ask him. I understand the plane is no longer producing income, is that correct?"

"Not right now it's not, but I should have that straightened out in a few months, hopefully."

"I can appreciate future earnings, but we need to know how you intend to qualify for this loan at present," Bob stated.

No way could I qualify for the loan on my own, and I suspected Bob Mitchell knew that.

"I don't know that I can, but if I keep the payments up what difference does that make, Mr. Mitchell?" I asked.

"The used airplane market is off. Without your co-signer, we have an unsecured loan. The bank doesn't like to be in that situation. I'm afraid we will need additional collateral or we must call the note."

"How long do I have to correct this?"

"Thirty days, or you will be in default."

"What happens then?" I asked.

"The bank will start a proceeding to foreclose on your house and your retirement with AeroMax Airlines, both of which were used as collateral for the note. The plane will be sold and you will owe us the difference. When can we expect the money for the note?"

"I'll work on it, thirty days from when?"

"Thirty days from today, Mr. Thomas. Have a nice day."

Have a nice day--What the hell was that about?

Jack Hastings had been a friend for a long time, but unless he had a very good explanation our friendship was down to its last few seconds. I dialed his number in the same amount of time.

"Jack, this is Cape Thomas. Why did you remove yourself from the note? You said you would wait until I got this straightened out."

"Cape, things change. The market has been hot—but I had some bad picks. I needed to shore up some other things, I--."

"Bullshit, you never put money in the market. You said yourself that real estate never shrinks. Something doesn't--."

"Cape, I've dealt with this bank a long time. They insisted I get off the note or they would call some other loans I have. I don't know what's going on, but I can't be a partner with you anymore. I'm sorry, but I have to look out for my own interest."

"Well, thanks for nothing, Jack."

"Hey, old buddy, don't blame me. You've gotten on the wrong side of some very high placed people. I think you better sell the plane. I hope you understand, it's just business."

I did understand. The W. Cronus Kress team had just shown up, and the rulebook was the first victim.

I called Sarge to see if he could sell the plane. If anybody could it would be Sarge.

"Sarge, I need to sell my King Air, quickly. Do you know anybody that would take it?"

"Cape, you can't even give a turboprop away right now. Just hang on, the market will sort out in a few months. Everybody's into V L J's (Very Light Jets) right now."

"I don't have a few months, Sarge. I'll sell it cheap."

"Sport, I haven't had an offer on a prop plane in two months. The market has just dried up. You need to hold it."

"If you hear of anybody, keep me in mind. When's my next trip?" I asked.

"Son, I've got a little bad news for you.... I got a call from the FSDO office this morning. They've suspended your commercial ticket. I can't keep you on without it."

I thanked Sarge and hung up the phone. These guys play hard ball. Influence with the bank was one thing, but when you can move the government? Now that's power. I knew it would be a tough fight, and I thought it might be dirty, but I never expected it would be so one sided.

The phone rang again--Tom Butterfield, my attorney.

"Cape, this is Tom. I received a call from Johnston Ballard & Hearst. If you don't let them know something soon, they'll retract their offer. I need to deposit the check. It's your call, but I need to let them know something right away."

"I'll call you tomorrow with an answer."

"Do it by tomorrow, Cape, because I don't think you have much more time than that."

Tom hung up. I called Michelle. "Michelle, this is Cape, can you get the same message to Ally? I need to talk to her right away."

"Good morning to you, too, Cape."

"I'm sorry, Michelle. I apologize for calling you at work, but I really need to talk to Ally."

"How did things go in Greenville?"

I wasn't thinking about Greenville, Laura, or even Jana. W. Cronus Kress was dictating my thoughts and actions now.

"Michelle, I did find out some things, but I have some other things to take care of immediately. I'll call you back when I have more time, okay?"

"Cape, is everything okay? You sound like a man being measured for the gallows."

"Close, but think trophy case."

"A what?"

"Nothing. Contact Ally, please?"

"I will. I know you don't want to talk about Jana right now, but you should know. My bureaucratic information has dried up. Oklahoma is as far as I've gotten."

"Michelle, I might have some ideas on that, but right now I have my own problems. We'll talk later."

"Are you sure you want me to call Ally? Playing with W. Cronus Kress possessions can be dangerous."

"I can appreciate that, believe me, but I'm not playing with his possessions. I'm just trying to keep a few of my own. Call her, okay?"

I waited until lunch for Ally to call. While I waited, I thought about putting my house up for sale but the note would prevent my selling it. Finally at 1:30 p.m. Ally called.

"Hi, Spy Master."

"Ally, thanks for calling. Look we have to move our plans up. I've just had a broadside volley from the W. Cronus Kress juggernaut."

"What do you mean?"

"Ally, in less than an hour I've had a note called at the bank, lost my commercial ticket, and received a call from my attorney. The offer Johnston Ballard & Hearst tendered will be retracted if I don't sign on in a hurry."

"Which bank called your note?"

"BancEast. I'm sure it's in Walter's portfolio."

"Yes, it's a bank he and some others founded. My father is involved, too," Ally said.

"Thank Walter and your father for me."

"That's not fair, I'm on your side."

"I know, I'm sorry. I guess I just want someone to be mad at, I can't help it."

"How much is the note for, Cape?"

"It's a pittance in your circles. It's a lot of money in mine," I said.

"Don't put me in their camp. You're better than that. How much is the note for?"

"Eight hundred thousand dollars. I know that's about what Walter pays in club dues each year."

"Actually it's closer to a million, but who cares. Is the note in your name?" Ally asked.

"Yeah, mine and a guy named Jack Hastings. Well, I guess it's just in my name now. Why?"

"I could loan you the money."

"Ally, you are not going to be a wealthy woman much longer, keep your money."

"You know it's not unheard of for people to help one another. Haven't you ever been close to anyone or ever needed someone?"

"My grandfather. But he couldn't rub two nickels together, because he was always helping the unfortunate. Doing the Lord's work made him a poor man by anybody's standard. He was a hard man, but fair, and when he gave his word…" I thought of Jack Hastings. "Damn it….He kept it. I guess that's why I respected him."

"So your family can't help you."

"Ally, I don't have a family, and after today....Damn few friends."

"Your grandfather was a good man. You know what else, Cape? If he knew what you are doing to help me he would be proud of you. You don't think of yourself as a good person, but you are. I want to help for that reason. I owe you something and I want to help."

"It's called charity, Ally, and I don't need it. You don't owe me anything. I made this choice. Besides, if our plan doesn't work, I could never pay you back. Someone accused me of being a fake recently. I don't want you to feel that way about me. Keep your money, trust me, I'm not a good investment. I have thirty days, I think maybe I can work things out by then, but thanks for the offer.

"In the meantime, let's put our plan into action and see what happens. Did you talk to Ken Bateman, yet?"

"Yes, and he was most helpful. Is your next move to meet with William Johnston?"

"I don't see any choice. Looks like they've decided to start the game, and they definitely have the home field advantage."

"What do we have, Cape?"

"We have a chance to join a very select group. Have you ever heard of the immaculate reception, the Miracle Met's, or the 1983 N. C. State Wolfpack basketball team?"

"I don't know much about sports. I'm afraid I don't understand the analogy."

"We are the impossible dream with a one-in-a-million shot of overcoming impossible odds."

"That's it?" Ally asked.

"At least it's something, as the man said, 'Let's roll'--we can do this, Ally."

"Is this where I should say, Rah! Rah!"

"Loud and long. Call me tomorrow."

"RAH! RAH, my captain."

I had to put my plan into action, because one more unanswered volley from the Kress team and the game would be over.

I called Ken Bateman. "Ken, I need to see you. Will you be in your office?"

"Sure, Cape, come on by."

I jumped in my car and was in Ken's office in ten minutes.

"Ken, what these people are doing--is it legal?"

"Cape, it really borders on extortion. I don't know that you could prove it, though. They have set it up to look like you are doing a favor in return for a favor. I doubt they would cross that line."

"I have to meet with Johnston, any ideas?"

"Johnston will insulate Kress from any involvement. If you could get Kress involved, maybe the whole thing wouldn't be so convoluted. Anything short of that and Kress will deny any knowledge. I know you don't want to hear this. Mrs. Kress is my client. I'll do everything I can to protect her. You're my friend, and the way I see it, you don't have to have a dog in this fight. It's a marital problem let the courts work it out."

"Ken, I can't think of one reason why I should help Ally. Other than I like her, and she's innocent. If I don't do this, Johnston will just find someone else under Kress's thumb to set her up. I've been set up before, Ken, and I didn't like it. We're a team, you, Ally, and me. Let's start thinking in those terms. How can we win?"

"When are you meeting with Johnston?"

"I'm going to call him today. I suppose he will want to meet quickly. I need for you to come up with some gumshoe strategy," I said.

"Wear a wire. We might not be able to use any of it, but it couldn't hurt. Try and get Kress involved. He has political aspirations, so maybe you can get something that could embarrass him."

"What if Kress does show up, what does that mean?"

"If Kress shows up he figures the game is over," Ken said.

"Is it?"

"Probably, unless you can get something on them at the meeting."

"OK, wire me up, and wish me luck."

I called William Johnston. " Johnston, Cape Thomas, I'm ready to talk."

"Meet me in my office in Charlotte, be here by six."

I was right, the game would be played on their home field. Johnston wanted me to know he was in charge.

"I'll have to drive, so I might be a little late."

"Why not fly, Mr. Thomas?"

"I had a little problem with my pilot's license."

"Oh, that's right, I heard about that. No matter, I'm sure it will all be taken care of very soon, Mr. Thomas." I didn't like Johnston. When this was over win, lose, or draw, I was going to hit him.

The traffic was heavy going into Charlotte and I arrived at Johnston's office at 6:15. His receptionist was still there. "I'm Cape Thomas, I have an appointment with William Johnston." I'd be damned if I was going to call Johnston Mister.

"Wait here, I'll tell Mr. Johnston you're here."

If one had any doubts about this firm's wealth, they vanished once you entered the double glass doors etched with the Johnston Ballard & Hearst name. Johnston's office dripped with the accoutrements of success and money. Walnut paneled walls bordered by ten-inch wide crown molding supported a walnut ceiling. Strategically placed halogen beams highlighted original portraits and sculptures. Leather sofas and chairs sat on a solid hardwood floor covered by expensive rugs.

The receptionist returned. "Mr. Johnston will be with you shortly. Have you eaten yet, Mr. Thomas?"

"No."

"What would you like?"

"Whatever you have--candy, popcorn--anything's fine.."

"We have fois gras, roast duck, and leg of lamb."

I was already impressed. Johnston wanted to make sure I was very impressed.

"Do you have a sandwich?"

"Turkey, ham, or club?"

"Club," I decided.

"Would you prefer wine, coffee, or soda with that? We also have imported beer, if you would like?"

"Do you have water?" I asked.

"Bottled, Perrier, or tap?"

I ate my sandwich and eyed the casino-styled camera pods overhead. Detection equipment, I hadn't thought about that. What Ken had called a wire was nothing more than a voice activated tape recorder taped to my leg. My worries subsided. If the office had detection equipment, it was much too sophisticated to detect a low-tech tape recorder.

Johnston's assistant led me to his office at 7:00 p.m. There was no apology for the long wait. I was just hired help now, no more niceties. Johnston stood when I entered his office. I assumed he had stood to greet me, but I was wrong.

"Follow me," Johnston commanded.

I followed Johnston down the long corridor. We stopped in front of a door marked Conference Room, and he pushed the heavy wooden door open. I walked inside. The room was much like the front office--heavy wooden paneling and the same style of crown molding. One entire wall was glass and afforded a panoramic view of the Charlotte skyline. The opposing wall was covered with oil portraits of Johnston and two other men.

I assumed one was Mr. Ballard, and the other Mr. Hearst. In the center of the room was a solid mahogany conference table. Down each side of the table were twelve tufted leather chairs. Two similar armchairs sat at either end of the table. In one of the chairs sat a man in his late forties, early fifties. He was slightly built and balding, but his suit was tailored.

Johnston introduced us, "Cape Thomas, Mr. Walter Cronus Kress."

I hadn't expected W. Cronus Kress to be here. I hoped Ken's tape recorder was working and his prediction of the game being over was wrong.

"Mr. Kress, how do you do?"

W.Cronus Kress didn't stand to greet me, either. "Have a seat, Thomas. I offered you a favor. I am not used to waiting so long for a response. I take that to mean you've had doubts about accepting my generosity. If you have any thoughts of double-crossing me, let me assure you, Thomas, you will never fly again, not even an ultra light. Do we understand one another?"

W. Cronus Kress didn't mince words. He wanted to me to understand in no uncertain terms that he was the boss.

"I apologize for that, Mr. Kress. I've been busy."

"Well, I don't think you have that problem anymore, do you, Mr. Thomas?"

If I had any doubts at all about who was behind my recent troubles, they were erased immediately. "No I don't have that problem anymore, but you'll forgive me if I don't thank you for my little vacation."

W. Cronus Kress moved to the window and stared at the street below.

"Thomas, I don't care for smart asses. I particularly don't care for you. Step over here to the window." I complied with Walter's instructions.

"Do you see those little people down there, Thomas? They remind you of little bugs from way up here, don't they?"

"Yes."

"Let me explain the difference between you and me, Thomas. You see, when we go back down on the street below, those people will look like normal-sized people to you. To me, they will still be little bugs. If there is one of them that I chose not to like, I can crush them, just like a bug. I don't need a reason to justify why I would do something like that. I can do it simply because I want to do it. I will then go home, and have a good night's sleep. You see, Thomas, crushing bugs is my hobby, I relish it.

"You, on the other hand, don't have the balls to do something like that. I've known people like you before, Thomas. You pull for the underdog. Every now and then your long shot comes through for you. I only bet on winners. I don't suffer many losses that way. I expect to win. You hope to win. Hope, however, is a very fickle mistress, Thomas.

"I'm telling you this for a reason. I'm a winner. If you bet on me, you will be a winner, too. You bet against me, and you won't ever be able to afford to bet again."

"Mr. Kress, do you remember who won the 1969 World Series?"

"I'm not a fan of baseball, but it was the New York Mets. Miracle Met's, I believe they were called."

"Do you remember who won the 1970 World Series?"

"No, I told you I'm not a baseball fan."

"I don't know who won either Mr. Kress. They say everybody loves a winner. I suppose that's true, but everybody remembers the long shot."

"What is your point, Thomas?"

"I may not win as much as you do. But, I get to savor my victories much longer."

"Does this mean you intend to bet against me, Thomas?"

"No, I guess you were right. I don't have the balls to bet against you, Mr. Kress. You have a marked deck. I can't win."

"I don't know if I should be happy or sad, Thomas. I enjoy winning, but I was so looking forward to crushing you."

W. Cronus Kress turned to William Johnston. "It seems as if your beast is nothing more than a paper tiger, Bill. He's all yours, he won't give you any trouble, will you Thomas?"

"No." Not right now, not right here, but you son of a bitch, I'm a bug that bites.

"Just no, Thomas?"

"No, Mr. Kress, I won't be any more trouble." I won't be any less, either. Walter, you just earned yourself a butt-kicking along with old toad frog Johnston over there when this is over.

"You see, Bill, I told you Allison would pick us a loser."

"I never doubted you, Walter. Mr. Thomas isn't so tough on your turf. Thanks. I can handle it from here."

W. Cronus Kress left without speaking. I wanted to grab the little bastard and sling him across the table. But that wasn't the way to fight Walter Kress. If crushing people was his game, that was the game I wanted to play. Like my grandfather said, "Time and place, always choose your time and your place, son."

"OK, Thomas, let's get down to business." Johnston had gained some bravado I hadn't seen before. No more Mr. Thomas, I was just their whipping boy now.

"We need more photographs of you and Allison, or Ally baby, as you know her."

I wondered if Johnston would have had the balls to say that in the presence of W. Cronus Kress.

"Why can't I just commit perjury on the stand? Why do I have to meet Mrs. Kress again?" I wanted to restore Ally's honor since I couldn't defend her.

"Because, Thomas, I'm an officer of the court. I can't instruct you to commit perjury."

Shit, maybe Ken and I could edit that statement from the tape?

"You know Mrs. Kress won't have an affair with me. Isn't that the same thing?" I asked.

"With the pictures and your testimony we won't have to prove anything else. The burden of proof will fall on Ally baby. That's the beauty of a civil trial."

"My false testimony is all you'll have, that doesn't bother you, Johnston?"

"Well, Thomas, it's the best we can hope for. You're right, though, Ally baby won't have an affair with you. You're not her type, she more interested in Jungle Bunnies."

I wasn't just going kick his butt when this was over, I was going to beat the hell out of him.

"How do I know you won't double-cross me, Johnston?"

"To show good faith I'll get your Part 135 certificate back right away. If you are a good boy, after you make arrangements to meet Ally baby, I'll call the dogs off at the bank."

"You said you could get me back in the 747 at AeroMax. I can't take your word for that," I said, "Once I set up this fictitious affair with Mrs. Kress, I'm on my own, so we need something in writing." Please be working, tape recorder, I thought.

"We can't put anything in writing. You'll have to trust us," Johnston said.

"I don't think so. Bugs get really uncomfortable in a roomful of wingtips, Johnston. I'll need some assurances."

"Let me do a little thinking on this. Walter doesn't like paper.... Especially paper tigers." Johnston laughed, and left the room.

I found my way back to the lobby. "Good night, Mr. Thomas."

Well, at least the receptionist was nice. "Good night, ma'am."

CHAPTER EIGHTEEN

Losing a Friend and Finding a Lover.

I received two calls the day after my meeting with W. Cronus Kress. One of them was anticipated, if not expected. The FSDO office called to tell me their lawyers had met with my lawyers. It seemed that the FSDO in Florida had acted arbitrarily with regard to my Part 135 certificate. Effectively immediately my Part 135 was reinstated. The matter would be adjudicated in my upcoming hearing. There was no apology, and no compensation would be forthcoming for the period of time I was denied my Part 135. The FSDO office also informed me they were looking forward to meeting me again during my hearing. I took that to mean they weren't happy to be making the phone call.

The second phone call was totally unexpected, Bob Mitchell with BancEast called and thanked me profusely for paying off my eight-hundred-thousand dollar loan. He would send me the cancelled note same day delivery. Bob also wanted me to know that anytime I needed anything, anything at all, from BancEast I should just call. He personally would be happy to work with me. I thanked old Bob for the call, then told him where he could stick BancEast.

Johnston had told me if I was a good boy he would call the dogs off at the bank. He never mentioned paying the note off. I suspected I now had eight hundred thousand and one reasons to like Ally.

I sold my Jaguar and Suburban to Lee's Used Cars. I purchased an old mint-condition Cadillac convertible they had on the lot. I was relatively debt free. I would take every penny I made and pay Ally back.

I called Michelle. "Michelle, sorry about yesterday."

"That's okay, Cape, I hope everything worked out for you."

"Things are much better. I need to talk to Ally, but I need to talk to you first. I want to see you. I have a file I want show you. I think we might have a way to get the codicil."

"Hey, that's great. I've got a little good news, too. I have a friend that might be able to help us find Jana. I hope you don't mind, but I want her to be at our meeting."

"Are you sure she can help us?"

"I think maybe she can, but you decide after you meet her," Michelle said.

"When can we meet?"

"Tomorrow is good for us. How's that for you?"

"It works."

I called Sarge before he gave my job away. "Sarge this is Cape. I have my Part 135 back, but I still want to keep my job. It'll take a while before I book some flights, but I'll still have some duty hours to fill. I want to work every chance I get. I'll haul bodies, skunks, and anything else nobody wants."

"I can work that out. Sport, speaking of skunks. There is something in my office that smells to high heaven. I can't find where the smell is coming from. It smells an awful lot like you did when you returned from that skunk flight. I don't blame you if you did what I think you did. Just tell me where you hid that little stinking son of a bitch. I can't get my paper work done."

The words were those of a penitent man, and Sarge had suffered enough. "Sarge, look on top of the ceiling tiles in your office. I didn't put those clothes up there, but I saw who did."

"You lying bastard! I knew it was you. I told Betty it was you. I'll hire you back, Cape Thomas, but consider this fair warning. I'll get you back if it's the very last thing I do."

"Sarge, if you pay me back you'll be punishing an innocent man."

"That may be, but I can live with the mistake."

"Sarge, have you got freight going south?"

"I've got some medical equipment going to a hospital in Savannah, you want it?"

"If I pay for the fuel and plane, can I use it to go to Augusta?"

"Damn, Cape, you've been back on the job for less than five minutes, and you're already looking for benefits. Hell yeah, take it, use it like it's your plane.

Forget I'm in business to make a living. Sorry-ass pilots, never have met one that was worth a damn, and you're the sorriest of the lot."

"Thanks, Sarge. What time do I leave?"

"I told them the plane would be there by eight. Now if that conflicts with your beauty sleep, I can change the delivery time. I wouldn't want my prima donna to have to work on my schedule."

"I think I can be there by eight, it shouldn't effect my beauty sleep too much."

"Cape Thomas, you be on the lookout. I'm after your ass."

"Sarge, I didn't know you liked men. Does Betty know about this little fetish you have for men's asses?"

"Cape Thomas--Ah....Go to hell, damn pilots."

Sarge never got to pay me back. He died in his sleep that night. I didn't learn of his death until I landed in Savannah. I've never been emotional, never had much reason to be. When the owner of the FBO told me what had happened, I found a quiet spot in between the FBO and a museum on the field. There under the pines of the South Georgia town I remembered my friend.

When I was a kid hanging around the airport, Sarge never coddled me because I was Allen Thomas's son. Just the opposite, really. My first job with him was washing airplanes for flight time. I never washed the planes correctly, he could always find something wrong, but he always gave me flight time. Other student pilots trained to plus or minus 10 degrees in turns and 50 to 100 feet on altitude deviations. The old codger was tougher on me, my training was to airline standards 0 to 5 degrees and 0 to 50 on altitude. I got so good that I could even fly to those standards inverted, he never told me I was good. But few pilots ever passed through the Goldsboro Airport without hearing a story about the "Flyingest little stick and rudder SOB that's ever lived." And when it was time for professional training he made sure I went to the best school,

Emory-Riddle. Not because I deserved it, but because he didn't want me to, "Kill my fool self," doing stunts in old planes at his airport.

The first trip I made as a Captain on an AeroMax commuter, Sarge booked a round trip with me to Augusta and back to Charlotte. I asked him about that. His answer was what I had suspected. "Cape, you fooled these people at AeroMax into thinking you can fly, I know better. I figured I'd better ride along just in case you got the urge to loop this damn thing."

"What if I had?" I had asked.

" Well," Sarge had said, "That's why I came along, to knock the shit outta you."

Sarge was a lot like my grandfather. He didn't believe in giving gifts for Christmas, but each year in December he found something he didn't need. A new leather bomber jacket, that didn't fit. Or a new flight bag, some dumb-ass pilot mysteriously left in his office.

Ally was right, a good man was hard to find, and Sarge Bishop was a good man: a man that made a difference in a lot of peoples lives, including mine. He gave, and never asked for anything in return. I wouldn't miss the things he gave, but I would miss the hell out of the man that never gave them.

I landed in Augusta at nine. Michelle was there to meet me. "Why are your eyes so red, Cape?"

"I didn't sleep well."

"You look like you've been crying."

"It's just lack of sleep. I think the plane might have an exhaust leak. Where's your friend?" I asked.

"She's at my house. Let's go there, the kids are back in school, and my husband is at work. It'll be quieter than a restaurant."

"What about your job, don't you need to be at work?"

"I work two days a week from my home. I've also asked for some time off so I can spend it with my friend," Michelle said.

"Good, maybe you can come up to Greenville during your time off. I think I'm going to need you."

Michelle's house was huge, not your basic two-income house. Either Michelle had some old family money or she married well, very well. I walked in the door behind her. Her friend was sitting with her back to us. I walked toward her to introduce myself. She stood to face me. It was Ally. I didn't shake her hand, I grabbed her and hugged her tightly. She hugged me back. My body shook as I choked back the lump in my throat. Both women looked at me in surprise. Ally spoke softly, "Cape, what's wrong?"

"I lost an old friend this morning. I apologize, I didn't mean to hug you, I'm sorry. I shouldn't have done that."

"Do you want to talk about it?" Ally asked.

"I guess I should....Michelle, it's not what you think. I've never even held Ally's hand before, I don't know why I did that. Ally, I didn't mean to embarrass you."

Michelle spoke softly now, "Cape, you had a human moment. Sharing the pain helps ease it, are you--."

"I'm fine, it's hard, he was--." I picked up my flight bag and retrieved Bianca's file.

"Michelle, look this over, and see if you come to the same conclusion I did."

Ally moved by her side and held my arm. "It's okay to grieve, why don't you sit down?"

I nodded. "Bianca was everything you said she was, Michelle. Look at this."

I placed the open file on the table, and both women gathered around to look at it.

"Cape, where did you find this?" Michelle asked.

"I got it from Bianca's Townhouse." I explained how I did it. Not that it mattered, but I didn't want Ally or Michelle to think I had slept with Bianca.

"Well, this doesn't surprise me. I guess I can add one more infamous attribute to Bianca's character--blackmailer," Michelle said.

"There's more. She made me a deal that if I promised to work with her, she's going to have the codicil changed before it's probated."

"Cape, can she do that?" Michelle asked.

" What kind of offer did she make you?" Ally asked.

"Whoa, one at a time. Ally, how much do you know about this?"

"Michelle has told me everything. What kind of offer did she make you?"

I explained the situation as I knew it.

"She'll never give you two million dollars, Cape, and you can bet Jana won't get a dime either. I hope you don't believe that," Michelle said.

"I didn't, but that's not important. Finding the codicil is."

"What about the University, she can't take their money, can she?" Ally asked.

"Look, this is the way I see it. If she had the codicil, she would have already changed it. She wouldn't have a need to work with me. Wherever the document is, it's safe for the moment. Michelle, Jim Rogers, what kind of person is he?"

"Cape, I know what Jim Rogers did to Laura was wrong, but he's a fine person. You wouldn't believe how hard he tried to make things up to Laura. He would never let Bianca change that codicil, I know that. Besides, he was a judge once."

"Yeah, but you said you'd asked him about the will and he wouldn't tell you anything. If Bianca has this over his head, maybe he could be persuaded to do something he doesn't want to do?"

"What if we blackmail him, too?" Ally asked.

Michelle and I both looked at Ally. "What?"

"I don't mean for money, but maybe we could use this file to make him show the codicil," Ally said.

"I was thinking of that, too, but not in the terms of blackmail. Although I guess it's the same thing," I said. "I've looked the letter over. It's the original."

"What if Bianca has a copy? This letter will have less meaning to him if that's the case," Michelle said.

"I've had more time to think about this than you all have. If Bianca had a copy, she would have put that in this file. The original would be in a safer place. I don't think she has a copy. Look at the checks, she copied those before she cashed them. If copying was on her mind, she would have a copy of the letter with the checks, not the original."

"That makes sense," Michelle said. " What do you think, Ally?"

"I agree, but she's going to miss this file."

"I thought of that too, Ally, but I don't think she'll miss it until September. Look at the checks. All of them are dated in September," I said.

"Okay, we know we have to show it to Jim, but who does that?" Michelle asked.

" I will, but I want you to be with me when I do, Michelle. He'll be less threatened by you, he trusts you. You've kept his secret all these years even after Laura's death," I said.

Michelle received a text, so Ally and I waited in the family room while Michelle answered it. "I have to run to the office for a few minutes. Can you wait here until I get back? Oh, Cape, before I forget. Ally thinks she might be able to help us locate Jana. She also told me about what Walter is trying to do, so maybe I can help you with that stuff, too. We'll talk about that when I get back, bye."

Ally and I watched as Michelle backed the minivan down the driveway.

"I know what you did at the bank," I said, " I appreciate it, but I can't take your money."

"Cape, I didn't pay off the loan. You said you didn't want charity. I would never go against your wishes."

"I know you wouldn't, but if it's all the same to you, I want to sign the plane over to you. You don't have to send the paperwork in to the FAA. I can't sell the plane without the paperwork, so in effect, you will own the plane. Sarge says….Sarge said, the market would come back on planes in a few months. He knew things like that….The plane will be your collateral. If you need the money, sell it."

I handed her a bill of sale for the plane. "I was going to give it to Michelle to send to you."

"Cape, I don't care about the plane or the money. I do care about a man that won't show pain, I want to--."

"Pity me? I had a dose of that when I was a kid, I promised myself that would never happen to me again," I said.

"It wasn't pity, I just wanted a chance to show you that someone cared, is that so bad?"

"Ally, there were two people in this world who ever cared about me. My grandfather was one, and Sarge was the other. They were both tough men, hard as bullets. I loved them, but I never told either one of them that. I…I can't talk about this, if I do I'll start blubbering like a baby, sorry."

"Cape, you can't keep the world out, caring for people is part of life."

" Look, we have to talk about something else, I'm not good at this."

"You've never told anyone you loved them? Not even your mother and father?" Ally asked.

Like all kids I had followed the rules to protect my mother. I never stepped on a crack or killed a frog, since either would bring harm to my mother. The night before my parents died I was awakened by a nightmare; in retrospect, it was probably a premonition. In the dream my parents had left me, and I was alone. My mother had come into the room to comfort me, and I told her about the dream. She rubbed my head and sang a song until I calmed down. Before she left she kissed me on the head. "I love you, Mama," I told her.

"Why Cape, I do believe that's the first time you've ever told me that without my having to pull it out of you. It must be a sign, a good sign." My mother said.

It wasn't, and I never said those words again to my grandfather or anyone else.

"Cape, did you hear me?"

"Sorry, Ally….Yes, I told my mother that once…it wasn't a good idea."

"What about Grace, you told her you loved her, right?"

I shook my head.

"So that's why she didn't choose you, isn't it?"

"Yeah, Grace said that if I loved her, I would shout it from the highest mountain. But I couldn't take that chance, words are powerful."

We didn't talk for a while, but the silence wasn't awkward, just the opposite. Somewhere in the quietness we found each other.

"Cape, I came here to help, but I really came to tell you something. I care about you--"

"Ally, I--."

"You don't have to tell me you care about me, one day I'll understand why you can't, but I had to tell you that."

"I'm glad you said that, I--."

Michelle's phone rang her recorder answered the phone. It was Michelle. " Hi, guys, I picked us up some lunch, I'll be there in a sec."

Ally looked at me. "You were saying?"

I kissed Ally, long and hard. Then the door slammed on Michelle minivan.

"A man of action, I like that," Ally said. As she stepped away from me before Michelle made it into the house.

" Sorry, I hope you two found something to talk about while I was gone," Michelle said as she came in the door. "You know, you guys would make a good couple if things were different."

Ally and I both nodded, then smiled. " I need to get back to Goldsboro, Betty and Sarge were married for sixty years. She'll take this hard, and I need to be there with her," I said. "Michelle, do you mind if I shower before I leave? I want to go straight to Sarge's house when I land."

Michelle and I made arrangements to meet in Greenville the following day. We decided it was best if Ally didn't ride back to the airport with us. Michelle hugged me good-bye on the ramp. "Cape, just so you don't feel guilty. If I were a man I would want Ally, too. She reminds me of Laura, there's a goodness about her."

"What do you mean?"

"Oh, nothing. Did she tell you about her plan to call the Governor of Oklahoma?"

"No, I guess she forgot."

"I'm sure she had other things on her mind. She likes you, Cape."

"Did she tell you that?"

"She didn't have to, I'm a woman and women know these things."

"Michelle, thank you."

"For what?"

"For inviting your friend down," I said.

"No problem, it's always good to see old friends, and I'm sorry about your friend."

I ignored her offer to talk about Sarge. "So, do you think the Governor can get information that a top-notch bureaucrat, like yourself, can't?"

"Cape, Laura died of kidney failure. It may be an hereditary condition. If we can convince the powers that be of that, there's a chance we can get more information onJana. I've tried it from my angle. Ally will probably have more luck with the political angle. Keep your fingers crossed."

"I will, take care of yourself, I'll see you tomorrow. By the way, Michelle, what

does your husband do?"

"He's a doctor."

I thought of Linda and her search for a doctor. "Good for you."

"It's not what you think. I put Ray through medical school. We were childhood sweethearts."

"So, what was I thinking?" I asked.

"That I snagged a doctor, got the kids and the mansion."

I smiled again. "You did. You know the best part?"

"What's that?"

"You did it for the right reasons."

CHAPTER NINTEEN

Liberating a Lawyer.

The winds were favoring runway two-three at Goldsboro. I was on a northerly heading, and in a hurry. I announced my intentions over the unicom frequency and lined up for a straight in for runway five. No traffic acknowledged my call, nor did anyone inside the FBO. I taxied to the ramp and stared at the wreath of flowers hung on the front door of the terminal. The airport operated every day except for Christmas. I thought for a moment the schedule had changed because of the death, until I saw the line boy moving behind Sarge's desk. I walked inside the office. The skunk smell was gone, but the aroma of Sarge's cigars still lingered.

In the display case of the terminal where various pictures of Wayne County's industries were kept, was a familiar sight. Sarge's old World War II leather jacket was folded neatly at the bottom of the display case. I knew who had lovingly folded the jacket and placed it there. It was Betty's way of accepting Sarge as a memory. I knew it was something I would have to come to terms with, too. I thought of old man Fisher and how he only thought of Laura as living on her birthday. I wanted to think of Sarge as one of the living. I would see Betty tomorrow, and she would understand my change in plans. In the days ahead Sarge would become what he was, a memory.

I stopped by Ken Bateman's office to play the tape from my meeting with W. Cronus Kress. We both avoided talking about Sarge, it's a tradition in aviation. You lose a pilot and for a while you forget the event. To remember them only reminds you that it could have been you.

Ken and I listened to the entire tape. "Both of them are pricks. Did you hear anything that might incriminate them?" I asked.

Ken weighed his reply. "Cape, if there was a law against being a prick, I would leave right now for the D.A.'s office because these guys would be guilty. Unfortunately, it's still perfectly acceptable to be a prick in this country. Johnston is an officer of the court, and he flirts with a reprimand of some sort for not counseling you on committing perjury. Other than that, there's nothing here."

"How about abuse? Hell, I feel violated," I said.

"Cape, they aren't demanding payment from you. You are returning a favor for a favor. That's the way they would paint the picture. Now as for a case against you for committing perjury…that's one I could take to the D.A."

"So, all I've done is insure I'll get into more trouble than either one of the slimeballs will?"

"That's the way I see it."

"Damn, I knew I was in over my head. I'm trying to beat these guys at a game they invented," I said.

"You're angry because they humiliated you. Remember when you taught me to fly? You said no matter how hectic things get in an emergency, fly the airplane, do the job of the pilot. That's what you have to do now, fly the airplane."

"Since you remember that. Do you remember what I told you when you asked what happened if the engines quit and the wings fell off the plane?"

"I sure do. Bend over and kiss my ass good-bye."

"Well, Ken, I have this uncontrollable urge to pucker."

We laughed about the old days. I liked Ken. If he had wanted, he could have been an airline pilot. He was smart, a quick study, cool under pressure. Just like he was now.

"Cape, they aren't going to give anything away. How's Mrs. Kress doing on her project?"

"She said she's made a little headway. I didn't go into details with her. I figure you would be better at assessing her information."

" I think our focus should be on getting inside information. W. Cronus Kress has a formidable empire. So was the Roman Empire, but it crumbled from within, let's remember that," Ken said.

Ken was right, I was about to abdicate my position as top spy to Ally. If we had a chance, Ally was the key.

I called my answering service. A businessman in Greenville had booked a charter flight on the King Air. I would have only one day with Michelle in Greenville before I left. I made a list of things to do. My time would be limited from here on out. I needed to be as efficient as I could.

I ditched my plan of not going to see Betty. The charter from Greenville would cause me to miss Sarge's funeral. Betty had been around aviation for a long time, and she knew that missing holidays and special occasions was the norm; still I owed her an explanation.

Betty had accepted Sarge's death, and I think in a way her own. We talked about Sarge and the good old days, then she asked me to help her run the business. As much as I needed the money, I offered to help for free. Sarge had never asked me for payment for all the favors he had done for me. I wasn't about to ask Betty for any now.

I needed to check on my King Air before I left for my upcoming trip. Michelle and I agreed to meet at the Kinston Airport so we could ride together to Greenville

Michelle arrived at nine as promised. "Cape, I know Jim is busy, so I made us an appointment. We need to be there at ten."

We arrived ten minutes early for our appointment. Jim Rogers had a nice office, but it paled in comparison to the luxury accommodations of Johnston Ballard & Hearst. The receptionist was friendly and offered us something to eat or drink. I was curious. "What do you have?"

"We have bagels and cream cheese or fruit. We also have coffee or Pepsi, can I get you something?"

Michelle wanted a bagel, I asked for water. The receptionist disappeared into a small room that was a makeshift kitchen.

"You know, Michelle, the last time I was asked that question in a lawyer's office, the choices sounded more like a five-star restaurant."

Michelle was curious about the choices. I described them to her.

"Maybe next time we can go there. Ooh, fois gras, wouldn't that be good?"

"Personally, Michelle, I'd rather have the bagel."

The receptionist returned with Michelle's bagel on a small paper saucer with a dollop of cream cheese on the side. My room-temperature water was in a Styrofoam cup sans ice, but it was better than the chilled Perrier I had had in Charlotte.

At precisely ten o'clock the receptionist escorted us into James Howard Rogers, III's office. Jim Rogers hugged Michelle and shook my hand after Michelle introduced us.

"How are your folks, Michelle?"

Jim and Michelle caught up on each other's family then we got down to business. "So, Michelle, what brings you back to Greenville?" Michelle turned to look at me. I nodded for her to begin. Instead, she asked another personal question. "Jim, aren't you a judge?"

"I was, District Court Judge. As you know, it's an elected office. I'm afraid I'm not a very good candidate. I hope to be appointed to a federal judgeship. My chances are good, but we'll see," Jim said, smiling.

I couldn't imagine Jim Rogers not being a good candidate. He was tall, handsome and affable. I suspected there was another reason. I was fairly certain of what, or rather who, it was.

"I'm sure you were a good one, too, and I hope you are again," Michelle said.

"Well, you know how fickle voters can be. How can I be of service to you?"

Jim Rogers had the right stuff. Not being a good candidate still didn't register.

Michelle began, "Jim, I've asked you before about the unrecorded codicil pertaining to Laura's will--."

"Michelle, you already know the answer, I can't show it to you. I have a fiduciary responsibility to my client, even if she is dead."

"I know Laura told you about the child, but I don't think you know this. Before she died she asked me to help her find the baby."

"Michelle, that's not the way I understand it."

"You mean Bianca?"

"Yes, she told me Laura's last wishes were for the child to remain a secret."

"Jim, you and I both know Bianca can ask a lie. She's good at it. It comes naturally for her," Michelle said.

"We both know why you don't like Bianca." Jim Rogers looked at me and I suddenly wished I wasn't a party to this conversation.

"Then just tell me this. Is the child provided for in the will?"

"Even if I knew, I couldn't tell you. Sorry."

"You drew up the codicil, how could you not know?"

"Michelle, because you're an old friend, I will tell you this. I have never seen that codicil. I hired a paralegal from Goldsboro to come over to meet with Laura. She provided the information to the paralegal, then sealed the document at my request. It's here in my office but I swear to God that I have never seen it. I was too close to the situation, so I recused myself."

Michelle and I looked at one another--we needed a sidebar in legal terms.

"Excuse me, Mr. Thomas, I know your name, but who are you, a lawyer?" Jim asked.

"No, Mr. Rogers, I'm just a friend."

"Just a friend of whom, Michelle, Laura? What interest do you have in this?"

I couldn't justify dragging this out any longer. "Mr. Rogers, is Bianca Jenkins blackmailing you?"

"Hell, no. What would she have to blackmail me for? I don't know what you're talking about. Get out of my office." Michelle spoke quickly to calm Jim down. "Jim, we have reason to believe she might be coercing you."

"Michelle, you promised. You've told him, haven't you? Damn you! Damn you both."

"Jim, calm down. I'm going to tell you something, and I want you to listen." Still angry, Jim Rogers sat back in his chair. Michelle continued, "What Bianca told you is a lie. Laura wanted to find the baby. She never said, but I think she had almost gotten up the nerve to tell Mr. Fisher. We think Laura wanted this child to share in her estate. We also think Bianca is determined for that not to happen."

"What, pray tell, makes you think that? Give me one good reason."

It was my turn to talk. "I can do that, Mr. Rogers. Bianca offered me two million dollars to stop my search for this child. She offered to draw up a document stating the same. She also indicated that the codicil would be changed before the will was probated.

"If she hasn't already contacted you, I think she will. Of course, she may have someone else draw it up, after meeting with you. I don't think you would be willing to go along with her plan to change the codicil, either."

"Well, thank you for that vote of confidence, Mr. Thomas. But I'm not going along with your story, either. It's hearsay and…and I know who you are. You're the guy that's been at the courthouse looking at the will. Michelle, tell me you're not involved in this. This guy's a scam artist. He's after the money, don't you see?"

"No, Jim, you're wrong, he's just trying to make sure the will is probated like it should be," Michelle said.

"Good god, Michelle. I know you've been away from Greenville a long time, but this happens a lot. Your friend is a crook."

"I also found this, Mr. Rogers." I said as I removed the letter and checks from my flight bag and handed it to Jim Rogers.

"Mr. Rogers, I'm going to forget that you called me a crook. All of this is yours to keep no matter whether you help us or not. You made a mistake a long time ago. I think you've paid enough. We need your help, but the letter is not our leverage. We could have used it to maybe force your help. You loved Laura once, and you hurt her. I don't think you want to do that again. If you don't help us, that will be exactly what you are doing. Laura loved that child. Don't ask me how I know, but Laura Fisher needs your help."

Jim Rogers sat at his desk and held the letter like the Pope would hold the Holy Grail. He didn't speak for a few minutes. Finally he found his voice. " You're right, I never stopped loving Laura. I begged for her to forgive me, but

Laura was fragile. She entrusted me with her heart once, and I foolishly broke it. She could never find the courage to give me that chance again. She blessed me with her friendship, but that's as far as she could go. Bianca put my dreams, my hopes, and my aspirations on hold. She has controlled me ever since. Today, you have given everything back to me that bitch took away. I may be disbarred, but I won't hurt Laura again."

"Jim, I hope you don't mind if I call you that?" I asked.

"No please, Jim is fine, and I'm sorry I called you a crook earlier….How did you get this? I know Bianca wouldn't have given it to you."

"Jim, I want to be honest with you, but I can't answer that question. I think you know why I can't," I said.

"It wasn't a legal question, of course you can't answer it. It's just that I looked for this so long….Was it--."

"Once this is all settled, I'll answer your question, fair enough?" Jim nodded. "But I do have a question I would like to ask you, and I'll extend you the same courtesy. You don't have to answer it if you don't want to, I'll understand," I said.

"Ok, what's your question?"

"Has Bianca seen this codicil?"

Jim was slow to answer. Perhaps my question was legal in nature and one he couldn't respond to, I thought.

"Yes, she has, but she read it in this office. I put it back in the safe, she only read it. She had that right as the executrix."

"She didn't discuss it with you?" I asked.

"The only comment she made was that the child must be kept secret. I didn't want to discuss any of it, but she made that remark before I could stop her."

"Why wasn't she allowed to keep it?"

"My fiduciary duty to Laura. She made it perfectly clear the will was not to be probated before a certain date. Bianca knew I wouldn't breech that trust," Jim said.

"One more thing," I said, "I don't know the law, but wouldn't the statue of limitations for statutory rape have run out by now?"

"Yes, but the political ramifications have no expiration date. You see, when I ran for Judge and won, it incensed Bianca, because she couldn't stand for me to find happiness. She wanted me to understand that she controlled me. She threatened to make my letter public if I won the next election. The federal judgeship I told you about earlier? I would never have been able to accept it. Bianca has already told me that. I left my name in the running, but not for the judgeship. I would've had to turn the appointment down. My happiness would have been in knowing what could have been, not what would be."

Jim Rogers walked over to the office safe and pulled out the codicil, then donned his glasses. "If you all want to pull up a chair, I'll go over this document with you."

We went over the codicil, and Jim explained each section. Bianca was to have made every effort to find Jana. If she were unsuccessful, Laura's entire estate would become hers after Jana's twenty-fifth birthday. East Carolina University School of Medicine wasn't mentioned.

"I guess this explains why Bianca didn't insist on keeping the codicil. Once the May 1st date passed, there would be no need for the codicil to be changed," Jim said.

None of us was surprised by those revelations. Bianca had held true to her character. The difference now was that we had factual evidence instead of innuendo.

Jim Rogers finished and removed his glasses. "Is there anything else? If not, I'll ask you to excuse me, I have to visit an old acquaintance. After that I'm going to savor the moment."

I knew the old acquaintance as well as Michelle, did. I couldn't blame Jim for wanting to confront his jailer, but we needed time. " I know what you want to do. I can't blame--."

Michelle finished my thought, "Jim, we need to find Jana before you confront Bianca. She may know nothing, but she may be able to slow our search. Twenty-five years is a long time, can a few more weeks matter?"

Jim folded the letter and put it in his wallet. "I'm sorry, I wasn't thinking. Suddenly for the first time in a long time I felt like a whole man. I am a whole man." He patted the wallet that held the letter. "I understand, but when you call to let me know all is clear--that bitch will know I'm a man. What can I do to help? Surely you can use a lawyer."

"Jim, I think we have things in hand now. But the offer you just made? Does it pertain only to Laura's situation?"

I looked at Michelle after I asked the question. She nodded her approval.

"Cape, right?" Jim asked.

"Yeah."

"My offer is to help. You decide where and when."

"You may not feel that way when I mention this name," I said.

"Try me."

I obliged, "Johnston Ballard & Hearst. Still interested?"

"Well, I guess we jumped right to the top of the legal hierarchy. I'm just a country lawyer--."

"I know. They're a powerful firm with very powerful clients. I just thought I would ask," I said.

"You didn't let me finish, Cape."

"Sorry."

Jim continued, "As I was saying. I'm just a country lawyer, but my grandfather is a retired federal judge. My father is on the North Carolina Supreme Court, and since we're all friends here now.... You're looking at, as of May 2002, a newly appointed Federal Court Judge. I don't know what this is about, but tell Johnston Ballard & Hearst to bring it on, Cape."

Michelle and I said our good-byes to Jim, and promised to be in touch. Michelle spoke first, "Cape, you don't follow the script very well, do you?"

I smiled. "Guess not."

"We agreed to use that letter for leverage if we had to, but I'm glad you handled it your way. Where did that come from anyway?"

"Have you ever been backed in a corner?"

"I know what you mean, but I think that's more of a male thing."

"Maybe, but I have. I wanted to fight my way out and couldn't, because people were depending on me to remain calm. That's a hard thing for a man to do. When I saw Jim a little while ago, it reminded me of that. I didn't like it when it was being done to me. I didn't want him to have to feel the same way I did. I'm happy things turned out right. I'm happier knowing even if Jim refused, you would have been okay with that."

"Well, thank you, Cape. That was a compliment wasn't it?"

"Yeah."

"I thought so. Let's do lunch," Michelle said.

Michelle and I ate Chinese and discussed our next move.

"I know Laura's room will be locked. How am I supposed to get in there?" Michelle asked.

"You said it didn't have a padlock on it, right?"

"Right."

I reached into my flight bag and pulled an old plastic chart plotter. It was pliable enough to bend double, but firm enough to push a door lock back into the housing. I gave it to Michelle to look over. "Cape, you want me to draw an angle on something?"

"No, that's just what it looks like you should do with it. Michelle, what you hold in your hand is a key to half the FBO's in America."

"What are you talking about?"

"When you haul freight, most of the time the offices are locked. I've used this to get in plenty of places. All you have to do is slide it along the doorjamb and press it against the door latch. Press down firmly and turn the handle, it should pop right open."

"I don't believe you," Michelle said, leaning back in her chair.

"Go to the ladies' room and lock the door, I'll show you."

Michelle locked the door and I quickly popped it open.

"You go inside and lock the door, and let me try it," Michelle said.

I stepped inside the empty ladies' room and locked the door. Michelle slid the plotter in to the latch and opened the door. "I'll be. That's amazing."

An old lady in the hallway called us perverts as we passed by. "Great, that lady taught me in high school and she knows my mom. I'm glad she didn't recognize me," Michelle said.

"Michelle, is that you?" the old lady asked.

"Yes ma'am, Miz Potter, how are you?"

"I'm fine. Where are Ray and the children, errr….and why were you in the restroom with that man? He's after the Fisher fortune, you know."

"It's not what you think, Mrs. Potter. Cape was just showing me how to break into a room."

"I see, that's nice, dear. Good to see you,… I think."

We sat back down at our table, and Michelle whispered, "Mom will definitely want to go into more detail tonight. Mrs. Potter is bound to call her. Let's go before I lose my nerve."

Michelle had learned from a friend that Gustavo Jobim played golf every Friday from noon until five. I couldn't be sure but I had a gut feeling Gustavo was tied to Bianca's sudden appearance at the cemetery on the day I visited Laura. Gustavo's absence would also ensure that Michelle would have less chance of being detected in Laura's room.

She was certain she knew where to find the diary if Laura had kept one. It was one of the two hiding places she and Laura had used as kids to hide cigarettes and other contraband Laura had kept to herself. Mr. Fisher was looking forward to Michelle's visit. He had known her from childhood, and was still fond of her.

While Michelle was at the Fisher house, my job would be to check the second hiding place, the mausoleum at Forest Lawn. I knew the door would be locked. According to Michelle above the ledge over the doorway there should be a small alcove with a loose shelf at the bottom.

I didn't remember the exact width of the doorway, but with any luck at all I thought I might be able to reach through the locked door and above to the alcove. If that failed, I would have to return at night after the gatekeeper had left to break and enter, not an endeavor I was looking forward to.

I drove by the gatekeeper and parked near the mausoleum. The flowers I had placed in the sconce had wilted. I pressed against the wrought iron gate and grabbed for the top of the doorway. My fingers could reach the bottom of the shelf. Even if I were able to lift it, though, I wouldn't be able to put my hand inside. I surveyed the cemetery for something that would extend my reach. One of the plant urns at the entrance to the mausoleum should provide enough height, if I could move it. I grasped the urn and tried to pick it up, but the weight was too much. I pressed my back against a column and pushed the urn with my feet. I was able to move it only an inch or so. I repositioned myself and tried again. This time it moved twice as far. I was ready to attempt another push when the gatekeeper called out, "Do you mind if I ask you what you are doing?" I stood to address him. "I need to get into this building, I'm glad you happened by."

"Just why would you need to do that?"

It was dark in the back of the building, then I remembered the reason for my last trip to the mausoleum, my lighter. "I lost my lighter in here and I need to get it back." The gatekeeper pressed against the door and peered inside. "I don't see no lighter."

"It's in the rear of the building. I know it's there." The gatekeeper shielded his eyes and looked back in the building. "I'll get my flashlight and a rake." Good. That would give me time to put the lighter inside. "Why don't you just get the key?" I asked.

"I don't know that we have a key."

"How do you get inside if you don't have a key?"

"Why would I want to get inside?" he asked, looking at me strangely.

"To clean it, a funeral, I don't know?"

"Been here ten years, and nobody has asked me to clean it. The old man that comes here has a key, why don't you ask him?"

Because, Einstein, I don't think he would want me to be here.

"I don't want to bother Mr. Fisher just to get my lighter. Can't you see if you have a key?" I asked.

The gatekeeper headed off in the direction of the office. I tossed my lighter in the rear of the building, and waited for him to return.

He arrived with a box of old keys and a big-beam flashlight. After numerous attempts, one key slid into the lock. "I don't think I better do this without calling Mr. Fisher," he said with a scowl.

I didn't want that to happen. "Look, I don't want to bother Mr. Fisher. How about if I give you a hundred dollars, and you let me inside?"

"My job's worth more than that," he said.

I decided to come back after dark as much as I didn't want to do that. "Okay, fine, I'll run by Mr. Fisher's and pick up the key."

The gatekeeper didn't want to lose the hundred, but he wanted a little more incentive.

"You say that lady on the Lexus ain't your girlfriend or wife, right?"

"No."

"I'll do it for a hundred, and her phone number. You think I might have a shot at her?"

I thought about Bianca, and couldn't see why I would need to see her again. "Well, she did ask me who the hunk at the office was the other day."

"Likes younger men, does she?" he asked.

"I couldn't say, but I do have her card." I pulled my wallet out and removed Bianca's card and a hundred. "Here, you give her a call. Don't tell her I gave you the number."

The gatekeeper crammed the hundred in his pocket then read the card. "Hot damn, a doctor. Wonder if she'd go out with me?"

"I understand she's quite social," I said.

He nodded his head and grinned. The key clicked and the door was open. I stepped inside grabbed my lighter, and lifted the shelf on the alcove.

"Hey, what are you doing now?"

"Looking for my cigarettes," I said. I held the shelf up with one hand, and used the other to feel in the space under the shelf. I felt a package too small to be a diary. I pulled out an old pack of Marlboro cigarettes.

"Well, I be damn, I thought you was lying."

I smiled at the gatekeeper, then slid my hand the entire length and width of the space. A cellophane bag crackled to life as I pulled it from its hiding place. The gatekeeper looked at the bag. "Is that what I think it is?"

I opened the bag and smelled the pungent odor of marijuana. "Sure is, do you want it?"

The gatekeeper reached for the bag. "Hell, yeah, you won't tell nobody, will you?"

"Not if you don't tell where you got the number."

"You got yourself a deal, Mister."

Michelle and I both had the same luck, none. The ride back to Kinston started out in silence--we were both disappointed. "Cape, why do we need the diary if there is one?"

"I don't know, Michelle, I guess because we found the key in the locket. Maybe the key fits something else?"

"I looked at some diaries the other day. I'm fairly certain it's a diary key. Besides, Cape, if it's not a key to diary how do we find out what it fits?"

"I don't know."

I wondered why Michelle had access to Mr. Fisher. Especially since no one else did, including his daughter.

"Michelle, why does Mr. Fisher like you? Everyone says he has no friends. He told me he left the house only to visit Laura, doesn't sound like he cares about anybody."

"I practically lived there when Laura and I were kids. I guess he likes me because I was so close to Laura."

"Bianca said he demanded perfection from himself and his family. Was he a mean man, or is that another lie of Bianca's?"

"I don't mean to take up for Bianca. I can see where she would think that. But, back to your question. No, he wasn't mean, not to us anyway. Cape, if you could have known him before Laura died you would have seen a different person. He was tough, but nice in his own way."

"What changed him, Laura's death?" I asked.

"Partly, or mostly I guess. That bitch he married didn't help."

"Bianca's mother?"

"Yes, she hurt him. Laura never told me the whole story, but it wasn't good."

I knew about the affair. No need to go over old ground. "I wonder how he would feel if he knew he had a grandchild."

"I don't know, Cape. I don't want to hurt him because Laura didn't. Hard choice, isn't it. The old man or the child, so who do you protect?"

"I've thought about that, too. Laura made that choice, and I think she regretted it. If we find her… Jana, I'm going to introduce them. She's been without him this long if he rejects her. How much can it bother her?"

"That's one way to look at it. But how much would it bother him? We could destroy the only thing he has left," Michelle said.

"Yeah, I know, the memory of Laura, and maybe Jana's estate."

"Why do you say that?"

"Bianca says if Mr. Fisher finds out about Jana, she won't get a dime," I said.

"Let's assume that's just another one of her lies, so we burn that bridge when we cross it, right ?"

"Michelle, if we blow it by introducing Jana to the old man, remember we helped somebody, Jim Rogers. At least that's one good thing that's come out of this crazy vision."

"I can think of one more thing?"

"What's that?" I asked.

"Ally, she told me everything, Cape. She's like a schoolgirl talking about you, don't hurt her."

"I think I may have done that already."

"Cape, don't tell me that, because I won't feel the same way about you."

"I don't mean like that, Michelle. Ally makes me feel like I'm walking on air. I think about her all the time. What I did was stupid."

"Why would you say that?"

"Michelle, Ally and I are in a hell of a battle. I think I might have destroyed our best weapon."

"What's that, Cape?"

"The truth."

CHAPTER TWENTY

Let the Game Begin.

Michelle dropped me off at the Kinston Airport. I promised to call and make sure she arrived home safely. I took the King Air up for a test flight, and as expected the plane did well. Beech builds good airplanes. I called it a day, then headed home to do my flight plan and fill out the passenger manifest.

Checking my messages was becoming an adventure, so I plunged in. Dr. Benson had called with results from her toxicology test and wanted to go over a few things. I erased the message. No need to try and explain the high salt content I was sure she had discovered.

The second message was from William Johnston, no surprise there, either. Instead of erasing the message, I left it on the machine as a reminder.

What had happened in Augusta should have been a pleasant memory, but it wasn't. If W. Cronus Kress had gotten pictures of Ally and me, all of our plans would be useless. The kiss in Raleigh was innocent, and even with the photograph it could possibly be explained away. If one existed from Augusta--it would make a hell of an exhibit A. And after seeing the Raleigh pictures, anything was possible.

Our new relationship was a cruel paradox. Being with Ally had been the most wonderful experience of my life, and possibly the worst. The perfect game scenario was out the window; by being undisciplined, I had single-handedly given W.Cronus Kress everything he needed.

I looked at my watch, Michelle should be back in Augusta by now. I called, but there was no answer.

Then I made a call I was dreading.

"William Johnston speaking."

"I'm returning your call."

"Ah yes, the paper tiger. How are you, Tiger?" Johnston teased.

"I don't think you really give a shit how I'm doing. You called?"

"Well, now, where was that bravado when you met with Walter, Tiger?" Johnston asked.

I had plenty I wanted to tell William Johnston, but like Ken had said, I needed to fly the plane. "Did you come up with a solution to securing my services?"

"I think we've worked something out, Tiger. Do you want to go over it with little Tommy Butterfield?"

"If you don't mind, I'd rather have a friend of mine look over it, and don't call me Tiger," I said.

"And if I do?"

"And if you do, I'll be calling you Fat Ass Johnston."

"Very well….Mr. Thomas, but I demand the same courtesy."

"Okay, Mr. Johnston, but let's keep this short."

"Short it is… and it won't be in writing."

"Then I would like my friend to be there when you present the deal," I said.

"Why don't we arrange your meeting with Ally baby first, then we'll talk about the deal?"

"You know something, Fat Ass, if you call Mrs. Kress that one more time, I'm going to forget about the affair, and the FAA. I'm going straight down to Charlotte and kick your butt. I don't think Walter would be happy about that."

"Mr. Thomas, let me remind you I'm an Officer of the Court."

"Then act like it." There was a tension filled-pause.

Then Johnston continued, "As I was saying. First let's arrange the meeting between you and Mrs. Kress."

Johnston had blinked, and my little victory was intoxicating. Overplaying my hand wasn't what I needed to do, but why stop now?

"I like your tone a little better, but I don't like what you said. Our deal first, then the meeting with Mrs. Kress. I have to be out of town over the weekend. I'll be back Tuesday. If you don't hear any different from me, meet us in Greenville at 4:00 p.m. Tuesday afternoon."

"Where in Greenville?" Johnston asked.

"The law office of James Rogers."

"James Rogers? That name sounds familiar. Isn't he a Judge on the N.C. Supreme Court?" Johnston asked.

"That's his father."

"I see. 4:00 p. m. Tuesday. Until then, Mr. Thomas."

"Oh, and just so you know. I assume this insurance is in cash, or no deal," I said.

"That won't be a problem, Mr. Thomas, I can assure you."

Johnston and Kress were giving me the rope to hang myself. No deal I could conjure up would trip them. Something, or someone, would have to even up the odds, and Jim Rogers was my best chance. Tom Butterfield was a good man, but even Tom admitted his expertise was limited to aviation. Jim Rogers had a pedigree and a personal vendetta against an extortionist, just the background I needed. Johnston Ballard & Hearst might have practiced law in the U.S. Supreme Court like most attorneys practiced in district court, as Tom had said. Just the same, I was also sure they had cases pending in the N.C. Supreme Court as well.

William Johnston would accept Jim as the intermediary, because he couldn't afford to offend James Rogers II. Something would have to be put in escrow. I didn't want a check, considering W. Cronus Kress's connections to banking. The amount was the only thing I wasn't sure of. How hard I could push was another matter. It would have to be enough that even Walter Kress wouldn't want to double-cross me. Jim would have ideas on the amount that someone like Kress would be willing to pay. I would give him a heads-up on the meeting. That would also give him time to develop a strategy for the situation.

I called Michelle again, and this time she answered. "Hi, Michelle, I just called to make sure you arrived safely."

"I've been here a while, I had some errands to run."

"Have you talked to Ally?"

"Yes, she's back in Charlotte. She told me to tell you she missed you."

It had been along time since someone had missed me. It felt good.

"Tell her I miss her…. That might not be good to say over her phone, so just--."

"Don't worry, Cape. We pretend you're a puppy."

"A puppy?"

"Yes, when we say the puppy's name that means you."

"Code, I like it. What is this puppy's name, by the way?" I asked.

"Batman," Michelle said.

"Batman, why Batman?"

"You can't guess?"

"I don't have a clue, Michelle."

"Batman, The Caped Crusader. Get it? Caped for Cape."

"Cute, tell Batgirl I miss her."

"Oh, Cape, guess what else. Ally called some friends in Oklahoma. She hasn't found any more out about Jana yet, but she did find out the stepfather's name."

"What is it?"

"John Kirkland, and she also has his address and phone number."

"How the heck did she do that?" I asked.

"Once she located the right person, she found out that he's a registered sex offender. Seems like Mr. Kirkland didn't stop with Jana."

"That's great--that she found him, not that he--."

"I know what you mean," Michelle said.

"Do you want to call him, or do you want me to do it?" I asked.

"I'll call him. I won't say I'm from Georgia, but I'll use my social services title. Criminals don't particularly care about getting on the wrong side of the system once they are out."

"Good idea. I don't suppose you know if Ally's made any headway on inside information, do you?"

"Cape, Ally has been around you too long. I went with her to a Lowe's hardware store. She picked up a peephole. You know, like people use on the front door?"

"Why would she do that? Doesn't she already have a peephole in her door?"

"That's the good part, she told the guy she wanted to put one in her wall. He helped her get an adjustable one. Isn't that neat?"

"Michelle, you lost me. Why would she want a peephole in her wall?"

"Oh, I forgot to tell you. Walter and Ally don't share the same bedroom, but they have adjoining closets. Walter has a wall safe in his closet. Alley is putting the peephole in her closet wall so she can get the combination to Walter's safe when he opens it. Good idea, huh?"

"Yeah, unless he finds the hole."

"He has wallpaper in his closet. According to Ally the pattern hides it well."

I didn't have to abdicate my spy position to Ally, she had just taken it away.

"That's great, but what does she think she might find if she gets into the safe?"

"Ally thinks if Walter has anything to hide it's in the safe. He uses it quite often."

"Let's hope he has something to hide, we don't have much time left. I talked with William Johnston tonight. They want to get the game started, I'll keep you posted."

I commandeered one of Sarge's copilots to make the trip to Atlantic City for my client. Casinos are designed to dilute reality. There are no windows and no clocks. Without a chronograph, it's impossible to know if it's day or night. Money is replaced by chits or markers to complete the illusion. In times past I had gladly joined in the fantasy, but this time was different.

The boardwalk provided the reality I needed to fine-tune my plan. Like a chess player, I tried to think three moves ahead. All my moves ended with the same results, a loss by checkmate. I talked to Jim Rogers a few times, and his moves weren't any better than mine. Jim and I both decided that. Chance would make our next move. We would play it by ear. Chance, like Hope, was too fickle for W.Cronus Kress and William Johnston to bet on, they would be well prepared instead.

Ally had been with Walter a long time, long enough to subscribe to his philosophy of only betting on winners. Smart money plays with the house, losers bet the field. But every now and then the long shot comes through; even Walter had admitted that. What was it about me that had made Ally buck the odds?

I tried to think of the positive things Ally could see in me. I came up with a few minor things, then ran smack dab into reality. I was a man who for his whole life had thought only of himself, with the possible exception of Grace. Even with Grace I hadn't been willing to validate our relationship, much less fight for it. I hadn't left Grace with much of a choice. I was sure Jon had said he loved her a thousand times. But he had never cared for her--words were cheap, and I wondered if Grace realized that now. Still I had to give the guy some credit, even if he was an asshole. He had committed, put his heart in someone else's hand, and that took balls.

What could I offer Ally? If I didn't get back on with AeroMax or at least retain my Part 135, I would be unemployed. Aviation was the only field I knew. She would be getting an ex-airline pilot with no job potential. Plus the fact that I was in her debt for almost a million dollars.

W. Cronus Kress was a jerk, but his lineage was long and his wealth immense. Even with my job back at AeroMax, the best I could do was provide Ally with a middle-class living. The bright side? Ally might not have the same feeling I had for her, and with my track record there was good chance she never would.

We landed back at Kinston at 2 p.m. on Tuesday. By the time I finished my paperwork from the trip it was almost three. I headed to Jim's office in order to be there before William Johnston arrived. Jim felt it was best if we let Johnston put his plan on the table. We could always reject it.

Johnston arrived at four on the nose, and with him was a man I had never seen before. He was young, perhaps thirty, clean-cut, and well dressed. Except for the duffel bag he carried, he could have been on the pages of G.Q. magazine.

"Hi, Jim, good to finally meet you. I saw your father a few weeks ago, fine man, fine man. He's doing a good job on the court, we need more judges like him," Johnston said. He and Jim talked politics until we finally got down to business. I guess Johnston assumed I had not told Jim the entire arrangement, but he assumed wrong.

"Jim, we want to make sure that we hold up our end of the little arrangement with Mr. Thomas." He pointed at the duffel bag. "That's why I've brought this." The young guy placed the bag on Jim's desk. Johnston opened the bag. "I apologize for this, Jim, but your client insisted that we not use checks." Johnston opened the bag and dumped the contents onto Jim's desk. " One million dollars cash. Yours to keep, if Mr. Cape Allen Thomas doesn't get his job back with AeroMax and the rating required to hold that job. Provided, of course, that Mr. Walter Kress receives a divorce from Allison on the grounds of adultery. Which, by the way, your client has committed with Mrs. Kress." Johnston then directed a question to me, "Isn't that right, Mr. Thomas?"

Johnston was smug, smug enough to know about Augusta....No, if he knew, the offer would have never made it to the table. Lady Luck was still smiling, Johnston was just baiting the trap.

Freed from the confines of the duffel bag, the pile of cash on Jim's desk grew. A million dollars in cash was much more than I would have asked for. These guys used real money like kids used Monopoly money. I looked at Jim for his reaction. Outwardly, he was calm, but his enlarged pupils gave him away. As badly as I played poker, it was still hard to miss the telltale signs of a player impressed with the bet. Johnston's eyes darted from Jim's to mine. The money had served its purpose, we were impressed with the ante.

"Isn't that right, Mr. Thomas? You and Mrs. Kress have committed adultery?"

As hard as it was, I moved past the money and answered Johnston. " I guess that depends on how everything works out."

"Your client is very coy, Jim. That's why I included this affidavit that Mr. Thomas must sign before he receives his ratings from the FAA. Agreed?" Johnston asked.

" My client and I will discuss that in private and get back to you, William," Jim said.

Johnston kept pushing his product. "We don't want it to be a messy trial, Jim. We only need the pictures to verify the truth. We are certain Mrs. Kress will deny she has had an affair, even under oath. The truth of the matter is, Walter still loves Allison, dearly. He's the aggrieved party here, so don't make him suffer anymore Jim." Johnston reached into his briefcase. "Jim, I brought these to show you." Johnston laid the photographs of Ally and me on the desk. I scanned the photos to make sure he didn't have any from Augusta. Good, just the ones from Raleigh. Jim gave the photos a quick glance, then placed them back into the envelope.

"William, I'm not a judge. You don't have to prove your case to me. What assurance does my client have that you won't pressure the FAA into going back after him?"

"Good question, Jim. You're a chip off the old block, sharp just like your father. I've brought a signed affidavit from W. Cronus Kress and my firm stating just that. Plus you have my word on it, Jim."

Jim nodded. "Okay William, I'd like a little time alone with my client." Johnston nodded, then he and G.Q. left the room.

Jim spoke first. "Damn, Cape, for a million dollars they could have Mrs. Kress killed. I get the funny feeling they may know people who do those types of things."

"Maybe she has a story to tell they don't want told?"

"Cape, dead people don't tell tales."

That was the second time I had heard that old adage in as many weeks. I knew better. The dead had plenty to say, understanding them was the hard part.

"Ever think they'd bring that kind of cash?"

"Hell, no," Jim said.

“Me, either. What’d you think of the deal?”

“Cape, it’s not logical. Why would a man help someone get his rating back who has had an affair with his wife? Johnston must think I’m a fool. If you didn’t want your ratings so badly, I would have stopped this dog and pony show right there. But another thing bothered me more. Adultery has nothing to do with divorce law in North Carolina. Maybe it has some bearing on child custody, but this isn’t about infidelity. ”

“Well, other than that, what do you think?” I asked.

“They could exert force from other areas that wouldn’t violate the intent of these documents. I doubt they’re worth the paper they are written on, sorry.”

“You saw the pictures. Could they prove anything with those?” I asked.

“It depends on the jury. I’ve seen people lose cases with less evidence.”

“Jim, with or without this insurance, Ally will probably lose. I’ll lose with the FAA. I know it’s a false panacea, but it will buy me a little time. Let’s do the deal.”

“I just wanted to point out the obvious. If I were in your shoes I’d do the same thing.” Jim added, “How’s the search coming along for Jana, that was her name, wasn’t it?”

“It’s been about as fruitful as this deal, I think we might run out of time before we can find her.”

“Well, I wish I could tell you to look on the bright side,” Jim said.

“It’s just as well, I wouldn’t know where to find it.”

CHAPTER TWENTY ONE

Flight to Memphis

I stopped at Billie's DownTown Restaurant in Goldsboro and ate a light meal at the bar. Emma, the owner of Billie's, was taking advantage of some free time before the dinner crowd arrived. "Didn't see you at the funeral, Cape. Did you have a trip?"

"Yeah, Atlantic City, I just got in this afternoon."

Emma was one of those people who could settle a bar bet, tame a drunk, and burp a baby while holding a tray of drinks and never spill a drop. She knew people because she understood what made them work. I didn't want to talk about Sarge. Emma picked up on it and steered clear of the subject. " Can I buy you a drink?"

"Thanks." I asked for a Diet Coke, straight up in a shot glass, then knocked it back in one gulp.

"You call that a drink?"

"I do now," I said.

"Does it make you feel any better?"

"No, but it keeps my head clear."

"Well, hell, maybe I'd better try one of those. Give me one just like Cape had, Joe…But, make mine a double." Emma knocked her Coke back and turned the shot glass upside down. "Yeah, I see what you mean, a real eye opener."

Little things like that made Emma easy to talk to. "You're in the people business." I tapped my shot glass for a refill. " How do you handle people that like to crush people like a bug?"

"You mean people that are powerful enough to crush people like a bug?"

"Yeah, rich, powerful, and cruel as hell," I said.

"I think I'd just try to avoid them."

"What if that's not possible--how do you get to them?"

"Cape, people like that are bullies. You can be nice to them, and hope they change. If that doesn't work you can't back down. If they sense fear or weakness you're done."

"Have you ever known people like that to lose?" I asked.

"Sure."

"Really? How were they beaten?"

"They bumped into someone who was richer and more powerful."

"That's what I thought…. Thanks, for the drink," I told her and she handed me the half-empty can.

"It's still half-full--want to finish it off?"

"Naw, I better not. I'm driving."

When I called Michelle, the excitement in her voice was hard to miss. "Cape, I talked to John Kirkland."

"Did you find out where Jana is?"

"No, he's not talking, but he's still lying. Says he never adopted a child. He wanted me to think I had the wrong guy."

"Do you?" I asked.

"No, he's the guy. Ally confirmed that with the Oklahoma Attorney General."

"Where does he live?"

"Muscle Shoals, Alabama, and you'll never guess where he works."

"I give up."

"Northwest Alabama Regional Airport," Michelle said.

"Don't tell me he's a pilot?"

"No, he has his own business. He details airplanes."

Pilots are a wild bunch, but I liked to think they're decent. Michelle's statement let me keep that option open.

"What's he call his business?"

"Spit Shine Aviation Cleaning Service."

"I'm going to talk to him," I said.

"I don't think it will do you any good, he has a terrible memory."

"Well, Michelle, we'll just have to jar his memory. Have you talked to Ally?"

"Yes, she needs you to get a copy of Laura's death certificate. If the cause of death is kidney failure, she stands a good chance of being able to get around the sealed adoption records. Can you pick up a copy in Greenville tomorrow?"

"Call Jim Rogers, I'm sure he wouldn't mind doing that for you. If Jim doesn't have the time I'll get it, but I'm lost in the courthouse. Besides I won't be around tomorrow."

"Do you have another charter flight?"

"Yes, a trip to Muscle Shoals, Alabama. I need to get my King Air cleaned," I said.

"Kirkland is not worth it, he doesn't know anything. We don't have extra time for you to validate your manhood. You can whack his balls off after we find Jana, hell I'll help you, but right now we have other things to do."

Michelle was right. Nothing good would come from my making a trip to Muscle Shoals. Except maybe the satisfaction of knowing that Kirkland would suffer some pain. Not nearly as much as Jana had suffered, probably, but the retribution would have been good for my soul. "Michelle, how long was he in prison for, do you know?"

"He never went to prison for what he did to Jana. He did go for molesting another little girl. That's how he became a registered sex offender. Even though he changed his name the predator requirements stay with him."

"Not even one day?"

"No, his wife sided with him against Jana and Social Services. She was abused and afraid, Kirkland is a pretty nasty character."

"How can a guy like that run a business?" I asked.

"If you took your plane there to have is serviced by this guy you might find him charming. It's a trait of a pedophile. In Social Services, we like to say they are the nicest people you never want to meet."

"Michelle, you need to knock the rust off your nursing skills. When this is all over we're going to Muscle Shoals, Alabama. I'll hold him, and you surgically remove 'em."

"Now you're talking!"

"Has Ally had any luck on inside information?"

"She thinks she might have some information on Walter. She wants to talk with you about it."

"She needs to get the information to Ken Bateman. He'll know how to analyze it. I doubt that it will help us, but Ken will know for sure. Tell Ally I want to see her, but Walter and Johnston want me to set up the meeting between Ally and myself. We should stay apart until then," I said.

"She's one step ahead of you, Ken Bateman already has the information. Why don't you run by and have a look at it?"

"I will, I'll go by Ken's office first thing in the morning. How about the key, do you have any more ideas?"

"I'm sure the key in the locket fits a diary. Either Bianca or Mr. Fisher have it, but with our luck, it would be Bianca," Michelle said.

"Keep trying. I'll call you tomorrow. Tell Ally I miss her."

Ken was going over a ream of paper when I arrived at his office. "Cape, Mrs. Kress sent me a copy of this ledger. I'm out of my area here. I do divorce cases and employee thefts, I'm not an accountant."

"Why would Ally send you a ledger?"

"It came from Walter Kress's personal safe. She also said there were large sums of cash money in the safe."

"I could understand that. Remember the escrow money we talked about? They brought a duffel bag full of cash yesterday."

"How much was it, Cape?"

"One million dollars."

Ken let out a low whistle. "Whew, I guess the rich really are different than the rest of us."

"That's what I'm thinking, Ken. But what would be unusual about someone like Walter Kress having money and a ledger in the safe?"

"I don't know, Cape. Mrs. Kress seemed excited about it. Maybe she knows something we don't. Do you know an accountant who could make sense out of this information."

"No, but I know a lawyer who might."

I called Jim Rogers and set up an appointment. I had expected to have to wait a few days to see Jim. He wouldn't hear of it. I would have to drive fast to be there in time for our appointment.

Jim went over the ledger again and again. "Interesting, very interesting."

"Jim, what's so interesting? I'd be surprised if Walter didn't have a ledger. He's a banker."

"Cape, in the old days I would agree with you. Bankers use computers now even on a personal level. Why wouldn't Walter use Quicken or some accounting software to keep up with this information?"

"Maybe he's an old-fashion guy," I said.

"Security. He knows computers aren't failsafe. Let me show you something. These are large amounts of cash. The money comes into the ledger without check numbers on the income side, but look on the out going side. The debit side has check numbers. Take this line for example. Ten million comes in, no check number, on the debit side eight million goes out with a check number. Don't you find that strange?"

"I find it very strange."

"I thought you might get it," Jim said.

"I don't get it. I find it strange that a guy gets ten million dollars in one day. To me that's very strange."

"I've seen examples of this before. You know we have a fairly lucrative drug trade on our coast. When these drug guys get caught they claim indigence, and are then appointed an attorney by the state. I'm on the list of lawyers who represent those defendants. In addition to the drug evidence, there is usually a ledger or some type of document to keep track of the transactions. No matter how despicable we find these people to be, they are business people, in a sense. They need records," Jim said.

"What do they have to do with Walter? He's not a drug dealer."

"Cape, there is an enormous amount of money generated by the illicit sale of drugs. You wouldn't think that would be a problem. Remember the money William Johnston delivered? That was a million dollars in cash or ten thousand one-hundred-dollar bills.

Can you imagine how much space ten million dollars would take up even in hundreds? Now imagine how much space it would take up in smaller bills. Ten million dollars in twenty dollar bills would be five hundred thousand twenty-dollar bills."

"You think Walter is laundering money, drug money?" I asked.

"I don't know the source of the money, but look at the ledger. Ten million comes in no check number. Let's assume that's because it's cash. Eight million goes out by checks to various companies all of which, I'm sure, Walter has a hand in. Two million disappears to the bottom line of Walter's ledger."

"So Walter is charging twenty percent to turn bulky cash into checks you can easily handle," I said.

"Bingo, but that's not all. Some of the checks are stubbed consultant fees and legal fees. Then there are some entries for miscellaneous items."

"What does that mean?"

"Well, I can't be sure, but I suspect the legal fees are checks to Johnston Ballard and Hearst. It wouldn't surprise me if the D.C. firm uses some of the cash to buy Walter's political connections. If I'm right, not only is he cleaning dirty money, he's cooking the books and contribution laws. The checks show up as legitimate business deductions, they're tax deductible. Uncle Sam wouldn't like that, if it's true," Jim said.

"How do you prove this?"

"You see the initials by each entry? One set of initials on the income side, a different set on the debit side."

"Yeah, but how do you find out who they belong to? There must be thousands of people or entities with those initials," I said.

Jim ran his finger down the list. "There's another book or sheet somewhere in that safe. Can you contact Mrs. Kress?"

"In around-about way."

"Contact her. We need that codebook. The initials we have here should show up as names in the code book."

"Anything else?" I asked.

"Yeah, tell her to be careful. This isn't a game of he-said she-said anymore. While you do that I'm going to make a call to the cavalry," Jim said.

"I'll bite, who's the cavalry?

"The U. S. Treasury Department. I have a feeling that they would like to look at this information. Something is most foul in the Queen City, Cape."

I left Jim's office on a high. Today I wouldn't need an airplane to get above the clouds, and I could thank old crooked Kress for the updraft.

I called Joy to contact Ally because she was closer. If Ally's phone was tapped the code book conversation would set off alarms. Joy could meet Ally at the club.

My cell phone rang, it was Michelle. "Cape, Ally called. She has the name of the family Jana was last adopted by, can you write this down?"

"Sure. Hold on, let me pull off the road."

I grabbed an old envelope from the pocket of the vintage Cadillac and prepared to write. My hands trembled as I waited for Michelle to give me the information.

"Mr. & Mrs. Sebastian Smith, 100 Dawson's Circle, Memphis, Tennessee. Do you want their number?"

Michelle gave me the number. I promised to call as soon as I found something out.

I headed straight for Kinston and my King Air. Sarge's Lance would have been much cheaper to fly. But I wasn't in a thrifty mood today, I wanted speed, cost be damned. I filed for flight-level two zero, or twenty thousand feet. As is usual on east to west flights, I would be bucking a head wind. Forty knots on the nose. I should still make Memphis in four hours. Memphis Center cleared me to ten thousand feet, and then handed me off to Memphis Approach Control. I was treated with a beautiful view of Memphis as I maneuvered for the initial approach fix for the ILS runway nine.

The approach brought me over the Mississippi River. I could see tugboats churning against the river's current pushing long rows of barges. The ribbons of interstate highways and main thoroughfares were crowded with afternoon traffic. I decided to wait at the SegFlight FBO until the traffic cleared before beginning my drive to the Smiths' house. I called Mr. & Mrs. Sebastian Smith. We agreed I would meet them at their house at seven. I followed the directions they had given me and arrived just after seven.

The house was a ranch style split-level, with a fenced-in back yard. The Smiths were a couple in their late fifties or early sixties. I wondered why they had adopted Jana at such a late age. I also knew she hadn't lived with them in five years. The Smiths welcomed me in and offered me coffee. We chatted about the weather and sports. I noticed pictures on the wall of their living room of a beautiful girl in a cheerleader's outfit. "Is this Jana?"

"No that's our biological daughter, Carmen."

"Beautiful girl, I know you are proud of her."

"Yes, Mr. Thomas, we were proud of her. She died shortly after those pictures were taken."

"God, that's terrible, I'm sorry to hear that."

"She was killed by a drunk driver. You don't drink, do you, Mr. Thomas?"

"No." For the first time since I had quit drinking, I didn't feel the need to explain my choice.

"Good, we used to drink, but after Carmen's death, we quit."

"How old was she when she died?"

"She had turned just sixteen, we bought her a car for her birthday."

That had been a long time ago but the sadness still remained, neither time nor anything I could say would ever change that. I waited as the Smiths looked at the pictures. "How old was Jana when you adopted her?"

"She was almost sixteen. We were the fourth family to have Jana. Did you know that, Mr. Thomas?"

"No, to be honest with you, I don't know much about Jana at all?"

"You mentioned her mother was trying to find her before she died? I imagine she was young and in financial trouble when she gave Jana up?"

I hated to lie to this couple, but Bianca, as bad as she was, had made sense. No need to call attention to Jana. "Yes, I'm sure she was, but I think she loved her daughter very much."

"We thought you might be a friend of the family?" Mrs. Smith asked with an air of suspicion.

"Friend, of a friend of the family might be a better way to describe me."

They nodded. I noticed Mr. Smith looking at his watch. I didn't want to impose any longer than necessary. "I don't want to take up a lot of your time. If I could just ask you a few questions?"

Mrs. Smith spoke next, "Mr. Thomas, we aren't in a hurry. Sebastian didn't look at his watch to clue you that it was time to leave. He worked for the railroad for thirty-five years. It's an old habit. I've tried to break him of it, but it's no use."

Mr. Smith had a question, "What line of work are you in, Mr. Thomas?"

"I'm in aviation. I was a captain for AeroMax Airlines."

Mr. Smith smiled. "You guys beat us out of the passenger business, but we can still beat you in the freight department."

I liked the Smiths. You could tell they were good and decent people. I looked at the pictures on the wall again. I could see why Carmen would cheerlead, but there were other pictures of her playing softball. I noticed Mr. Smith and thought of his statement. He was a competitor, probably an ex-jock. I had to get him involved in the conversation that had been pleasant but uninformative so far. "I bet you played sports, Mr. Smith?"

"How did you know?"

"Just a guess, am I right?"

"I was a middle linebacker for the Vol's 1959 to 1962. Good guess. But you didn't come all this way to talk football?"

"No, you're right. I was just curious. Why did Jana leave? You seem like a nice couple to me."

Mrs. Smith replied. "I'm afraid that was our fault. Carmen had been dead about five years when we found Jana. She and Carmen looked very similar. I've had a lot of time to think about this. We didn't accept Jana for who she was. We tried to make her into Carmen."

"I see."

"I know you think we're terrible. To be honest, I don't think either of us realized it until it was too late," Mrs. Smith said.

"You don't have a picture of Jana, do you?"

"I thought you might ask that question, Mr. Thomas. I have some pictures for you to look over."

Mrs. Smith handed me a thin picture album. I opened it. The first picture in the book was what must have been Jana's senior high school picture. Her image was the same image I had burned into my mind of the woman on my deck. Except for the hair color, Laura and Jana looked like twins.

"You look at her as if you know her, do you?"

"No, it's just that she looks like her mother. What type of person was Jana?"

"She was a sweet person, but very reserved. She and I got along well, but she never seemed to care for Sebastian. I don't know the reason for that, he tried so hard to be close to her," Mrs. Smith said.

"She just left, no explanations?"

"Jana had a beautiful voice. The Glee Club was the only extracurricular activity she participated in during high school. She wanted to sing. We wanted her to go to college."

Mr. Smith spoke up. "University of Tennessee, of course."

Mrs. Smith smiled and continued. "We didn't argue about it or anything. One day just after her eighteenth birthday, she left. We received a few postcards and letters, but after a while they stopped. It became painfully clear that she didn't want us in her life."

"When was the last time you heard from her?" I asked.

"Letters or cards, maybe four years ago. I would give them to you, but they won't help you find her."

"Why do you say that?"

"There's no return address on them. As I said she didn't want us to be a part of her life. I'm afraid she knew we would try and find her," Mrs. Smith said.

"Thanks for your help. Does she use Smith as her last name?"

"I would suppose so."

"No offense, but that really narrows my search a lot." I thought of how many Smiths there were just in the Memphis phone book.

"I know we haven't been very helpful, perhaps this will help in some way? This letter came for her about three years ago." Mrs. Smith handed me a letter. "I never opened it. I thought she might come back one day, and I would give it to her."

The letter was addressed to Jana Smith, Personal and Confidential. The return address was The Dix-E-land Music Company, Nashville, Tennessee. "Do you mind if I keep this?"

"No, by all means keep it. I also had duplicates of her pictures made. If you do find her, Mr. Thomas, ask her to call. We still care about her. Maybe we could at least explain our mistakes."

CHAPTER TWENTY TWO

Address on Topsail Island.

I decided to stay in Memphis and leave early the next morning for Nashville. The hotel nearest the Memphis Airport was the Radisson Inn, a familiar haunt for me. AeroMax had used this inn for its close proximity to the airport. My preference for the site was steeped more in nostalgia than practicality. The Radisson had been the first place Grace and I had slept together. I even remembered the room number, 108. Back then hotels had keys. Grace had taken the key as a memento. Somewhere in a box labeled mistakes, I was sure she still had it.

I plugged in the coffeepot, filed my flight plan for the next day, then turned my attention to the object responsible for the trip. The handwritten letter addressed to Jana was an invitation to cut a demo record for Dix-E-land Music Company, and Tate Harris, President had signed it. Something told me the record hadn't gone platinum, but if I could find a copy, she would have one more sale.

Wisps of scattered ground fog rolled off my wingtips as I lifted from the runway and banked toward Music City. Easterly winds at altitude shorten the flight and I landed just as Nashville was waking up. SegFlight FBO hooked me up with a rental car and within thirty minutes I had located the Dix-E-land Music Company off Music Row.

Nothing about the dilapidated brick building screamed music industry icon. A patch of mishmash bricks covered what had once been a freight door. Windows along the front of the building had been replaced by bricks set in the same haphazard manner. A wooden door protected by a metal security gate served as the main entrance.

Any illusions about the success of Dix-E-Land Music Company faded as I entered the building. The lobby area floor was covered with a well-worn beige carpet. Sections of a faux mural that passed for wallpaper clung precariously to the wall. Gaps in the seams of the paper had peeled away to revealed dingy orange paint underneath. An overweight woman in a receptionist chair was engaged in hand-to-hand combat with the retreating hemline of her clingy red dress. Tired of the skirmish to maintain her dignity, the woman grabbed the dress with both hands and jerked so hard she knocked over a plastic flower arrangement that sat on her stained plywood desk.

Beyond this battlefield of futility lay the waiting room, bare except for five ladder back chairs with woven cane bottoms. Each chair was occupied by what I supposed were aspiring artists.

I listened as the size 24 woman in the size 14 dress explained the Dix-E-land Music Company policy to a prospective client. The policy required a one-hundred-dollar deposit for a consultation with, Mr. Harris. For this fee, Mr. Harris would evaluate the client's talent. If the client was good enough, she would receive an invitation to cut a demo tape, which required a one-time five-hundred-dollar charge. I suspected Roseanne, singing her rendition of the Star-Spangled Banner, could have easily passed the vocalist aptitude test Mr. Harris conducted. The letter Jana received was a con. The only product Dix-E-land Music was selling was a long-shot dream.

I didn't want to wait in the lobby, and I wasn't going to pay the fees. "Hi, I'm an old friend of Tate's, I'll just be a minute." I started for the door labeled Tate Harris.

"I'm sorry, you can't go in there, Mr. Harris is conducting an interview."

I flicked the receptionist a casual wave. "It's fine, Tate and I go back a long time."

I pushed the door open. A young girl barely in her teens turned to look at me. Her blouse was opened and her breasts were partially exposed. I nodded to the girl then looked at Tate Harris, a man in his early fifties dressed like a much younger man. His shirt was unbuttoned at the top and a heavy gold chain hung from his chicken-sized neck. Harris's body had the tone and pallor of an underworked galley slave.

The girl opened her blouse, fully exposing her breasts. "Do I have the body to be a dancer, Mr. Harris? My breast will grow some more, mama had big breast. I really need the five hundred dollars, I'll dance real good. I know I can sing, I just need a chance."

Harris's eyes locked on to the girl's breasts. With his eyes still on the girl Tate Harris addressed me, "You can wait your turn. I haven't finished this interview yet."

"I'm not here for an interview. I need to ask you a question," I said.

The girl wanted an answer to her question. "Are my breast nice enough?" Her accent was thick southern Appalachia, chockfull of extra syllables.

Harris handed her a business card. "From what I've seen you might make it. Call me tonight, I'll have a little better look and let you know."

The girl gushed her thanks, buttoned her blouse, then headed back into the lobby.

"What the hell do you mean barging into my office? There're certain people you don't piss off in Nashville, pal, and Tate Harris is one of them."

I wasn't in the mood to deal with a slimeball like Harris. "Cut the shit, Harris, I'm not one of those starstruck suckers in the lobby out there." I took the letter addressed to Jana and laid it on his desk. "I want to know if this girl came in here. If she did, I want to know her current address."

Harris thought about impressing me with his importance again, then thought better of it. He was used to dealing with artists, not hostile ex-airline pilots.

"Are you her father, Mr. Smith?"

"No, but I need to know where she is," I said.

"Well, I can't help you. It says right here on the envelope: Personal and confidential." Harris jabbed his finger on the envelope for emphasis. " I can't give you that information, it's company policy."

I grabbed him by his collar and lifted him from his desk. "I don't give a damn about your company policy. Those people in your lobby don't know you are running a scam. All they want is their fifteen minutes of fame. If I leave here without her information I'm going straight to the State Attorney General. I don't think you want that."

Harris sat back down in his chair. "Sir, I can assure you we run a legitimate business here."

"That's fine, then I'm sure you wouldn't mind if the Attorney General talks with you," I said.

"Maybe I could have my secretary search for you? I don't want no trouble. Are you with the police?"

"No, but a very good friend of mine is a United States District Court Judge. He wants to talk to this girl. If you don't cooperate with me, I can promise you, Mr. Harris, he's not going to be happy. He might also be interested to know you recruit under-aged girls as topless dancers in exchange for the demo fee."

"I just try to help them get a job, what's wrong with that?" Harris asked.

"Let me guess. If they can't get a job dancing, I bet you can help them find jobs as prostitutes? Do you see anything wrong with that? I do."

I was guessing. But I must have been close to the truth. Harris curled his lip and wanted to talk.

"What was her name again?"

"Jana Smith."

Harris looked in his filing cabinet, and finally pulled a dog-eared file from its slot.

"Jana Smith, she cut a tape and was booked to do some singing in Atlanta. See, I told you I run a legitimate business."

I snatched the file from his hand. "You won't be needing this anymore." I started to walk out then stopped and faced Harris. "A little piece of advice, Mr. Harris."

"What's that?"

"Don't ever used the word legitimate again. Stick with words you know, piece of shit and asshole come to mind."

I was done with Harris, and I left without closing his door.

As I drove back to the airport in Nashville I wondered if Jana was subjected to the same treatment that the young girl in Harris's office had been. When I found her, I intended to ask. If she had been, Mr. Harris was going to get one more visit from me, of that I was certain.

I read bits and pieces of Jana's file. She had signed with a talent agent, Robert Krump, and I called his number on my mobile. A professional-sounding woman answered the phone. I explained my situation. For the first time since I had started this quest, I was on the right track. Jana had worked for them in Atlanta, but the agency hadn't had contact with her in a few months. The woman gave me the name of the club where Jana had last performed. Smokie's Blues Lounge off Piedmont Avenue in Buckhead was the name and location I needed. I filed an IFR flight plan from my car. Twenty minutes later I was cleared direct to PDK. An hour later I touched down on two zero left.

Linda was at the desk. The FBO lobby was empty except for SegFlight personnel.

"Cape Thomas, aviation's answer to Casanova."

I didn't feel like sparring with Linda today. I was tired but excited. My long search was almost over, I could feel it. "Hi, Linda," was the best I could do.

I headed for the men's room and flushed my face with cold water. Linda was waiting when I came out of the men's room. "Cape, what's wrong? You look tired."

"I'm beat, Linda. Cut me a little slack today, will you?"

"Come on in my office and have a cup of coffee with me."

We went into her office. I explained everything that had transpired since I had seen her last. Laura, W. Cronus Kress, Ally, my search for Jana, and the FAA, I told her all of it.

"Cape, I'm off, and I know Buckhead. Let me drive you there, and you can rest." I wanted to go alone, but I did need to rest. I reclined in the seat in Linda's Jaguar and fell asleep.

When I awoke we were parked in front of Smokie's Blues Lounge. No other cars were in the lot, and only two cars were parked in the rear lot. Linda and I walked to the front door, but it was locked. I didn't say anything, but Linda sensed my disappointment.

"Cape, let's try the back door. Maybe someone is in there."

We walked to the back of the building. The back door was propped open with an empty beer keg, so we walked inside. It took a few seconds for our eyes to adjust to darkness of the building. A man was sitting behind a baby grand piano, a woman stood in front of it.

My eyes weren't fully focused, but the woman looked a lot like the picture of Jana. I called her name. The woman at the piano answered. "No, I'm not Jana, I'm Lisa, can I help you?"

"Do you know Jana Smith?" I asked.

"No."

Just the answer I didn't want. I sank down on a barstool, leaned back against the bar, then closed my eyes. Another wild goose chase.

"I know Jana, but not Jana Smith," Lisa said.

I sat back up, and started to describe Jana. Lisa stopped me. "I get the picture. Who are you, her parents?"

Lisa was making sure that if Jana didn't want to be found by these two particular people, she wouldn't be.

"No, we aren't her parents, but I need to talk to her."

"Jana's not here anymore."

I was tired of the detective game. I explained all I knew about Jana and the reason I wanted to find her. Lisa walked away from the piano, and came over to sit down at the bar with us.

"You must be for real, Jana told me she was adopted. She never mentioned her natural mother, though." She looked at Linda. "Are you her mother?"

"No, no mother," Linda stammered, "but I can tell you this. This man doesn't mean her any harm, he's trying to do something very wonderful for her. Can you help us?"

Lisa was stoic, but thinking. I was curious about something. "What last name does she go by, if not Smith?"

Lisa decided to talk. "Jana and I were roommates. We helped each other get singing jobs. I asked her about that once. Her legal name is just 'Jana'. I thought it was an entertainment ploy. You know, like Madonna, Cher, one-name entertainers? That wasn't it. Jana dropped her last name because she said they all belonged to someone else. She stayed with four different foster families. She never felt like any of the names were hers. That's why I told you I didn't know Jana Smith. She would never answer to anything but Jana."

I went for broke. "Do you know where she is?" I closed my eyes again as I waited for her answer. "Yes, she's in a little place called Topsail Beach, North Carolina. Bet you never heard of it?"

Lisa was wrong, I had spent a lot of my childhood on Topsail Island. I knew it like the back of my hand in those days. "Lisa, if I had taken that bet, you would've lost. My grandfather had a little cottage there when I was a kid. Do you have her address?"

"I do, but I don't know if I should give it to you or not? I don't mean because I don't trust you. Jana is sick, very sick, I don't know if she would be up to having visitors," Lisa said.

I knew what her illness was. "Kidney failure, right?"

"No, Jana has non-Hodgkin's lymphoma, it's a very rare form of cancer." I was shocked. I don't know whether I was shocked that Jana was ill, or that she didn't have the kidney disease that had killed Laura. We had played the disease card to find her, but now our little ruse had become way too real. I would find her if she was on Topsail Island, that wasn't a problem, but I wanted to know something of Jana's life. "Lisa, you're a friend of Jana's. Did she, or does she have a good life?"

"Singing is a hard way to make a living, Mister. I mean, when you see people on a stage you think they are doing great. It's much harder than it looks."

I wanted to hear all about Jana, but I was more interested in her childhood. "I mean, when she was younger, was life okay for her?"

"Jana didn't talk about her childhood much. I know some bad things happened to her, but she didn't like to talk about it. You know, all she ever wanted was to have a family. She wanted kids, lots of them. It's sad, I don't think she will live long enough to see that.

I would give anything to see Jana happy, she's a wonderful person. She could never catch a break, though. She was signed to sing at one of the hottest clubs in Atlanta but then she got sick and couldn't make it."

"Lisa, if you want to help Jana you don't have to give anything except her address. Jana's natural mother loved her. She had some issues she couldn't deal with when Jana was born. She wanted to find her, she wanted Jana more than anything else in her life." Lisa wanted to speak for her friend. "Yeah, but how can her mother help her now? It's a little late, don't you think?"

"Lisa, Jana's mother is dead. She died sixteen years ago, but I can assure you she can still help her."

"How can a dead person help her now?" Lisa asked.

"Jana's mother was a very wealthy woman, she came from a very wealthy family. If I find Jana before her twenty-fifth birthday she will be a multi-millionaire. That won't give her health, but it won't hurt her odds either. I'm running out of time, I need to find her." I was no longer worried about a kidnapper. If Jana was on Topsail Island no one could find her before I could. Lisa was writing the address and phone number down before I finished talking.

Linda parked in front of SegFlight and I grabbed the door handle on my side.

"Cape, before you go there's something I want to tell you." I waited for her to finish.

"You remember when I told you didn't have too many husband qualities?"

"Yeah, I know the loyalty thing. You know, Linda, I think I might get a badge made up: 'Women, be careful. This man is hopeless and doesn't play well with others'… I get it, trust me."

Linda looked hurt, and I was sorry for getting angry.

"No, it's not that. I was wrong. You would make a good husband. I wish you could have seen that a long time ago. I wish you could have seen the real me. I--."

"Linda, I've spent most of my life trying to find reasons not to be close to people. I hurt you, and I didn't realize it until a few weeks ago. You weren't looking for just anyone to marry. You were looking for someone to love. We all are, it's our purpose in life. I think you loved me. I pushed you away after I found a pigeonhole for you, 'gold digger'. It was easier to forget you after that. I'm glad you're happy and I'm sorry I was a jerk," I said.

Linda started to cry and I braced for her anger.

"Thank you," Linda said.

"Huh?"

"Thank you, Cape."

"For what?"

"For seeing the real me, after all these years." Linda rolled her hands around the steering wheel. "The day you gave me the prospector's outfit, you know, the miner's helmet and the little gold shovel?.... That hurt Cape, I thought your gift was a ring wrapped in a large box. I wanted you to stop me. I thought you would ask me to marry you."

"Linda, I--."

"I didn't tell you that to get another apology....Lord knows I'm grateful for the first one. I did it for myself. I needed to clear my mind," Linda said.

"So, if a ring would have been in the box, would you have accepted it?"

"Nope... I was never that desperate." Linda kissed me on the cheek.

"Smart woman....Bye, Linda."

"Cape, one other thing."

"Yeah?"

"You don't look half-bad in shining armor."

I left Atlanta hoping Linda would have it all, like Michelle. The doctor, the mansion and the kids. She was a good woman.

CHAPTER TWENTY THREE

A Mother and Child Reunion.

The lights of Charleston, Savannah, and Wilmington glowed in the eastern sky like harborous ladies-in-waiting. For centuries seafaring souls had struggled to find these Grand Dames of the South for the safety of the deep-water ports nestled in their bosoms. Twenty-one thousand feet up negated the limited line of sight imposed by the earth's curvature as well as the need for navigational instruments. Like a mariner on a stormy night, dead reckoning was the only talent I needed to find Wilmington, the middling little sister of Charleston and Savannah. Exposing the mysteries of the vision of Laura would have proved no more difficult than using rudimentary piloting skills to locate the Port City, had I just been able to read the signs.

Laura, Jana, the locket, and even the Indian on the deck, now fell into the realm of logic, a port in the storm.

The Indian was a clue to find Jana, that assumption had eluded me until his importance was illuminated by circumstance. Years ago, a Native American flight attendant from Oklahoma had given me the answer. Oklahoma means 'home of the Indian'. The Indian in my vision had clutched his chest and held his hands to his heart. If Oklahoma was the home of the Indians, that had to be what it meant. We had missed that clue, even though I'd had the answer for years and it hadn't mattered. The locket or key had yet to reveal its secrets, unlike the Indian. I was certain the diary held clues we could ill afford to ignore.

What I could no longer be certain of was the connection between the vision, or more specifically Jana, and Madame Marie's riddle. Since my visit with Madame Marie, I'd applied her riddle, You will find what you have lost, what you will lose cannot be found, to any manner of things that had gone missing. As much as I had wanted to believe the old woman could predict the future, the truth was as plain as the city lights on the windshield of the King Air. The riddle, like the predictions of Nostradamus, made sense only after the fact. I was going to find Jana, and there was nothing that I was going to lose that couldn't be found. Madame Marie was a charlatan, an old Gypsy who had tried to rob a kid of five dollars. The supernatural lived, but not in crystal balls. Even MarKay, steeped in the mystical essence of the bayous, had admitted as much.

Atlanta Center cleared me direct to ILM and down to ten thousand feet. Requesting Augusta as a final destination passed through my mind. Michelle would want to know about Jana, but there was no need to get anyone's hopes up. The next time Michelle heard from me, the search would be over.

Life was good, I had a charter on the books and the ratings for the job. The one thing I didn't have was duty hours to fly the charter. In the old days that wouldn't have been a problem, I would have forgotten to log the hours, and flown the charter anyway. That wasn't the case anymore, rules were rules for a reason. It wasn't my job to question them, it was my job to obey them.

I called Shane and asked him to help me out, and as expected, he agreed to suffer propellers one more time. Being home-based in Wilmington was one reason he had agreed to help, I was sure about that. But Shane would have made the same decision if he had been based in Alaska. Distance should never be a barrier between friends. Shane had learned that lesson from me, and I wouldn't forget his loyalty.

The charter trip to Charleston was a short hop. Shane performed the duties of pilot in command while I daydreamed about my 747 job just around the corner. The return trip was a deadhead leg, short in flight time, but long in hours. Finally, Shane intercepted the localizer for three five at ILM, Wilmington. We broke out before we hit the initial approach fix. From my seat on the starboard side I could see the familiar sights of Wrightsville Beach and Figure Eight Island. Further to the north, the blue water tower of Topsail Island peaked from the gray haze. Somewhere on that sliver of sand between the Atlantic Ocean and the mainland was a little girl lost, soon to be found.

The plane rocked violently and negative g's pulled me from the seat. "Mother F....What the hell are you doing?" I screamed at Shane.

"Paying you back, for sleeping on the job."

"I wasn't sleeping, besides I'm paying you so I can daydream. You crazy bastard."

"Oh yeah, I forgot. Hey, one question, though, was that Mama or mayday, Cape?"

"Neither, I was thinking out loud what I'm going to do to one of your family members once we land."

"Ah, come on Cape, admit it, you were scared."

"747 captains don't scare that easily, kid."

"Holy shit, you got your job back, right?"

"That's right, and if you hadn't pulled that little stunt I was going to get you on with me, but I see you're not mature enough to handle a big job like that." Shane put on his puppy dog face and complied with the Wilmington tower's next command. "King Air six niner Bravo Charlie, cleared to land runway three-five."

"I'm sorry, boss, it was a dumb stunt."

"Cheer up, you whipped pup. If I go back with seniority, you'll get on the line. You may have to work for a feeder line first, but I'll make sure you get your shot at the heavy iron."

"Thanks, Cape, you won't be sorry, I'll…."

"You'll be a pain in the butt, and an embarrassment. Just remember this, I fly with you on your first trip as a captain. You may fool AeroMax into thinking you can fly, but I'll know better. You pull a stupid stunt like you just did, and I'll be there to knock the shit out of you."

From the Air Wilmington ramp I watched the King Air until it disappeared into the northern sky. Shane's short trip would end in a known destination, Kinston, mine was yet to be decided. Laura had brought me this far and MarKay had helped me understand why. Bianca and Jim were wrong, not only do the dead have tales, but they can take you on one hell of ride if you listen.

As much as I wanted to be in charge of my own destiny, a seat in coach and a tight seatbelt were the best I could hope for. Jim Rogers, the FAA, Ally and W. Cronus Kress had the controls from here on out.

Salt air from the marsh flats drifted through my open windows and smothered the realities of the mainland. Island time on Topsail is not measured in minutes, nor are hours limited by clocks. Events on the island were planned around the tides, and timepieces were set to coordinate with the swing drawbridge that opens on the hour to let the Intercoastal Waterway traffic pass. To the masses enslaved by an atomic clock at Greenwich, island time would be a mystery. To me, this land without time made perfect sense. Parked in front of the open bridge high above the sparkling waters that separated the island from the mainland, I became one again with Topsail. Like it or not, we were both connected to the world. The island, for better or worse, owed its connection to some engineer; I owed mine to Laura Fisher. Unlike my debt to Ally, my debt to Laura would soon be paid in full.

I rented a room at a small motel on the Island, then stopped by the IGA to buy food and toothpaste. Nothing about the address Lisa had given me rang a bell. Sea Shell Drive only sparked confusion in the cashiers at the IGA. One was certain north of Surf City would put me in the vicinity, the other was just as sure the opposite direction would work. By consensus, I came to the conclusion that north or south were my choices. Fortunately, as with most islands, only one road ran the entire length of the island. There was a good chance the road of Jana's address would intersect the main road. Tails came up on the coin toss and I headed in that direction. Besides, if the choice proved wrong, I could always stop by the Surf City post office and ask for better directions. Four miles south of Surf City I spotted the road.

Sea Shell Drive was nothing more than a shell path covered by a canopy of wind-swept coastal oaks. I ignored the no trespassing signs posted at the entrance to the road that snaked along the access until it abruptly ended in a clearing under the trees. Three separate paths led to as many houses perched atop pine pilings. Only one car was parked in front of a house. I climbed the steps and rang the doorbell. "Hi, I was trying to find a lady who is staying here?" I said to an older gentleman who answered the door.

"No ladies here."

I pulled the napkin from my pocket and read the address aloud, "181 Sea Shell?"

"That's next door, but she's not home," the old man said as he pointed to an A-frame cottage to his right.

"I don't suppose you know where she is, do you?"

"Her boyfriend left in the car. I think she walked over to the beach, she goes over there almost every day." Before the storm door closed the old man hurried out helpful directions, "Go to the end of the path, there's a public access just up from there."

I parked the rental car in a public parking place, pulled my shoes off, and plunged my bare feet into loose sand warmed by the midday sun. On the steps of the access I observed twenty or thirty people walking in the short, choppy steps of those jelled by age. Retirees from my old planet Up North, I thought. Conversations inflected with faux Southern accents floated on the wind and confirmed my hunch. Emboldened by the presence of brethren with my own secret heritage, I hit the beach and began to walk north.

Translucent ghost crabs oblivious to the blowing sand sidled from hole to hole in the dry grit above the tide line. Flocks of ravenous seagulls made quick meals of sand fiddlers in the shallow waters of the receding surf. Far up the beach I spotted a woman walking with a graceful gait. I picked up some shells and began to toss them into the waves until the woman drew closer. Long blonde hair whipped by the wind covered her face and I turned to follow her. As if cued by a higher power, she stopped and looked at the ocean, the wind blowing the hair from her face.

Island time stood still, and for a moment gave me back the long-lost woman of my dreams. My time and place with Laura had finally come. "No," I shook my head and spoke the obvious to the only person who would understand. " Laura, I've found her. I've found your May Day Baby"

"Excuse me, did you say something?" The woman asked.

"Jana, you don't know me. But I've been looking for you for a long time."

"What are you, some kind of freak?" Jana looked up at the cottages that lined the shore. "I'll scream, go away."

"Jana, I'll move away, but I need for you to listen to me. I was a friend of your mother's. I'm not crazy or here to hurt you--"

"How do you know my name?"

"It's a long story, and it starts before you were born. That would be in 1977. You were born in Augusta, Georgia, and you were adopted." She moved closer.

"The Smiths sent you. Look, they were nice, but tell them I'm Jana, not Carmen."

"Jana the Smiths didn't send me. They are concerned about you, maybe you could just give them a call, you know, let them know you're okay."

"Maybe I'll do that, see you."

I watched as she walked further down the beach, then I blurted out,

"Jana, I'm here because your natural mother wanted me to find you."

She stopped and turned to face me, and I became the object of her ire.

"You're lying. Adoption records are sealed, I know. I've tried to find my birth mother. I find it hard to believe that someone who knew her could find me."

I eased a little closer, hoping she wouldn't leave again.

"Jana, I know what you went through. I've had a heck of a time finding you. I know how hard it is to get through the red tape."

"So, what does she want, a reunion on the Jerry Springer show?" She turned to face the ocean and continued her thoughts, "Is that how she plans to get enough money for her next fix, or is she some pathetic drunk that couldn't deal with the responsibility of a child?"

"Not exactly. I think her plan was a little more thought out than that," I said.

"I've got a better plan, tell her you didn't find me, I don't want to see--."

"Jana, you can't see her, even if you wanted to. She died sixteen years ago." I watched her face to see how she would react to my statement. Her physical reaction and her conversation were conflicted. "It's just as well, I wanted to thank her for all the hell she put me through, that's the only reason I wanted to find her." Jana was putting up a tough front. Misery loves company, I thought.

"Jana, I know it's hard to understand why someone would give you away."

"How would you know?"

"Nobody gave me away, Jana, but my parents were taken from me when I was five. So I sort of know what abandonment is. It hurts whether it's accidental or planned."

"I'm sorry--I didn't know."

"I'm fine with it, but let me finish, okay?" Jana nodded, for the moment we had bonded.

"Your mother loved you, she searched for you before she died. She had her reasons for giving you up," I said.

"So, was she was a drug addict or a hooker? No, don't tell me let me guess, both."

"Not good at guessing, are you? Your mother was a doctor."

"A doctor, and she couldn't afford to keep me? Well, let's see if I can get this one right. I was in her way, she didn't have time to raise a little girl, so she let some pervert in Oklahoma do the job for her. Getting a little better at the guessing game, huh? " she asked.

"Jana, can hating her make things better for you?"

"Why shouldn't I hate her, just because she's dead that makes everything right?"

"I've thought about this a lot before I found you. I knew there would be questions you wanted to ask. The thing is, I don't know that I'm the person who can answer them," I said.

"Yeah, well if it's all the same to you, I just don't won't to hear any more. Please tell whoever hired you, I'm doing fine. I don't need them any more than they needed me. Good-bye."

I couldn't let her walk away, not with out hearing the story as I knew it. "Jana, no one hired me. I got caught up in this. Even if I could explain why, you wouldn't understand. I'm here because someone loved you. Because someone never stopped loving you, even in death. If you'll give me just a few minutes of your time, I can explain. If you want to walk away after you hear what I have to say, I'll never tell a soul where you are, deal?"

She dug her toe in the sand and slowly nodded her head.

"You may find some of this hard to believe, but it's the truth. I won't sugar-coat anything. Your mother and I met briefly. I knew her for only one night. I never saw her again, alive anyway, then one night a few months ago she came to me in a vision. I know what you're thinking, that I'm a nut case. So did I for a while. I won't go into the story of how I found out who she was. Instead let me tell you about your mother. She was a doctor, as I said. She came from a very prominent family in Greenville. When she found out she was pregnant with you, she had a choice to make.

"She believed her father, the only person who loved her, would reject her if he found out she was pregnant. She hid the pregnancy from him and put you up for adoption. She wasn't a bad person. She was scared, confused, and young, almost as young as you when you left the Smiths."

"How do you know about the Smiths?" she asked.

"In due time, I'll get to that. Your mother--Laura was her name--wanted to please everyone--."

"Except me, did she think of me? No?"

"Jana, she made what she thought was the right choice at the time. Later, according to her friend, Michelle, she realized she had made a terrible mistake. She began a search for you that was cut short by her death--."

"Just because she searched for me doesn't mean she loved me."

"I could see why you would think that, but what if I can prove she loved you?" I asked.

"How?"

"Your mother left a very sizable estate. Her estate cannot be probated until May 1, 2002."

"That's my birthday, May the 1st ."

"I know, and you're the reason the will can't be probated. The will is the reason I know she loved you. She wanted to make sure you were taken care of, I think it was her way of saying I'm sorry to you," I said.

"How large was her estate?"

"I'm not sure. I think it would be safe to say if you show up before your twenty-fifth birthday you'll be a multi-millionaire."

Jana started to cry. I put my hand on her shoulder.

"I need some time to think about this. You don't know how I've dreamed of having a mother, a family. Just to know that someone really loved me. Now you tell me I've always had that, not to mention the money. Life is so cruel...I don't even know your name?"

"My name is Cape Thomas."

"Mr. Thomas, I'm dying. I have cancer. Do I have brothers and sisters?"

"No."

"Is there any other family?"

"I guess it depends on your definition of family. If you mean warm and caring people that care about you, then the answer is, no. You do have an aunt, your mother's sister, but I'm pretty sure she won't welcome you with open arms. You see, if you don't show up, your aunt gets all of your mother's estate. She was directed by the will to find you at any cost. To be honest with you, I don't think she ever looked one day for you," I said.

"That's it?"

"No, your mother's father, your grandfather, is still alive. I don't know how he would feel about you, either. He has no idea that you are alive. I wish I could paint a better picture for you, but these are the facts. I know your mother wanted you to have her estate. I'm sorry she couldn't have been here to tell you herself."

"What about my father? Don't I have a father?"

I thought about not answering her question, but she deserved some answers. How she handled them was my concern.

"Jana, your mother was engaged to be married. Her fiancé cheated on her, and it hurt her very much. She acted out of anger, she wanted revenge, she sought comfort in the arms of different people. I'm afraid no one knows who your father is."

"Are you one of those people?"

"Yes."

"My mother, what did she look like? I used to dream about her when I was a child, she never had a face, though," Jana said.

"Do you have a mirror?"

"Not with me."

"The next time you stand in front of a mirror, you will be looking at your mother. She was just as beautiful as you are."

"Do you know where my mother is buried? I know it's a strange question, but dying has been on my mind a lot lately."

"Yes, I do," I said.

"Will you take me there?"

"Sure, we can go tomorrow, if you'd like."

"I want to go today. I don't know how much longer I'll have strength enough to travel. Will you take me now?"

"My car is just over the dunes. Do you want to change clothes first?" I asked.

"No, I want to go right now."

The traffic had increased as Jana and I headed out for Greenville. As a rule I don't like to drive slow. Today was different. It gave me time to talk with Jana. She had no problems talking about her adult life, but stayed away from her childhood. I wanted to find out about John Kirkland. I decided to test her depth of trust on Tate Harris, first.

"Jana, do you remember a guy named Tate Harris?"

Equal parts of shock and surprise spread across her face. "How in the world would you know Tate Harris?"

"I met him briefly," I said.

"So, what did you think of him?"

"I didn't care for him, I thought he was a slimeball. As a matter of fact, I told him that in so many words."

"Good for you, I'm glad somebody did."

I wanted more information, I thought for a moment that she wouldn't tell me.

"He's really a pervert, I arrived in Nashville flat broke. I wanted to be in the music business. He made demo tapes. Thank God, my voice was good enough to get me a singing job."

"You didn't have the money to pay for the tape?" I asked.

"How do you know about paying for the demo?"

"Doesn't matter, did you have the money for the tape?"

"No."

I knew the rest of the story and didn't need to push her any further. Tate Harris was on my list. Now the big question. Something from an area she steadfastly avoided, her childhood. "How about a guy named Albert Rannor? He changed his name to John Kirkland, is he the pervert from Oklahoma?"

Jana slid over to her side of the car and pulled her long legs up against her body.

"Yes, he adopted me when I was a baby. He was Albert Rannor to me."

"Jana, if you don't feel comfortable talking about this--I'll understand, but I have my reasons for asking."

"He molested me.... It hurt so badly. I told my teacher about it in kindergarten. Social services removed me from the home. I was just a child when we went to court. He and his wife said I was a liar. They made it sound like the whole thing was just something that I made up. I was confused, and I didn't help the case very much. A doctor examined me and said I had been abused. The Rannors blamed it on a retarded boy in the neighborhood. I think he went to jail. I don't think they ever did anything to the Rannors. I guess little girls don't make good witnesses. It's not fair that bad people don't get punished and that the wrong people do sometimes." Jana tucked her chin on her knees and stared straight ahead. "I've never talked about that with anyone before, not even my boyfriend. What else do you know about me, anyway?"

"First off, I think little girls make good witnesses. Even if I didn't know the truth, I'd still believe you. You know something else, Jana? You're right, sometimes bad people get away with things for a long time. Whether you believe it or not, justice catches up with them."

"Got an example?" she asked.

"Well, I know this rich banker that hasn't gotten his yet, but it's coming. I also know that John Kirkland or Albert Rannor did time in prison for being a child molester. I suspect the prisoners made him pay a little more than the justice system extracted."

Jana buried her face in her legs and sobbed softly. She looked like a small child as she sat in her little ball. I wondered if she cried like that after Kirkland or Rannor hurt her.

I choked the steering wheel until my knuckles turned white, and calculated the time it would take to fly to Muscle Shoals.

"Hooray for the prisoners. I hope they hurt him, like he did me."

"I hope they hurt him more," I said.

She smiled. "You know, Mr. Thomas--."

"It's just Cape, Mr. Thomas is some old guy in Florida playing shuffleboard."

"Cape, I like you. Do you have kids? I bet you have lots of kids," Jana said.

"You know you really need to work on your betting and guessing skills. I don't have any kids."

"Do you have a wife?"

"Are you betting or guessing?" I asked.

"Asking, I've learned my lesson."

"Good, there's nothing more attractive than a beauty with brains. Well, if you had to bet, what odds would you give that I have a wife?"

"Two to one?"

"Jana, stay out of Vegas, I'm not married."

We turned onto Greenville Boulevard on our way to Forest Lawn. Jana pointed at a small strip mall and ordered me to stop. I quickly pulled in and stopped the car. My God, don't let her die, not now, not this close to the end of the journey. Have a heart, Big Guy.

"Jana, I can get you to hospital if that's where you need to go. There's a fine medical school here."

"No, I'm fine. I want to buy some flowers for my mother's grave....Oh, Jeez, I forgot my purse."

I reached into my wallet, and gave her a hundred. "I guess I can make a future multi-millionaire a loan."

She smiled. "I'll pay you back."

"It's okay, a lady made me a loan when I really needed it. She didn't ask for terms, and so I wouldn't feel right asking you for payment. We'll leave it like she did, pay me when you can."

"She must be a nice lady?"

"Very nice, I hope you get to meet her one day," I said.

"Sounds like someone is in love."

It was my turn to smile. "I am, but it's one of those high-rent-district-low-rent-district romances. They never work out," I said.

"I wouldn't feel that way if I loved someone. Money wouldn't matter."

"You know, you may feel differently in a few days. You'll be rich then. I bet you wouldn't give a poor guy a second thought."

"I'm glad you didn't get to lay a bet on that, Cape, you would have lost."

I waved at the gatekeeper as we passed by on our way to the mausoleum. Jana pulled down the mirror on her sunvisor and wiped away the black circles of her mascara. "It's funny. I know she won't be able to see me, but I want to look nice for her."

"I'm sure she would love you just the way you are, but I'm glad you spruced up a little bit."

"Why?"

"I don't want the gatekeeper to think I'm removing a body from the graveyard. You were beginning to look a little scary." As soon as the words left my mouth I regretted the remark. I had forgotten how close Jana was to death.

But instead of being reminded of death, Jana started laughing. She had a beautiful laugh and a good sense of humor. I couldn't bear the thought of this wonderful person dying so young. Jana held her flowers in front of her as we approached the mausoleum. I held her arm as we stood at the gate.

"Laura Fisher, that's her name?" Jana asked.

I remembered that I had never told Jana her mother's full name. "Yes, she died when she was twenty-nine."

"Did she have cancer, too?"

"No she died of kidney failure, but medical science might have been able to save her today."

"I wish they could save me."

"Jana, why can't they? You hear all the time how we are beating cancer. Besides, you look healthy to me, maybe you need a second opinion?"

"I'm supposed to start Chemo next week, that's why I still have my hair. I have a rare form of cancer, non-Hodgkins-lymphoma, and I need a bone-marrow transplant. That's why I asked if I had any brothers or sisters. You see, sometimes siblings are exact matches."

"How about your aunt or your grandfather?" I asked.

"You would think they would, but family that aren't siblings can be a long shot. Besides from the way you described my aunt, I don't think she would be willing to help."

"Well, we'll see if they are willing to be tested. It wouldn't hurt, right?" I could see Bianca kicking and screaming all the way to the hospital as I dragged her along for the bone marrow test.

"It wouldn't hurt, but I won't get my hopes up. If I don't find a donor, I don't think I'll ask for any treatments," Jana said.

I left Jana at the mausoleum alone. This might be the only time she would have to be with the one person who had loved her. I walked around the graveyard then made my way back to where Jana was. She had her arm through the door and was stroking Laura's sepulcher.

I eased up behind her and placed my hand on her shoulder. "Are you ready to go, Jana? You can come back anytime you like, I think your mother would like that."

"Cape, when I die, do you think they may let me be buried beside my mother?"

That did it, if the news of Jana killed the old man, then too damn bad. This girl had suffered enough. We were going to the Fisher house. He would have to answer his granddaughter's question. I didn't give a damn what it did to his memory of Laura, and I was certain Laura didn't. As for losing Jana's estate, let the old bastard take that decision with him to his grave, this woman was his blood, damn it.

We drove up to Fisher's home. Jana's eyes widened. "Cape, is this where you live? It's beautiful."

"No, Jana, this is where your grandfather lives. You are going to meet him."

"What if he doesn't like me?"

"I'll like you enough for the both of us. Are you willing to do this?"

"Yes."

I stopped the car and rang the doorbell. Gustavo came to the door. "You, you look like Miss--."

"Doesn't she though, Gustavo? We need to see Mr. Fisher," I told him.

"Mr. Fisher cannot be disturbed. You must leave at once, or I will call the police."

I pushed Gustavo aside. "Then call the police, Gustavo, and call Bianca while you're at it."

I started yelling at the top of my lungs. " MR. FISHER, MR. FISHER. HELLO, MR. FISHER." I heard a door close in the back of the house and I pulled Jana along behind me down the hall.

Mr. Fisher appeared in the hallway. "It's you, leave now."

"I will leave, Mr. Fisher, but first I want you to meet someone." I pulled Jana from behind me and thrust her in front of the old man's face. I wasn't prepared for what happened next, and I was certain Jana wasn't. The old man grabbed her and started crying, "Laura, Laura, my precious child. I've missed you, oh God.... Laura."

Jana hugged the old man back, then spoke softly to him, "I'm not Laura, Mr. Fisher, I'm Jana."

The old man regained his composure. "I'm so sorry, young lady. I'm just a foolish old man. I...you look just like my daughter. I knew it couldn't be true, but I wanted you to be her. Who are you, then?"

I moved beside Jana. "This is your granddaughter, Mr. Fisher, Laura's daughter."

"It can't be. Laura never had a daughter."

"You're wrong, Mr. Fisher. I can call Michelle, and she will explain the whole thing to you," I said.

Jana spoke up. "I don't know the whole story, but I know the woman in the graveyard is my mother."

Mr. Fisher cradled Jana again. "Where have you been, child? I don't need proof, I'm looking at it. You have to be Laura's, there is no difference in the two of you."

Gustavo made good on his promise. Greenville would be a good city to live in if you needed fast police protection. Two Greenville police officers followed Gustavo's instructions and tackled me to the floor. I was handcuffed before I got my wind back.

Mr. Fisher roared, "What are you doing? Let that man go immediately." The two officers lifted me from the floor and looked at Gustavo. "He is the intruder, Mr. Fisher, you told me to keep him away from here."

"I don't give a damn what I told you. Let him go now, he is a guest in this house. A welcomed guest, and someone to whom I owe a debt of gratitude. Look, Gustavo, doesn't she look just like Laura?"

"I see a little resemblance," Gustavo mumbled.

"A little resemblance? Open your eyes, man. Come, my dear, come to the drawing room with me."

We all filed back up the hallway and headed into the large room with the fireplace. The policemen still held me, one on either side. The old man stopped in front of the fireplace and placed Jana under the oil portrait. "Look, look at the picture, who is this, officers?" he asked.

The policeman looked at the portrait, then at Jana. "Mister, all I know is if this was a Wanted poster, I'd arrest this lady. I'd say they're the same person."

The cuffs were biting into my wrists. I was glad for the positive I. D. but I wanted out of the restraints. "Mr. Fisher, do you think it's okay to get me out of these things?"

"Officer, I'm Nathan Hale Fisher, and I own this house. Release this man at once."

The police apologized to me. Mr. Fisher excused Gustavo then asked Jana and me to sit down. "Mr. Thomas, I want to hear the whole story, please make yourself comfortable. Jana, my dear, please sit over here by me. I think you might want to hear this, too."

I told the story in its entirety even the part about the vision and included the Indian this time. Mr. Fisher didn't care about Jana's pedigree. He was happy to have her home. He insisted that she move in immediately, but Jana wanted to say good-bye to her boyfriend. Mr. Fisher offered for Jana to stay longer, then offered to have Gustavo drive her home. I nixed that idea and insisted I drive Jana home. I didn't trust Gustavo Jobim.

CHAPTER TWENTY FOUR

One Down, One to Go.

I dropped Jana off and met her not-so-serious boyfriend. Nothing about her friend impressed me, and I made no attempt to hide it. The guy was a loser, Jana could do much better than him.

It was late when I checked out of my room. During the drive back from Topsail I tried to call Michelle a few times but didn't get an answer. I arrived home a few minutes before ten and played my new messages.

William Johnston had called, and wanted me to hold up my end of the bargain. Dr. Benson had also called, and wanted me to return her call. I left both messages on the machine and called Jim Rogers, instead. The news about Jana pleased Jim, especially when I explained how much she looked like Laura. Jim never said, but I got the impression he was planning a reunion more than a meeting. He suggested Jana make an appointment in the near future, and I agreed. The U. S. Treasury Department was on the case, but due to the complexities of the investigation, we could forget about the Feds running interference for Ally and me. After the conversation with Jim, I had a satisfying thought, provided by one of my grandfather's old sayings. "The wheels of justice grind slowly, but they grind exceedingly fine." I was all for the wheels grinding exceedingly fine, though it would have been nice if they could grind a little faster.

The phone rang during my comforting thought,--Tom Butterfield. "Cape, I need to know something on the Johnston Ballard & Hearst check. Your hearing is in two days. It's your call."

"Do it, Tom. I just needed to make sure the interest wasn't too high on the favor."

"I'll tell you, Cape, the case is in the bag. The FAA seems to have lost interest. I'm more focused on the AeroMax deal. I've already sent them a letter. Grace, the lady that signed the affidavit?"

"Yeah."

"She's agreed to testify that the statement she signed was false. The bartender in the pub that night has an incredible memory. He and a barmaid have signed statements as well. Both of them picked your picture out of a book of AeroMax pilots. They are absolutely positive it was you in the bar that night. They remembered setting the clock up."

"I don't understand the FAA, I really thought they were above reproach. I guess money talks?"

"The only money that talked was the money Johnston Ballard & Hearst spent to hire detectives in London. Once the FAA saw the truth, they backed off. Those guys are tough, Cape, but fair. You could have done this three years ago, and walked," Tom said.

"Three years ago Grace wouldn't have signed that statement."

"Yeah, I hadn't thought about that, I wonder why she changed her mind?"

"Tom, that's uncharted territory. A place too dangerous for two simpletons like us, so let's don't go there."

"Yeah, if I had to figure a woman out, you could never afford me. By the way, when this is all over where do I send my bill?" Tom asked.

"Maybe you can get another advance from Johnston Ballard & Hearst?"

"I don't know, Cape, they're the ones who handled everything in London. They've spent a bundle just running down the bartender and the barmaid. One was in New Zealand, the other was in the United States."

"I thought they weren't going to do anything until they heard from me?"

"So did I, but I thought maybe you talked directly to their firm," Tom said.

"Not Guilty. I was hoping it was something you had pulled off."

"Nope, but I'd hate to know what this has cost them. They've even prepared the case against AeroMax, and it's a winner."

"How much is my bill?"

"Damn, Cape, you are out of the loop, I've been paid in full. Provided I get to keep the Johnston Ballard & Hearst check."

"You mean it's over?" I asked.

"The FAA isn't going to contest your right to get your ratings back. That part is a formality. The AeroMax case is a slam dunk, but I can take it on a contingency basis, you won't have to spend anything out of pocket, how about it?"

"How much percentage-wise?" I asked.

"Does forty percent sound fair?"

"Hell, no….Not for a slam dunk."

"What's fair? It could drag out a long time. It could take years," Tom said.

"To hell with AeroMax, if I get my ratings back I can afford to wait. Besides, I can use Airline Pilots Association lawyers."

"Cape, I'll do it for ten percent. They don't have a case, and they know it."

"Done, good-bye, Tom."

I could think of no good reason why Johnston and W. Cronus Kress would get me off before I delivered my end of the bargain. I suspected my call to William Johnston would verify what I already knew. The pre game warm-up was over, it was show time. I hated to help them but if these worms could live up to their word--I didn't have much choice.

I called Michelle, tonight might be the last free time I would have for a while.

"Cape, I've got some good news for you. You won't believe it."

"I've got some news for you too, Michelle."

"Let me go first, this is important. I've just had Laura's diary delivered to me by UPS. I have it right now in my hands. We were right, the key in the locket fit. I've been reading it."

"How did you get it? Where did you find it?"

"Well, I've gotten so caught up in this spy game of yours, that I wasn't thinking on my own. I asked myself if I wanted to see Laura's diary how would I get it. Then the answer hit, just ask Mr. Fisher. I did that, and as quick as you can say 'Race the big brown truck, Dale' I had the diary." Michelle laughed, "I know it's not as fun as breaking into Laura's room or digging around in the graveyard, but it's a lot more effective."

"Great, I'm glad the direct approach worked for you." I said, " It's just as well I'm getting out of the spy game. I guess that's just proves it's not my forte."

"Why do you say that?"

"Michelle, I'll be a Captain for some airline in a few days. I've got my ratings back. Well, I haven't paid for them yet, but I have them, anyway."

"So you get your ratings back and now you're going to quit on Jana. I can't believe that, Cape, I thought you were a real stand-up guy. I see I was wrong, you bastard."

"Michelle, before you pass judgement on me let me tell you my news. Remember I had some, too?" God, women will turn on you in a minute. Just when you think you can trust them….Bam!

"I hope I feel good about this news, but I've got a feeling it won't change my mind about you."

"I bet it will. I found Jana," I said.

"Where….How? Is she okay? Do you want me to call her? She might take this better from her mother's best friend."

"She took it just fine, Michelle. So did Mr. Fisher, by the way. Jana will be moving in with him."

There was a pause and I waited for Michelle to respond. Nothing. "Hello, Michelle, are you still there?"

"I'm here, Cape, I was just thinking of the best way to apologize to you."

I savored the moment. After all, whether we like to admit it or not, it's rare for a man to be one up on a woman. It's rarer for a man not to gloat. " I suppose your silence is penitence enough…. I accept it."

"Cape, I swear you surprise me at times. I was expecting some--."

"Smart-ass remarks?"

"Yes, and globs of male bravado."

"Don't lose faith in me. That comes with your next question," I said.

"If I wasn't so curious….I'd skip the question."

"Ah, come on! It's just a big dose of humility--take it like a big girl."

"Okay, how did you get all of that done?"

"Well, Michelle, I'm glad you asked…finally. I got tired of this spy game stuff, too. So I called information and asked for Jana. Presto. The next thing you know I have her number and we meet; the rest, as they say, is history."

Michelle squealed, "You lying dog, I want all the details, but I have to tell you about the diary. It's so wonderful, and I owe Bianca an apology. She took care of Laura right up till the end. It's all in Laura's diary. I was having a lot of difficulty with my pregnancy and was confined to bed. I couldn't be with Laura, I'm so glad Bianca was there. I'm going to apologize when I see her."

"How about not looking for Jana?" I reminded her.

"I'm not going to apologize for that, but at least she did one good thing."

"Does the diary mention Jana?" I asked.

"It's beautiful. Laura has written so many things to her personally. She explained her feelings about her decision to give Jana up. She went into details about trying to find Jana, her Will, everything. Jana has to read this diary. She will know how much she was missed."

"Did Bianca promise to find Jana?"

"Cape, I think Laura was really sick at the end. Most of the last few pages tell what Bianca did for her during those last terrible days--I feel bad for disliking Bianca for so long. I know she knew that Laura wanted Jana. Greed makes people do strange things, but that doesn't mean she didn't love Laura."

"I can understand that in a way. I guess that much money could have an effect on a lot of people."

"Isn't this wonderful? It's like a fairy tale, and they all lived happily ever after."

"I like the ending, but I didn't tell you everything." I said.

"Oh, God, I knew there had to be more."

"Jana has non-Hodgkins-lymphoma, cancer. She doesn't have long to live unless she can get a bone-marrow transplant."

"God, and she doesn't have siblings either. I remember a little about that from my nursing days."

"I know, but she's a fighter. I spent some time with Jana, and she's a wonderful person, Michelle. Too wonderful to die this young. Will the money help her get better medical attention?" I asked.

"Cape, it couldn't hurt, but it's all about a donor for her now. Is that what made you take her to see Mr. Fisher?"

"Yeah, I took her to the mausoleum to see Laura. It was her idea. She wanted to know if she could be buried beside her mother. That did it for me. I want Jana to read that diary, and I want you to answer her questions about Laura. Can you take some time off?"

"Tomorrow, I'll be there tomorrow," Michelle said.

"I don't know about tomorrow or even the next few days, I think I'm going to be busy."

"I want to see her, soon. I can't wait much longer than a day."

"Michelle, I've told Jana about you, and she wants to meet you, too. She was in Topsail with a friend of hers. She has to drive him back to Atlanta and pick up her things. Why don't you give her a call, see if she can spend some time with you in Augusta?"

"That's a great idea, but do you think she would?"

"If she doesn't want to, call me back. I know she wants to see Mr. Fisher, but I don't want her in Greenville alone. I don't trust Bianca, but I really don't trust Gustavo. When she goes back there, I want us all to go together, if you know what I mean."

"Cape, I don't think Bianca will cause any trouble. You should have read Laura's diary, Bianca went above and beyond."

"I understand the way you feel. I hope it works out, too, but I've seen a darker side of Bianca. Once she finds out the money is gone, she may be different. If Jana can't stay with you, call me, and I'll talk her out of going back to Greenville."

"You're right, one right doesn't make up for all of Bianca's wrongs. Besides, I've got a ton of stuff here for Jana to see--Laura's pictures, yearbooks, and even some old clothes. I want to give her the Coptic Cross. Do you think she'll want it? After all, if it hadn't been for the Cross we may never have figured out all of this."

"Hey, and don't forget the diary," I said.

"I'm going to hold off on that because I want you to be here when she reads the diary."

"Good idea. Maybe Ally could come down, too. You haven't heard from her, have you?"

"She's going to meet Walter in Edenton. They have a big farm up there…I've gotten so caught up in Jana, I forgot about you and Ally. That's why you said you haven't paid for your ratings, isn't it? You have to meet Ally, right?" Michelle asked.

"I don't know for sure, but I think that might be the case. If it is, I guess they can't start without me. Just the same, I'd better give William Johnston a call, it's getting late."

"Does Jim know about the meeting?"

"No, I don't know for sure myself. I'll call Jim when I know it's on….I have to go. Call me back if Jana can't stay with you. And Michelle--."

"You don't have to say it. I'll take good care of her. I'll tell her to bring her medical records, so we can put her in the bone marrow database."

"Don't you think she's already in there?" I asked.

"She may be, but she's never had a crazed bureaucrat helping her before."

CHAPTER TWENTY FIVE

Death on the Albemarle

I was right, it was show time. By phone, Johnston confirmed my hunch in esoteric bits of information. "Drive, do not fly--wear light-colored clothes, no sunglasses, arrive by, but not before six."

Then he gave me a number to call for directions once I arrived in Edenton. There was no confirmation read back concerning his instructions or the number. Johnston made no mention of my ratings, Ally, or the purpose of my trip to Edenton. I suspected the brevity of the call was partially because of the disdain we had for one another, but the remainder of my suspicions weren't as clear.

I stopped by the airport to check on Betty and let her know I would be gone for a day or two. I also put in a call to Jim Rogers, but no luck. He was in Federal court and wouldn't be back until the next day. It was just as well. There was nothing he could do but advise me to smile for the camera. But Jim's read on Johnston's terse message would have been nice, though.

I decided to take the back roads and enjoy the season. Highway 17 was tough driving if you were in a hurry, scenic if you weren't. I fell into the latter category. Anxious to see Ally, but cursed with too much time, I stopped in Little Washington for a late lunch. Small river towns in the tidal basins of North Carolina can provide orgasmic culinary experiences, and Washington was no exception. I ordered soft-shell crabs and a side order of steamed oysters and ate them on a patio overlooking the Pamlico River.

The peacefulness of the moment made it hard to think about the double-cross that was sure to come. No matter who drew first blood, there would be no winners. Walter could savor his pictures, but even his victory would be short lived. Ally's testimony and the Treasury Department investigation would see to that. Walter and Johnston, if convicted and jailed, still had the resources to retaliate. My rating would be history, and life as Ally knew it would be over.

All my life I had thought of the legal system as a means to finding justice, yet often it wasn't. What kept the scales balanced was equal suffering, a draw. I could live with that, maybe Ally could, too. But not winning would drive Walter Cronus Kress crazy; a Pyrrhic victory, my grandfather would like that.

I crossed the Ablemarle Sound on Highway 32, thirty minutes before my deadline. If Walter's house was on the water I should be in the neighborhood. I stopped for a Coke and called the number Johnston had given me. A payphone on the side of the building rang. The man who answered the phone wasn't a stranger, even though I didn't know him. I remembered him as the clean-cut GQ guy that had carried the money into Jim Rogers office.

"Where are you?" he asked. I almost gave him the answer Michelle had given me in Augusta when I first met her. But something didn't add up. Why was I calling a payphone, and if this guy worked for Walter Kress why didn't he have a cell phone?

"I'm coming in on Hwy 64, where are you?" I asked.

"I'm on the road. Maybe you should pull over, I have some directions for you."

I let a few seconds pass then lied, "Okay, I'm stopped now, go ahead."

The directions were explicit, down to the tenths of a mile I should go before I found a path off a secondary road. I wrote down the directions. "Is that it?"

"Yeah, one other thing. Be there by six, but not before, got it?" GQ asked.

The same phrase Johnston had used, and what was so magical about six? Maybe it had something to do with the lighting or some other accommodation for the photographer?

"Yeah, I got it, but how do I know when this little photo shoot is over?"

"Oh, you'll know, that won't be a problem," GQ replied.

"Yeah, but how will I know?"

There was no answer, GQ hung up and drove off without seeing me. I waited inside the store for a few minutes, then headed for my car. I drove slowly to see whether anyone was following me, then remembered my instructions to Ally and made a turn around the block. No one was following me.

The path to Kress's house split two stands of timber with an open gate at the entrance. After entering the gate, I drove down the path with my eyes on the rear-view mirror. The thick woods played out and the path continued across an area planted in bunch grass interspersed with long leaf pine. I had seen places like this before in South Georgia, quail plantations. Through the thin stand of trees I could see Albemarle Sound glimmering in the setting sun. The path went on for a few thousand yards before I saw the hunting lodge. A black BMW 840 was parked in front of the lodge. I looked at the directions again. Satisfied I was at the right place I blew my horn. Ally came out on the veranda of the lodge. "Cape, thank goodness you're here, I thought it was going to be dark before you arrived."

"Are you alone?"

"Yes, Walter was supposed to meet me here, but I knew he wouldn't. I guess this is the setup," Ally said.

"Guess so, want to do the kissy, kissy and go have dinner?"

Ally put her finger to her lips and motioned for me to come up the steps.

"What is it?" I whispered.

"Something's wrong, Cape. When it started to get dark I decided to call you, but the phones in the house don't work."

"Maybe they cut the phones off after the season--."

"I know that, I come to this place only when I have to, but I do know that. My dad comes hunting here, that's not what I'm talking about," Ally said.

"What is it? You look like a ghost."

"I came into the lodge to use the restroom when I first arrived, and that's when I heard footsteps upstairs in the main bedroom."

Ally was a city girl, so the quiet of the countryside wasn't setting well with her. I looked around the house. Ninety-foot loblolly pines swayed gently in the breeze. "Ally, I have pines in my yard. Sometimes when the wind blows, cones drop on the roof--they sound an awful lot like footsteps."

"The main bedroom is on the south side of the house, and the sun was shining through the window....I saw the shadow of a man--he had a knife in his hand."

"Ally, you're letting your imagination run away with you. Look at the trees, the limbs make shadows....Shadows are like clouds if you look at them just right and you can see all types of things."

"Cape, I left the house, then thought of my phone in the car. I ran back to the car--my phone was gone. I was going to call you, but it was gone. That's when I decided to leave, but the car wouldn't start."

Nothing was going to calm Ally down until I explained away her fears. "Let's have a look at your car." The BMW was new, so for it not to start was a little strange. But Ally could have gotten excited when she realized she was alone and had no way to call. She could have left her phone at home, I'd done it a thousand times myself. We walked to the car, I opened the door for Ally. "Pop the hood and try to start it," I said.

I lifted the hood, saw that the battery cables had been neatly cut. Blocked from Ally's view by the raised hood, I studied the soft ground in front of the car. A fresh set of boot prints led from the car into the side door of the lodge.

"Do you see anything wrong?" Ally asked.

"Looks like the battery is dead. It's getting late. I saw a neat little restaurant on the way out here, let's go get a bite."

I leaned close to Ally and whispered, "Put your arm around me, walk with me to my car. It may just be kids or vandals, but we're leaving. Walter and Johnston will just have to get pictures in the hotel we'll be staying at, come on."

Ally slid into the seat from the driver's side. I turned the car around and glanced into the rear-view mirror, just in time to see a man bolt from the side door of the house and run to the rear of the lodge.

"Cape, I'm not imagining things."

"I believe you, we're safe now. You look great."

"Thanks." Ally grabbed my hand. "That place gives me the creeps, I'm glad you came when you did."

"Yeah, me too. It pays to be early."

"You mean late, right?"

"What time were you to meet Walter?" I asked.

"No later than five, Walter acted as if we were going to finally forgive me. He told me to change into something comfortable and meet him at the river to watch the sun set. I was going to the bedroom to change. When we were younger, Walter would hide in the room and watch me change, because it excited him. I thought he was probably hiding in the bedroom. I almost went upstairs, then I saw the shadow with the knife." Ally closed her eyes. "I knew better, but I thought Walter had second thoughts about ending our marriage."

"I thought that might be something you would have liked."

"Cape, I have no love for Walter, but if he could have forgiven me--maybe we could have parted as friends. I know it sounds crazy, but our families are--I hate conflict--"

"Ally, even without rose-colored glasses the world's not so bad, but it won't ever be perfect."

"I know, but at least in my world men don't have knives."

"Maybe the guy was the photographer? Maybe the knife was a camera?"

"Cape, I'm not wearing those rose-colored glasses, now…it was a knife, and what was wrong with my car? You saw something that made you want to leave."

"The cables were cut, Walter must know how jumpy this places makes you. They cut the cables to make sure you didn't leave, that's possible isn't it?"

"I don't know, but I'm glad your timing was off."

"Funny Ally, but for the first time in my life. I think my timing was perfect."

I drove a little faster than I did coming in, but not fast enough to look suspicious. The sun hovered over the tree line and illuminated a large yellow gate that covered the path where the thick woods began. "Damn, I didn't see that gate when I came in. There was one up at the main road--"

"Something's wrong, isn't it--."

"Here Ally, take my phone dial 911. I'll have to back up."

Ally punched at the phone while I tried to back down the darkening path.

"Darn."

"What is it?"

"You don't have a signal," Ally said.

I whipped the car into the bunch grass and bottomed out. "Damn….Hold on Ally, I'm hung on something." I floored the big Cadillac until smoke came from the wheels, finally the heavy tank began to move. The automatic lights came on. I killed them and gunned the car. "Cape, where are you going?"

"Back to the lodge, is there a gun cabinet there?"

"I don't know, I hate guns. Don't go back….Run through the gate."

"Ally, this car is heavy, but there's no way it'll break that gate down. We're trapped.
We have to go back."

"Can't we stay in the car?"

"Is there another road out of--" Before I could finish the windshield on the Cadillac exploded, and silica from the glass sprayed into my eyes. "Son of a bitch, I must have hit a limb, the sun had me blinded, are you okay?" I jammed on the brakes and grabbed Ally by the hand.

"Yes, the hole was on your side."

"What hole? The limb knocked a hole in the windshield?" I asked.

"No! It was a bullet hole--someone's shooting at us--"

"Come on." We tumbled from the car and found cover in the bunch grass. I pulled Ally's ear close to my mouth and whispered, "Ally we have to get away from the car, I can't see. Low crawl. Hurry! I'll hold onto your foot."

We crawled for ten minutes before we spoke again. "Cape, I can't go any further-- we're in some briars."

"Okay, we're in the deep woods, we'll be safe here. Ally, we--"

"Your eyes, blood is coming from them, were you shot?" Ally asked.

"No, but some grit from the glass must have gotten into my eyes. I can see a little out of my left eye, but nothing from the right eye." Ally cupped my face with her hands. "We need to rinse your eyes out. If there is debris in there you could damage them more by opening and closing your eyes."

"Can you get us to the river?"

"Yes, maybe-- I don't know it's so dark, but if we wait the moon is supposed to be full tonight."

"Now how do you know that?" I asked.

"Full moon, the river, even a bottle of '86 Chateau Margaux. If I was going to have an affair….I was going to do it right."

We sat in the dark and waited for the moon. Birds roosting in the trees made noises like steps in the woods. Smells of the new spring foliage took the edge off of the noises and our predicament. "Sounds like it would have been a nice evening, but are you sure you didn't bring the bottle for Walter?"

"Cape, Walter and I were over years ago, besides why would I bring wine for a man who hates it?"

"Yeah, but I don't drink anymore."

"Wine makes me more amorous, you would have benefited by proxy, trust me."

I did, and as I sat blinded in the woods I savored the thought.

"It's a dumb time to bring this up, but how were they going to get pictures of us in the dark?" I asked.

"I almost asked Walter about that, wouldn't that have been funny?"

"Yeah. You know, Jim Rogers mentioned something to me. I guess you already figured it out."

"What was it?"

"Well, two things actually. The adultery grounds, they're meaningless under North Carolina law," I said.

"I know, I knew it was for political reasons. Walter figures all of the angles. Pity is a worth a few points in a poll, I guess. Walter, a pitiful little darling! That's one for Believe it or Not. What was the other thing?"

"Jim mentioned that….Well, is Walter capable of murder?"

"Planning murder, yes. Committing murder, no."

"Did Jim talk to you about the Treasury Department?"

"Yes, without my testimony their case would be weak."

"How about the ledgers?" I asked.

"I gave Jim copies, but they need my testimony to verify Walter owns them."

"How about handwriting experts? Hell, Matlock caught people all the time with handwriting?"

"Walter's ambidextrous. He could take notes in school with both hands, at the same time. He could fake it." Ally patted her blouse around my eyes. "Cape one more thing."

"Yeah."

"Do you remember the loan you thought I made to you for the plane? Walter made that loan, I'm sure of it now."

"Why, why would he make it easy on me?"

"He didn't. He gave the jury a million reasons why you would kill me."

"Ally, there's not even one reason I would kill you."

"Cape, not that you would, but Walter has created the perception that you would, don't you see? When you arrived, I was supposed to be dead."

"Ally, why would he bring you all the way down here to kill you? Why not just have it done in Charlotte?"

"Because, Cape, spouses are always the prime suspects in the murder of their spouses. Think about it. If I'm dead, I can't testify. Then for the sake of argument, let's say our affair went badly. I pressed you for the money, you--."

"Shit, I get it…Motive. Damn, I've got us circling blocks and playing spy games--and all the while Walter is planning the perfect murder."

We sat still until Ally saw the moon rising in the east. "Cape, I think I can find the river now, but it will take all night if we have to crawl."

"I can see a little better, I'll follow you. Ally, if something happens and we have to run--don't use the path. Wait until daylight and pick your way through the woods."

"I can't leave you, how can you run?"

"I can't, Ally, but don't let me slow you down. Hit the thick woods we just left and wait for daylight. Somebody has to tell what's going on, I'll try and hold this guy off as long as I can."

"What guy?"

"The one you saw in the house," I said.

"I thought it was a shadow!"

"We both know shadows don't shoot. Someone's trying to kill us."

The blood around my eyelids had started to congeal and crust over. The side of my head hurt and my equilibrium was gone. Ally walked, as I stumbled along behind her.

"Ally, my right eye is in bad shape, though I think my left eye just has blood in it. If we could clean it out, maybe I could see enough to walk faster."

"Lie down."

Ally spit on my eye and dabbed it with her blouse, again. Some vision returned but everything was blurry.

"How's that?"

"I can see you, not well, but enough to follow you. The pain in my other eye is awful--I'm not going to make it very far."

Ally led us across the woods and down to the brackish water of the Chowan River. I stuck my head in the frigid water and opened both eyes. Pain shot though my head like hot coals had been dropped into my eye sockets. I jerked my head from the water and Ally covered my mouth to muffle my scream. "Just sit here for a minute. The water is like a saline solution. If this doesn't help we're in big trouble," Ally said. We sat on the bank with my head in Ally's lap. The faint light from the moon spun in a lazy circle.

"Hey, I forgot to tell you thanks," I said.

"For getting you into this mess?"

"No, I'm man enough to take credit for my own mistakes. I found Jana."

"That's great, how is she doing?"

"She's a good person, Ally. We couldn't have found her without your help."

I closed my eyes and tried to extinguish the flames with my eyelids. "That's it? Tell me about her--Do your eyes still hurt?" Ally asked. I nodded my head, Ally slid down to the riverbank. Cool water splashed on my face. "Open your eyes." The water eased the pain and flushed more grit from my eyes. I told Ally about the search for Jana after she brought back more water and repeated the rinsing. "What's that you're putting water in?" I asked.

"My bra--sorry about the cup size. I'm a charter member of the I.B.T.C."

"You got me, what the hell is the I.B.T.C?"

"Itty Bitty Titty Club, Walter tried to get me to super size, but I'm happy with what I have."

I had super size pain, but I bit my lip to keep from laughing out loud. Countless trips around the world and I had just come across one of the funniest phrases I'd ever heard, yet I couldn't laugh. Ally dabbed my eyes dry with her blouse, and mistook my stifled laugh for a groan. "Are you okay?"

I didn't answer right away. The humorous I.B.T.C. remark and Ally's kind ministrations reminded me of what a perfect woman Walter had. Anger from the thought that he was trying to kill her rushed right over my affection and smothered it.

"Yeah, I was just thinking, you wouldn't have made a bad nurse."

"Funny, that's something I always wanted to do," Ally said.

"Why didn't you?"

"Mrs. Walter Cronus Kress, working? No, I was allowed to do charity work, but nursing would have been below the Kress standard. I just hope this water doesn't cause you an infection."

"I don't know, there's something to be said for holistic medicine," I said.

"I wouldn't have thought a modern-day aviator would believe that."

"Well, when I was a kid, I got really sick. The doctor came by, shoved a few needles in my butt, and gave up on me. This old lady in our neighborhood, I guess she was a nurse. Not trained like you, but she helped deliver babies, and generally took care of people in odd ways."

"Sort of like a midwife?" Ally asked.

"Yeah, but she cared about people, you know, like nurses do. I mean I don't have anything against doctors, but nurses cure people."

"So how did this nurse cure you? A magical concoction?"

"The concoction, as you say, was probably nothing more than snake oil. Maybe it helped, maybe it didn't, but she cured me by giving me something else," I said.

"What was it?"

"She gave me the sky. Pretty neat gift, huh?"

"So that's your sky up there?"

"Yep, I let people use it from time to time, but it's mine thanks to Miss Minnie, midwife, shaman, and nurse. I guess what I'm trying to say is you might rethink your decision. You'd make a great nurse," I said.

Slowly the image of Ally began to materialize. I sat up and looked around through the haze of my compromised vision. Our temporary haven was an old landing on the river. A small dock jutted into the water for about twenty feet, then made a ninety-degree angle and ran parallel to the shore.

"Ally, can you tell if there are any boats tied to the pier?"

"No, it's too dark, but they duck hunt here, there have to be some somewhere."

We crawled out onto the pier where we found three small boats tied to the dock. All were chained together and padlocked to a piling. I felt for the 5/8-inch chain, wrapped a loop of it around my hand, and yanked. The sound of the chain rattling on the aluminum boats traveled long and loud across the river. "Damn, that was smart! I can't see--how secure are these boats?" I asked.

Ally climbed into the bow of one of the boats. "They have eyelets, but the bolts have been flattened on the ends….Cape, lights, flashlights, coming in our direction!"

I looked toward the shore. I could make out the lights, but my depth perception was shot.

"How many?"

"Two."

"How close?"

"Close, three, maybe four blocks away," Ally said.

"Blocks, urbanite?...What kind of measurement is that?"

"The only one I know, I hate the country."

"Ally, they're hunting us, covering the escape routes. How many landings are on the farm?"

"I don't know, I've been here only once….twice, I came with my dad, the last time was with Walter. They were shooting ducks, I stayed in the lodge."

"How many people came for the hunt?"

"Why does that matter? Thirty, maybe a few more if you count the women, why?"

"Three boats wouldn't carry that many people, there must be more landings. Did you see any blinds?" I asked.

"Blinds?"

"Yeah, duck blinds?"

"You mean the little houses made out of cloth?"

"Yeah, how many?"

"Ten, maybe more," Ally said.

"Okay, each boat would holds three people. I'm guessing that's how many would be in each blind. There must be a few more landings here. How far are we from the lodge?"

"You're not going to like this, but five, maybe six blocks."

"We have to make our way back to the lodge, is there a boat landing there?"

"There's a boathouse there, and another building by the water," Ally said.

We slid from the dock into the shallow water near the shore. My plan was to walk along the shore until we came to the lodge. I hadn't considered the temperature of the water or the reeds bedded in the muck of the Chowan River bottom.

"Hey, I heard something down by the river."

"You stupid ass, if you'd killed the bitch we could be home by now. I did my part. I didn't get a clean kill, but I hit that bastard, there was blood all over the car."

"You check out the river, I'm going to double back to the lodge." The voices of our predators rolled over the river. I pushed Ally under the pier. "Cape, I'm freezing," Ally whispered.

"I know, but it's going to get colder."

"Why?"

"Because we have to get under the water." I grabbed two bamboo shafts from a canebrake and pulled them from the soft bottom, then cut one into foot-long lengths and fluted them out with the small end of the cane. "What are you doing, Cape?"

"I'm making us a big pea shooter."

"Are you serious?"

"No, breathing pipes, we can't get back to shore without him hearing us, we'll have to hide in the water."

"My knees are already aching from the cold, I can't do it," Ally said.

We moved under the pier to the deeper water. I sharpened one end of the largest cane and gave it to Ally. "Ally, you stay under the pier take this, and see if it will slip between the cracks in the boards."

Ally found a large gap and pushed the cane up through it. "It does, now what?"

"If the guy comes out here shove the cane spear into him."

"Shove it where?"

"Aim for his balls, I'll get under the water. You tap me when you have a shot at him."

We waited until we heard footsteps on the dry wooden planks. I sank under the water and gripped a steel lag spike attached to a piling. My first pull on the makeshift pipe was full of water, I spit it out and moved the cane higher. Ally's aim was good--the man on the dock crumbled into a withering heap. I jumped from the water, grabbed a handful of clothing and pulled him into the water.

He fought back to the surface and opened his mouth to scream. I used the cane as a makeshift garrote on his neck and pulled until the cane snapped. The face sinking into the dark water belonged to the GQ guy who had been with Johnston at Jim's office.

"Is he....Is he dead?" Ally asked.

"Yeah, poor bastard." Dizzy from the fight I sank into the water. A pair of hands grabbed my neck and pushed my face into the mud. I fumbled along the piling until I found the lag bolt and pulled us to the bottom of the river. GQ struggled for the surface, but I pulled him down by his hair and held him under the water until no bubbles came from his mouth.

River water ran from my mouth and nose, as I sucked for air. Ally pulled me under the pier and into the shallow water.

"Ally, we have to get to the lodge. His friend will come looking for him in a few minutes. Let's go back into the woods-- we're going to have to crawl some more."

Ally led the way and I low crawled behind her with GQ's gun. The light from the other man was near the river, and out of range of the shotgun. "Ally, the hole in the windshield, was it just one hole or a bunch of them?"

"One hole, a big one."

I ejected a shell from the gun. My hands shook violently from the hypothermia caused by the water. Between my blurred vision and my shaking, the cartridge looked more like a red bird than a bullet. "Look at this shell see--see---see what number's on it."

"You're freezing."

"Fro--frozen. The num--number, read it."

Ally rolled the shell in the moonlight until she could read the numbers. " Four shot, high velocity, it could be a nine, I don't have my glasses with me."

We made it back to the lodge, and the faint voice of the other man calling for his partner echoed off the sides of the building. Ally wrapped the throw on the couch around me and rubbed until my shivers subsided. "Ally, I need a rifle, see if you can help me find the gun cabinet."

"Here it is, but there's a chain….like on the boats."

"Shit, see if you can find some buckshot--12 gauge," I said.

Ally shuffled through the cases of ammo "7 ½ , will they work?"

"No, see if you can find something lower."

"4's, that's it."

"Four shot, duck ammo, it'll have to work….Give me a box, let's get back outside and find the other guy," I said.

Ally ran upstairs and brought back some dry clothes and a clean pillowcase. Then she ripped it into strips. "I can't find a first aid kit, hold on."

Ally walked to the bar and grabbed a bottle of Scotch.

"Thanks, but I'm trying to quit," I said.

"It's for the bandages, your head is bleeding. I think you may have been wounded….This might sting."

It did.

"Put these on, they may be a little short for you, but the waist should fit."

We put on the clothes and headed for the boathouse. An ATV was parked under a shed near the house. I felt for the key, but it was gone. "Ally, do you know where the key for this thing is?"

"No."

"He must have the key with him, engine's still warm. How far can you run?"

"About three miles, I do it every day. Why?"

"Can you still see the flashlight?"

"Yes, he's way off. Maybe ten blocks," Ally said.

"We need to keep this vehicle here." I jammed some broomstraw into the ignition switch.

"You take this gun, and run down the path to the gate. When you get there jam the padlock like we did here. I'll check out the boathouse while you're gone."

"Cape, the gun won't do me any good, you keep it. Besides, it'll just slow me down."

"Ally, it's like a computer, point and click."

"I can't kill someone, I'm sorry. It doesn't seem to bother you. You keep it."

I crossed a wide strip of grass then noticed a white aviation cone. Warm blood ran back into my eyes. I dabbed at my left eye and found the next cone, then another one--a landing strip. The building beside the boathouse turned out to be a hanger. Inside was a Cessna 172, with the key. I sumped the tanks, opened the door, and waited for Ally.

"Cape, the other guy's coming back, close, five blocks," Ally panted.

"Have you ever had flying lessons?"

"No."

I explained the rudimentary instruments and Bernoulli's law to Ally.

"Why can't you fly?"

"Ally, I can't see far off, and everything close up is still blurry. I can help you, but I can't see to fly."

"The guy's closer, four maybe three blocks."

"Let's get over by the path, we need to get close to get a shot at him. You take the shot, I can't see well enough to aim."

"Can't we just leave?"

"Ally, he has a rifle. If he gets a shot at us, we're finished. You can do this, come on."

We hid behind an oak tree near the path, and gave Ally the gun. "Cape, I won't hurt someone, it's not my way. I was trained to help, not hurt."

"Okay, but you have to give me distances….In feet would be nice?"

"I could do that, but men have messed up my ability to measure in feet."

"Now, how did we do that?" I asked.

"Oh, something to do with five inches being almost a foot long."

"Oh, yeah….I think I've contributed to that confusion….Hey, car lengths--will that work for you?"

"I can do car lengths."

Ally counted down the distance in soft whispers…. "Seven, six, five."

I pressed the gun against the tree to steady the shot, and raked the blood from my eye. The muzzle flashed and the fuzzy light fell to the ground. We ran for the plane, Ally on the pilot's side, me on the copilot's side. "Ally, air speed and altitude. Don't let the speed get below seventy and keep the wings level."

"How do I do that?"

"The gauge that says airspeed, keep your eyes on that, and steer with your feet. The yoke won't help you until we get airborne. You call out the speed I'll tell you when to rotate."

I felt around the panel, found the master switch, and hit the starter button. Ally lined the plane up on the runway. I set the flaps, pushed the throttle to full forward, and we were rolling.

"Thirty, forty, fifty--."

"Pull back on the yoke, easy….Get the nose off the ground."

"It's going to the left, it won't turn," Ally said.

I kicked in some right rudder. "How's that?"

"More, we're heading for a tree."

I kicked in more rudder and turned the yoke to the right as we lifted off.

"God, we just missed the tree--."

The stall warning came on, so I lowered the nose to build airspeed. "Ally, keep us level call out the airspeed."

"Sixty-five, seventy--more trees, big trees….Higher, higher--eighty."

I pulled the nose up, just a touch.

"Tree--tree….Whew!"

"Altimeter--how high are we?" I asked.

"I don't know, over the trees, maybe ten stories."

"You did good, take the plane, keep us level and hold the airspeed at eighty. We should be climbing, read this instrument." I tapped the altimeter.

"The long hand is on four, the little fat hand is just past zero."

"Hold it just like this until the fat hand is on three." I said.

"Okay, what now?"

"Wait till we get to three thousand feet, then stop the climb, lower the nose."

Ally fought with the altitude, while I reduced the power and helped her trim the plane for straight and level.

"What now?"

"One more thing, set 109.6 on this instrument then turn this knob until to comes up on the little window."

"Okay, I have 'to' in the window."

"Turn the knob until the little white needle centers," I said.

"It says 'from', but the needle is in the middle."

"What's the bearing at the top say?"

"Zero fifty."

"Put two-thirty on the top and make a turn until the heading indicator reads two thirty."

"Where's that?"

"The gauge with the little plane on it, watch your altitude."

"Okay….One-eighty, two hundred, two-twenty--."

"Stop the turn, level your wings," I said.

"Okay two-thirty, now what?"

"Hold that heading, we're home free, you're locked on to the Kinston VOR. Damn good job!"

CHAPTER TWENTY SIX

Family Reunion.

Ally and I bounced to a landing in Kinston in the wee morning hours. Calling the police was a must, but that wasn't going to happen without a lawyer, and R.H. Carter came to mind. He had relatives in Greenville, and if they were in law enforcement, I was sure I'd get the death penalty.

We decided to get a motel room and call Jim Rogers the next morning. I borrowed the airport courtesy car and Ally drove us to Wal-Mart to pick up some medical supplies. The bullet had grazed my head over my right eye. Ally bandaged the wound and rinsed my eyes out again. Other than the bandage over my right eye, I wasn't too bad for wear. While Ally doctored, I talked.

"Ally, I've got something to say. It's something I've been thinking about for a while now."

"You rest. You can talk later."

"No, after tonight I understand how precious life is, and I want to say this. It'd be a lot easier if you just let me talk. I pretty much know what I'm going to say by heart."

"Well, if you insist on going against my medical advice, go ahead," Ally said.

"Ally, I know we come from different worlds, and I don't think I've ever seen an ant farm. As for being an artist, I can't paint--not even my house. No one has ever accused me of being a sensitive guy, but who knows? Maybe I'm more sensitive than I've gotten credit for. Then there is the money thing. You know as much about my finances as I do.

"It's no secret, I'm not a rich guy. I can't buy you a private jet. We may have to sit in the back of a theatre because we can't get the best seats. Hell, we might not even be able to get seats. But if all that means so much to you, Ally, I guess this next part won't matter."

"I'm listening," Ally said.

"Well, I guess you need to know something about my family. I'd like to be able to introduce you to all of them, but my grandfather is the only family member I ever knew. He was a good guy, but hard. He came from good stock, he was a lawyer. Not a greedy lawyer. I don't know for sure, but I'd bet he ranked right up there in the top ten as far as pro bono publico goes. Which made him a poor guy, too, but he was also one of the richest. He had something at one time in life that was a treasure. Something no man could buy, or charm away from him. That treasure was my grandmother. I never knew her, but she must have been a wonderful woman. My grandfather never wanted another woman after she died.

He said they were meant for one another. He loved her, and when she died, he loved her memory. He attended church for thirty-five years, and never missed a Sunday. I asked him about that once when I was older. He told me he knew Sarah--that was my grandmother's name--was in heaven, and he wanted to be sure to be there with her. I was by his side when he died. He took his last breath, and died. Then he smiled….I know it sounds impossible, but I was there, and he smiled. I know why he smiled now, because Sarah was there again.

"When I'm on my deathbed, I want to smile after I die. If you're here after I'm gone, I'll smile because I know I'll see you again. If you go before I do, I'll smile because I know we'll be together again. I don't want to be on my deathbed regretting that I never told you this. I--."

"That's a beautiful story, but are you trying to tell me you love me?" Ally asked.

"Well….Yeah, wasn't that in there somewhere?"

"No."

"Ally, I love you. If that's not good enough I'll rent a plane, and write it in great big letters across the sky "

"Cape, I know we haven't known one another very long. That concerned me. Then I remembered I've known Walter my entire life. Tonight, the thing you did, killing those men, it bothered me. It scared me, but I know why you did it. When you pulled that trigger, I realized it was us or them. Not many people have to do something like you did tonight. I hope they never have to, but we're alive and we're together. I don't know how things can get much worse, but for good or bad, I want to be with you."

"Wait a minute. Are you trying to tell me you love me?" I asked.

"That wasn't in there?"

"Close enough, come here."

Ally didn't ask how she compared to anybody after we finished making love. I was glad she didn't, but the answer was easy. There was no comparison, Allison Tyra Moore Kress was in a class by herself.

The next morning I called Jim and explained what had happened in Edenton. Jim promised to call the Chowan County Sheriff's department and arranged a time when we could meet to tell our story. Then he gave me some real news. "Cape, Michelle's been trying to call you, Jana wouldn't stay in Augusta. She headed back for Greenville--."

"Jim, you have to find her. I don't--."

"Hold on. She's here in my office, and she's safe. Michelle is here, too, with her whole family. We're going to Mr. Fisher's, and we want you to come with us."

"I can be there in forty minutes. Can someone pick us up at the airport?"

"I'll let Michelle do that, Jana and I will meet you at Mr. Fisher's."

We didn't talk until we were airborne, and at first I didn't understand Ally's question.

"So how does it feel to be a hero?"

Nothing about what I had done made me feel like a hero. Just the opposite, in fact. I thought of GQ and how hard he had fought to hang onto life. Had Ally not been able to stab him with the cane, or if I hadn't known where the lag bolt was under the pier, the outcome would have been different. Maybe we could have flown out without having to shoot the other guy, but who could have known? He was using a rifle, and that made him a good shot, plus he could see. Maybe the police in Chowan County would understand my choices. Then again, they could see things the way the presumptuous R.H. Carter had seen things in Florida. If they did, they would be wrong. There were choices to be made in Chowan County, and GQ and the rifleman had made the wrong ones. No matter what anyone said.

"Ally, what I did in Edenton wasn't something I'm proud of--to be honest it's something that will take me a long time to forget."

Like a kid erasing an Etch-O-Sketch, Ally shook her head to erase the memories of our nightmare.

"That wasn't what I meant, but since we're on the subject, I want to say this, and then let's never mention it again. The two killings were some primordial instinct that revived itself in you or maybe it wasn't natural, but it was necessary."

I patted her hand. Nothing that the police would believe mattered anymore. Ally knew, and that was enough for me.

"I like the way you put it, now let's put it in the past."

"Done, but I was talking about you finding Jana. That was pretty heroic."

"Ally, when I started the search my reasons were selfish. Laura was a part of my youth that I had lost, I wanted her or maybe I wanted my youth back. That didn't happen, but Jana and you did. I thought she was my child. I don't think that's the case anymore, and I haven't for a while. It's funny the way things turn out sometimes."

"How's that?"

"Well, all of this started with me searching for my child. I guess I didn't find him or her, but I did find my grandfather and you."

"Cape, you've lost me. What does all this have to do with you finding your grandfather?"

"My whole life I never understood him. He was a lawyer, he could have made tons of money. Hell, a boatload of his colleagues did, but my grandfather always made time to help other people. When I grew up I promised myself I would never be like him, and for a while I did a damn fine job of it. Ally, this is the first time in my life that I've helped people for no other reason, than that it was the right one. It's a good feeling, but more than that, it made me understand why my grandfather was like he was. I don't think he was ever very proud of me, but for some reason I think he is now."

"I think a lot of people up there are proud of you, Cape."

We taxied up to the Greenville FBO, where an attractive woman stood on the ramp. I recognized her, but couldn't remember from where. She walked directly up to me. Ally gave me a funny look. I shrugged, and held Ally's hand tightly.

"Mr. Thomas, I'm Doctor Benson, do you remember me?"

"Yes, yes, I do."

"What happened to you?" Doctor Benson asked.

"Doctor, it's a long story, but what brings you to Greenville?"

"I've left you several messages, and you didn't return my calls. I had some concerns about your toxicology test."

I knew what it was about and I should have told her earlier. "Doctor Benson, I can explain the salt. I have this adverse reaction to salt tablets. I took them to make myself sick. The reason I did won't make any sense to you, but it worked. I'm sorry I didn't call back."

"It's not the salt I was concerned about, Mr. Thomas. Have you been to Brazil lately?"

"Not since my AeroMax days, and that's been almost six years ago."

"Have you ever heard of a plant called Baburau?"

"Doctor, I can't spell it, much less say it," I said.

"It took me a while to identify the toxin in your sample. The plant grows only in Brazil. We don't see many cases in North America. At first I thought the oysters were bad. I called the Pitt County health department. They secured all the oyster shells from the Mess restaurant the night you were there. No other patrons reported food poisoning. Then I tested each oyster shell. Out of two hundred and sixty shells only six tested positive for the toxin. How many oysters did you have that night?"

"I had one order of Oysters Rockefeller. I can't be sure, but I think it was six," I said.

"Do you know anyone that might want to poison you?"

"Doctor Benson, I know someone that wasn't happy with my search for a person. I find it hard to believe she would try to poison me."

"Did you ingest any other food that night or the next day before you saw me?"

"I had a bowl of soup." I said.

"I know a lot of time has gone by, but could you find the bowl it was served in or maybe the utensil it was cooked in?" She asked.

"No, I washed everything after I ate--there was something a little strange, though. The woman who made it wore rubber gloves while she prepared the soup. I remember that because I wear the same gloves when I preflight a plane. You know, the little flimsy numbers. I call them doctor's gloves."

"Mr. Thomas, it's a good thing you took those salt tablets. Had you not become nauseated, I'm certain you would have died," Dr. Benson said.

"That bitch."

"Do you know where this person is now?"

"I sure do, and if you don't have anything else to do you're welcome to come with us. We have to make a stop first, and then I can take you to her office."

"I'll go with you. Did this take place in Greenville?" Dr. Benson asked.

"Yes."

"I'll need to talk to the District Attorney. I've brought my results with me."

"Dr. Benson, Jim Rogers will be at this gathering. He's an attorney and I think he can help you with that."

We all piled into Michelle's mini van, and then headed for Mr. Fisher's house where we would meet Jim Rogers and Jana. While Ally and Dr. Benson talked about my eyes, I explained to Michelle what the doctor had found, and what her suspicions were. "Cape, did you say soup? Laura mentions that Bianca fed her soup every day. You don't think she could have killed Laura, do you?"

"Did you bring the diary?"

"I brought everything, and I can't wait to show it to Jana."

"Let's wait until we get to Mr. Fisher's. We can read the diary then," I said.

Gustavo met us at the door and led us to the drawing room to join Jana, Mr. Fisher, and Jim Rogers, then Gustavo left.

Mr. Fisher and Jana were seated on a couch looking at photographs. Jana jumped up from the couch and came over to hug me. "What happened to you?"

"Got a bug in my eye. How are you?"

"Must have been a big bug!"

"Naw, but he was an ornery cuss," I said.

"Guess what? My mother was Miss Greenville."

"I heard about that, so are you thinking about running? You know, keep the old tiara in the family?"

"No, but guess what her talent was?"

"I don't have a clue," I said.

"She was a singer, just like me. Mr. Fisher said she wanted to be a singer."

"Jana, I thought you were going to call me Granddad," Mr. Fisher said.

"Granddad.... Cape, can you believe it? I have a family. Guess what else? I'm changing my name to Fisher because that's my name, not someone else's."

"I'm happy for you, Jana."

"Anyway, Granddad said he pushed Mom away from her dream of being a singer." Jana turned to Mr. Fisher. "But you won't ever try to rule someone again, right?"

"Never again. Whatever you want to be, Jana, I'll support you." Then Mr. Fisher looked at us. "Mr. Thomas, I want to thank you. Michelle, you too, thank both of you so much."

I eased Ally in front of me. "Mr. Fisher, you haven't met Ally, or Allison Kress, but I think you owe her some thanks, too," I said.

Ally stepped toward Mr. Fisher to shake his hand. Mr. Fisher had another question.

"You're not related to, the Kress of banking, are you?"

"No, sir, actually my name is Ally Moore, and I'm glad I could help."

Michelle walked over to Jana. "Jana, I'm Michelle. I was your mother's best friend. I have two things for you, one you can keep, the other we need for just a little longer." Michelle gave Jana the Coptic Cross.

"Antique jewelry, I love it. I collect it. What's the other thing?" Jana asked.

"It's a diary, your mother's diary. Most of it is written to you. I want you to read it." Michelle smiled. "You'll see that Laura never stopped loving you, Jana.... But do you mind if we look at it first?"

Jim Rogers and Doctor Benson were in a corner of the room having a conversation, they stopped talking to join us. Michelle read aloud from the diary. From April 20 to April 27, 1986, Laura chronicled the details of her last days. The last entry in the book read:

"I have very little time left. I wanted so much to see my daughter before I died. I'm afraid that is not to be. Bianca has promised she will find her, and I love her for that.

Dearest Daughter,

If you were found I know you have read this diary, and you know why I did what I did. If my father is still alive, don't be angry at him. The choice I made was mine. It was a mistake, a terrible mistake. I'm sure that you will make mistakes in your life. We all do. But I want you to know I forgave you the minute you made them, and I hope you can be as understanding. There is a question I am sure you would have wanted to ask me. I don't have the answer for you, but if I did I would write it now. I can tell you this much. I met your father only once, please don't judge me harshly. There were circumstances that led to our encounter that will, and should remain private.

He was young and handsome, full of himself. I thought he would call one day after that, but he never did.

If you decide to search for him, this is all I can tell you about him. He was from somewhere in the southeastern part of the state. He wanted to be a pilot, that's all he talked about, it was his dream in life. His name was Cape, I never knew his last name. You will know him if you find him. In spite of his cockiness, there was a kindness about him. He had a warm, loving heart. I don't think he realized he possessed this trait, though. I knew him for only a short time, but his eyes revealed his soul. Maybe, one day even if you don't find him, he will find himself. I love you, Jana, Mom.

Ally squeezed my hand, and Jana moved toward us. In that moment Laura's wish for me came true. I found myself, but much more important I found my daughter and the woman I loved.

Jana asked the question softly, "Is that the day my mother died? April the 27th?"

Michelle answered her. "No, Jana, your mother died on May 1st 1986. I think she held on until your birthday."

Before we could take in what had happened, Bianca stormed into the house. "Jim Rogers, I'm glad you're here. That woman," Bianca pointed at Jana, "is an imposter, she's after Laura's estate. I demand that you do something at once. If you don't, you know what I will do. Don't think for a minute that I won't."

Jim Rogers stepped from behind the sofa to face Bianca. "Is this what you want to show everyone, Bianca?" He held the letter over his head.

"Where did you get that?" Bianca snapped. "You, you stole that letter, that's what you were doing in my bathroom." Bianca looked at me. " And after I took care of you when you were ill."

Before I could answer Jim Rogers, had his day. "Bianca, shut up and sit down. That's right, Bianca, I'm quite a tiger once I've been released from bondage."

I thought of the leather cuffs and whip I had found at Bianca's. Jim was her sex toy.

"Mr. Fisher, forgive me. Bianca is the reason Laura and I broke our engagement. I had sex with her when she was a minor. That's what this letter is about. You know, for twenty-five years my biggest fear has been that this would come out. Now, it feels good to say it that I made a mistake. But I had a little help, didn't I, Bianca?"

"You're so pathetic, trying to act like a man. You're a fool, Jim."

"You're right, Bianca, you played me for a fool, even then. Oh, I know you were younger, but you knew exactly what you were doing. You finally had something of Laura's."

"Shut up Jim! All I had was something Laura never wanted, you sniveling bastard."

"That may be, but I don't care anymore. Ever since Cape and Michelle gave me this letter, I've become a little stronger each day. This may get out. I may never be a judge. But, at least I will be my own man. Bianca, you took Laura away from me, but that wasn't enough, you had to have my life, my manhood. I've been on hold all this time. I couldn't marry because you said a wife would get in our way. I couldn't run for office, because that would get in the way, too."

"Well, my little Jimmy-acting-like-a-man, what a surprise," Bianca said.

"Guess what, Bianca, I am a man. Man enough to stop you, anyway. I suppose your next step is to prove that Jana is not Laura's daughter. Well, since everyone else was trying to find Jana, I did my own little search for her. I didn't find her, but I know you tried hard to find her, Bianca."

"Shut up, Jim--."

"I couldn't understand it at first, I thought maybe you were trying to do the right thing. But after talking with, Dr. Benson, I've figured it out. I think we all have now. You wanted to find Jana so you could poison her. You tried to kill Cape, and I believe with all of my heart you killed Laura."

"You are crazy, Jim Rogers! I tried to find her because Laura wanted me to, and this woman is not Jana. I'll prove it in court if I have to, you're all wrong, this is not Jana. I never tried to kill anyone. I loved Laura. That man, Cape Thomas, is a liar. He is making up this story so he can get the money. I earned that money, it's mine!" Bianca shouted.

Jim continued, "Bianca, I'm going to call the police. I guess you don't remember the little plant in your house. You know the one you call your deadly little darling. You said it was like keeping a deadly animal, remember? You still have that plant, a Baburau plant. Gustavo brought it to you after one of his visits to Brazil."

"Shut up, Jim, or I'll--."

"What, poison me? Ask Dr. Benson what poison was used on Cape. You sprinkled it on Cape's oysters when he went to the restroom at the Mess. When he was sick all night, you were sure he would be dead when you returned. That's the reason you didn't mind him being in your house. What you didn't know was that Cape was sick from salt tablets he was taking. The poison didn't stay in his system long enough for it to kill him. When you got back that morning, he was still alive, so you had to finish him off. You made him a bowl of soup, a deadly brew. Cape doesn't like soup, Bianca, and he poured it out. Your little plan failed.

"You almost got away with murder, but I am going to have Laura's body exhumed. Dr. Benson is going to do a postmortem to determine the cause of death."

"Are you finished with your wild tale?" Bianca asked.

"One more thing, Bianca--if I were you, I'd hire a good attorney, you'll need it."

Gustavo came from the hallway with a pistol. "Nobody will call the police. My daughter will not go to jail."

Mr. Fisher turned to face Gustavo. "Your daughter? You, Gustavo, you're the one!"

Gustavo turned to face Mr. Fisher. "That's right, Mr. Fisher, Mr. High and Mighty. Maria wanted a baby, but she didn't know you're weren't man enough to do it. Tell them how you can't have children. Laura wasn't yours any more than Bianca was. You can't have children. I watched you dote on Laura and ignore Bianca. I didn't say anything to you, but long ago Bianca knew the truth. We both kept quiet after that, because one day, somehow I was going to see to it that my daughter got what was hers. So for forty years I pretended to be your faithful manservant. Ha! I was only watching over my child."

The old man rose. Like a broken man, he told his story. "It's true Calis and I couldn't have children. We wanted children but it wasn't to be. I understand Laura's dilemma now. She gave up what Calis and I would have done anything to have, a child. I loved Calis--she was my angel, my darling angel. We had all that life could give. Our world was complete except for a child. Calis went to the doctor one day for a routine checkup. Instead, she learned that she was dying. At first, she kept the secret to herself, Calis was like that, she would do anything to spare me hurt. I found out the truth from the doctor. I became a man possessed. I wanted some part of Calis to live forever. The fault was mine that we couldn't have children.

"I was young then, lucky, and always I had my way. I was going to have a child. I was determined that some part of Calis would live forever. I devised a wicked plan. Calis was shocked--and hurt at first. Unable to believe I could have such thoughts. What I'm about to tell you, please understand, was my doing, so think badly of me, not Calis.

"We knew a couple who couldn't have children, either. They wanted a child as badly as we did. The woman of the couple was infertile. It seemed to be the perfect solution to our problems.

"I couldn't bear the thought of my Calis being with another man. But I could bear less the thought of losing Calis forever. The deal was struck. Calis was to have two children. One for each couple, that was our arrangement. Then God blessed us with twins. I say blessed because one union was all I think I could have suffered. Late in the pregnancy, the doctor informed Calis and I that she might not live long enough to give birth".

Mr. Fisher stopped his eyes were brimming with tears. " She died the day Laura was born. There were two babies, one a boy, the other a girl. I had to choose. I wanted them both, but in my day a man's word meant something. I couldn't put Laura down because she looked exactly like my Calis."

Michelle said, "Mr. Fisher, Laura never mentioned she had a brother."

"She didn't know, Michelle. No one in Greenville ever knew Laura had a brother."

"What's his name?"

"Michelle, you don't know him, none of you do. It was--is a secret--but I want to tell the whole truth now. His name is Robert Hale Carter, he knows me as his Godfather."

"Where does he live," I had to ask, the name rang a bell.

"He lives in Orlando, and he is a police detective there. I think you would like him Mr. Thomas. He reminds me of you--a fine man. But let me finish my story…where was I?"

"You left town, granddad."

"Thank you, dear--yes--town--we left the town shortly after we found out Calis was pregnant. I know you must think it was some evil thing that we did. But you have to understand. There was no such thing as artificial insemination back then. What we did was done out of love.

"Maria became pregnant--years later." Mr. Fisher pointed at Gustavo. "I guess that's where you come in the picture, you…you…scoundrel." Mr. Fisher glared at Gustavo and then at the gun in his hand. "Anyway, she insisted the child was mine, and that's when I told her the story I have just told you. She hated me after that, said I should have told her I was sterile. Maybe I should have. She threatened to expose Calis, Laura and me if I didn't accept the child. She wanted an heir to this damned, cursed Fisher Fortune.

"What she did was not done out of love but out of greed. I agreed to her demands, but I insisted she leave this country and never come back. I paid her handsomely, but in installments. She understood that if she ever broke her promise, the money would go away. I raised Bianca as my own. I tried to love her, but as you can see today, Bianca is not capable of love." The old man stopped and looked at Bianca. "I should have let your mother have you then and told the truth to everyone in town."

"You blabbering old fool! Oh, you kept me all right, physically. But you never, never loved me."

"That's not true, I loved you as my own," Mr. Fisher said.

"No, that's what you told people, but you raised me to fail. 'Your slut mother,' remember saying that to me? You wanted me to be a slut. How could Nathan Hale Fisher be wrong? I hate--."

"Bianca, that's not true. I wanted you not to be like her. I wanted you to be--."

"Like Laura, and Calis. Well, your prediction came true, old man. I'm just like my slut mother. All you are to me is a meal ticket, and I hate you!" Bianca shouted.

As Bianca talked, I watched Gustavo. The gun in his hand was a Ruger single six .357 caliber. The hammer was cocked and ready to fire. The ends of the hollow-point rounds were visible in the cylinder of the revolver. Gustavo waved the gun and motioned for us to move to one side of the room.

Gustavo stood alone in front of the room. "Mr. Rogers, you will not send my daughter to jail. Bianca is the rightful heir. This woman, Jana, is an imposter. It cannot be proved otherwise."

Jim Rogers moved in to the front of the group. "You're wrong, Gustavo."

Gustavo pointed the gun at Jim. "You will call me Mr. Jobim from this day on. I am Mr. Jobim. Bianca and I, by our patience with this fool, have earned his house, the money, it is all ours. You are wrong about Bianca, I poisoned Laura and Mr. Thomas. I should have poisoned the old man, too, but I never knew if Bianca was in the will, he would never tell me."

"Gustavo…."

"Shut up, Fisher. You live today because I thought one day you would tell me Bianca was the only heir. I should kill you now."

Jim Rogers stepped in. " Mr. Jobim, you need to calm down. You're an innocent man right now. You didn't have access to Laura or Cape Thomas. Your daughter is a murderer."

"No, it was I."

"No, it was Bianca, Mr. Jobim. Let justice be served. If you think Jana is an imposter, that's easy enough to prove, we can obtain a DNA samples from Laura. If you're right, Bianca gets the money."

That's good, Jim, you said enough. Oh shit, don't say anymore, Jim, let it rest, don't be a lawyer here needing to uncover all the details.

" But I don't know what good the money will do her. She'll be in prison," Jim said.

Damn, you had to say it…Just couldn't let it go, could you?

Gustavo aimed the pistol at Jim, but Bianco rushed in front of him. The gun fired and Bianca fell to the floor. Gustavo stood in shock as a pool of blood spread under her lifeless body.

"No, my child, why? Why save him?"

I felt sorry for the old man, and in some odd way, I felt sorry for Bianca. I didn't respect or like her, but I didn't want her to die, either.

I knelt beside Bianca. "Gustavo, put down the gun. Let Dr. Benson help her."

Anger replaced the shock on Gustavo's face. "No! You, Jana, you caused all of this, why do you not stay lost? None of this would have happened." Gustavo pointed the gun at Jana. Hold on Mister, you can kill your own daughter, but not mine. No wait…Don't be stupid. It's a single shot six, he can't fire it again until he cocks the hammer. How long will that take, a second, then another second to pull the trigger. Two seconds, long enough to score in a basketball game. I can do this. I sprang from my position next to Bianca's body. One thousand one, one thousand two, almost there, it's over, you bastard. I could see Gustavo's finger as it became rigid on the trigger--then a beautiful white light.

CHAPTER TWENTY SEVEN

Complete the Puzzle

I recall the night when I was delirious with fever on the porch with Miss Minnie I imagined myself floating in the sky. The words she spoke that night, "Yours, boy, the sky is yours, always will be," are no longer an enigma, but a truth as tangible as the last piece of my grandfather's jigsaw puzzle.

The old woman wasn't crazy. Just as she predicted, the things I saw did come to mean something. But as for so many others, it took me a while to figure out that *Sometimes what you looking at--ain't what you see.*

Laura was never simply a vision of the past, as I first thought. She was one piece of a mosaic of my life, our life--our future. Everyone we meet, if for only an evening, enhances the potential for us to fulfill our destiny. We're all connected, and even the dead remain a part of our circle of life. I see that now, Miss Minnie.

MarKay's riddle:

Lost for now

In days of dark

Fated doom will soon enkindle

Eternally yours in lifeless heart.

Was a simple acrostic. To find the secret word use only the first letter in each line. L.I.F.E. though the price of enlightening a stranger spelled Death for MarKay.

That troubled me until I thought about how calmly MarKay accepted her fate. She knew even before we met that her time was close. There are many documented cases of soldiers preparing for battle who express their premonitions of death. With that intuitive knowledge many of them are inspired to do heroic or charitable acts. Some soldiers are rewarded with medals and other people, like MarKay, gain only the humble gratitude of an unworthy survivor.

I was wrong about MarKay not being on Madame Marie's psychic level, she was light years ahead. I'm not saying MarKay saw the future but she saw something in me I didn't know I had. MarKay made me promise to continue my search because she saw me as a man who would keep his word. A trait no one else had ever believed about me, and for good reason.

My chance meeting with R.H. Carter must have been more than a coincidence, Carter turned out to be a perfect donor match for Jana. The transplant was successful and Jana and her doctor husband (I was right about a poor guy not having a chance) have a beautiful set of twins, Laura and Cape "T".

Little Laura is just as beautiful as her namesake, and sings like an angel. Most people think she gets her talent from Laura and Jana, and I'm sure she does. But the sweetness in her tiny voice belongs to a woman who once held me close and sang to me-- Catherine, my mother.

"T" (The T. stands for Thomas, but his nickname is Trouble)--well, he spends most of his time piloting a swing, just like the one in my backyard. One of these nights, when the sky is cold and clear and the stars are brighter than he will ever remember. He too will learn of Orion, the hunter killed by the woman he loved; Ursa Major, the Great Bear and keeper of the Big Dipper; Ursa Minor, the keeper of the Little Dipper.

Laura and Cape "T" will learn many things, but the most important lesson will be to keep their promises--after all, that's why they are here.

Though Bianca's death was tragic, ironically her death benefited the school she hated. At Mr. Fisher's death, Bianca's portion of the Fisher Fortune will be used to fund the Bianca Jenkins Wing at the East Carolina School of Medicine. The old man toyed with the idea of removing her from his will, but he never did.

Promises kept don't mean good things for everyone. Tate Harris and the Dix-E-Land Music Company are no longer part of the Nashville music scene because Harris is a ward of the Tennessee Prison System.

John Kirkland is a man on the run. But no matter where he moves, Michelle and Jana find him and put up more billboards with his picture and this caption: **Warning Child Molester!**

Walter Cronus Kress and William Johnston have moved, too. Both are inmates at the Federal Penitentiary in Atlanta. William Johnston is busy filing appeals, while Walter spends his days crushing bugs that no one else can see.

Ally, sweet Ally, donated the bulk of Walter's fortune to charity. She also made a sizeable contribution to N.C. State University earmarked for the entomology department. I think it was her way of making up to all those little bugs Walter hates so much.

Mr. Fisher spends a lot of his time at the mausoleum when he's not doting on Jana and the twins. The family is worried about him. Not because he spends so much time at the graveyard, but because of the long conversations he has with the occupants of the mausoleum. There is no need to worry, Mr. Fisher is not crazy. He understands, maybe because he is so close to death, that the debt he owns for his happiness is to the dead. I guess that's why he had some engraving done on the old structure. Laura's sepulcher now reads: Laura Fisher--Loving Mother. The sepulcher next to Laura's reads: Captain Cape Thomas--Loving Father.

Over the door of the mausoleum is engraved:

Here lie those immortal dead who live again

In minds made better by their presence.

THE END

In Remembrance of Walker Taylor, an alumni of Auburn University School of Forestry and a War Eagle for eternity.

July 23 1986—May 8 2009

Coming Soon:

The Last Kincaid

By Ted Miller Brogden

Scheduled for Distribution 2011

Made in the USA
Charleston, SC
30 November 2010